SOMEONE ELSE'S SON

By Sam Hayes

Blood Ties
Unspoken
Tell-Tale
Someone Else's Son

SOMEONE ELSE'S SON

SAM HAYES

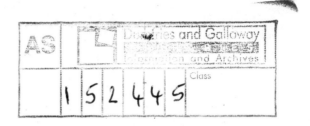
headline

First published in 2010 by
HEADLINE PUBLISHING GROUP

1

Cataloguing in Publication Data is available from the British Library

ISBN 978 0 7553 4987 6 (Hardback)
ISBN 978 0 7553 4988 3 (Trade paperback)

Typeset in Plantin Light by Avon DataSet Ltd,
Bidford-on-Avon, Warwickshire

Printed in Great Britain by Clays Ltd, St Ives plc

Headline's policy is to use papers that are natural, renewable and
recyclable products and made from wood grown in sustainable forests.
The logging and manufacturing processes are expected to conform to
the environmental regulations of the country of origin.

HEADLINE PUBLISHING GROUP
An Hachette UK Company
338 Euston Road
London NW1 3BH

www.headline.co.uk
www.hachette.co.uk

For Polly, my beautiful daughter, with all my love.
You are an inspiration.

ACKNOWLEDGEMENTS

Grateful thanks as always to Sherise and Anna for your dedication, hard work, insights and experience – it's all so very much appreciated. Many thanks to Sam – it's a pleasure working with you (your enthusiasm is contagious!), and also Celine for keeping me organised. Sincere thanks, of course, to everyone at Headline for getting my books on the shelves.

Much love to my dear family, Terry, Ben, Polly and Lucy, and to Grawar for Bat-phone talks and Avril for keeping my feet off the ground.

Finally, to Sandra who is still waving her magic wand . . .

FRIDAY, 24 APRIL 2009

Before she knew what was happening, the knife was in and out of his body. Over and over, sinking deep. It cut through the air, mesmerising them, slowing their lives, condensing everything to the beautiful moments just before it happened, just before it entered him, just before their worlds changed for ever.

She didn't know how to make it stop; *couldn't* make it stop.

They stared at each other one last time. A love affair packed into a second. Blood flowed between them. What was he telling her?

'Shit!'

'Fucking twist,' one of the youths yelled, already running. They danced on brilliant trainers; a pack fleeing. Their shiny tracksuit bottoms dragged in the puddles; their liquid eyes gleamed from adrenalin, drugs, alcohol – any fuel for their fire.

The vinegar from the chips still stung her lips. Slow motion, he dropped to his knees, then his body folded to the ground. She couldn't believe he'd stood this long. She tried to catch him. His head hit the tarmac. She screamed but nothing came out. His eyes bulged.

She pressed her hand to his ribs, his stomach, but there were too many holes. Scalding blood flowed between her fingers, although she could already feel it cooling.

'Don't die,' she sobbed, dropping her head on to his body. Where *was* everyone? 'Help me!' she screamed. All in class. No one else bunking off today. 'I'll get help,' she said frantically, not daring to take her hands off his wounds. How had it come to this?

His chest suddenly heaved up with a bubbling wheeze before it collapsed again, as if it was the last breath he would ever take. Otherwise, he didn't make a sound.

'*Help!*' she cried again, scrambling to her feet. She had to do something. She spun around, desperately looking for someone, *anyone*. All she saw were the blank faces of the ugly buildings, the empty school grounds – a desolate wasteland. She pulled her phone from her pocket. She dialled 999. Gave details. Screamed for them to hurry. He was dying. *Please be quick.*

'Don't leave me,' she begged. She was beside him again, applying pressure as the operator had instructed. His expression was blank, empty, staring – not even showing any pain. It was so far removed from just ten minutes ago when they'd shared a joint and a tray of chips.

'I can't live without you,' she cried, thinking of everything. She couldn't do it alone. Tears fell from her face and melted into his blood. 'I *won't* live without you.' The sobs burst from deep inside. Spit and phlegm, tears and blood choked her words. '*Bastards,*' she screamed out.

'Stay with me. Stay with me,' she said, panting, rocking, pressing. Where was the ambulance? She tried to pull herself together, scanning through the fragmented memories of the first-aid classes she'd taken last year. Quick-fire revision for a real-life exam no one wanted to take. 'OK, OK.' She helped herself first. She was no good to him in a panic. She fought hard to keep the shots of breath down. She would pass out if they got any faster.

What had she done?

'Shock,' she whispered, refusing to think of it now. Quickly, she let go of the wound on his side and pulled her arms from her jacket. Her limbs shook as she struggled free, draping the coat over him. He was shaking every few seconds – a deep vibration that she felt resonating up through her arms and straight into her heart.

She'd never told him that she loved him.

She saw the pool of blood, dark as death, seeping through the coat at the same time the siren reached out to her.

'Oh, thank God,' she cried. 'The ambulance is coming. Please don't die.' Her arms shook from the strain of clamping his wounds. She was leaning on him, her left forearm tracking a series of deep bleeds while her right arm took care of several more under his ribs.

Suddenly, she heard voices, all around her.

'Young male, about sixteen, seventeen . . . multiple stab wounds to the chest and abdomen. Major blood loss, blow to the head . . . BP falling, pulse weak . . .'

She heard all these things as she was prised out of the way. 'Fifteen,' she whispered from the periphery of the scene, but no one heard. 'He's fifteen.'

'What's going on?' a male voice suddenly snapped at her. Was she in shock too? She couldn't move. A hand fixed round her arm. 'Jesus Christ, tell me what's happened, girl.' He yanked her round, their faces close. Then he was on his phone, calling for people to come, calling for more help, gripping her as if she was getting a telling-off for bunking lessons. 'Jack, it's serious. Get down here now,' he barked into his phone.

She looked up at him. Mr Denton. Her maths teacher.

'Well?' He shook her. His face was red.

'I . . . I don't know,' she whispered. 'I was coming back from the sports centre and . . . and I just found him lying here all messed up.' She swallowed. Her mouth was dry. What was she supposed to tell him?

How could she tell anyone?

Her entire body shook. She stared down at the blood-soaked ground. He had help now, and that was all that mattered, wasn't it? She'd say she didn't know what happened, that she'd had nothing to do with it. She would just go home, call the hospital later to see how he was. It would all be OK. Not as bad as it seemed.

'Did you see anything? A fight? Was anyone else around? Speak, girl!'

She shook her head. She saw the stretcher being lifted away, sealed inside the ambulance.

'*Fucking hell*,' someone said. Another screamed at the blood clotting on the ground. Hands clapped over mouths, eyes wide, people gathering and gawping.

She looked up. The headmaster was striding across the school grounds towards the mayhem. The buildings – our *ship*, as he called it in assembly – had faces crammed at every window. Pupils and staff spilt out on to the far end of the rectangle of dull tarmac that caged twelve hundred teenagers during mid-morning break and lunchtime.

Police swarmed through the school gates. They raced down to where he had dropped, gauging the blood, the denim jacket, the spread of chips, as if that would tell them exactly what had happened. They took control. Everyone was ushered back. Somehow, Mr Denton let go of her arm; somehow, she got swallowed up by the crush of students, teachers, people off the street, and somehow she managed to slip out of the school grounds without anyone knowing she'd gone.

She reckoned, as she ran and ran, that it was all going to be fine.

AUTUMN 2008

Carrie Kent smiled routinely. As if she damn well needed telling. She touched her earpiece. The director was telling her to dig deeper, push harder. *Get him to crack, Carrie.* She wasn't going any easier on the guy because of his age or the circumstances. She knew exactly what she was doing – toying, entertaining, making great TV.

There'll be a fight, she thought, she *hoped*. A quick glance as she turned and paced the set for effect told her that she was flanked offstage by security – two burly men dressed in black with shaved heads, arms folded. All good. She swung round to face camera two, dividing her gaze between an audience that had barely breathed in ten minutes, the row of Britain's best no-hopers that her researchers had dealt her this week, and the viewers. *Classic Carrie*, the producer had once said. She liked that.

'So what you're telling me, Jason . . .' She paused, pulled a concerned face, then continued. 'Is that your baby nephew is actually your son and you're claiming this little family tree gem in order to get back at your brother?'

She walked up to him slowly, with the camera zooming in from behind. She knew the skirt looked good. 'Get back at him for what, exactly, Jason?' she whispered, bending down. The mike would still pick her up. 'Because, forgive me, but I still don't quite understand. We've seen the report. Watched your family . . . er . . . dynamics at work in your home . . .' A quick turn to the camera, an exasperated look. 'There aren't any, are there, Jason? Your family is dysfunctional and, at sixteen, you're already a loser.' She thought of her own son, only a year younger, but immediately refocused, not wanting the viewers to pick up on anything personal. Then, bordering on a yell, she said, 'Did you or did you not sleep with your brother's twenty-seven-year-old wife when you were just fourteen?'

She stepped back, gave the youth the stage. It would go one of two ways – he would cry like a baby or fend off an attack from his brother, who was sitting only five feet to his left, perched on the edge of his seat and waiting to pounce.

Oddly, the boy didn't do anything.

'What we want to know, Jason, is who should little Tyler call Daddy? You or your brother?' The expected rumble of audience disapproval flew around the studio.

Good work, came through her earpiece.

That did it. The brother, who hadn't said much so far, launched himself at Jason, swearing, yelling, toppling him backwards off the chair that was designed to be just a little unstable. Carrie waited a beat, knowing security had been briefed to do the same – they wanted a scuffle, but not bloodshed. People might still be eating breakfast.

Carrie stepped back as security marched on stage and pinned the brothers back in their chairs. 'Now just settle down, the pair of you.' Her voice was commanding. The studio silenced. She spoke first to Jason, then to the camera. 'I think it's time we brought on Bobbi-Jo and heard what she has to say about all this, shall we? Followed by the results of the DNA test.'

Carrie allowed the strand of blond hair to cut across her cheek. *Nice*, she heard the director say in her ear. 'Join us back on *Reality Check* after the break to find out who little Tyler's daddy really is. Don't go away.' Then her famous eye-hand signal, warning the viewers that she was watching them, that her cameras could soon be delving into their lives.

'Off-air,' the director called out. 'Two minutes forty-five.' It was three minutes in reality, but they always ran fifteen seconds ahead. Working in live television, despite the unpredictable contents of the show, suited Carrie perfectly. Everything was precise, controlled and scheduled. Just the way she liked things.

The audience shuffled, mumbled and whispered. Carrie ignored the line-up of dysfunctional guests on her stage. She strode off set, sat on her own chair, sipped specially imported Swiss mineral water, allowed the make-up girl to touch up her cheeks, her eyes, and the stylist to set back that loose strand of hair so that when she tipped her head a certain way, it could fall free all over again.

'One minute ten,' she heard in her ear. Just how would she get this tough little nut to crack before the results? She stood, stared at him sitting rigid with fear on stage. Bobbi-Jo was in the wings opposite: fat, red-faced, eager to get on television to brag about sleeping with an underage boy.

Carrie felt for them, really she did, each and every one of her guests. She was all too familiar with the burning deep inside her chest – the guilt, the sadness that their lives, despite appearing on her show and the help they offered afterwards, would never really change. Then came the rush; the warm lake of security that swept through her, that kept her going, that made her so damned good at her job.

I'm not like them.

Gloss was slicked across her lip. She strode back on stage, faced the camera, smiled and prepared to take apart the miserable family sitting behind her.

Brody Quinell was lying in the dark wondering what stank. Maybe it was the takeaway cartons from the other night, or it could be the drains again. Perhaps it was coming from the flat above. They were pigs. He didn't really care. He liked lying in the dark, feeling the autumn sun stream in through the window, warming his skin, imagining he was on the beach. Jamaica. He could hear music – the dull thud-thud of a bass line. But it wasn't reggae and there were no steel drums. Some emo punk dirge. But he quite liked it. It made him resonate. Down the hall, someone screamed and a toddler wailed. The music went up louder.

Brody's mobile phone vibrated in his shirt pocket. 'Yeah,' he said. It would be the university. He didn't want to think about work today. He just wanted to lie in the dark and be left alone. He sat up suddenly, finding the floor with his feet. 'He did?' He wiped big hands over his tired face, reigniting himself. 'Are you sure?' The slow, definitive *yes* brought Brody fully upright. 'Shit,' he said. He felt around for his clothes. 'I'll be there in twenty minutes. Hold fire. Don't let this get out, right? Don't talk to *anyone.*'

Hopping into his jeans, Brody called Fiona. 'Come on, come on . . . answer . . . Fiona, you have to get over here right away. Something's happened.'

'Of course,' she replied in her usual hyper-efficient manner. 'Everything's in hand, Professor.' Then there was a knock at the door. With the phone still pressed to his ear, Brody fumbled his way across the room and answered it with one leg still out of his jeans. He wasn't wearing a shirt.

'I see you're all ready,' Fiona said, striding in. She snapped her phone shut. 'It stinks in here, Brody.' She sniffed her way to the kitchen and knocked the top off the bin. She pushed down the contents and tied the bag.

'My housekeeper's been off sick.'

'You don't have a housekeeper. But if you did, I'm pretty certain that, yes, she would be sick.'

Brody heard Fiona pull the rubbish sack from the bin and dump it outside on the concrete balcony that ran round the

8

interior of the block, connecting up the hundreds of dismal flats. A group of kids jeered from one end of the run, calling out obscenities to Fiona. She shut the door.

'Do you want me to dress you or are you going to do it yourself?' she said.

Brody lit a cigarette. 'I'm going to think first.'

'Don't you want to get straight down . . .' Fiona stopped. She knew better than to interrupt him, he reckoned. If what he'd just been told was true, then he damn well deserved a smoke. He'd discovered a genius.

'Like I said, when I've finished my cigarette.' Brody felt around the floor for the ashtray. He knew it was around there somewhere. When he couldn't find it, he flicked the ash out of the tiny window opening. It blew right back in, but he didn't notice.

Fiona paced Brody's small living room. He knew she hated coming inside. Usually he was ready and they would head straight out. She said it was depressing with its sickly orange and brown carpet, nicotine-coloured walls and dark, dusty furniture. Nothing was put away. He'd lost count of the times she'd tried to get him to move out. He flatly refused.

'Can't you suck a little harder?' she said.

'I'm thinking.' Brody put on a shirt, belted his jeans and walked around the room, knowing every square inch. He leant on the back of a chair. 'Thing is,' he said slowly, 'what do I do with him now?'

'Write the introduction, publish the paper and give him another one to do.' She rattled her car keys. 'Which you're never going to be able to do unless you put that thing out.'

'It's the bigger picture we're looking at now. What this solution means for the rest of the mathematical world.' Brody was getting excited. 'Even fucking Einstein couldn't do it, Fi.' He strode across the room, catching his leg on the coffee table. He took

Fiona's slim shoulders between his big dark fists. 'Correction. It's not a big picture any more. It's an enormous one. That boy's sat silent in my class for months. I knew he was different.'

'Thanks, but I quite liked my suit without the cigarette ash.'

Brody was sweating, perhaps with anticipation, perhaps with fear of what it all meant. Ricky was his responsibility now. He was the one who had slipped the unproven statistical theory into the student's assignment in the hope that the sullen, shy and friendless boy would rise to the challenge. 'This is life-changing,' he said, dropping the butt out of the window.

He linked arms with Fiona and allowed her to take him to the car. He belted himself in and heard the engine tick over. He heard the mid-morning news on the radio, quickly followed by a click as Fiona turned it off.

'Hurry,' he said. 'I want to get there now. I want to see it for myself.'

Then there was silence. The engine cut out.

'What's going on, Fiona? Drive me to the university.'

'No,' she said quite simply. 'I want you to move out of this dump.'

'What?' Brody was incredulous. He banged the door with his fist. 'Just get driving, Fiona. I want to see Ricky before the story breaks.'

'No.'

Brody heard the keys being taken out of the ignition. 'Now don't be stupid, woman. This isn't what I damn well pay you for.'

'You don't pay me. The university pays my salary.'

'Same darn thing.' They both knew that what he meant was, without him, she wouldn't have a job. 'Drive me or I'll walk.'

'Then, unless you agree to getting a new flat or a nice house somewhere, you'll have to.'

Brody heard her little gasp. She had just told him to walk to work and clearly regretted it. He said nothing.

'Oh God, I'm so sorry.' She jammed the keys back into the ignition and started the engine, but Brody was already out of the car. He leant back in through the open window.

'Fine. You want me to walk, I'll walk.'

'No, no . . . don't. I just don't like seeing you living in . . .' Fiona hesitated, '. . . in there.'

'Honey, then don't look.' Brody laughed. 'I don't.' He turned, snapping a telescopic white stick out of his bag. Like a beagle, he sniffed the air. He angled his face skyward, paused for a moment, then swung through a hundred and eighty degrees.

He knew Fiona would be watching, stunned how he knew the exact direction of the university. So he didn't get killed on the road, she tailed him in first gear all the way.

Half an hour later, Brody gave up and was back in the car.

'I did say white, Martha.' Carrie spoke softly, which was, as Martha knew from experience, worse than yelling. '*White*.' A whisper. She really didn't want to shout.

Carrie pressed the pedal of the gleaming bin and allowed the Swiss chocolates to fall from her hand.

'But the box was white, pet.' Martha shrugged.

'The chocolates. I wanted white *chocolates*, Martha.' Carrie shook her head and brought her vibrating phone to her ear. 'Yes, Leah. What's up?' She walked across the kitchen to the vast expanse of window that gave way to a view of the garden with its steel waterfall, glass walkways and Japanese plants. 'Me? Uptight?' Carrie laughed. 'Why on earth would I be uptight?' She paced through the vast hallway and into the drawing room, making sure Martha was out of earshot. 'The stupid woman got milk chocolates. Not white. This whole cooking thing is getting to me.'

Carrie kicked off her shoes and curled up on the leather chaise that had recently been delivered. She was glad Leah had called. 'Do I really *have* to do it?' she begged – and Carrie rarely begged – her mood softened by her friend and producer's lilting Irish accent. It reminded her of her country house. Of the garden. Of grass. Of everything green and lush. Of when things were normal.

'Can't you come over early? You know I don't do kitchens.' Carrie examined her hands, wondering if there was time for a manicure before they arrived. 'Five o'clock, honey. Please. And get some nice white chocolates on the way over. Swiss.'

Carrie disconnected before Leah could argue. She joined her housekeeper back in the kitchen. Things needed to be sorted.

Martha was virtually invisible, her white uniform blending against the glossy white cupboards. All that stood out was her grey-black hair, her blue eyes. Eyes that didn't believe what Carrie had just done. That little box would have probably racked up fifty pounds on the food hall account.

'You really don't want them?' Martha swallowed and blinked. 'I need a thank-you present for my surgeon. The tumour hasn't spread.'

'What?' Carrie glanced up. She smiled and waved her hand. She was on the phone again. 'No, no. Take them, Martha.' When there was no reply, she left her phone on the stone worktop. 'And I'm sorry. I didn't mean to sound ungrateful before.' She reached out for her housekeeper's shoulders, her hands hovering above the older woman. Martha had been with her for nine years. She knew a lot about her. Too much, she sometimes thought. 'What time are the caterers coming?' She folded her arms across her cashmere sweater. Touching her wouldn't be right.

Martha's skin paled, making her even more invisible. 'Caterers?'

'Yes.' Carrie laughed, bordering on nervous. 'The caterers. I told you to book them a week ago for this wretched dinner tonight.'

'But . . . but you said you wanted to cook for yourself. That home cooking was in fashion and everyone was doing it to save money.' Martha held her breath. 'The ingredients are being delivered later, pet.'

Calmly, just as Martha had seen her do on TV before she let rip at one of her guests, Carrie fell silent. She made a slit of a smile before narrowing her eyes. Her chin jutted forward just a little more than normal, and her shoulders tensed. A single vein on the side of her neck – not usually visible – ticked in time with her heartbeat.

'When I said home cooking was *in*,' she said slowly, 'I didn't mean that I would be doing any actual cooking.' She allowed a little laugh, knowing that she was unable to lose her cool in front of the housekeeper. If she sacked her, she'd probably sell her story to the papers, despite the confidentiality agreement.

Carrie sighed. Television had taught her control, if nothing else. Keeping her voice level was easy. Things could still be sorted. Just. She had people. She had enough money to book an entire restaurant – hell, *buy* an entire restaurant – if necessary. Leah had said that the producer from the States would appreciate some English hospitality. English hospitality was what she would give him.

'Where's Clive today?' Carrie thought fast. Was her Hampstead house, all four thousand white square feet of it, really enough English hospitality? It was a little Spartan. She hadn't thought this through properly. 'Damn it, Martha. Get me Clive.'

Carrie went to lie down. It was only eleven thirty. Things could be done. This could be sorted. She reached for the remote control and drew down the blackout blind. She felt a headache coming on. Moments later the phone beside the bed rang.

'Clive, thank God. Can you fly three of us to Charlbury later? You're an angel. You and Sally go somewhere nice this weekend on me. Love you.' She hung up. Then she touched the direct dial button to Charlbury Hall. 'Answer, answer . . . come on.' She breathed deeply, just how her therapist had shown her. 'Daniel. I'll be home for dinner tonight with two others. Can you make it English? *Very* English . . .' She was about to hang up. 'And you have my permission to use wines from the second cellar.'

Carrie nodded, satisfied the evening was sorted. She flopped back on to her bed, smiling as she tried to imagine herself in the kitchen, jiggling plates and ingredients, making a meal. *Ridiculous*, was her last thought as she dozed off, dreaming about *Reality Check* going Stateside.

Dayna Ray doodled on the cover of her exercise book. She'd scalloped all four edges in blue, coloured them in, and now she was doing it again in green. In the middle of it all she'd drawn a heart. She thought she might write that new kid's name inside it, but not yet. She wanted to mull him over some more first, find out who he was, where he'd come from.

The teacher was harping on about something. Stupid equations. Quadratic something or others. Who cared? She hooked her foot around the strap of her pack and slid the bag towards her. She pulled out a packet of crisps, coughing loudly as she tore it open.

'Give me one,' Neil whispered across the gap between their desks. Dayna pulled a face that told him to get his own, but the idiot's hand shot up above his head. Dayna rolled her eyes and passed across the packet when whatshisface up front wasn't looking. Denton was off sick.

'Don't bloody take them all,' she spat.

'Who's talking back there?' The teacher swung round to the class. None of them was paying attention or taking note of what was on the whiteboard. Most were texting under their desks, some were reading magazines, one was asleep. 'What's the matter with you lot?' he barked. 'Lazy little sods.'

Dayna glanced up. There was a knot of laughter from the kids to her left. Maybe something good was going to happen, like when the last supply teacher ran out in tears and they had the whole lesson to mess about.

She always listened in English, though. It was the only subject she liked; the only reason she bothered coming to school at all. All those stories; all those crazy lives, some even wilder than her own. 'Give them back, you idiot.' Dayna leant across the gap and snatched at the crisps, but her chair toppled and she ended up on the floor. The class howled and whooped. Bits of balled-up paper rained on her head.

'What's your name, girl?'

Dayna looked up. The teacher was looming over her. His skin was pockmarked. He had small hands. 'Dayna, sir.' She stood up and righted her chair. Her hip hurt. 'Dayna Ray.' She slung her pack over her shoulder. She'd be sent out for sure. *Good*, she thought.

'Well, Miss Ray, you can pay a visit to the head's office for being so stupid.' There was a rumble of disapproval around the class. Not because the others didn't want her to get slammed by Jack the Crack, no. They were annoyed because they knew that she'd effectively just been given the day off.

'Not fair, sir. If we all fall off our chairs, can we go too?'

'Silence, you idiot.' The supply teacher scribbled something on a piece of paper. 'Take this to Mr Rushen. Let him deal with you, you stupid girl.'

'Are you allowed to call me that, sir?' Dayna stared up at him through eyes rimmed with kohl. What was she saying? 'To call me stupid.' Another ripple of laughter. A whistle. No one had ever seen Dayna cause a fuss. She reddened and distracted herself by seeking out that new boy, whatever his name was. He wasn't joining in with the predictable catcalls. She couldn't help it that her eyes narrowed to focus on him; to check out what he was doing over there in the corner. Reading, she thought, as she walked towards the door. He was reading a book and it didn't look like a maths textbook. Her stare fixed on him as she turned the handle to leave the class.

At that exact moment, the boy looked up and caught Dayna's eye. He didn't smile, didn't frown, didn't make any smart remarks like the others did as she left. Slowly, the new boy in the corner with his black hair and his skinny neck and his ripped jeans offered a flicker of a wink before turning back to his book.

'Get out of my sight, stupid, stupid girl . . .' Dayna heard the teacher say as she walked out. She had no intention of going to the head's office, but equally she had no intention of going home or hanging out at the shops either. It was English after break and she wanted to go. She'd written an essay. Besides, she wanted to find out more about New Boy. It had been a week since term began and he hadn't said a single word to her yet. She wasn't sure he'd said a single word to anyone.

'A loner,' she said to herself in the mirror, leaning against the sink in the girls' loos. 'We have lots in common already.'

The door banged open. 'Who you talking to, freak?' said one of a pair of sixth-formers. They came up to Dayna, who was pretending to wash her hands. She'd hoped to hide out for a bit.

'No one.' Dayna shrugged and looked at the floor. She knew the routine. Her cheeks were burning and her mouth went dry, a bit like when she'd had to taste bleach. There were no paper towels so she wiped her hands on her school trousers. She bent down for her pack.

'What we got in here, then?' The older girls yanked it from her and unzipped it. They rummaged through the contents.

'Hey,' Dayna said, lunging for it. 'Give me that back.'

'Uh-uh,' the blonde one said. They disappeared into a cubicle with it, leaving Dayna kicking and thumping the door.

'Yuk, that stinks,' one of them said. 'Jesus, look at that.' Then she heard paper ripping and what sounded like the contents of her bag being emptied out. A couple of pages of a precious book fluttered out from underneath the door.

'Just fucking stop it, will you?' Dayna fought back the tears. Not much made her cry. She'd learnt to be tough, to hide it all away, to keep the bad stuff inside. It generally worked. She gave one extra hard kick on the door just as the girls came out.

'Dirty little emo,' one of them said. They left the loos arm in arm, their straightened hair falling in highlighted lines down their backs.

In the cubicle, Dayna found most of her belongings stuffed down the toilet. What wouldn't fit was trodden into the filthy floor. She pulled her pack from the pan. It dripped on to her sweater. A couple of books – including the one she'd been decorating in maths – were sodden and fit for the bin. Her make-up bag had been emptied into the sanitary disposal unit, and the little bit of money that was in her purse was missing.

'Bitches,' she said. Then she felt it start – a burning in her chest, speeding through her body with every banging heartbeat. She grabbed the edge of a basin. 'Breathe slowly,' she told herself when her chest rose and fell in increasingly shallow bursts. The room started to spin. She dropped to the floor, anticipating the blackout that would follow. She didn't want to smash her head on the tiles. This didn't happen often but when it did, she knew she'd been pushed to her limits.

'It's OK, it's OK, it's all OK,' she repeated. Everything suddenly appeared colourless, washed out, unreal. As usual, her eyes fogged and her limbs tingled. The inside of her mouth was dust and the beginnings of a migraine buzzed across her forehead. She breathed. She stared. She counted. She focused, just as the books had told her to do.

Don't let them win, something told her. *You're better than they are.*

Her mouth suddenly filled with saliva. *Please don't be sick*, she prayed. Dayna gripped on to a dusty old pipe that ran behind the basins. It was warm. It sent ripples of comfort through her hands, up her arms and down to the rest of her body. She screwed up her eyes and carried on counting – up to ten over and over again. She rocked. She nursed herself through it.

Then, as quickly as it came, the attack subsided. She'd won. It was the only thing in her life she could control.

When the bell rang, Dayna got up off the floor and left the toilets. In another thirty seconds, the break-time stampede would begin. It marked the start of half an hour's mayhem.

She walked briskly through the building, went outside and slipped round the back of the science labs. She pulled the half-finished joint from her pocket and stared at it. She glanced around, full of the feeling that someone was watching her. They were always taking note, scrutinising her, laughing at her, telling her what a loser she was.

'Don't cry, you silly bitch,' she said, digging her nails into her palms. She kicked the wall of the building, lighting the joint and sucking slowly. She wanted it to last. She'd sold the silver bracelet her real dad had given her as a baby on eBay for this hoard. It was worth it. A couple of lungfuls and she felt better. She glared at a couple of younger kids who dared come near, willing them to leave her alone. She hated them all. A chilly early autumn wind cut between the science block and the boundary fence, making her shiver.

Dayna pulled her mobile phone from her pocket and stared into its mirrored back. She licked her finger and wiped beneath her eyes, trying to get rid of the smudged make-up. She saw the black and orange streaks of her hair in the body of the phone. She thought she looked like a wildcat as she put the mobile away, disgusted with herself. She finished her smoke.

When it was time for English, she skulked back into school,

eyeing groups of kids as they thickened into impenetrable packs in corridors and classrooms. She sat at her usual desk and opened the books she'd salvaged – books that the teacher had given to her because he'd said she'd got an eye for language, that she should experiment, read a lot. She got her head down to work, making character notes on *Romeo and Juliet*. She chewed her pen and glanced across at the new boy. He was working too. She wondered if he was anything like Romeo, if they would fall in love.

She went back to her books and made a list of the cast, circling her favourites in red, jotting notes across the page, highlighting the bits she loved, frowning at the bits she didn't understand, the language that occasionally passed her by in an unintelligible string of gobbledygook. *An eye for it* . . . She pondered her teacher's words, wondering how it was that she could understand everything about the lives of fictitious characters yet nothing about her own.

Carrie Kent was majorly under-impressed with the producer from the States. Was he really here to talk business? She nudged Leah's foot under the table. Leah glanced up and scowled. Carrie scowled right back and hoped her best friend, her producer, her right-hand woman, was happy that she'd wasted an entire evening without the tiniest glimmer of a US series to be had.

The dreadful man was nothing more than a tourist with some half-bit show on an obscure cable channel. He had only come to gawp, to say he'd spent the evening with the famous Carrie Kent while visiting London. And then there was the cost of it all – the helicopter fees, the food, and, oh, the *wine*. Rich she may be, but she didn't like wasting money. It went against every fibre of her being. Some things were genetically programmed.

'So,' she said, leaning forward on her arms. She might as well play him like a guest on *Reality Check*. Bob Dane or Dole or

Dreary . . . she couldn't remember which – put down his knife and fork. He virtually melted on to his rabbit fricassée at the sight of Carrie's smile and her low-cut dress. 'Silly old me thought you came here to talk about a US version of my show, Bob.'

He laughed and dabbed at his mouth. 'Bill. My name's Bill.'

Carrie glanced at the mantel clock. Nine forty-five. Would it be horribly impolite if she wrapped things up by ten thirty? She was good at wrapping things up. She did it every week on her show, usually to the detriment of her guests, right at the point of no redemption. She wondered if he would notice if she disappeared upstairs to watch a movie.

'I'm so sorry. *Bill.*' Carrie leant to the side while her waiter went round with the wine. 'Don't open any more,' she whispered in his ear, wistfully eyeing the level of the Château Latour specially brought up from the reserve cellar for what she believed was going to be a very special occasion. Wasting such a treat with this jerk was a travesty. At best it deserved to be drunk in the company of her closest friends – three, four, five bottles of the stuff, deep into the night. At worst – better than this – she'd have settled for it on her own, crashed out on her bed, allowing the velvet of it alongside a platter of French cheese to quieten her mind.

'So what do you think of my little show?' Carrie noticed Leah's raised eyebrows, the dab of her lips to cover the smirk, the jut of her angled jaw. Oh, they'd probably laugh about this later, but for now it was painful.

'I haven't yet had the pleasure of viewing your show, Mrs Kent.' Bill forked up rabbit with one hand and hovered his wine glass near his lips with the other. 'But I've heard so much about you, I couldn't resist calling you up for a meet.'

Leah, what the hell were you thinking arranging this? Carrie shot a look at her friend.

20

'And I'm just loving your English hospitality.' He stuffed his mouth. Carrie looked away.

'I'm so glad. Nathan will be in the car waiting to drive you back to London in twenty minutes. Isn't that right, Leah? Will you call him and check he's on schedule?' she said pointedly. She'd be damned if she was flying him back to his hotel.

Leah gave a salute. 'Yes, ma'am.' She grinned and left the table.

'To be honest, Mrs Kent—'

'Ms Kent.' She couldn't take another Mrs.

'To be honest, since I have been in your company this evening, since I have had the pleasure of meeting you in person, since . . .' and he shifted his chair closer to Carrie and trailed a finger along her wrist. She snapped her arm away. 'Since I have come to know you—'

'But you don't know me.' Carrie used her show voice, the one where the guest has no way out. He was messing with the wrong woman. How tiresome.

'I would like to take you for dinner—'

'All set with Nathan,' Leah said. She grasped what had been going on in a second. She wheeled round behind Carrie's chair and threw her arms around her bare shoulders. She bent down and delivered a fond kiss right on her lips. Carrie took her cue and grabbed her friend's arms, pulling her closer. The two women eyed Bill pitifully and raised their eyebrows, smiling. He sat there for a moment, perhaps considering whether to ask them both for a date, before reddening and excusing himself.

'Don't even *go* there,' Carrie said when he'd left the room. She shoved Leah off her back. She dropped her head on to the table, suddenly hit square on the jaw by the huge empty space that was her love life.

She groaned, 'Things must be really bad. *Really* bad.'

'Oh?' Leah pulled a face and waited for her friend to continue.

Carrie lifted her head. 'Part of me actually considered accepting his offer.'

Max Quinell stared up at the dismal block of flats. The dingy concrete merged with the sky. He liked it; liked the red, black and green slashes of graffiti shouting out through the murky weather. He liked the fact that there weren't any trees or lawns or neatly clipped bushes outside stupid front doors. He liked the sense of danger that clawed around his body as he walked deeper into the tenement.

He pulled up his hood and bent his head parallel to the pavement. The box was tucked under his right arm, a little crushed but he knew the contents were fine. He shoved the other hand deep inside his pocket, fingering his fags, his lighter, the cash his mother paid directly into his bank account for the taxis he never took. The key was there. His phone was in his back pocket, probably ripe for nicking given the groups of youth that hung around here.

But what he didn't feel in his pocket, and sorely wanted to, was a knife. The compact, silky-smooth handle wrapped around its hidden blade; the effortless protection whipped out in an instant at the first sign of trouble; the look on their faces when it glinted; the power, the shock, the safety. Everyone else had one, didn't they?

But he just couldn't bring himself to get one. No one would sell him one without ID and, while he knew he could probably buy one off some of the kids who hung around his dad's estate, he wasn't brave enough to do it. Would owning one, he wondered, invite more trouble? He didn't want that. Then again, he thought, taking the stairs two at a time, not having one could be asking for trouble too.

Max banged on the door. He waited a while. His father might be . . . doing something. With someone. That woman, Fiona. When there was no reply, he let himself in.

'Jesus fucking—' he said, retching. The stink was overpowering. He covered his nose with his sleeve and went round the tiny flat opening curtains and windows. He'd not visited in a while. No one had, he reckoned. So much for his dad's stupid assistant.

He put the box down on the table in the living room. 'Dad?' he called out. He wandered around, kicking old cans and empty food cartons, tripping on strewn clothes and shoes, picking up CDs and gadgets that he'd given him over the months. He eyed the box he'd brought with him today, wondering if his father would even want it.

Sighing, Max began in the tiny kitchen. It was the worst. He pulled off his hoodie and draped it over the back of a chair. He lifted the stack of congealed plates and takeaway cartons from the sink, sorting what could be thrown away.

He's managed to take the rubbish out at least, Max thought, noting the empty bin and fresh liner. He pushed his earphones into place and turned up his music full volume. Somehow, it made the stench seem less. Then he set to washing up, plunging his skinny arms into soapy water that soon became greasy and brown. He emptied the sink, dried up what he had washed so far, then began again. After that, he wiped down all the surfaces, spraying everything with some cleaner he'd found under all the junk in the cupboard. It was that easy, he thought, unable to understand why the place was such a . . .

'Hey! Jesus, you fucking scared the sh—'

'Doesn't your mother teach you any manners at all?' Brody Quinell released his son, but received a face full of suds for creeping up on him and grabbing him round the chest. 'If you will deafen yourself with those stupid things then expect to be pounced upon.' His father roared with laughter, apparently in a good mood.

Max pulled out his earphones and heard the tss-tss of the music in his palms. He turned off his iPod and stuffed the thin wires in his pocket. He wiped his hands down the front of his jeans and followed his father into the living room. 'I haven't tidied in here yet.'

'Good,' Brody replied. 'Then I won't be losing anything.'

'You can't leave it like this. Doesn't that woman of yours do anything?'

'Firstly, she's not my woman. Secondly, I see no logical reason for you to refer to her in that tone and, thirdly, you're a teenage boy. You should understand and embrace the disorder. Don't tell me your mother makes you keep your room tidy?' Brody lit a cigarette.

Max wondered if it would matter if he smoked too. Would his dad even know?

'Help yourself.' Question answered. Brody threw the packet at him, aimed perfectly in his direction. How did he do that? 'And don't pretend to me you don't smoke, either.' He shook his head and went round closing all the windows. 'I often smell it on you. Bloody cold today,' he complained.

For the next ten minutes father and son sat in silence. Max watched as his father's cheeks hollowed with every pleasurable suck on the cigarette. There was something about the way his lips curled round the slim stick, the way his large hands ridged with veins deftly bent around it, holding it at his mouth. Max copied his dad. He stared at his own hands, smaller, a bit paler, smoother. He switched his cigarette between his thumb and forefinger but dropped it on to the dirty rug.

'Don't burn the place down,' Brody said.

Max laughed, picking it up and flicking his ash. 'Here,' he said. 'I brought you a present.' He touched the box against his dad's hand. Brody took it and shook it. He felt the size of it while holding the cigarette between his lips.

'Not another blood-pressure monitor, I hope.'

For a second, Max looked crestfallen. 'It's an electric whisk. You can beat eggs with it. Or froth milk.'

'Why the fuck would I want to do that?'

'Omelette? Cappuccino? I dunno.' Max felt like taking it back. But his mother wouldn't want it either. 'I'll put it in the kitchen cupboard. Get Fiona to show you how it works. It could be useful.' He tried to refer to her with less resentment. Thing was, while she was in his father's life, there was no chance of a reconciliation between his parents. A crazy idea, he knew, and although he didn't want to dislike Fiona, he simply couldn't help it. She was the one who had replaced his mother when things had gone bad.

'No space in the kitchen 'cos of all the other shit you gave me. No more kitchen gadgets, son, OK? Don't mind the mobile phones or the music, and the weekend break was a nice touch. But no more electric griddles or bread-makers.'

Max squinted. They'd always been honest with each other. 'Sure, Dad.' He stood. 'I'll get on with the washing-up.'

'Fuck you will,' Brody said, rearing up and grabbing his son with a lucky lunge at his arm. 'We're going out to celebrate.'

'Celebrate what?'

'That my little protégé cracked something that simply shouldn't have been cracked by a kid. And you, son, have a new woman.'

Max stopped dead. 'New woman?'

'Don't deny it, Maxie. You smell like a duty-free shop. Calvin Klein? Armani?'

'Beckham.' Max pulled on his hoodie.

Brody grinned, white teeth flashing, proud as hell. 'She hot? Got big—'

'No, Dad. You're wrong.' Max sighed heavily. He threw his father's leather coat at him, gathered the bunch of house keys from the window sill, quite unable to explain why he was suddenly thinking of that weird girl at his new school again.

THE PAST

Carrie Kent had worked in television for only three years – first as a news anchor woman and then as assistant presenter on *Crime Hits*, a late-night satellite production tailing the Met as they made live arrests – when *Reality Check* first went to air. That's how she'd met Dennis. With a few years' experience and a desire to succeed, she pitched her show idea to the station and it was snapped up, leaving the senior commissioners wondering why they hadn't thought of it before.

Carrie, they said, would become a household name. They would make her a star. She would be the most talked about female presenter with the highest rated daytime show ever. And it was true. It happened, and quickly. Never once did she consider that the price she paid for fame would far outweigh her astronomical earnings.

Reality Check first aired on 3 September 1999. It was initially commissioned for a twelve-week run but was so popular, it hadn't missed a slot since it began. When Carrie took a holiday or was ill, re-runs were aired to sate the public's hunger for real-life drama, misery and crime.

'We just hit the formula,' Leah boasted as Carrie's best friend and producer. Having pursued a career in journalism, radio production and then children's television, Leah was Carrie's right-hand woman. The women were inseparable both in and out of the studio. 'It's all about the presentation and style. That's down to Carrie's talent. Without her, we wouldn't have a show, we'd have a news bulletin.'

Every women's magazine in the country had run interviews with Carrie Kent over the years. Each time they'd attempted an insight into her private life, the secret side of Carrie Kent, and each time they'd failed. Her divorce from Brody was covered with double-page splashes of speculation, but she refused to be drawn into the gossip that her ex's blindness was a factor in their break-up. Carrie's lack of comment fuelled further stories about a dysfunctional private life – how she'd shipped her young son off to boarding school because she couldn't cope.

'That's what happens,' she was told by an older presenter at the station, 'when you get so famous. There comes a time when simple, honest celebrity is no longer enough. They have to know about that line of coke or that you once paid for sex. They want to bring you down, Carrie. Always remember that.'

Those words stuck with her, became her mantra, and not a day went by when Carrie didn't have cause to believe it. *They want to bring me down.*

Four years into the show and with enough cash in the bank to buy her own television station – there had been spin-offs, too, plus her ever growing fee – Carrie decided, no, *needed*, to get away.

'It's only for a few days. Just me. Alone.' She didn't give Leah the chance to argue. She hung up and switched off her mobile from Friday evening until Wednesday lunchtime. She had no idea what the following week's show would hold and neither, at that time, did she care. She could hazard a guess: pregnant teen, battered wife, unfaithful husband, missing person, drug addict, alcoholic spouse, shoplifter or car thief. There was no end to human depravity. Rehearsal not needed. She'd deal with the brief on her return.

Carrie spent an hour trawling the internet for somewhere to go. This time she didn't want five-star luxury and she didn't want to stay anywhere she'd be recognised. Airports were out of the question. She just wanted to be normal, to get excited about being alone, to take long, deep breaths of fresh air that weren't filled with stress, crime or rumour.

That rules out most of the United Kingdom, she thought, flitting from one website to another, but she persevered. She liked the look of a log cabin on the far side of Loch Lomond. It was vacant. She emailed the owner and booked under a false name, promising cash on arrival.

The drive was exhilarating. She'd requested that a hire car be delivered – her personal plate was too recognisable – and the Jeep was perfect. She sped non-stop up the motorway, having stocked up on water and food before she left. After Glasgow, she stopped in a lay-by, ate and folded back the soft top of the vehicle. It was a starry night, warm even for Scotland, and she liked the moonlight on her shoulders, the moths swimming through the high beam as she wound round the edge of the loch to her cabin.

When she pulled through the gates of the park, everything was silent. Eight cabins sat nestled in private wooded areas at the loch side of a large estate. She had booked cabin number six. Driving along the track, the headlights barely picking out the worn-down earth that denoted the way between the trees, Carrie inhaled deeply. The air was brimming with oxygen, the scent of nature and peace. She was conscious of the rattling diesel engine disturbing the quiet, although there didn't seem to be any signs of life from the other cabins she'd spotted.

'Three . . .' she said to herself, catching sight of a plaque nailed to a tree, but then the next number she saw was five at the edge of a clearing. Beyond, she saw a simple rectangle of logs and shingle silhouetted against the moonlit water. The thrill of being totally alone for a few days was comforting yet dangerous. Something had taken her beyond a point she never usually reached. If she hadn't escaped, she believed that her mind and body might have imploded. Leah hadn't liked it, and her agent had kicked up at the cancellations he'd have to make, but they'd manage without her, they finally said, knowing arguing was futile.

'At last,' Carrie said to herself. She steered round behind a tree, heading towards cabin number six. 'It's cute.' She switched off the engine. She thought of leaving the headlights on to guide her to the door but decided that she'd prefer to walk through the darkness. It was easy, navigating her way through the trees with the moonlight reflecting off the loch. By the look of it, she'd have a first-class view of the scenery from the veranda that spanned the end of the cabin. Her heart skittled with excitement. Five whole days of solitude. She would do absolutely nothing except walk, think, sleep and read.

She tripped on the step up to the door.

'Shit.' Her voice ricocheted through the woods and skimmed over the water. It was incongruent in the serene place. Something rustled in the undergrowth behind her – a fox, a badger? Because the booking was at such short notice, the owner had emailed to say that a key would be left under a pot of flowers beside the door. There was no pot.

'Damn,' she said. Again, her expletive cut through the still night. Carrie squinted through the darkness and thought she saw a pot further round on the veranda. The wood beneath her feet creaked as she felt her way along the cabin's side.

Something came crashing down – sticks and poles. Something wound round her, getting caught in her hair and nails.

Carrie squealed. 'Bloody stupid—'

A light came on. The door opened.

'Who's there?' The voice was deep and commanding.

30

Despite being tangled up, Carrie spun round to see a male figure to accompany the angry words.

'What?' She tried to fight the things off. 'Who are you? What are you doing in my cabin?'

There was laughter – something suddenly warming about it, but laughter from another person that she hadn't expected. She'd wanted to be alone. Totally alone.

'*My* cabin?' he asked, approaching her.

Carrie squinted into the light behind him. She pulled a wire or line from her hair. 'Ow!' she cried, sucking her finger when something sharp stuck it.

'Well now, just look what I caught.' The man came close. He was about her age and, even though it shouldn't have been her primary thought, she couldn't help noticing his good looks.

'Caught?' Carrie tasted blood. Did he recognise her?

'You're all tangled up in my fishing gear. Helping yourself, were you?'

'No! Of course I wasn't.' She yanked what she now knew to be fishing line from around her arm. 'You were supposed to have vacated this cabin today. I'm the new occupier.'

The man laughed again. 'I don't think so. This is my cabin.'

'Then you should know that I booked cabin six for five nights.' Carrie finally rid herself of the tackle.

'You did, did you?'

'Yes. I was looking for the key when your stupid stuff got in my way.'

'And where was that key meant to be?' The man leant, rather infuriatingly Carrie thought, on the cabin wall. She noticed his very white teeth as he grinned.

'Under the pot.'

The man casually peered around. 'I don't see any pots.'

'Exactly. I was emailed lousy instructions. Can I see inside? I'm only paying if it's satisfactory.' Carrie suddenly had visions of sleeping the night in the Jeep, which, she thought, might not be too bad. Already her plan to escape from people had gone wrong. Was there nowhere in this country to hide?

'Sure,' he said, turning, expecting her to follow.

From the light spilling out of the cabin, Carrie could see that the area around the lodge was dense woodland. She loved the way the trees gave way to water. Once she'd got rid of this man, she would slip from the shadows into the depths of the loch for a midnight swim. It would help her forget this false start.

'Welcome,' he said, holding open the door.

Carrie stepped inside. It didn't look quite like the pictures. How could the simple white New England style in the website photos look anything like this eclectic mix of big dark furniture, old woven rugs and sports equipment – everything from wet-suits to sails to walking boots and even a bicycle propped by the door.

'I think there's been some mistake,' Carrie said. Not hers, though. Cabin six, Kinlochburn Hall. The directions to the estate on the north east side of the loch were unmistakable.

'I think you're right. Can I get you a drink?' He reached over the kitchen counter and produced a bottle of single malt.

'I just want you to go. This is a disaster.' Carrie was deflated. She looked round the cabin. It was OK but not what she'd paid for. And she wasn't *alone*. She felt close to tears and hated herself for it. Was she incapable of a normal existence outside the boundaries set by her celebrity lifestyle?

The man shrugged and poured from the bottle. 'Can't do that.'

'Why the hell not? Is this some kind of set-up?' She half expected a camera crew to appear or the wretched man to produce a tape recorder. Oh, why didn't she let her secretary take care of the booking?

'Don't think so, nope.' He fell down into a large leather settee that was draped in furs. His arms spread along the back of the chair. He drank his whisky. He stared at her.

'So what am I to do?' Carrie's voice quivered. People usually did as they were told.

The man shrugged. 'Guess if it were me, I'd apologise, leave without any further fuss, and drive a little way along the track until I reached cabin number six.' He grinned and downed the last of the whisky.

'This isn't six?'

'Nope.' He stood and walked past Carrie, the smile still there. He put his glass in the kitchenette sink. 'The number plaque's a little weathered. This is number eight.'

'Do you know who I am?' When he realised, he'd be sorry.

'Nope again.' He was right in front of her now, all big and tanned with his Scottish accent weighing down his words so Carrie could hardly understand him. No wonder wires had been crossed.

'I'm Carrie Kent, for God's sake, and you have entirely ruined the start of my break.'

'Pleased to meet you, Carrie Kent. I'm Jason McBride.' He held out his hand. 'I own the estate. My family have lived at Kinlochburn Hall for three centuries.'

Carrie was vaguely aware of her hand being drawn into his, only half conscious of him explaining why he lived in the cabin for part of the year, how he needed the solitude, but fully alert when his mouth suddenly came down on hers.

As he kissed her, she was already reading the trashy headlines: *Carrie's Secret Snog . . . One-Night Stand For* Reality Check *Star . . . Kent's Secret Lover Spills All . . .*

Despite what was going on in her head, she didn't immediately pull away. She listened to the voice telling her all the things that she'd come to Scotland to do – be alone, relax, unwind, escape, recharge – but her resolve was waning with every inch more of him that pressed against her.

'Stop!' she managed, gasping for air. 'I can't do this. Do you know who I am?' She knew she sounded ridiculous. Briefly, she was reminded of Brody, felt a pang of regret as she recalled their first passionate night together seemingly a lifetime ago.

'You just told me. And you know who I am. So we're even.'

Oh no we're not.

And he pulled her close again, attempting a further kiss.

'Turns out,' Carrie said to Leah just before the next show went to air, 'that he doesn't even own a television. Imagine, in that great mansion. So he hadn't got a clue who I was.'

Leah glanced over the top of her glasses and shook her head. A smile threatened but she fought it back. 'And you're honestly telling me that you didn't sleep with him?'

'Not even a little bit. But we swam together. We fished. Cooked and ate the catch. We went for walks and he showed me the big house.'

'I thought you wanted to be alone.' Leah handed over several files to her assistant as she passed through the set.

Carrie was about to defend herself, but there wasn't time. She paused for a moment then walked out on stage. There was applause from the studio audience. She stared at them – hundreds of people all here to see *her*.

Then it hit her, beneath her ribs in a spot so sore it hurt right up to her throat.

It was true. She *had* wanted to be completely by herself, to enjoy the solitude, just as Jason McBride did for a few months each year. Technically, she had failed on every level. And Leah clearly didn't understand. Whether live on air being watched by millions, or in the company of just one other person, Carrie Kent was *always* alone.

AUTUMN 2008

'What do you mean . . . no?' It came out as a squeak, she was so unused to being refused. The phone was hot against her ear. Sun cut across her right cheek, magnified by the glass. The engine was ticking idly, her foot poised to hit the accelerator, but he'd said *no*. It appeared she wasn't going anywhere.

'Look, Dennis . . .' God, she hated that name. It reminded her of cardigans and golf. 'Detective Chief Inspector,' she tried. 'This has been arranged for over a week. I have a film crew on standby. I have slots to be filled. A show to produce.' Carrie felt the beginnings of a sweat break out. This family were box-office news at the moment. She had to see them. Wait another couple of days and it would all be over. Or, worse, someone else would get to them first.

'Listen, Dennis darling, unless you can conveniently arrange another stabbing for me by ten thirty tomorrow then I'm going to have to find myself another friendly det—'

Grim laughter drowned the line. Then there was silence. 'Just kidding.'

A pause. 'What?' She jammed her foot on the accelerator and, before she snapped the phone shut and threw it on to the passenger seat, she called him a stupid fuck.

The car was hot and airless, even though it was a cool day. Carrie sat in the front while DCI Dennis Masters drove. He'd put on the siren because he knew she loved it. Another detective sat in the back with his knees pressed into Carrie's spine.

She opened the window and leant her arm out, enjoying the wind as they pushed through the tide of cars that bumped up on to kerbs and panicked on to the central reservation as they approached.

'Makes me laugh,' she said, unwilling to admit that she'd felt helpless when Dennis had said the meeting was off. 'Such a thrill, all these people getting out of our way.' She spent the rest of the journey pondering how she could achieve this effect with the rest of her life, but, just before they arrived, she came to the conclusion that she already had.

'This is it,' Dennis said grimly. He peered beneath the sun visor, looking at the row of council houses. He pulled the keys from the ignition and glanced at Carrie. 'Whatever you may think, Ms Kent, these people have just lost their only son. Be—'

'I will be nice. I'm not completely without feeling.' Carrie pulled a sympathetic face and pushed her sunglasses on top of her head. Deep in her chest, she felt something – was it sympathy? she wondered – as she fleetingly tried to put herself in the position of the bereft mother sitting within those grim walls. She shook her head. It was too awful to contemplate. 'OK. Let's get this over with.'

Without these meetings, the exploration into the homes and lives of her victims, as Carrie called them, *Reality Check* wouldn't be the show it was. It was infamous for its unforgiving style of reporting – a journalistic gash into lives ripped apart by tragedy. The production team also prided itself on the aftercare and counselling offered, as well as the usefulness of the police hotline that was always onscreen to offset the gawping at misery. Carrie had once described her show as a car crash. People just couldn't help but stare.

'Is he coming in with us?' Carrie asked. She'd not seen this young detective before. Carrie had what she called a special arrangement with the Met. 'Don't ask,' she'd urged Leah when the first show aired. 'It's complicated.' She meant her relationship with Dennis and the benefits that afforded. That was nearly ten years ago now. A heated fling – him wanting more, her killing it dead before he got too needy. Soon she would reach her five hundredth show. Carrie suddenly felt incredibly old; incredibly lonely.

'Let's go, Mr Plod.' She tapped the young cop on the shoulder.

'My mate used to live around here.' He was doleful, suddenly grey-faced, staring around the desolate rows of pebble-dashed buildings. 'Got killed. Drugs deal screw-up. Fifteen, he was.'

Carrie smiled. This was good. A cop with a conscience. 'Then you'll have lots in common with Mrs . . .' She glanced at her notes. 'With Mrs Plummer, won't you? Her kid was stabbed in the neck when he refused to give up his mobile phone to a gang of youths.' She walked off, shaking her head, wishing she had a pair of those plastic shoe covers that surgeons used. The path was littered with dog muck and she didn't reckon the house would be much better, if the outside was anything to go by.

It was as the door eased back by a couple of inches, while Carrie was focusing on the thinnest, most gaunt and unbearably sad woman she had ever seen, that her mobile phone rang. Automatically she pulled it from her jacket pocket. She glanced at the screen. It was her son. With a swallow, she cut him off. Now was really not the time.

Max Quinell liked to be on his own. With parents like his, he figured it was OK to escape for a few hours. No one knew the shed was down here.

Inside, as his eyes adjusted to the dimness, he glanced around as always. Nothing was missing. It was all in perfect order, unlike the rest of his life. OK, so the shed was dilapidated, the wall timbers clinging to each other with rot, and the roof dry-lined with an old tarpaulin, but for Max it was a home away from his homes. *This* was his real home. No one bothered him, no one else had yet staked a claim on the ten-foot square shack that sat forgotten beneath the railway bridge – a workers' store once, he presumed – so therefore, by rights, Max considered it his. One day, he thought to himself, I might move in for good.

He sat down in the old car seat that he'd dragged up from the canal bank. Ford, he reckoned. He pulled a packet of fags from his pocket and lit one, using the same match to light a scented candle on a wooden crate. It had been part of a set – lavender bath oils, face mask, the candle in a blue glass jar. He was going to give them to his mum for Mother's Day, but really . . . He laughed, coughing as the smoke coursed into his lungs. That particular runner's-up gift pack would have been better off going to Oxfam – or not, he thought, as he remembered how the face mask had stung his skin. Crap quality, he reckoned. It had given him a crop of spots for a week.

'So,' he said, gazing lovingly at his stuff. 'Who and what next?' He pulled the list out from under the crate. It ran into six pages now. Thirty items per page, that's what he reckoned – going on two hundred items. Two hundred strokes of luck – or genius and skill, he preferred to think. Especially the ones with the captions. He usually won those; had always been good with words.

The boxes were stacked as high as the old tarp clinging to the roof. Big ones at the bottom, smaller ones at the top. It made sense. It was order. He'd learnt that from his mother. The stuff that didn't come in boxes was piled in the corner as best he could manage. It annoyed him, the lack of square edges, of stability, of dependability. He knew that if he piled the toasters, the juicers, the hairdryers, the fridges, they would be in the same spot the next day. Randomly shaped packets, long tubes, soft squashy toys often took a tumble and greeted his feet when he opened the door.

Max chewed a pencil and ran his finger down the list. His nails were long. Best for the guitar, except his mother didn't like the din. She told him to stop. 'It's like dirt on the floor, darling. You'd take off your muddy shoes if I asked, wouldn't you?' He regretted it now, but he'd left the guitar on the railway line for a train to mash. Part of him wished it was him that was splintered and scattered – just an echo of a life once loved left behind.

'The bread-maker,' he said, businesslike. 'Or the pressure washer.' But who? he wondered. His father was always ungrateful and Fiona . . . well, he wouldn't give her the shit off his boots, let alone one of these prized babies. He'd done most of his teachers and some of his classmates. They just mocked him and sold the loot on eBay. Used the money for booze and fags. He could do the same, of course, but he preferred not to. He didn't want to devalue the hope they represented.

'That girl.' He winced as the words sounded louder than he'd intended. 'That. Girl.' He broke her down, as if That Girl was her name. 'Miss Girl. Miss That Girl, I would like to give you this bread-making machine as an act of random friendship. May we be friends, Miss Girl?' Max pulled a face. It wasn't right. Not the bread-maker, he decided. He pulled the white and orange box that contained the pressure washer off the pile. He'd not opened it yet. Virgin goods. He liked that. 'Miss Girl, I have this pressure washer, and I'd like you to have it.'

In his mind, Miss Girl's face lit up. She dropped the heavy pack that she always carried – full of books, he'd noticed – and she gratefully took the box from him. 'Just what I've always wanted,' she said, beaming. 'Now I can clean the drive. Now I can hose down my dad's car. Now I can strip the graffiti off the garage wall. Thanks, Max. Thanks so much.' And Miss Girl stood on her tiptoes and gave him a kiss. A long, slow, wet, lingering kiss full on the mouth. He got an erection.

He shook his head and stared at the list. Pressure washer. Yep, he remembered that competition. Judge must have had a sense of humour. The local hardware store had been doing a promotion in the car park. Ten uses for a pressure washer, the girl in the bikini had said, waving a leaflet at Max when he'd popped in for a light for his bike. Have a go. He'd leant on someone's bonnet, filling out his ten suggestions. The last one, he distinctly recalled, was *Cleaning all the shit outta my life.*

'Pressure washer it is then,' he said, putting a line through the item. Next to it he wrote *Miss Girl. To be delivered. By hand.*

Dayna Ray was crying when she felt the tap on her shoulder. She flinched. They'd come back to get her. Bitches. Her breathing quickened as another panic attack welled inside her.

'Hey.' It was a boy's voice. She didn't recognise it. She looked up from behind the curtain of her hair. Her fringe was too long and she let it hang over her eyes to conceal the black mess that she knew ringed her lashes.

'What?' she said. Her breathing slowed.

'I was gonna ask you the same.'

Dayna sat bolt upright. It was *him*. Shit. 'You don't need to sit down, you know.' Best get rid of him. She looked such a state.

At this, the boy kicked a crumpled Coke can out of the way and dropped down next to her in the gutter. He offered her a fag. She shrugged and took one.

'Bad day?' he asked.

'Bad life.'

'You'll be needing this then,' he said, sliding a box across the alley to her. It was wrapped in yellow paper.

Dayna frowned. 'It's not my birthday.' She touched it. Ash fell on the paper. 'You weird or something?' She brushed off the ash. 'Did you follow me?'

The boy stared at her, shrugging. She could see the tiny flicks of his eyes as his gaze ran around her face. She knew she looked a mess. He laughed. 'You look like a vampire. A ghoul or something.' He blew smoke at her. 'Go on. Open it. It's for you.'

Dayna frowned and sighed. 'Shouldn't we at least introduce ourselves? It wouldn't be right otherwise.' Then she thought, is this a set-up? Is the box full of crap from the bin?

The boy leant across with his hand outstretched. 'Max Quinell,' he said. 'Year eleven no-hoper and all-round outcast. Pleased to meet you.'

Dayna felt her cheeks burning. She relaxed a little. 'Dayna Ray. Year eleven punchbag and also all-round outcast. Delighted to meet you, too.'

They shook hands.

Dayna felt it. Up her wrists, along her shoulders, straight into her heart.

By the look in his eyes, the deepening of their chocolate colour, she reckoned he felt it too.

God.

'So. What is it?' She sniffed. She hadn't got a tissue. She pulled off the paper and stared at the box. She tilted her head round to read. 'Xtreme-Force Pressure Washer including rotating head and six-metre hose.' Dayna looked up at Max. 'Nice,' she said, nodding. Then she started laughing. A laugh that tore the fear and hate from her belly, a laugh that rang between the walls of the dank alley where she sometimes chose to sit, a laugh that announced to the universe that everyone had better watch out because she'd got a new pressure washer.

'You like it?'

'Love it,' she said.

41

'Now you can clean up your life.'

'It's already working,' she said, hardly able to wait to get the thing out of the box.

Fiona Marton usually ate her lunch alone. It wasn't by choice, rather because Brody insisted on eating *his* lunch alone, holed up in his office forking noodles from a carton, thereby leaving her on call and unable to go with the others to the canteen or that new place round the corner. She didn't care. She could watch him through the glass partition, hunched over his desk, just thinking, just eating, occasionally drawing half a bottle of water in one gulp. She'd eat her sandwich – always cheese and lettuce – studying him as she chewed thoughtfully, imagining, wondering.

Today, however, was different. 'Let's go out for lunch,' Brody said mid-morning. He'd just finished a lecture. Fiona nearly fell off her chair. She was typing up some letters he'd dictated earlier, all part of her job.

'You mean us?' She couldn't look at him. Blind or not, the man seemed to know when she blinked. He was sure to feel the heat of her blush.

'Of course us.' He waited for her response. 'Well?'

'Yes,' she replied, wondering what the catch was. He went back to his office. She watched as he typed on his laptop. The talk-back facility was turned down so low she could barely hear it. Brody, she knew, heard every syllable clear as a bell, confirming that what he had entered was correct. 'That would be very nice,' she called out. She wished she'd worn her new blouse.

By one o'clock they were seated in a booth in what Fiona could only describe as a greasy spoon caff not far, she noted dismally, from the estate where Brody lived. Sticky red plastic benches bracketed an equally sticky laminated table. 'God, you should see this place,' Fiona said. 'It's trying to be all fifties diner, but actually I think everything here literally *is* from the fifties. Including the food.'

Brody grunted.

She sighed and picked up the menu. It wasn't what she'd had in mind. 'There's bacon and eggs. Bacon butty. Egg butty. Scrambled egg and bacon, with or without tom—'

'I'm having Chef's Special.'

Fiona glanced at the menu, then looked around the diner and saw it written up on a chalk board. 'You're right. There's a Chef's Special. What is it?'

'Different every day.' He stopped, turned to his left, paused for a moment. 'How's it going, Edie?' His face rippled to a smile.

'Just wonderful, thank you, Professor. I'm a grandma for the sixth time.' Edie smoothed out her apron proudly.

Fiona saw that there were a couple of other waitresses buzzing about. How, then, had he known this was Edie? He must have been in before, but when?

'Two Chef's Specials and two coffees please,' Fiona said. She just wanted to get this over with and get back to work. Lunch wasn't exactly what she'd hoped it would be – time spent with Brody in a classy restaurant, perhaps him finally telling her how he'd felt about her all these years. She sighed and unrolled the cutlery from the napkin that Edie left on the table.

When they were alone again, Brody cleared his throat. 'I brought you here for a reason, Fiona,' he said.

'Oh?' Stupidly, her heart missed a beat. Just one, but enough to make her catch her breath, enough for Brody to hear.

'Don't be concerned,' he added.

'I'm not.' Fiona tensed. What was it about her that a blind man could see but she couldn't?

'I need you to tell me who's in here.' The words came out bitter and short. Brody didn't like to ask for things, let alone use the word *need*. He accepted Fiona's help grudgingly. He wanted her to drive him around, he'd said at the interview years ago, and assist with some administration work. Fiona didn't mention the hundred other things she did for him, from helping with his students to making sure he had toilet paper in the bathroom at home. She's my assistant, he told everyone. *I'm your eyes*, she thought.

'Tell you what about them?'

'Start with the table by the door. Four people, right?'

Fiona swung round, resting her arm along the back of the banquette. 'Yes.' She would never understand how he did it. She'd often wondered if he really was blind. 'Two men, two women. Probably in their twenties. They're a bit, well, alternative. One's got a beanie on. One woman's got a long patchwork skirt. They look nice enough.' She turned back to Brody when one of the men glanced at her. 'Would you mind telling me why?'

'Next table,' he ordered. The one running along the window.

Fiona sighed. 'Man on his own. Old. Late sixties probably. Looks as if he lives alone and—'

'That's enough. Go round every table. And don't speculate.'

'Next one has a young mum. Girl with a pushchair. She's got a friend with her too. They're drinking tea. The next table has a couple of school kids and the one beside that has a couple of builders—'

'Stop. Go back to the table with the kids.' Brody leant forward. He reached out for Fiona's hand and halted it before she wrapped it round the mug of coffee the waitress had brought. 'I want to know every single detail about them. Right down to the colour of their socks.'

Fiona stopped, speechless. She stared down at her hand. It was the first time during the eight years she'd worked with Professor Brody Quinell that he had ever touched her. The first time she had ever seen him look scared.

Carrie wasn't sure what was more shocking, the way the woman lived or that she'd lost her only son. She'd been sedated by her GP since it happened and, even with four days' worth of diazepam inside her, she was still agitated, angry, hysterical, and lashed out at the cameraman when he filmed the photos of her boy adorning the mantelpiece.

'Jimmy was my life,' she wailed, her face lifting from the puddle that she'd formed on the foul carpet. Two boxer dogs and another rather illegal-looking canine slumped beside her. They seemed to understand her grief.

'Mrs Plummer, I'm so very, very sorry about your loss. Words can't explain the pain you must be feeling.' It was almost a script, but not quite. The story of Jimmy Plummer had been headline news since it happened several days ago. He'd been cycling home through the estate after soccer practice. He'd found an old man beaten up and lying in the road. He stopped to help. His mobile phone showed he'd called for an ambulance. The operator heard Jimmy being stabbed repeatedly when the gang came back.

Carrie sat down, even though she really didn't want to. It was all being filmed. Turning her nose up at the disgusting state of the sofa would lose her sympathy. The skirt could go to a charity shop afterwards.

'Tell me what Jimmy was like, Mrs Plummer. He loved football, didn't he?'

Slowly, the bereaved mother lifted her head. Her face was swollen, her cheeks red, and her hair splayed across her forehead in greasy streaks. As well as the mother, they were going to get some of Jimmy's friends on the live studio part of the show. Talk about the gang culture in the area. Dennis would help with a reconstruction, too. The phone-in results were usually phenomenal. The ratings would be through the roof on this one. She needed to get this interview exactly right. Being in people's homes was what made *Reality Check* unique.

'Jimmy was Jimmy,' Mrs Plummer said. She brought herself up to a sitting position. 'He was fourteen. He liked football. He were good at it. He liked his bike. He loved Dollar here.' Mrs Plummer rested her hand on the ugliest of the three dogs. 'And he went to school. He ain't got no ASBO or nothing.'

'Was Jimmy part of a gang, Mrs Plummer?' From the corner of her eye, she could see Steve zooming in on the woman. Perfect.

'No, no, he weren't part of any gang. Jimmy weren't like that. He just got on with things, you know?' Mrs Plummer hauled herself to standing. She clenched her fists, looking for someone to take it out on. Carrie patted the spot beside her. An intimate moment on the sofa. Fabulous.

The woman sat.

'Do you have any idea why anyone would want to kill your son, Mrs Plummer . . . or can I call you Lorraine?' Carrie's voice was low, gentle, coaxing. She reached out and took the woman's hands. Steve moved in front of the sofa and caught every second on film.

'No,' she whispered. 'But I want the police to find them.' Lorraine Plummer glanced across at Dennis and his detective. They'd edit in a quick shot of them later. 'I want you to catch them bastards who did this.' And she fell forward, breaking into a thousand pieces on Carrie's new wool skirt just as her phone vibrated in her jacket pocket again. The skirt was definitely for the charity shop.

'What do you think?' Carrie fished antiseptic hand cleanser from her bag and squirted half the bottle into her palm. 'Think she knows anything?'

Dennis pulled a face. They were going nowhere fast in this

traffic. 'Why would she? Just another gang having a bit of sport. They do it for entertainment, you know. The kid interfered and he got it. Simple as. We'll probably make an arrest or two for show, but that'll be that. Many of these cases get binned.' DCI Masters yawned. 'Fancy dinner?'

'No, of course not.' Carrie stared out of the passenger window. Thank God they'd left that dreadful place. As the last of the derelict – or perhaps they weren't derelict – houses gave way to more habitable properties, Carrie felt something loosen inside her, something that was usually fixed down tight. She was nauseous and shaky, quite unlike anything she'd experienced in a long while. She pulled her mobile from her pocket, remembering the calls from her son that she hadn't taken earlier.

'Den,' she said thoughtfully, fingering the phone.

'Yeah?' Dennis was vague, concentrating on a right turn at a busy T-junction.

Do you ever think what it would be like if it were you? Carrie wanted to say. *If this was your life?* she swallowed. Shit. 'Nothing.'

Dennis glanced across at her a couple of times, steering between the traffic. He laughed. 'Nothing's something.' He put on the siren.

Carrie made several attempts to call her son. Each time, it went straight to voicemail.

Brody lay on his bed and stared at the ceiling. Black. He imagined there were thousands of stars glittering above him – his own private constellation. No one else saw what he saw inside his useless eyes. He smoked, the last one before sleep, and he drank a little brandy to help him reach a place of isolation, of desolation – the place that was filled with visions of a life long gone.

Max was a clumsy six-year-old the last time he'd actually set eyes on him. Barging around their comfortable house, Brody watched as his little boy tore round the furniture on skates, annoying his mother when he sent ornaments and photo frames flying as he grabbed on to furniture. He'd been given the skates for Christmas – his idea – and the joy he'd got from them was priceless. Worth much more than the stupid things that got broken.

Brody growled long and low. Those days were gone. He shifted on his bed. It creaked beneath him. He wondered who was living in that house now, if they sensed the happiness left behind.

The house was a far-fetched dream – not, admittedly, where he'd seen himself ending up when he was a student, but life was like that. How everything could change in a moment, like when he'd first set eyes on his future wife. Things like that couldn't be mathematically worked out; they just *were*, they just existed and had to be accepted. The property they chose was in an up-and-coming area in North London. It had an apple tree in the back garden. They'd saved hard for the down payment. They'd moved in with no furniture, just a mattress on the floor and a few bits of crockery. But it was home, it was theirs, it was perfect. Brody worked long hours and sat up all night studying, researching, preparing lectures for the days he taught at the university. He became well-respected, an eminent researcher in statistical theories with papers published across the world.

Two years later, Max arrived, along with a highly paid research and teaching position for Professor Brody Quinell at the Royal London University. Six years after that, he was blind.

A few months later, divorced.

He'd hardly spoken to his ex since. But he'd heard her. Oh yes, he'd heard her.

Morning had somehow come – he knew from the warmth on his face. Damn, he hated it when that happened. It seemed as if he'd only just been taking a look at Max, at life back then – a photo

48

album of precious memories playing through his mind – but he must have fallen asleep. He was still in his clothes, ashtray balancing on his belly. His feet were cold. Someone was banging on the door.

'Brody, Brody, are you in there?'

He recognised Fiona's voice. He was tempted to stay in bed. She had a key but he always put the security chain on. Kids went round kicking doors in for the hell of it. 'Coming,' he yelled out, easing himself up. His back was stiff. Someone banged the floor in the flat above. *Shut the fuck up.*

Brody let her in. He'd been thinking about this. 'We're having lunch together again today.' It wasn't a request.

'Not at that place again, please no.'

He knew Fiona would prefer the pair of them lingering over a panini at that new deli, or Sebastian's Bistro above the music shop, or even bloody McDonald's. He wasn't completely blind to everything.

'No, no. No,' she reiterated.

'I'll take that as a yes, then.' He noticed her perfume. It was new – spicy yet sweet. What if Max was right? What if she was 'his woman'? Instinctively, although there was no concrete reason behind it, he knew Max would kick up at the prospect of Fiona as a potential stepmother. He'd hated her presence in his father's life from the start; saw her as a mother replacement. Fiona, however, had no reason to dislike Max, and she didn't. She bought him Christmas presents, sent birthday cards, and was always polite when they met, which wasn't often.

He shook his head. 'I need to shower.'

'You do.'

He left her in his living room. Max had tidied up since she'd last been. He'd cleared out the rubbish, picked up the dirty clothes, re-boxed the CDs. He was the only other person Brody allowed in his flat, and Fiona had told him several times that she was sure if he could actually see the place he wouldn't let anyone in at all, including himself.

The water poured down his body. Brody made quick work of washing. He wondered how much older he looked now than when he'd last seen himself clearly. He remembered exactly when that was and, ironically, it hadn't been clear at all. He'd been making Max laugh at the fairground hall of mirrors and his torso appeared ten feet wide with a tiny head and stumpy legs. Even then, he knew something was wrong. His son jumped about, giggling at the sight of his unrecognisable father. Some last memory of myself, he thought, turning off the tap and wiping his hands over his hair. An image frozen in time.

Brody dried himself quickly and dressed in fresh clothes. 'Take them from the left,' Fiona told him every time she put away his laundry when it came back from the cleaners. 'If you take a pair of trousers from the left and a shirt from the left, they'll match. I organised them that way.' He didn't like to admit he needed her.

'Nasty,' he heard her say when he came back into the living room, towel-drying his hair.

'What is?'

'This book. *How to Survive the Playground*. It's grim what goes on.'

'A metaphor for life,' Brody roared. 'You're going to read it to me. After we've had lunch at the greasy spoon.' He let his towel fall on the floor. He heard Fiona sigh.

'Why do we have to eat at that dump? My insides still haven't unclogged from Chef's Special.'

'We're going to study some youth.'

Fiona stood, jangled her car keys. 'Spying on kids again? I don't get it. And what's with the book on bullying?' She picked up her bag. 'I want to know.' There was silence. 'Are you collecting data for some new research paper or is it simply Professor Quinell going insane?'

'Neither,' he said. 'But if you put up with another greasy lunch, I'll tell you.'

They had to wait a while. Half of the tables were occupied by kids from the comprehensive a couple of blocks away. The rest were populated by the usual group of old folk, workmen and single mums cluttering up the small space with pushchairs. Edie was waitressing again. She wiped her hands down her front when she saw Brody and Fiona; gave them a sticky menu to peruse as they waited in line.

'They're not here yet.' Brody leant against the wall. More customers pushed in behind them, getting trapped in the doorway. 'Can't hear their voices. I can't *smell* them,' he snarled.

'Who's not here yet?'

'The ones we're going to watch. The year elevens. They're in class until twelve forty-five. By the time they've packed up their books, taken a piss, and walked down here, it'll be one o'clock easily.'

'Brody.' Fiona cleared her throat. 'I don't mean to sound off or, you know, at all doubting of your motives, but . . .' she paused. 'But it's a little creepy that you know the local school's timetable. Eating here is bad enough, but stalking children?'

'That's where you're wrong. We're monitoring, not stalking.'

Fiona dropped her face into her hands.

'And because I have you with me for cover, no one will think us suspicious.'

'Your table's ready, Prof Quinell,' Edie sang in place of Fiona's retort.

They sat, drank tea and waited. The café was noisy, steamy and hot. Fiona put off ordering food as long as she could, telling

Brody that service was slow, that their waitress kept passing them by, that she'd signalled she'd be over to them soon.

Brody touched his watch. He stood up and yelled. 'Can we get some service here, please?' The café fell silent.

'Brody, sit down. You're making a scene.' Fiona pulled his sleeve. 'They've just walked in. Same youths that were here last time.' Edie came up to their table. 'Chef's Specials twice,' Fiona said resignedly. She just wouldn't eat hers.

Brody leant forward across the table. His eyes were intense, scanning like radar; useless. Fiona could hardly believe they saw only blackness and was convinced he'd developed a sixth sense.

'Tell me about them. I want details.'

Fiona hesitated. She was torn. She wanted to help Brody with whatever craziness was going on in his mind, but it just didn't feel right spying on school kids for no reason. She sighed, trying not to admit that it was her feelings for Brody that made her comply. 'Three of them. All boys. Two dark-haired, kind of shaggy cuts, medium brown, a bit greasy. One of them has awful acne. He looks hard. You know, sort of tough-eyed, as if he's seen too much in his life already.' Fiona took a sip of tea.

'Don't stop.' Brody was breathing in short quick bursts. His fingers knotted together on the table. He stared directly at Fiona. No one would know he was blind; no one would know he wasn't just an ordinary guy chatting with his girlfriend.

'The other dark-haired boy is a bit boring looking. Pursed mouth, an earring in his left ear. They're all laughing about something. Looking at a mobile phone. The third boy is dark blond I think, but his head is quite closely shaved. He's wearing jeans below his school blazer and shirt. No tie. The others are wearing school ties.' Fiona sighed. 'That do?'

'More.'

'There's a bag on the floor by the shaved head boy. Black and red backpack. They're pulling open bags of crisps. One each. Drinking Coke. Oh, but Shaved Head has a Tango.'

'They still got that phone?'

'Yes. Spotty's texting, I think.'

Brody took his mobile phone from his jeans pocket and dialled a number. He held the phone beneath the table. Seconds later he said, 'Hear that?'

Fiona scowled. 'Not really.'

'Look at them. Are they answering the phone?'

'Yes. Spotty has it to his ear looking puzzled. Did you just call them?'

'Uhuh.'

'Why?'

'To make sure I've got the right kids.'

Fiona leant back, puzzled, as Edie dumped sauce, napkins and cutlery on the table. 'It would seem you have.' Fiona spoke quietly, watching both Brody and the boys alternately.

'Good,' Brody said flatly. He turned his head in the boys' direction. 'Because I wouldn't want to mess up.'

FRIDAY, 24 APRIL 2009

Carrie had given up trying to contact her son. It wasn't unusual for him not to pick up his phone, if he'd even bothered to charge it. As ever, he'd called her at an awkward time – she'd got up early, being a show day, and had been in the shower – and he hadn't bothered leaving a message. She felt as if she hadn't seen him for days. She tried calling one more time, but his phone went straight to voicemail. 'It's me. Telephone tag and you're on. I'm home early this evening. Join me for dinner if you like.' She hung up.

Martha had bought croissants for breakfast. Carrie ate staring out across a drizzly rear garden from the end of a long kitchen table capable of seating a large family, if only she had one.

'You home?' she yelled out, wondering if he'd slunk into his room last night and she'd not noticed. Her voice echoed around the empty house. She couldn't hear any music or smell the cheap rubbish he doused himself in. 'All the lads wear it,' he'd told her. 'Chick magnet.' He'd grinned, knowing he was disgusting his mother to the core.

What, she thought, eating a tiny bit of pastry, had the thirty-grand-a-year boarding school actually done for him? She made a mental note to call the headmaster. Yet again. They must be able to work things out. As it stood, the situation was intolerable.

Carrie tipped half the croissant into the bin and went into her office. She booted up her computer. It was still early and, before going to the studio for this morning's show, she would spend half an hour catching up with what the researchers had sent her. She skipped through the reports of the disaster zones that these people called lives, remotely gawping at their misery from her comfortable home, reading about their poverty, their downright depravity, her dismay at their misery tempered, as ever, by relief that she wasn't one of them. *Reality Check* could only help people so far.

'How do people exist like this?' she asked herself. Lorraine Plummer's name was on the potential studio list again. Last autumn's programme about her son's stabbing strangely hadn't stimulated much phone-in response and, as a favour to Dennis, she'd agreed to run a follow-up show. They were popular with the viewers – the ratings confirmed this. They were living soaps; a real-life glimpse into tragedies most people were fortunate enough to never experience.

Lorraine Plummer's second out-of-studio segment had already been cut and edited and would air within the next month. Carrie prayed, for the mother's sake, that the show would bring in a few useful calls to Dennis's incident room. Since the lad's death, there had been a spate of stabbings in the area, shockingly close to her own home, Carrie realised, wondering how two vastly different communities, Hampstead and Harlesden, could exist within a few square miles.

'Poor little sod,' she said, clicking off the face of the dead kid. She took a second to stare at Lorraine Plummer's image in a scanned newspaper clipping. Empty eyes, hollow cheeks, gaunt expression; most of all, she could see that the woman's soul was gone. She knew it would never come back.

Carrie fired off a high-priority email to Leah insisting they get Lorraine Plummer on air next week. There was something about the case that chimed with the way she'd been feeling recently – the creeping void, the unsettling state of mind, the loss of control. Normal feelings for the parent of a teenager, she assumed.

To block out all the misery, Carrie picked up a silver-framed photograph of her son. Smartly dressed in a suit and his school tie, it had been taken at the end of his final year at Denningham College, just before he'd decided he wasn't going back.

'You silly, silly boy,' she mouthed at his image. 'You could have finished your GCSEs at least.' She recalled her total horror when he announced that, as well as leaving Denningham, he was dropping half the subjects he'd spent the last few years studying.

'What do I want with Latin and German?' He'd leant against the kitchen counter. Carrie remembered that his hands were grubby because he'd left smeary prints on the work surface after he stormed out – the same little hands that used to wring out her heart when he was a baby with his cute dimples and cheeky giggle.

'A place at university?' Carrie called out after him. 'A decent job?' His Oxbridge chances had gone down the pan since he'd left Denningham. Three meetings with the head, countless emails, thousands of harsh words with her son had got her nowhere.

'I don't want to turn out to be a superior rich kid with a famous mother,' was his closing argument. No more to be said, he spat, slamming into his bedroom.

'And no son of mine will turn out *inferior*,' she'd whispered, pouring shot after shot of vodka in the hope it might fill the hole in her heart.

She'd got him. With the footage of him flying into a rage when they'd filmed him with his two-year-old at home, with the fresh bruises on his wife and his girlfriend's faces, with him upturning the stage furniture and security restraining him on set, there was no doubt that today's star guest was a complete shit. Carrie despaired of society. She also loved it.

'Look me in the eye, Vincent.' She traversed the studio effortlessly. Security had him pinned into his chair. He was a small, weasely man. She wasn't scared. She crouched down in front of him, half facing him and half turning to the camera that followed her closely.

'Tell me honestly, now. Did you ever smack your little girl around?' She paused. She knew he wouldn't answer. Not yet. 'Why were Social Services called out seventeen times in the first year of her life, Vincent? Why do the photographs in the police file show bruising across her back consistent with a man's hand delivering the blow? Why do your wife and girlfriend, God help them, have faces like rotten apples? Why, I want to know,' and Carrie stood and turned to her audience, 'was this little babe not taken into care ages ago?' She was shouting now; waving a photograph of the toddler above her head. She was a mother. None of this was her life, but it still hurt.

Total silence. Then one person in the audience clapped. Then another and another. Suddenly, the three hundred-strong studio audience were on their feet applauding. Too many kids had slipped through the net in recent years and the public wanted answers. When they had quietened, Carrie continued.

'Did you or did you not hit your daughter?'

More silence.

Carrie touched her earpiece. *Give him ten more seconds*, she was told by the director. She knew they'd be on the edge of their seats backstage. She'd been hammering him for nearly an hour. He had to crack soon. Even Dennis had come in for this one. A confession was what he needed. *Camera two get closer*, Leah ordered, overriding Matt's decision to go for a single camera viewpoint.

Vincent stared at his feet. He scuffed his toes together. 'She were naughty,' he eventually said. 'Everyone smacks their kids. It ain't a crime.'

The audience became a ripple of gasps and shock. Boos and

calls of abuse rained down on to the stage. The child's mother flew out of her seat and security barged on to the set to handle the fracas. Carrie allowed the scene to continue for a moment longer before turning personally to camera two to sign off to an ad break with her trademark gesture.

'Super, darling,' Leah said in a silly accent. 'You are truly Queen of Confessions.'

Dennis also muttered a couple of words of praise before heading backstage to question Vincent further.

Carrie sat in her usual chair for the short commercial break. The audience was still restless. The set behind her was filled with security guards and angry shouts of abuse. The atmosphere crackled with tension, but she ignored it. She had her job to do; let the others take care of the rest. There was more to come after the break; another set of wrecked lives to expose.

For a moment, Carrie was overcome with tiredness – not in the physical sense, but emotionally. This unexpected feeling – and she didn't like it – jolted her as if someone had shoved her sharply from behind. Dealing with these people was gruelling, she acknowledged that. They'd filled her life for the last ten years. If she was honest, she could do with a break from their misery, their tragedy, their hopelessness, the lot that wasn't hers but had almost become so by default. Every show was getting harder. But ironically, without their misfortune, she would still be a regional journalist eking a living from stories that occupied half a column on page ten of the local rag.

With less than a minute to go, Carrie needed to be in control for the remainder of the show. The ratings on this next item would be sky high.

The make-up girl fussed over her cheeks.

She smiled.

It was black and white. As clear-cut as the two-tone shoes she'd chosen for the show. Work was work. Home was home.

She took a call on her mobile.

She batted the make-up girl away.

Who was this?

Her mouth fell open.

She dropped her bottle of water.

She felt the cold liquid splash her ankles.

She ran.

Leah Roffe skimmed the report. It had not been a good morning. She took off her glasses and glanced at her watch. This week's show had been off air for an hour now and the station switchboard was still in meltdown. She frowned at Dennis. 'I can't make much out of these cases.' Their usual weekly brief in readiness for future shows wasn't providing the distraction from the earlier disaster that Leah had hoped for. She simply couldn't concentrate.

'Fine. I'll hand out a few knives and handguns to the local youth, ply them with booze and drugs, and see what that nets us. I wouldn't want your ratings to fall.'

Leah pulled a face. 'You know what I mean.' She shoved her glasses back on. 'I'll take the abortion. The boy who did it to his girlfriend.' She poured tea, hoping that might help her mood. 'Can we contact her parents?'

DCI Masters shrugged. 'She's in care. She's only fourteen. I can get you into the home if you like. We're working closely with her carers. She refuses to name who did it to her. The doctors say she won't be having any more kids.'

'Christ.' Leah shook her head. 'Want some tea?' Then she fell forward on to her elbows, chin in hands. What a morning. She couldn't believe Carrie had just walked off set during the ad break. No one knew where she'd gone and she wasn't answering her phone. They'd had to air a repeat for the second half of the show.

Dennis screwed up his face. 'Nope. I'm off. I have work to do. My life isn't all glamorous TV shows and celebrity tantrums, you know.'

Leah groaned. She appreciated his help, really she did. Without his cooperation, they wouldn't have the heads up on many of the topical cases that made the show so special. It was a symbiotic relationship. Masters' trickier cases gained airtime, community awareness was raised, and police crime-line numbers scrolled across the screen during the show. The Met had received leads on over eighty per cent of cases since it began, and thirty per cent more crimes had been solved thanks to Carrie Kent and her unique style of reporting. *Jeremy Kyle* meets *Crimewatch*, Leah told the media. The show was unique.

Dennis stood. He made to hug Leah but stopped. 'How's the girlfriend?'

'Gone.'

'Ah. So you're single?'

'Just go, Den,' Leah ordered. 'Get out of my hair.'

'I suppose dinner's out of the que—' Dennis's face went purple. 'Oww,' he wailed, rubbing his knee.

'Serves you right.' Leah's mobile phone rang. She lunged at it. 'Oh, thank *God*. Carrie, where the hell *are* you?' Her face relaxed a little, the dozens of lines she'd acquired in the last couple of hours relenting now that she knew Carrie was alive at least. 'It's her,' she whispered to Dennis unnecessarily, her hand over the mouthpiece. She rolled her eyes.

But then Leah's face fell serious and drained of all colour as she listened. 'Oh my God. Oh shit, no . . .' Leah's pupils dilated and her hand came up to her face. 'Carrie, no . . . Where are you?' Her voice became a whisper. 'I'll be right there.' Leah grabbed her keys, her bag, and ran out of her office without saying another word.

THE PAST

From the moment she met him, she knew she would fall in love with him. The interview was quick but seemed to fill most of her life so far, as if it was the moment she'd been born for. He'd questioned eight other women but he could see – *see?* – he'd said, that she was perfect for the job.

'How can you tell?'

Did he feel it too?

'Because you let me put my own sugar in my tea,' he replied, sliding a contract across the table. It crunched in the white granules that lay between them. 'Take it. Read it overnight. Send it back tomorrow if you agree.'

He didn't know that she'd spent the ten minutes of the interview staring into his sightless eyes; didn't know that she watched the way his lips parted as he thought what to ask her next; didn't know that she wanted to take hold of his hands, to somehow tell him that she *knew* this was right. It was a new start for the new millennium.

She smiled as she left. Some things just couldn't be reduced to a formula.

Fiona, when she got home, signed the contract without even reading it.

Her first day working with Brody Quinell was hardly taxing for a maths graduate.

'Blue or black?' She let him feel the different socks.

'These. They're softer.'

She imagined him pulling them over his feet, snugly fitting round his ankles, the little wheeze as he bent forward to pull them up.

'Ten pairs?'

Brody nodded. He bumped into a display of underpants.

'Guess we should get some of these while we're here too.' Fiona plucked several packs off the shelves.

By the end of her first morning working with Professor Brody Quinell – *the* hottest name in statistical research, both in looks and intellect, the man whose name sent ripples of confusion through the world's top mathematicians with his polemic papers – Fiona had pretty much restocked his underwear, bought enough toiletries to last a year, and filled his freezer with food he insisted she buy but that she wouldn't feed to her cat.

'I would have thought . . .' She hesitated. He sat at the tiny kitchen table while she unpacked the groceries. 'Didn't you ever . . . I mean . . .' She just wanted to look after him.

'What? Spit it out, Fiona. If we're to work together, then we must be entirely open with one another.'

'Nothing,' she replied. It's nothing. Crazy, she told herself. Inappropriate, too, she thought. He's my boss. Why am I feeling like this? But whatever it was that made the pit of her belly skittle like a teenager's, she didn't like the thought of him living in this flat. It was awful. Worse than awful. Didn't he realise?

'Your wife,' Fiona began again, wondering if there was a gentler way to bring this up. 'Did you live here together? In this flat?'

'Hell no.'

'Where then?'

'Somewhere nice.' Brody squinted, as if his lifeless eyes were trying to focus, to see the past. 'It was a house. With a garden. We had a shed and a swing for my kid. We had beige carpet and fresh flowers on the hall table. I didn't see it coming, all that domestic bliss.'

There was a pause; no noise apart from rustling as Fiona piled packets of cheap brand food into the freezer. She was wondering about his kid; suddenly feeling defensive. She hoped he wasn't going to be a problem.

'Wanna know the other thing that I couldn't see?'

Fiona turned; she forgot and just nodded. He somehow sensed her interest.

'I never once saw that it would all end.'

She finally got to go to the university – the reason she applied for the job in the first place. The mathematics faculty was set in thirty acres of landscaped grounds between Kew Gardens and Osterley Park. Fiona drove up to the security guard's booth and showed him her new pass. He peered into the car.

'Welcome back, Professor,' he said.

Brody raised his hand. Fiona drove on, following the signs to the staff car park.

'It's my first time,' Brody said as the engine silenced.

'First time what?' She liked being at the start of something fresh in his life.

'Being back at the department since . . . since . . .' He swallowed and stared straight ahead. So far, he'd refused to talk about how it happened. 'It's been a few months since I was here.'

'Well then,' she replied. 'Let's get in there, shall we?' Fiona was suddenly as nervous as the great man himself appeared to be. She went round to the passenger side as Brody straightened out of the car. She took his arm and closed her eyes for a second. 'Main entrance?' she asked.

'No,' Brody replied. 'Follow the signs to the rear. Look for the porters' entrance.'

Fiona didn't need to ask why he wanted to slip unnoticed

around the back; and she didn't need to ask why his hand was trembling as it gripped her arm for guidance. Nor did she question why Brody ignored every well-wisher, students and staff alike, who welcomed him back to work. And speculating about why he stood in silence as the elevator rose to the fourteenth floor was pointless because, she smiled to herself, she already knew.

Professor Brody Quinell was as vulnerable as she was, yet each of them chose to hide it from the world. Before the lift arrived, Fiona screwed up her eyes and tried to fathom the blackness. She felt Brody's warm hand take her arm as the doors parted. She opened her eyes again, amazed at what she'd seen with her eyes tight shut – a clear view right into the world of the man she hoped would make her whole again.

FRIDAY, 24 APRIL 2009

Carrie couldn't remember leaving the studio or flagging down a taxi. She didn't remember paying the driver or flying up the steps of the hospital and demanding to know what was going on. She was unaware that her legs were at the very last point of being able to hold her upright as she leant against the reception desk, panting and snapping at the woman behind the glass.

'Name of admitted,' the clerk said.

'It's . . . it's my son,' Carrie choked out. She tried to say his name clearly but the syllables got twisted. The woman listened, swallowed and typed. Then she paled, glanced at Carrie, and made a phone call.

'Just tell me which ward he's on. For God's sake, which floor is it? This is my son we're talking about. Do you know who I am?'

The woman nodded that, yes, she did know who the frantic woman the other side of the glass was, but she refused to answer the barrage of questions. Within another minute, a doctor – Carrie thought he was a doctor – was at her side, guiding her away from reception.

'This way, Mrs . . . Kent.' Carried noticed the man doing a double-take. Having a celebrity in his department would no doubt be gossip for the doctors' mess later, but at least it was getting her special treatment now.

'At last,' she said. 'Please take me to my son. I don't know what the hell's going on.'

The whole situation was ghastly. A bad dream. No, a terrible nightmare fuelled by a call from the school secretary that there'd been an accident and her son had been taken to hospital. The urgency with which she'd flown out of the studio had surprised her, scared her almost, given that she was in the middle of a show. Finding him with a broken arm, most likely texting from his hospital bed, was hardly grounds for walking out. There would be serious repercussions. She'd give him a serve, teach him a lesson and threaten to get him live on air to discuss wasting parents' time. Bloody kids, she thought.

As she was led deeper into the hospital, Carrie found herself wishing they shared the same surname; mother and child would then at least have one thing in common, somewhere to start afresh. As it stood, she wondered if the gulf between them – that terrible adult versus teenage void that had somehow spread between them over the last few years – was now too wide to even throw a rope.

'Do you know what's happened? Apparently there's been some kind of accident.' She almost had to run to keep up with the silent doctor. When he offered only a small smile and a shrug as a reply, Carrie reeled through the possibilities. Chemistry lab, perhaps. Some kind of chemical spillage or maybe an accident in DT with a band saw. Oh God. Did he take his bike to school today or was he on the bus? She had no idea. In fact, she wasn't sure he'd even stayed at her house last night. Had he been at his father's? Food poisoning, perhaps. He was always eating rubbish. Or perhaps it was just a sprained ankle. A cracked wrist from falling down a couple of steps. Why, then, Carrie wondered, had she fled the studio without a word to anyone? Why, then, was her maternal instinct – she thought that's what it was – rearing up inside her as hot as a furnace?

Carrie felt the grip of the doctor's hand tighten around her arm.

'This way, Mrs Kent. I'll take you to someone who will be able to tell you what's going on.' He smiled reassuringly.

Carrie was shown into a small room. It was white and had several stacking chairs set out around the edge. On the low table in the centre of the room was a plastic flower arrangement and a box of tissues. In one corner – although she chose not to acknowledge this initially – there was another table draped in a white cloth with a cross standing on top.

It took her a second to see, took a moment for her eyes to pull in and out of focus to check that what her brain was registering was in fact real. And then it hit her. Sitting like a great shadow against the anaemic wall beyond was Brody Quinell, head in hands, knees apart, his hair knotted down his back and about a foot longer than when she'd last seen him.

'Brody?' she said. Was it relief she was feeling, that she wouldn't have to deal with whatever this was alone? Maybe she could go back to work and leave him to sort it all out.

At the sound of her voice, Brody slowly raised his head. There was a woman beside him. Carrie ignored her.

'What's going on, Brody? Where's Max?'

'He's dead,' he replied in a voice that filled the universe. 'Our son is dead.'

AUTUMN 2008

Thirty-four kids in class and only five handed in their essays. Two of those were from Dayna. Max dropped his on top of hers.

'You've been busy,' he said.

'I couldn't decide which viewpoint to write from.' She slung her pack on her shoulder. 'So I thought I'd try both. It really made me think.'

Max stared at her, trying to fathom what lay beneath her dark eyes, but she suddenly lurched forward, falling against the lockers.

'Oi,' Max called out at the idiot who had barged into her. 'You OK?'

'Yeah. That was nothing. She burnt me with her fag last time.' Dayna pushed up her sleeve and showed Max the shiny red blister on her wrist. She shrugged. 'Still alive, aren't I?'

Max reached out to touch the wound, but Dayna pulled away. They were herded along in the flow of kids as the lunch rush began. 'Do you want to get something to eat?'

'Don't have any money.'

'Follow me.' Max allowed a small smile and took Dayna's arm. He led her through the crowds to his locker. Within the bustle, he took out a cold food bag.

'You're gonna get it bringing that thing into school,' she said, backing off.

Max shrugged; only winced a little when the boot came in the knee.

'*Fekkin' freako . . .*'

'Let's get out of here.' He pulled firmly on Dayna's hand and they ran along the clearing corridor as kids headed for the chip shop, the local greasy spoon or, if they were desperate, the school canteen.

Dayna and Max ignored the shouts of the duty staff ordering everyone to walk. They ran outside, through the car park and pushed through a gap in the wooden fence. At this end of the school, beyond the boundary, was an area of scrub land that eventually gave way to the street, a row of shops, and an industrial estate behind. They veered off before they got that far and continued through the scrub.

'There's a stream.' Max grinned. 'I know all the best places.' He urged Dayna to follow him, but she lagged behind.

'I dunno, Max.' She scratched her leg. The nettles had got through her trousers.

Max held up the cool bag. 'You wait,' he said. Dayna nodded and followed, muttering something about being starving, about not eating breakfast. Finally, they came to a depression in the scorched weeds, the building rubble, the tumbledown sheds from long-deserted allotments. They heard the sound of flowing water. Max dropped to the ground, legs spread apart, head thrown back in the weeds. 'This is the life.' He grinned, then sat bolt upright when Dayna tentatively joined him.

She stared ahead. 'Not much of a stream, is it?'

There was a rusty shopping trolley on its side in the three inches of water that struggled along the rock and broken concrete of a man-made drain. An old bike lay three feet away, strewn with plastic bags and rope that had snagged in the current.

'No, but at least it's not school. That's why I like it. And time enough to get back without getting reprimanded.'

'Reprimanded?' she said in a posh accent, smiling. 'You speak funny.'

'Thanks.' Max made a face and spread out his school jacket on the ground between them. He opened the cool bag and took out several plastic pots. He set them on the makeshift picnic rug. 'Lobster with crème fraiche and dill. Honey-glazed chicken with sesame seeds and watercress. Crab terrine. Crackers. Coke.'

'Bit bloody posh, isn't it?' Dayna poked the tub of lobster. 'I mean.'

Max laughed. 'My mother left a note telling me to take whatever I wanted from the fridge. So I did. She said it would get thrown away.'

'I've never had lobster. Or crab. I've had Coke though.' Dayna grinned and dunked a cracker into the pale pink mixture. She bit into it, waited to see what it was like, and scoffed some more. 'It's really good.'

Max shrugged. 'We only have proper food at Dad's. Burgers and stuff like that.'

'Divorced?' Dayna's mouth was full.

Max nodded. He hadn't started eating. He was watching her devour the picnic. He liked seeing her eat. 'Yeah, like for ever.'

'Me too. My mum remarried this lazy shit. Yours?'

'Nah,' Max said. 'Doubt anyone would put up with my mother. Dad's got this creepy woman. He denies he's seeing her, but she's got her claws in. She hates my guts. Sees me as, like, I dunno, like getting in the way. She'd rather I didn't exist.'

'Ouch. Who do you live with?'

Max shrugged. In truth, he wasn't sure. 'Myself,' he said, smiling, thinking it could be a good afternoon to bunk off school.

By the time they approached the shed, the sky had folded over with layers of cloud. A steady drizzle wet their hair and shoulders. Max felt himself rehydrating.

'I've got a stitch,' Dayna grumbled. 'Do we have to run?'

Max slowed to a walk. He had a sudden urge to tuck his arm round Dayna's small waist, to rub gently beneath her ribs and soothe away the sharp pain. Instead, he tugged harder on her sleeve. 'We'll get soaked if we don't. Come on.'

The railway was about a mile from school. They'd cut through the industrial units – Max holding up the barbed wire as Dayna slid beneath – and run between the racks of unsold cars at the back of the motor dealer. Then it was downhill for a good way until they reached the railway cutting. Max smelt coal smoke as the familiar row of terraced cottages came into view. When he saw them, he knew he was nearly home.

'Slow down!' Dayna shrieked as a train sped past them only twenty feet away, sucking up her words like litter as it disappeared down the line.

When Max reached the bottom of the slope, beneath the blue-grey brick bridge, he stopped and waited for her. Picking her way through the knee-high grass and scrub, he thought she looked beautiful. Her hair – shiny from the rain, black, some of it sliced through with a funny shade of orange – framed her pale face in a boyish style. Her nose was tiny, he noticed, as she drew alongside him, decorated with a barely visible dot of a jewel. Her skin was clear apart from an area on her forehead that was grazed with a few spots barely discernible behind her make-up. Her eyes were deep and thoughtful, as if she was drowning in whatever was kept secret inside them.

'Welcome,' he said proudly. The wooden shed wasn't really noticeable until he pointed it out. That's why Max liked it. That's how, when it came down to it, he preferred his life.

Dayna glanced around. 'It's just the bloody railway.' Then she noticed the hut in the shadows, partly obscured by the great curve of blue brick that formed one side of the bridge.

'Come in. Make yourself at home.' Max had the padlock off and was ushering Dayna inside.

'Cool,' she said, nodding as her eyes adjusted to the dim light. 'How come?'

'Just found it one day. It was empty apart from some old sacks of cement and a mattress. Think a tramp might have lived here. There were some old cider bottles. Stuff like that.' Max fought the grin. Dayna was impressed. His own place. 'Sit down.' He pointed to the car seat.

'What's all this stuff?' She stared at the boxes. They were dusty.

'My winnings.' Max ran his hand over the nearest one. A hairdryer complete with attachments and straighteners.

'Sweet.'

'Here. It's yours. Take it.' Max held out the box.

Dayna held up her hand. 'Don't use that kind of stuff.' She fingered her hair and laughed.

'What about your mum?'

'Nah. My mum's hair dries in all the hot air my stepdad spouts.' She tried to laugh again, but it came out as a hiccup. 'Thanks though.'

Max shrugged. 'Suit yourself.'

'Now really, where d'you get all this shit from?'

Max felt himself redden. There was no denying the need to be honest with Dayna. From the start, he wouldn't have it any other way. Whatever they were going to have – what he *hoped* they'd have – had to be see-through, honest, lovely. 'Won it all. You know, competitions and stuff.'

Dayna thought; narrowed her eyes. 'All of it?'

Max nodded. He sat beside her on the car seat. He wondered if anyone had made out on it before.

'Lucky then,' she said, frowning.

'Yeah,' Max replied. 'I s'pose.' He was thinking the complete opposite.

72

FRIDAY, 24 APRIL 2009

Carrie opened her eyes. Everything was white. All white. Dazzling.

'It's all right.'

She didn't recognise her own voice; didn't recognise the taste in her mouth. Someone was beside her. A dark shadow; a figment of her past. A glimpse of her future. Her head ached. A biting pain from one temple to the other feeding directly through her brain.

'It's all right, isn't it?' She sat up on her elbows. The sheet was stiff against her skin. She wasn't at home then. She was in a small room. One window. White. A hospital. It smelt like a hospital.

Had she been in an accident?

The dark figure spoke. No, he said. It's not all right, Carrie.

Oh, the sorrow. She felt it resonate through her bones, deep in the marrow. She ached, but didn't know why.

She recognised the voice. She turned. She saw, finally, through the opaque film that coated her eyes. She saw her ex-husband.

'Brody?' she whispered.

Something warm took her hand.

You fainted. Hit your head. She couldn't hear him exactly, but somehow the words were in her head.

She held on to the warmth. Vomit came into her mouth.

She turned her head and it spilled out. A nurse was there.

'Am I ill?'

No, Carrie. Brody talking again. Why couldn't she *hear* him?

Hear him like her own voice, like the voices that laced the rest of the room?

Because she didn't *want* to hear him.

'Brody,' she said.

His head fell on to the edge of the bed. She felt the weight of him.

The weight of their grief on the small bed.

Carrie allowed her head to push into the foam pillow. In her mind, the bed collapsed under the load of it all and they fell into the centre of the earth.

They walked slowly side by side. They weren't alone. Someone had mentioned a wheelchair. She recalled shaking her head. Until she saw him, she wouldn't believe it.

Prove it, she'd screamed. There was a warped vision of the *Reality Check* set. She heard herself yell out the same words, the audience behind her revving and baying in a sympathetic rage. She phoned Leah; tried to explain.

'No,' she said. 'No. No.' She went on, until a hand on the small of her back indicated she should turn left. There was a door. The mortuary. *No, no, no . . .*

'In here.' A voice she didn't recognise.

No, no, no . . .

And suddenly she was inside the room, beside a table. A white sheet.

'Are you ready, Ms Kent?'

No, no, no . . .

Carrie looked at the man as if she was staring at him through viscous liquid. *Who are you?* Her fingers tingled. She couldn't feel her legs. Her breath hurt in her chest. She nodded.

Slowly, the doctor pulled back the sheet. The long lump beneath transformed into her son. She was reminded of a stage magician. It was all an act.·

Saw him in half . . . the miraculous levitating boy . . . the vanishing teen.

Bile in her throat again.

His hair was so silky, as if he'd washed it that morning. A couple of spots on his cheeks, still plump.

'Why's he wearing that?' she asked. It was all she could think of to say.

'We put him in something clean.'

The doctor had probably done this a hundred times before.

'Were his clothes dirty?' He didn't look dead. Just asleep. She'd not noticed the red tint in his hair before. She hadn't realised he had an ear pierced; a tiny silver skull sitting on his lobe.

'Carrie, don't.' Brody's voice blanketed the room. 'Help me see him.'

Instinctively, Carrie took Brody's hands. The woman standing the other side of him stiffened, watching intently as she placed them on their dead son's head. Brody kept them there for a moment, then spread them over the boy's face. He pushed a finger either side of the nose and slightly parted the lips with his thumbs. He let out a single sob.

'Ms Kent, I'm going to have to ask you about identification. Can you confirm that this is your son, Max Quinell?'

'It's him.' Brody's voice was deep but empty.

'Ms Kent?' The doctor wanted confirmation from her. They couldn't accept identification from a blind man.

'Yes,' she said, suddenly feeling as if the spotlight was on her, as if she were on her own stage set, heart pounding, taking a grilling from that woman . . . the famous Carrie Kent; as if the audience were holding their breath for her reply, as if what she said would make a real difference – life or death.

No, no, no . . .

'Yes. This is my son.'

Detective Chief Inspector Dennis Masters had just returned from his curtailed meeting with Leah when the news broke. He sat before his team. Just a hunch, but he didn't believe it was going to be a good day. He sipped coffee from the polystyrene cup. It was too hot, but he desperately needed the caffeine. He'd commandeered the largest incident room for this one, hardly able to believe that another stabbing had happened on his patch. The public wanted answers, they wanted security, and they wanted, most of all, for it to stop.

He rubbed his eyes. Three a.m. he'd got to sleep. The Scotch hadn't helped; made it worse, if anything. Earlier in the evening, Estelle had called, egged on by her mother, no doubt. She'd cancelled their plans for the weekend. *Something*, her sorrowful voice confirmed, *has come up, Daddy*.

Masters put his glasses back on and refocused. All he could see as he glanced around the team were angry protesters marching through Harlesden, led by grief-stricken parents of dead kids; banners screaming out that enough was enough, the violence had to stop. Then he envisaged his resignation. The Brent Met had been his home for the last fifteen years and, in all his career, he'd never had to deal with as much knife crime. Carrying a weapon was a way of life for these local kids nowadays. They were too scared not to.

Dennis had already ordered his best detectives to switch cases. He didn't care who he upset in doing so. He would face the superintendent later, when word got back, but for now he needed to know he was doing whatever he could.

'What have we got then?' he said dismally to the woman beside him. Was this one for Carrie? he wondered. Would he be commended for taking action to publicise the crime or slated for glamorising it? He would call her later, see what she thought about putting it on the show.

'Little.' DI Jess Britton had two slim files set between them. A dozen other detectives were perched on the tables around the dreary room, waiting for their brief, impatient to get on. 'There's one possible witness according to a member of staff at the school. The security camera was broken so there's nothing much else yet. No weapon.'

'Who's the potential witness?' Dennis glanced at the clock above the whiteboard. Time was not to be wasted.

'Another pupil from the school. A girl called Dayna Ray.' Britton blew on her coffee.

'Has she been interviewed yet?'

'Nope.' She sipped and winced.

'Organise the usual set-up here, Jess,' Masters replied. 'Send a team out to the school immediately. Talk to everyone. Staff, pupils, caretakers, the lot. And I want the CCTV footage on all cameras within a three-mile radius of the school, and make sure I have a post-mortem report on my desk when I get back.'

'Where are you going?' Jess Britton abandoned her coffee.

'To speak to this Dayna Ray girl.' Masters slid the file across the table and nodded when he read her address.

'What about the parents?' Jess sighed, assuming that unsavoury task would fall to her.

'Sort it with Chris and Al.' DCI Masters bent his neck back. He heard something crack beneath his collar. He wanted the best to handle the key players in this one. He needed an arrest and quick.

Jess shrugged. She didn't want to go out anyway. It was pissing down. She kicked her boots against the chair leg. 'Talk later then, Chief.'

Masters nodded, stood and addressed the room. From behind, Jess Britton pulled a face, the exact same one that she made five years ago when she learnt the promotion had gone to him, not her.

Dennis knew what to expect. Council estate half a mile from the school with the usual area of wasteland disguised as a park housing a couple of burnt-out cars. With the racks of ugly pebble-dashed properties, it provided a fitting battleground for the local youth. 'Local youth,' he repeated out loud. God, it made him feel old.

He parked up outside number twelve and got out of the car. He pushed his radio and phone into the inside pocket of his leather bomber jacket and hitched up his jeans. There was loud music as a throaty car sped by; a dog barked; a woman with a chain of small kids walked through the rain. She stared at Dennis, no doubt sensing he was a cop.

Someone had made an effort to tend the front garden of the Ray household. Masters knew this only because there were no rusty washing machines, no piles of dog mess and no bags of split-open rubbish. He knocked on the green front door. He could smell food cooking. He was about to knock again when the door opened.

'Yes?' A small woman with pulled-back hair answered. She was mean-eyed, as if she'd just been shouting.

'Mrs Ray?' At the same time, Dennis flashed his ID. The woman's gaze flicked to it and then back to his face. 'Is your daughter home? I'd like to speak to her.'

Without hesitation, Mrs Ray nodded and stepped aside to allow him in. She slammed the door. 'What's she bloody done now?' She turned to the stairs. 'Day-na?' The yell was louder than someone so small should be able to produce. 'Stupid girl. She told me she came home from school ill. Just go up. The door to the right.' Mrs Ray went off into the kitchen with a dog bothering her ankles.

The tiny landing was littered with clothes and general mess, including toys, indicating there was a much younger child living in the house too. Dennis stepped over them and tapped on Dayna's door. He scanned the stickers and magazine cut-outs taped to the chipped paintwork. He hoped the younger child couldn't read yet.

'What?' a girl's voice finally answered.

Dennis put his mouth close to the wood. 'Dayna, your mother sent me up. My name is Dennis Masters. I'm a detective. You're not in any trouble, but I'd like to speak to you about what you saw at school today.' Silence. 'Is that OK?' Nothing. 'Dayna, it's really important that you help me. So we can catch the person who killed Max Quinell.'

After another few seconds the door pulled back slowly. A slim girl stood in the darkness of the doorway, her face ashen, her lips parted, her eyes filled with absolute fear. 'Max is *dead*?' Her words were sewn together with a tenuous thread; that if she spoke too loud, it would make it real.

'I'm so sorry. Yes.' Dennis waited a moment. He had assumed she knew.

The girl didn't cry. She swallowed and stared at the wall behind him. Then she swung the door wide open and went back into the dim room to fold herself on to her unmade bed. Dennis followed. When she said nothing, he shifted a pile of clothes and sat down on a wooden stool.

'I know this is hard for you, but I was hoping you'd be able to talk to me about what happened, while it's still fresh in your mind.'

Dayna lifted her head and dragged her gaze around as if it weighed a ton. 'But I loved him.' A sigh escaped.

Dennis sensed they were virgin words; a declaration, fuelled by loss, that – at what? Fifteen? – she had finally found the courage to say. Except it was now too late.

'I'm sure Max knew that.'

'No. No, he didn't.' She stared askew at Dennis.

'Were you his girlfriend?' He would have to work his way

gently. If he could have removed his notepad and pen without her noticing, he would have done. As it was, her eyes flicked to his hands. He rested the pad on his knee.

'Yeah, kind of.' Dayna's eyes suddenly glistened and rounded with tears. 'Are you sure he's dead? The . . . the ambulance came.' She smudged her sleeve across her eyes. 'They were meant to help him.'

'I'm sure.' Dennis sighed. He couldn't see a damn thing with the curtains closed. 'Were you close friends?'

Dayna nodded.

'Before we go much further, love, I want to ask you if you know who did this to Max. Who stabbed him? Who was holding the knife?'

Dayna focused on the detective. Her face slowly puckered into a gradual implosion of grief. 'No,' she whispered. The single syllable shattered into a thousand pieces. 'No, I didn't see.' She fell forward and cried fiercely into the duvet. Her fingers kneaded the wadding. She pushed her head deeper and deeper into sorrow, into the softness. Dennis Masters sat and watched, waiting until she was able to speak again.

She sat up. 'It was all over so quickly. One minute all normal. And then . . .' She squinted, as if reliving the scene in her mind. 'And then there was just so much blood. All that shouting. The panic.' Dayna wrapped her thin arms around her body, hugging herself. Dennis concluded that there was probably no one else going to do it.

'Are these . . .' Dennis glanced at a blood-smeared carrier bag lying on the floor.

'My dirty clothes. Covered in blood,' Dayna replied, blushing.

'I'll have to take them.'

Dayna nodded.

He heard the woman downstairs yell and then a young child's indignant wail.

'Little brother?' he asked.

Dayna offered a glimmer of a smile. 'Sister. Well, half-sister. Kev's not my dad.'

'Where's Kev now?'

Dayna shrugged. 'Pub. Someone's house. Bookies. Job Centre if it's Mum's lucky week.'

Dennis suddenly felt like a male version of Carrie Kent, prising out the grim truth of lives that most people would rather ignore. Lives filled with tragedy, poverty, neglect and abuse. It went on. He saw it every day.

Dennis pulled things back on track. 'Do you think it was a pupil at your school?'

Dayna shrugged.

'Tall? Short? White? Black? Asian? What was he wearing? You must be able to tell me something? You were actually there, weren't you?'

Dayna began to shake as if she wasn't sure. Her electric blue-tipped fingers snatched at the duvet cover. Her eyes swam with confusion and anger. 'Shut up! I didn't see them.'

'If you can give even a couple of shreds of information about Max's killer, Dayna, it will help enormously. Think back to this morning. Start with when you first saw Max. What were you doing?' Masters put pen to pad. He wrote *them*.

Dayna was repeatedly shaking her head. She was clearly traumatised. Victim support would be on to her soon enough, he reckoned, but perhaps immediate counselling was what she needed. Her head would be well and truly clogged. He'd dealt with young witnesses like her many times before. They either never shut up spouting lies, or they went in on themselves, like Dayna, somehow feeling that they were to blame, that they could have done something to help.

'We were bunking off. I was waiting for English. I'd got some chips.' She touched her lips, as if the taste was still there.

81

'Go on.' This was good. She was thinking about it.

'And then . . .' Dayna stood and went to the window. Dennis squinted as she whipped back the curtains. 'And then they were just there. Taunting him. Threatening him.' She turned. 'You're not meant to die bunking off lessons and eating chips.'

Dennis sighed heavily. 'What do you mean, you were waiting for English?'

'It's the only lesson I like. Max likes it too. Liked.'

'I can see you read a lot.' Dayna's room had more books in it than the average teen, he reckoned. Not that he knew much about kids' bedrooms these days. Not since Kaye had left with Estelle. Dealing with teenage girls particularly stung these days. He tried not to think about it.

Dayna nodded. 'We read to each other.' She was a silhouette between the gloom inside and the spring sun that had broken from behind cloud. 'Shakespeare and stuff.'

'Did Max have any enemies that you know of?'

The girl swallowed several times. As if the news had just hit her all over again, she puckered with sadness and fell on to the bed. 'I don't know. I don't fucking know anything any more.' Then she raised her head. 'I do know one thing though. I'm never going back to school.'

Her head sank into the bedding again. Even the detective's hand tentatively placed between her shoulder blades didn't elicit a response. He decided to allow her an hour or two more grieving; to come to terms with things before he really set to and grilled her. Meantime, he would catch up with what Jess and the others had rounded up.

He would also call Carrie or Leah. It would be incredibly useful if they could air a last-minute special edition show, he decided, wondering just how many strings he could pull. Perhaps a general round-up of knife crime to stimulate interest, then a focus on the Quinell case. They could do a reconstruction. He

82

needed answers and he needed them fast. In the past, it had been clearly proven that the sooner they got information out to the public, the better the results. And Jesus Christ, he thought sourly, did he need results.

Dennis left Dayna's bedroom and trod the stairs quickly. Mrs Ray didn't bother replying when he called out a goodbye, that he would be back later, that Dayna would need to come down to the station to make a statement. He hesitated by the front door, turned and opened his mouth. But then he continued outside, seeing no point in telling the woman that her daughter could use some motherly comfort.

THE PAST

'Don't write shit about me,' were Dr Quinell's first words to her. He didn't care for journalists, and he cared even less for the stupid photographer as she circled round him, snapping repeatedly. He batted his hand at the silly girl. 'Get away from me.'

'I'll only write shit if you choose to tell me shit.'

'All journalists write shit.' He flashed a crooked smile.

'I'm not all journalists.'

Before she could put pen to paper, he reached out and snatched her pad. 'What is this?' he said, turning the pad round and round. 'I can't read it. It's sh—'

'Shorthand.' She tried to grab it back, but Quinell whipped it behind his back. There was a ripping sound followed by the scrunching of paper. 'What the hell . . .' She darted behind him, but he spun round. 'Stop it! That's my notepad.'

'Full of shit, like I said.'

'I need to write the story up later and you have no right to—'

'Tough. Have dinner with me tonight and I'll tell you a story worth printing.'

'No, I—'

'Fine. Go tell your editor that you couldn't be bothered to report on one of the biggest breakthroughs in coefficient regression since Legendre and his least squares.' Quinell balled the paper tightly and bounced it back and forth between his large hands.

The woman watched as her notes teetered on destruction. He doubted she'd remember anything of what he'd told her. It was gobbledygook to the lay person.

'My mother always told me not to go off with strangers. I imagine that includes dinner with you,' she said.

'And my mama told me never to date a white girl, but that hasn't stopped me asking. I think you should go tell your mother—'

'Telling her anything will be difficult. She died two years ago.'

'I'm sorry.' Dr Brody Quinell's manner suddenly changed. His face became serious and one hand reached out to her shoulder although didn't quite touch. He noticed her face soften, her eyes open wide as her brow lifted.

'Thank you. But you still shouldn't have ruined my notes.'

He stopped playing with the paper ball for a moment and let out a noise, more a roar than a laugh. 'But you wrote—'

'Stop!' she said, half smiling, looking around for her photographer. Her pencil crept between her teeth. Brody could see he was winning.

'So what's your name?' he asked, reckoning she was about twenty-three or -four.

She swallowed. 'Caroline Kent,' she said quietly.

'Pleased to meet you, Miss Kent.'

Then Dr Brody Quinell – up-and-coming mathematician in the field of statistical science – spread his lips wide and stuffed the paper right in his mouth. Cheeks bulging, he chewed and chewed. 'Mmm, tha's goood shit,' he got out. 'Reckon I'm so stuffed full I won't be needing any dinner at all tonight.'

Carrie Kent, ace reporter with a final warning on a job that many young women fresh out of university would lose a few fingers for, her boss had said, decided she would try a tape recorder on Dr Brody Quinell. She knew she'd drawn the short straw by being given this story, but she was serving time under the science editor as part of her internship with a huge periodical conglomerate. She was determined to prove herself.

The recorder was hidden in a small evening bag. She lifted her napkin and set the purse down on the table with the half-open flap facing him. She'd expected more burger bar than expensive cuisine and was surprised at his tailored suit. He'd made an effort. Earlier, he'd perched on the wall outside the university wearing ripped jeans and a faded shirt. His research work over the last four years had resulted in a paper that was causing quite a stir in the States. It was Carrie's job to discover and report on the personal side of Dr Brody Quinell for *SciTech* magazine.

'The jeans aren't the only thing that's ripped, eh?' Leah, her photographer and best friend, had said when she saw Carrie eyeing up the doctor's lean physique.

'Not my type,' Carrie had whispered back, just wanting to get the story and leave. But gradually she'd warmed to the man, convinced him to take her notes from his mouth, flatten them out, and go over the technical points that she simply couldn't read any more. Eventually, she agreed to go to dinner with the persuasive maths star – he'd been working with NASA, he confided, and had once dated an astrophysicist. He promised her exclusive details of how his research was going to be used and he would even tell her what he had in his refrigerator. If it got back to the editor that she'd passed up the chance, her job would be on the line for sure.

'Nice restaurant.' Carrie glanced around at the elegant wallpaper and pristine tablecloths. Conversation hadn't exactly flowed since they'd arrived. She glanced at her watch.

'You think?' Dr Quinell replied, already appearing bored as if his great mind simply wasn't being stimulated enough.

Carrie smiled coyly, praying she wouldn't ruin things. She

smoothed out her napkin. 'Yes, I do.' This was awful. She wasn't going to get anything from him.

He shrugged. 'We'll find out, won't we?' He stared hard at her. Carrie was unable to look away. Something passed between them. She felt herself break out in a sweat. Finally, Carrie asked for some water. She fiddled with her hair – anything to override the bolt of electricity that shot out from her heart.

They'd barely finished their starters when he suggested they leave.

She sat in stunned silence but, inside her mind, it took her only a second to decide. It couldn't be worse than staying here, having him stare at her, break her down like one of his stupid equations. She didn't want to be something he could figure out. That was what she was supposed to be doing to him.

Then that shard of excitement again, straight through her middle.

He had an apartment, he said, with wine and plenty of food. *They could relax more.* It would be a glimpse into his personal life – for the article, she tried to convince herself as her mind forged ahead to other things.

Carrie swallowed, stood, and picked up her bag. She'd never done anything like this before. 'Sure,' she replied as if she were merely accepting another glass of wine. She would get the story – an exclusive – and then go home.

But there was something about Dr Quinell, she thought as they waited for a cab; something that made her stomach wring itself out. But that same something also made her want to slap him as hard as she could for unsettling her. He was infuriating yet intriguing, powerful yet oddly vulnerable, Carrie discovered, when she saw his apartment. It was basic. He's been single for a long while, she deduced. That or he made a point of not letting women influence him one bit. His living space was utilitarian and devoid of personal belongings. Not even a picture on the wall or a single cushion on the grey sofa.

Carrie stood alone in the sparse apartment and felt like a very small number in this great man's world. *His genius had aided the exploration of Mars.* Suddenly her article for *SciTech* seemed wholly unimportant.

Two hours later, Carrie was feeling as if she'd been to Mars and back. As for the process, she couldn't quite work out how it had happened. Just something about the man she was meant to be interviewing, something about the sum of them both after a few more words and a bottle of wine.

'Again?' Brody asked. It wasn't really a question. He clambered on top of her for the third time, his shiny black skin such a contrast to her milky white colour, and twenty minutes later he rolled off. 'Not bad,' he said, eyes closed, sheet tangled around his waist.

Carrie reached across the bed and slapped him hard. She felt utterly satisfied. Then she reached for her bag and took out the tape recorder. She spent the next four hours grilling Brody about his life, his loves, his achievements and ambitions. He was, not surprisingly, his most amenable yet. Carrie didn't even notice when the mini-cassette reached the end and clicked off. Eventually, exhausted, she drifted off to sleep. When she woke, quite against her better judgement and large amounts of good sense that usually dominated her life, she wondered if this was anything akin to love.

THE PAST

Max had grown up with something weighing him down and, try as he might, he couldn't name or identify it. He didn't like it – just as some kids were fat or had a limp, or spots or eczema. That was their thing. They got on with being teased and that was the end of it. No one wanted to be different.

One girl in his kindergarten class had an extra finger on her right hand. A little wiggly stump without a nail. Her parents wanted to have it removed when she was younger, but she'd refused. She thought it made her special. The other kids ripped into her about it, but Max loved her for it. She had something extra too, like him, only he wasn't sure exactly what it was he'd been born with, just that he knew he had it – something unusual sitting on his shoulder. Something heavy that he dragged around every day of his life; something that ate into him; something that watched him, spied on him, like his own personal god. Or demon, he concluded as he grew up.

During his early years, Max believed that he was special, that this *thing* somehow protected him. He knew he was different from the other kids – he was mixed race for a start, one of only a handful at his school. He knew his parents paid a lot of money to send him to Denningham College and wondered if that was the source of his angst. He was never happy there.

Teasing, bullying, racism, violence or plain nastiness is simply not tolerated at Denningham. Any pupil caught partaking of such contemptible crimes will be immediately removed from the school.

Here, we pride ourselves on good behaviour and tolerance of all.

The headmistress's words rang loud and clear at the start of every term. No one took any notice. Max still got his hair washed in the urinals; still had his possessions taken, broken or sold; still got the silent treatment as his entire year was cajoled into not speaking to him for a term. And he always slept badly in the dorm. He woke early to take his shower before anyone else was up for fear of being ridiculed about his skinny body. He couldn't bear it if he had to do those vile things in front of them all again.

Denningham College treats everybody the same. You are all equal.

During his school years, Max grew and matured and developed a strong bond with the Thing. It sat right there on his shoulder, watching him when he sobbed at night, criticising him when he was a fool, egging him on when he was shy, holding him back when he wanted to have a go. It interfered in every aspect of his life so that when he reached puberty, Max's school sent a letter home informing his mother that he talked to someone. Someone that wasn't there.

Carrie Kent had her secretary book him an appointment with a top Harley Street psychologist.

'And has this *thing* always been with you, Max?'

Max liked the way the woman said *thing* just like he did – as if it was real, yet unnameable. A thing not to be messed with, to be spoken of carefully. This thing was powerful. It ruled his life, didn't it?

'Sure.' Max was twelve. He was clever but never got good grades. 'Always.'

'And does this *thing* have a name?'

Now she was being silly. 'It's not a person. Of course it doesn't have a name.'

'But you talk to it as if it's a real person?'

Max shrugged. He kicked his foot against the corner of the

woman's desk. Was she a doctor? He didn't know. He stared at his mother, sitting next to him, keeping silent, knotting her fingers round and round in an annoying tumbling dance. He wished she'd go away. He didn't feel comfortable talking about the Thing in front of her, and worse, he'd been told to get a haircut before he came back to school. He would have to ask his mother, but he could already see her staring at her watch, rolling her eyes, instructing her driver to take him to some poncy salon full of women while she raced back to the studio.

'No one else to talk to, is there?' He felt his mother's frown bring the mood in the dismal room down even further. She had a knack of doing that. A certain way of commanding everyone around her. If Max did it, he'd be called spoilt and moody. When his mother did it, she got famous.

'How come, Max? Don't you enjoy school?'

'It's all right.' Max stuffed a hand into his pocket. He felt a packet of Polos, or what was left of them. Probably only about three, all warm from his leg. He salivated a little. The Thing told him to eat one so he did. His mother sighed. The other woman smiled and shook her head when he offered her one. Then she wrote something down on the pad resting on her knee. She had nice knees, Max thought, like Miss Riley at school. The other kids were mean to her, too.

'What I'm trying to say is, wouldn't it be better to talk to real boys your own age rather than this thing, rather than talking to yourself?'

There was a big silence. Max felt as if he could have fitted his entire life into the void that swallowed up the room. She actually believed he was talking to himself. What was he going to answer? He had no idea. The Thing sometimes surprised him, made him say stuff that either got his head kicked in during free time after supper or, more likely, meant he took to the dorm early, feigning illness, just to sleep, just to escape the great weight of everything.

The void didn't get filled. Instead, the psychologist put down her pad and pen and turned to Max's mother.

'I think your son's depressed, Mrs Kent.' She spoke in a low voice.

That was it. Her diagnosis. Depression.

At twelve, Max knew exactly what that was.

'Well. Thank you, doctor,' Max's mother said. Now they could get on with life again.

Max turned his head slowly round to his mother. She looked relieved – the way her eyes narrowed as if there was a smile beneath them. Well, there was, but not a smile of pleasure. More a smile of, what next? A smile thanking God that it wasn't terminal, that she could just send him back to school with a packet of pills and a few sessions with a counsellor and she'd never hear anything more about the whole annoying incident. That's what the Thing told him, anyway.

Max took the remaining Polo from his pocket. He crunched it slowly, not taking his eyes off his mother.

AUTUMN 2008

Max had no problem carrying the large box. The happiness in his heart, the grin on his face pretty much made it float weightless in his arms.

'I won, oh yeah. Knew it. Just knew it.'

The side of the box cut into his skinny arms, but he didn't care. This one rocked. This was the best yet. This one, thinking about it, had been *easy*. 'It's all about the purpose,' he muttered. He thought of Dayna's face when she opened it; thought about helping her lug it home after he'd surprised her with it at the shed when they met later. He could meet her family, maybe stay for tea. He'd do it all properly, make sure it was OK with her folks. They could use the computer too . . .

He stopped.

Up ahead was a group of four lads loitering at the head of the alley he wanted to take to get to the railway. He squinted, recognising one of them. He had a crew cut and was sometimes at school. Max knew they'd clocked him by the way they suddenly fell into formation and moved forwards. Shit.

Max glanced to his right. There was a shop. He started to cross the road, unable to see round the box very well.

'Oi!' one of the gang yelled.

The thud thud of trainers on tarmac fell into rhythm with his heart.

'Oi, fuckhead.' There was a hand on his shoulder just as he reached the middle of the road. 'What you got there?'

He was surrounded. Four kids about his age, one on each side of him, gave him no choice but to follow them back across the road and down towards the alley. The rear fences of a street of council houses formed one boundary of the narrow short cut. A mix of iron railings topped with spirals of barbed wire, kicked-in wooden slatted fences, palettes and junk, old settees and cars made an assortment of endings to the depressing patches of garden behind.

Max took all this in as he was frog-marched further down the alley. He'd never noticed the houses before as he'd dashed to his hut, eager to escape from the world. A world that really didn't understand him. But now, trapped, hedged in by four thugs who stank of booze and menace, time slowed painfully. He knew he was going to feel every kick, every jab, every cruel word as they relished taking what they believed was theirs – his soul.

'I said, what the fuck is it?' The hood was pulled over the youth's head. His shoulders were narrow, hunched beneath his clothes – a naturally aggressive pose as well as helping to conceal his face from the dozens of cameras that had already tracked their movements round the neighbourhood.

'Just a box.' Max's voice failed him and went high-pitched. The four youths laughed. The computer's brand and logo was printed on all sides.

'I'm pissin' myself, man.'

Then the kick in the back. A line of pain passed through his kidneys and spiralled down to his groin. He doubled over and the box slid from his arms, down his knees and on to the ground. His feet prevented a hard landing. It was a present for Dayna.

The box was yanked from him. They kicked and punched him some more before ripping it open.

'Don't. It's mine,' Max said, straightening up, trying to block out the pain. 'Just leave it, will you?'

They ignored him and pulled out the polystyrene. Their eyes

bulged as they hoisted the sleek machine from its housing. Max smelt new plastic as polythene bags of cables and instructions and discs fell on to the dirt. The flat screen monitor slipped from its packaging and tumbled back into the box.

'Shove it in and let's go,' one grunted. Yeah, they were all thinking. Let's fucking get it shifted down the pub. Two of them picked up the overflowing box. Max received another kick and got a streak of phlegm spewed down his jacket. 'Fuckhead freaking motherfucker . . .' and they strode off, trying to maintain their usual gait while scarpering with the loot.

Max stared after them. His body hurt. His head was worse still. How would he tell her? What would he give her now? Max began to shake. His fingers itched and burnt. The anger, the shame, the frustration, the stupidity, the inevitability boiled his insides until all he could do was run and run. His feet stumbled and scuffed up the dirt, his clothes snagged and tore as he ducked under the wire cordoning off the railway land, and the pain messed with his brain until he finally made it to his shed. His hands fumbled to get the lock off. He charged inside, bolting the door behind him.

Max fell down on to the car seat. He wept. He hated himself for it. When she came, he wouldn't answer the door. He'd promised her a surprise and had let her down. The only thing for it, that voice in his head told him firmly, was to pretend that he didn't exist.

Dayna didn't understand. The padlock was open and hooked through the bolt on the outside, but the door seemed locked from the inside. It wouldn't budge even when she pressed the toe of her shoe against the wood. She'd knocked of course, but Max wasn't in there. She checked her phone. One thirty, as they'd agreed. She'd raced out of English, knowing he'd already be down here. She keyed in a short text message: *where r u?* She finished with an X but deleted it before sending.

95

A kind of beetle thing crawled across her ankle as she sat waiting on the bit of raised scrubby grass next to the shed. The autumn sun flickered through a tree, making it the nicest spot to sit in the otherwise grim landscape. All she could see was litter, junk and greyness. The blue arch that miraculously held up entire trains as they clattered overhead appeared slightly beautiful when she thought of all the Victorian hands that had held every one of those bricks.

All dead now, she thought, feeling like one of the Railway Children. She cowered as a low rumbling turned into a deafening roar as a train shook the earth. Every cell in her body tingled and she whooped and cried out and screamed *hellooo* because no one could hear her, not above that din. She was free to yell out her deepest secrets when a train came, she thought, as her mind settled down after the flurry of wind and noise. Free to spill my guts as long as I can't hear it myself.

No text back from Max. She stood up and kicked the side of the hut. She had no idea why Max wanted to meet her here. He could have just seen her in the canteen, couldn't he?

My hut. 1.30 tomoz. b there.

The text had come in late last night. She was lying in bed. It made her feel wrong, reading his words in her nightie, lying beneath her duvet struggling to get to sleep when there was so much din downstairs from her mother and Kev arguing.

She decided to send another text, asking where the hell he was and, seconds later, she heard a shrill text alert coming from the hut. As she made her way closer, a second alert sounded.

'Max, you stupid twat, open the door.'

It took a moment, but there was rattling and then Max was standing there, looking gaunt in the shadows.

'Have you been crying?'

Max shrugged and Dayna pushed past him. She saw a lighted joint balanced on the edge of the car seat.

96

'Mind?' She picked it up and drew in. She felt her brain loosen from her body within seconds. She liked that bit. What she didn't like was being stoned; out of control. 'You'll set the fucking place on fire if you leave it there.' She dropped down on to the scorched plastic seat. Her heart missed a couple of beats, as it usually did when she got her first hit of the day.

'So what have you been crying about?' Dayna pulled out a book from her bag. She held it out to Max. '*The Great Gatsby*. I like them when they're new. It's the untouched and the unknown. And the smell.' She opened the pages and breathed in deeply. 'Mmmm.' Then she drew on the spliff again before handing it back to Max. He took it but not the book. 'It's yours. I said I'd give it to you. He gave them out in the lesson. Where were you?' Dayna set the book carefully on top of an electric grill box. 'Lean and mean,' she said with a twinkle in her eye.

'Have it if you want.' Max smoked. 'Have the lot.' He fell down into a squat. 'Would your mum like it?'

'No.' Dayna hugged her knees and let out an odd chuckle. 'She only does tins. Tinned tomatoes on toast. Tinned pies. Really. We have pie from a tin. Tinned fruit and tinned cream stuff that tastes like spunk.'

Max dropped down further and sat semi-cross-legged with one knee stuck in the air. He rested his forearm on it, spliff dangling between his thumb and first finger. 'How d'you know what that's like?' Beneath the red eyes, which, Dayna now realised, could be from the dope and not tears, a loose smile formed. It was one of those smiles that took its time coming, she thought, usually from embarrassment. Or was it disgust? she wondered.

She shrugged coyly. 'Just a guess.' She pulled out a can of Coke from her bag, cracked the pull, swigged and then handed it to Max. 'So what did you want me to come here for?'

Max stared so intently at her and for so long that she began to feel uncomfortable. Maybe he was going to say he liked her or ask her out or something, instead of sitting in a stupid hut. She could do with telling her stepdad that she had a proper date. A boyfriend. She liked the sound of that. A boyfriend.

'Well?' Dayna prised the can from his hand. She stood and looked at all Max's boxes. Dozens of them. 'Won't someone nick them?' Hairdryers, straighteners, blenders, coffee machines, heaters, a bike helmet, the grill, a toaster, a sledge, a massive furry toy that could be a camel or a bear, an art set . . . she couldn't see to the bottom of the pile but there were some very large boxes there.

'Yeah,' Max replied.

'Yeah what?' Dayna got a Christmassy sugar rush from looking at all the new stuff – nearly as exciting as sniffing a new book.

'Yeah, I was crying.'

Dayna turned. 'Why?' She set the Coke down and reached out for his arms. They were very thin.

Max shrugged as if admitting that he'd been crying meant he'd failed. She sensed he didn't want to talk about it. 'Do you want to, like, go to the cinema or something? Or we could just go . . . go to a library.'

Dayna looked away and scratched her neck. 'You're such a geek. You don't have to act all manly because I saw you crying.'

'I'm not.'

A speeding train cut through their awkwardness, shaking the shed, their bones, the boxes. Max rolled his eyes.

'I don't want to go to a library. The cinema's fine.' Dayna drained her Coke can.

Max nodded vigorously, almost exploding from the neck up. 'I wasn't crying because I wanted to ask you out.'

'I know,' Dayna said. She was suddenly reminded of Lorrell holding back her tears after a beating until she got upstairs for a sob on her bed. 'I know.'

FRIDAY, 24 APRIL 2009

Dayna's bare feet trod the worn carpet. She reluctantly slid her hand down the sticky banister rail. That cop had come back again. Her mother had barged straight into her room without knocking and dragged her by the arm on to the landing. 'Get down there and speak to him, whatever it is you've done.'

Dayna could smell her mother's hair – unwashed and smoky. It clumped in stringy bundles, grey at the roots, orange-brown at the uneven ends that hung around her exposed shoulders. She was wearing a mannish vest – wife-beaters, the girls at school called them, only in this case it was the other way round. Dayna thought it made her look like a scrawny bloke.

'I haven't done anything.' Dayna couldn't see properly because she'd been crying so much. No one understood. Was his body cold yet? she wondered. Had his insides trickled out? She'd read about decomposition when she'd skipped ahead in the biology textbook.

'Well, he seems to think you have. Go and tell him what he wants to know.'

Dayna reckoned it had only been an hour or so since his last visit; barely long enough to dry her eyes. She felt her mother's hand in the small of her back shoving her into the living room. She stared at her, praying for her to come in with her. She didn't. Wasn't it the law that you had to have a parent with you?

'Hello, Dayna. I thought I'd come back sooner rather than later to see how you're doing.'

The cop's voice was kind although Dayna knew it was fake. Why should he care about anything? There were two of them this time. Dayna's eyes flicked between them as they sat in the small front room – both of them men, neither in uniform.

'How do you think I'm doing? My best friend's dead.'

She sat down on the green velour sofa. They'd had it forever. Lorrell had weed on it, spilt milk on it, she'd been sick on it, food had been eaten on it, and her mother and Kev had shagged themselves stupid on it. Probably, if she thought about it, it was where Lorrell had been made.

'I want you to help me piece together everything you know about Max's life, Dayna. But first I need to clarify the events at school. It's important we don't waste any more time.'

How could a single morning in April span an entire universe?

'Do you think Max woke up this morning knowing he wouldn't get to see the evening?' Dayna got up and walked to the window, staring out of the grimy glass. It fogged from her breath. Grey cloud and drizzle shadowed everything. It was crazy. Worse than crazy.

'I—'

'Do you think he ate breakfast or do you think he thought there was no point? Or that it didn't matter if he never finished his coursework. Did he wonder that?'

'I don't think so, no.'

'What's your name?' Dayna swallowed. The shock of everything had made her forget.

'You can call me Dennis.'

Dennis the Menace, she thought. Max wouldn't have liked him.

'And this is Detective Inspector Marsh.'

A pause.

'What time did you get up this morning, Dayna?'

'The usual. About seven. Lorrell gets hungry.' She turned and went back to the sofa, slumping down and resting her chin in her hand. What could she say? It all had to change now that Max had actually died. 'Yeah. Seven.' Her face ached from crying.

'And did you go straight into school at the normal time?'

'After I'd got Lorrell sorted, yes.' A sob hiccupped from her throat.

'Did you see Max first thing in school?'

Dayna thought. She glanced at the ceiling. 'No, I don't think so.'

'It's important.'

'Well, maybe. I can't remember. Can I see him?'

Dennis glanced at his colleague. 'Probably best to wait for the funeral,' Marsh said. 'There are tests and things that need to be done.' His voice was croaky.

'An autopsy?' She'd read about those.

Both detectives nodded.

'So when did you first see Max today?'

Dayna drew a sudden sharp breath. It took her by surprise. 'Erm, like he was . . .' She picked her fingernails. 'He was in maths, I think. Yeah, I saw him in maths.'

'What was after maths?'

'Geography then science. Max skipped them. I just did geography then went outside. It was break after science.'

'Did you go outside to look for Max?'

Dayna shrugged.

'It's important, Dayna.'

'Maybe. I dunno. What's it matter, anyway? He's dead, isn't he?' She knew she'd have to say it a thousand times at least before the raw edges healed, like picking a scab. Eventually it would be skin but slightly different.

'I'll ask you again. When you went outside after geography, were you looking for Max?'

'Yeah, I guess.'

'Did you find him?'

'Not right away.' Dayna stood up again, unable to keep still. She paced to the window and leant on the sill. She stared out at the front garden. She'd tried to tidy it up after Lorrell got that glass in her foot. 'I went and got chips. I was hungry.'

'What time did you find him? It's important, Dayna.'

'Maybe about ten fifteen. Perhaps half past.'

'But geography doesn't finish until ten forty-five. I thought you said you were in geography.'

Dayna closed her eyes. Behind the blackness of her lids, the safest place she knew, she saw Max's face. He was grinning at her and, beneath his trademark smile, she knew his body was doing the dance he did when he'd won something. The shimmy that made his legs look ten feet long. His *body*, she thought, flashing open her eyes, gripping the sill.

Then, in the brightness beyond, Dayna saw the river of blood flowing from Max's hollow chest. Imprinted in her mind was the look on his face as he fell to the ground. She heard the whoops of the youths as they ran off, exhilarated, terrified; heard the ring of panic in her ears as she tried to save Max; heard the wail of the siren as the ambulance approached.

After that, not much was clear. She heard the pounding of her feet as she ran away; heard the breath of a stranger flying in and out of her lungs. Heard the sound of her own sobs as she realised what she'd done.

Carrie discharged herself. There was talk of concussion, sedation, monitoring until the initial shock had subsided . . . but how could anything compare to seeing your son's body lying on a morgue slab, thinking that if you just touched his shoulder lightly, a little nudge, he'd twist on to his side, bleary-eyed, and groan that it wasn't time to wake up yet, was it, Mum?

When no one would tell her what had happened to her

clothes, she left the ward wearing the hospital gown. She didn't have any shoes. She stopped a cab. She had no idea what she was doing, where her money was to pay the impatient driver as he waited outside her house, hooting the horn while she punched in security codes. She wasn't sure she even lived there.

Eventually, Carrie leant through the passenger window and dropped a fifty pound note on to the seat. She walked back up the steps of her house, shut the door and slid down the wall on to the floor. Her naked back pressed against the cold plaster.

Something was making a noise. Every few minutes, an electronic beep cut through her mind as she tried to shore herself up against reality. Her body was weaving itself up in a padded web to numb everything. Soon, she would feel nothing.

Where was Brody? He'd been with a woman, she recalled that much. She had a vague memory of his deep voice – once so dear and familiar – resonating down the hospital corridor, sweeping through her mind as she was wheeled away on a bed. He told her that he'd find her, that they'd face this together. He never came, so she left.

Carrie crawled through the hallway and along the corridor with its shiny wooden floor. She noticed the tiny dents of a thousand high-heeled footsteps. Hers, no doubt, walking through a life where everything was perfect. It was only up close that the dents were visible.

She felt as if she was swimming through treacle as she made her way to the kitchen. What drugs had they given her? Using all her strength, she hoisted herself up against a stool and leant on the glossy kitchen worktop.

'If they could see me now.' She felt as if she had flu. Her muscles ached, her eyes burnt in their sockets. 'The great Carrie Kent.'

The noise was coming from the answer machine. She plucked

the phone from its holder on the wall and automatically pressed the buttons. She shivered and tried to pull the wretched hospital gown around her but it refused to cover her properly. Carrying the phone, she headed for the stairs, leaning on the walls and furniture as she went. She pressed play.

Carrie, where the hell are you? Your mobile's not answering. Call me.

Hello? Pick up. Carrie?

Are you there?

Another five frantic messages from Leah asking why she'd left the show were punctuated by beeps.

Carrie, it's me. I've been to the hospital to look for you, but they said you'd left. Carrie, please call me.

More of the same. Then a message from her aunt. She obviously didn't know. Then a message from Dennis Masters. He wanted to talk about a new case for the show.

All these voices yet she was quite alone.

It was dark in her bedroom. She recalled leaving the house in a rush first thing that morning. Martha was having a day off. When she arrived, the woman would normally scoot around tidying, opening blinds, picking up things. Max's things.

Carrie ran to the bathroom and vomited. She washed her face. She lay on the bed and considered eating all the pills she knew were in her bedside cabinet. They would like that, the newspapers, the celebrity magazines. They hated her, she knew, even though she sold their publications, but she tried to pretend otherwise. Most of the country hated her too, but they still watched her. She was the most popular female television presenter this year, yet probably the most despised.

Profit from depravity: superstar's luxury lifestyle funded by Britain's poorest.

Carrie had laughed at the article. She'd agreed to the interview – a young chap, hungry for an inside scoop. She was reminded of herself years ago as a struggling hack, trying to make a name for herself. There was a spate of reports following the write-up, a couple of attempts to dig up dirt from her past – drugs, gambling, debt, prostitution, abuse. Again Carrie laughed. They found nothing. There *was* nothing.

'*Noooo* . . .' The scream pierced her body as if she'd been the one stabbed. She hurled herself on to her side and dragged the pillow round her head. Her nose was pressed into the goose-down quilt and she prayed she would suffocate. Through the other side of the wall was Max's room. Filled with his stuff. His smells. The leftovers of his life. How would she ever go in there again? Simple. She wouldn't.

The phone rang.

Carrie grabbed it. It was a connection to the outside world. She felt like the only person left alive.

'Hello?' It didn't sound like her voice.

'Oh Carrie, Carrie. You're home.'

'Leah.'

'Honey, I'm coming round. I couldn't find you. They wouldn't let me near you at the hospital when I came. When I did finally get past them they said you'd left.'

Silence.

'Carrie?'

'Just come.'

The two women sat entwined, rocking, comforting. Leah made tea, but it formed a skin and went cold. Junk mail rattled the letter box and fell on to the mat.

'It's all going on around me. Don't they know? Can't they stop?' Carrie blew her nose but she wasn't really crying. Her eyes were dry, emotionless, drugged up by the need to detach. 'Where are the bloody police?'

Leah rocked in time with Carrie. She held on to her

shoulders, guiding her back and forth to the rhythm of her breathing. 'Haven't you spoken to them yet?'

Carrie shook her head. 'I passed out at the hospital and hit my head.'

'They were perhaps waiting until you felt . . . better.'

Carrie stared straight ahead. 'It was just a call from school. Like he had a sprained ankle or something. The school secretary asked if I could go to the hospital. I didn't expect my son to be . . . to be . . .' Carrie didn't cry. She just swallowed. If she ignored the lump of pain, it would go down. 'There was a message from Dennis. I should call him.'

'Fuck the show,' Leah said. 'I'll call Dennis. He can send someone round to give us an update while he's at it. He must know something. I can't believe you're sitting here on your own.'

'Do you think it's because . . .' Carrie faltered. 'Leah, do you think Max got . . . do you think they did it because of me? Because of who I am?'

Leah was already shaking her head. 'No, no. Not at all.' She pulled Carrie against her chest. 'The police will catch the bastard who did this. He'll burn in hell.'

There was silence again, more rocking, no tears. 'I'm alone, aren't I?' Carrie asked, not expecting an answer. She thought back to when it was the three of them: Brody, her, Max. A happy family.

What were they now? Blind, divorced, dead.

Carrie broke down and cried, this time with tears.

He took the steps two at a time. Things were moving. He'd just left Dayna's house for the second time that morning and, after they'd pushed her as far as they dare, Dennis parted company with Al. Al, together with Chris, was off to make initial contact with the boy's parents. He'd left it with Jess to organise the details.

For now, he was more concerned with finding Carrie Kent and begging for an emergency slot on next week's show. With the immediacy of the stabbing, he knew his superiors would slate him for prioritising this, but it needed to be done. Besides, he was concerned for Carrie. Running off like that wasn't typical behaviour. He glanced at his watch for the hundredth time that morning. Where the fuck was she?

Leah had charged out of the studio in a fit of panic during their meeting, following the call from Carrie. He never even got to ask why she'd walked off stage and then his day had subsequently exploded with news of the stabbing. Now Carrie wasn't answering her phone and neither was Leah. He would need her approval, too. The secretary at the television studio hadn't a clue where either of them were but promised to pass the message on. He also left messages for the director and the assistant producer to call him urgently. If they didn't get this latest stabbing aired next show, even a five-minute slot, it would be pointless. As it was, he was hedging his bets and praying for an arrest before the end of next week. But contingency plans had to be set in place and he was doing what he could. The public reacted best when news was fresh, when emotions ran high. One little piece of information could score them the arrest he was determined to make, *needed* to make, for his community. For his bloody job, he thought, recalling the last grim meeting he'd had with the Commander over the borough's knife crime statistics.

He parked the car, got out and headed up Carrie's steps. He'd give up looking for her if she wasn't here. There were things to do. His phone rang just as he hammered on the door.

'Yep?' But he didn't catch what the caller said because another Met car pulled up behind him. Several voices yelled out.

'Chief, wait up. Thought you wanted us to take care of this?'

Dennis swung round, the phone a few inches from his ear. He saw Al Marsh and Chris Rowe. He half registered a voice saying something on his mobile. 'Al, Chris, what's up?' He forgot the phone call and hung up when he saw the looks on their faces.

'Have you been in yet?' Chris Rowe hitched up his trousers.

'What?'

'Carrie Kent. Have you seen her?' Al looked weary. They'd been at Dayna's house together only a short time ago and Dennis knew he'd been up most of the night.

'No. Not yet. Why are you two here? You were supposed to—'

'Chief.' Al nodded towards the door, glancing beyond Dennis's shoulder.

Dennis turned. Leah was leaning in the half-open doorway. Dennis frowned. She looked awful compared to when he'd seen her only a short time ago.

'Thank God,' she said, eyeing the three detectives. 'You'd better come in.'

Dennis stepped into the cool dark hall. 'Would somebody mind—'

'Shh,' Leah said. The exhalation contained grief, matching the forward droop of her usually straight, businesslike shoulders. She pulled the door to the drawing room closed. Dennis had been in the grand room many times. He was confused.

'Is she in there?' Al asked.

Leah nodded.

'How's she doing?'

'How do you expect?'

Dennis realised he was out of the loop. Which loop, he wasn't sure.

'I found her here, alone. It was awful.' Leah began to cry.

Dennis was getting impatient now. He put his hand on the door handle. He needed to speak to Carrie about the show.

Wait, he thought he heard Leah say.

His mind raced, the school, the proximity of the area . . . surely not. He dragged up the kid's name – what was it, Matt?

He opened the door and, sitting on a pure white chaise longue, her face wet and milky, was Carrie Kent. She looked tiny, he thought; a minuscule version of the powerhouse that millions watched every Friday morning.

'Carrie?'

Her eyes were scarlet. Her hair was flat and seemed to have lost its colour. She'd tucked her bare feet up under her and they poked from beneath the garment she was wearing. Her toenails were shell pink. Was that a hospital gown?

'Have you been in an accident?' he asked. *She'd* been in hospital. It was nothing serious by the look of it. Dennis visibly relaxed. He sat next to Carrie, causing her to lean towards him. She stared straight ahead. 'Are you hurt?' He touched her arm. Shock. What was the hospital thinking, discharging her in this state?

'My son was killed today.'

Flat words against a background of nothing.

'Killed?' Dennis's mind went blank. He recalibrated, started to think over. 'Jesus, Carrie. How?'

She looked at her watch. She wasn't wearing one. 'Is it still today?'

'It's Friday.' Dennis gripped both of Carrie's hands. They were cold.

'Was it only this morning that Max was killed?' Her voice was pathetic.

Max. Dennis's mouth went dry. 'I . . . I don't know.' He looked to the door. Leah, Al and Chris stood in the hallway, staring at the scene.

'Den, can we have a word?' Al Marsh beckoned to his boss. Leah swapped places with Dennis.

He wheeled Dennis down the hall; spoke in a low voice. 'Max Quinell, the lad that got stabbed at the school this morning. Turns out he was Carrie Kent's son. Jess gave us the address of the parents and . . . well, here we are.' He said her name as every-one says a famous person's name – with a touch of envy, of distance.

'Jesus fucking—' Dennis wiped his hands down his face. His stomach lurched. In all his time working for the Met, he'd only ever had to deal with something this personal once before. A girl in Estelle's kindergarten class had been the victim of a hit and run. Thinking of that only added to the chill that crawled over his skin. 'Jesus, now I understand.' Carrie's day fell into place with his. He nodded his head slowly. 'OK,' he began, his chest heaving then exhaling. 'Let's get on with it.'

Al nodded. With bowed heads, they rejoined Carrie in her drawing room. Like she had done to hundreds of guests on *Reality Check*, Dennis Masters prepared to question her about her son. He knelt down beside her and looked into her vacant eyes. He wasn't sure where to begin.

AUTUMN 2008

Neither of them wanted to admit that they'd seen the film before. They popped into a Spar to get some sweets and cans before going to the cinema.

'Do you like Revels?' Max asked.

'The coffee ones suck.'

'Maltesers then.' He picked up a large bag.

'Nah.'

Dayna fondled some jelly sweets. 'These?'

'Sure.' Max hated them. They reminded him of chemistry lessons at his previous school, but he wanted to please Dayna, saw the way her eyes lit up at the sight of the neon colours. They paid and stepped out into the sunshine. The pavement almost hissed with steam as the earlier rain evaporated at their feet.

'Indian summer,' Max said. They waited at the bus stop. The cinema was a five-minute bus ride away. 'One'll come soon.' He stared up the road, over the heads of an old couple who stood next to them.

'Not technically,' Dayna said. The can was cold and wet in her hand.

'Not what?'

'We haven't had a frost yet. You really need a frost for it to be an Indian summer. And then at least seven days of high temperatures.'

Max thought. 'There'll have been a frost in Scotland, I bet.'

'That's not here though, is it?' Dayna pressed the side of the can to her lips.

Max noticed her doing this and wondered if she was imagining what it was like to kiss him. She had nice lips and she knew a lot. He was desperate to snog her but had no idea how to start something like that. He stuck his arm out to stop the bus.

'What was it like then, that old school of yours?'

Max made sure his shoulder was touching Dayna's as they stop-started to Willesden. 'Depends.'

'On what?'

'Whether you're one of the popular kids or not.'

'Were you?'

Max laughed. 'Do I look popular?' He lifted up his sweater and smoothed his hands down his skinny chest, straightening out the words on the T-shirt hidden beneath. *Loser* started off huge at the top and was repeated over and over until it faded away.

Dayna glanced down. 'You are so not.'

Max suddenly felt silly, as if a tiny part of him might not actually be like that when he was in her company. 'Ah,' he said with a grin. 'But you haven't seen the back of it yet.' Max bit hard on the inside of his cheek. *Yet*, he'd said, as if it was a given his sweater was coming off.

'No, but really, what was it like, living at school?' She wasn't giving up. 'I can't imagine it.'

Max watched Church Road give way to High Road. He gripped the bag containing the sweets and his drink. 'It wasn't for me,' was what he settled on. He didn't want to put her off snogging him; didn't want to go into detail. The bus wasn't the place for dragging it all up from where he'd buried it.

'Your dad must be loaded.'

To avoid answering, Max imagined what Dayna's house would be like – maybe not even a house, but a small flat. He conjured an image of her parents – her stepdad perhaps working nights in a factory, her mum going mad at home trying to make the money stretch. He thought there'd be a couple of younger brothers riding around the streets on their bikes, and probably a dog or two taking up most of the space when they all watched telly at night. Then there was Dayna, shut away in a bedroom that she perhaps shared with two others, surrounded by the books that she'd saved up for or borrowed from the library. He liked to think of them reading the same school book, their heads filling with similar scenes.

'Nah,' he said, laughing. Since she'd said he spoke funny, he'd tried hard not to. 'My dad just lives in a shitty flat.'

'What about your mum?'

Max tensed. 'Don't really see her much.'

'Thought you lived with her?' Dayna cracked open her can of Coke. It fizzed up and she slurped from the rim.

Max shrugged. 'Technically I do but she's not around much. We don't really get on.'

Dayna nodded slowly. She was thinking. 'So who's got all the cash for that posh school then? Or was it left to you by a distant relative?' She shook her head and grinned.

'Got a scholarship.' He hated lying to her.

'You have to be really clever for that.'

Max felt a twinge of pain radiate through his chest. He opened his drink, even though he'd wanted to save it for the film. If he was sucking on that, perhaps he wouldn't have to answer. As soon as Dayna found out about his mum – or indeed if anyone at his new school found out about his mum – then it was all over. He would give up. He would run away, except there wasn't anywhere left for him to go, not round here anyway. Another bus went past in the opposite direction. When he saw it, Max sprayed Dr Pepper all over Dayna's jeans, choking, coughing, red-faced.

'Hey, what d'you do that for?'

'Sorry.' He didn't have anything for her to mop the mess with. He took off his sweater and rubbed vigorously at her legs. 'So sorry.'

As they stepped off the bus a few minutes later, Max didn't know whether to curl up and die because he had seen his mother's face as big as a house on the side of that other bus, or because Dayna was right behind him reading the back of his T-shirt.

'I fuck losers,' she said loudly, trying to sound amused.

Max pulled his damp sweater back on and led Dayna by the hand to Willesden Cinema.

She thought Max did everything funny. He wasn't like normal boys. He fumbled with his wallet, unable to open it and hold his can and the bag of sweets all at the same time. She laughed and helped him out. Then he insisted on paying for everything without directly looking her in the eye, as if he was ashamed or didn't want to embarrass her, before disappearing into the loos for ages without saying a word after he'd handed over a *gold credit card* to pay for the tickets.

'You OK?' Dayna said when he came out. Part of her wanted to put an arm round him. He'd been acting very weird since he spat that drink over her.

'Yeah, yeah. I'm fine.'

'Shall we go and get a seat then?' The popcorn smell filled Dayna's nostrils and reminded her of when things had been better. She stared at the booth, watching the woman scoop the buttery stuff into huge tubs.

'I guess.'

'What's up?'

Max hesitated in the middle of the foyer. He was flicking his gaze between Dayna and a woman with two small kids in tow at the popcorn counter.

114

'Just a minute.' Max went over to the kiosk.

She shrugged. It had been her idea to get the sweets from the Spar. She couldn't afford cinema prices but Max had paid for the stuff anyway.

A moment later, he came back with two of the biggest buckets of popcorn she had ever seen. It would last the rest of their lives. 'Jesus, Max. We'll be sick.'

'Sick together, then.'

Max handed one bucket to Dayna. There was a moment of fumbling, a panicked look exchanged when each thought the other had let go, but they managed to get themselves into the theatre without spilling the snacks. They sat right at the back. There were only four other people in there.

'You have a credit card,' she whispered. It sounded silly. The lights dimmed.

'Oh. Yeah.' Max stuffed his mouth full of popcorn. He stared straight ahead, his nose highlighted by the flickering screen.

'How come?'

Max shrugged in reply. The still-framed local ads gave way to a sudden rush of sound as the turn-your-phone-off film played. Dayna fished in her bag and switched off her ancient Nokia. She hid it away again. She watched as Max tapped his iPhone to silent mode.

'Prize?' she asked.

'Oh, yeah,' he said reluctantly but didn't elaborate.

Dayna watched as he shovelled popcorn in continuously. He didn't want to talk. She tried to convince herself that it was because they were in the cinema, not because he was going off her. Having Max in her life had lightened her days, given her a reason to get up each morning, made everything bearable.

'When you came down to the shed,' he suddenly whispered, turning to her, 'I was going to give you something. A present.' Dayna thought he looked wistful.

'Oh?' She was curious. Max often said strange things. That's what she liked best about him.

'But it got stolen. I was mugged.'

'Bloody hell. Did you go to the police?' She wanted to put a hand on him, to show she felt for him, to show she appreciated the thought, but she was frozen solid.

Max shook his head. A trailer for a film came on and he just stared at that.

'Why not?' When he said nothing, Dayna broke free from her reservations and pulled Max's sleeve. She shook his arm. 'What was it? What was the present?'

'A computer,' he replied without turning from the screen. The popcorn kept going in. Dayna had only tasted one piece of hers.

'You were going to give me a computer?'

She saw Max nod.

'That's crazy. You don't give computers to people you hardly know.'

Max shrugged. 'I do,' he whispered. Then, 'Shh, the movie's starting.'

Dayna chewed on her lip. There was a snag of skin. She tugged it with her teeth and waited for the burst of blood. Probably Max wouldn't kiss her anyway.

The movie began. Dayna stared intently at the American whitewashed house. Someone's dream home. A little boy and girl played in the garden. From the corner of her eye, she gave Max a glance. He was a mystery; not like ordinary lads. Slowly, she turned back to the screen and began to eat her popcorn. The chaotic music screamed that something bad was going to happen.

'Shaved Head's leaving.' Fiona pulled an elastic piece of bacon rind from her mouth. She felt sick. She scraped the pool of tinned tomatoes to one side, along with the remainder of the egg and fried bread and dropped her knife and fork on to the plate.

'Pay. Now.' Brody was urgent. He stood. '*Now.*'

Fiona thrust ten pounds into Edie's pocket as she carried a tray of dirty plates. 'Keep the change,' she said to the waitress. 'In case you're interested, Brody, the other two boys are leaving as well.'

'Follow them.'

'What?' Fiona hissed the words at Brody's ear. 'We can't.'

'You want me to do it alone?'

Fiona rolled her eyes. She took Brody's arm. It was rigid. She knew he worked out – she was there most times, watching as the personal trainer guided him around the equipment – but she didn't think this was from honed muscle. This was pure tension. 'What the hell's got into you?' These kids were upsetting him. She'd like to teach the little sods a lesson for whatever they'd done.

Brody said nothing but fell into step with Fiona. They had a way of walking, as if they were in a three-legged race, as if not only their stride became synchronised but their thoughts, too. Fiona liked to believe this, anyway. Working so closely with the professor for so many years, these things couldn't help but become second nature. That was what she told herself. What she couldn't stand to admit, though, was that in all the second nature, all the symbiosis and rapport they shared, the desire to take things further was purely one-sided. Brody Quinell was completely blind to the love that she'd grown for him.

'Are we close?'

'They're up ahead. About fifty feet away. There are some shops. They've stopped for a smoke. Spotty's kicking litter.' Fiona gently pulled Brody to a stop. 'We shouldn't go any further. They're probably just going back to school. What's the big deal with following a few manky kids?'

This would be as good a time as any, Fiona thought, to kiss

him, to distract him. She hadn't kissed a man for years, not since Daniel broke her heart and walked out two weeks before their wedding. She stared up at Brody's face, looming above her, his glazed eyes staring right over the top of her head. There were similarities between the two men, she thought. The same determined jaw bone, broad shoulders, full lips and a smile that didn't break often but when it did, it came direct from the heart. She shook Daniel from her mind. He had no place in her life now.

'It's personal.'

He did that mouth-rolling thing, where his lips became virtually nothing. He sucked them in before releasing them and then did it all over again.

Fiona had learnt very gradually about the silent battle Brody fought with his emotions. He worked tirelessly to keep anyone from seeing them. She often felt blind herself as she fingered her way through his life, waiting for her touch to stumble across an hour of sadness, a moment of desire. Usually all she felt was the rough brick of the wall that he'd built up around himself. Today, though, she sensed – almost *smelt* – the welling emotion seeping through the cracks. It was, she thought, an awful lot like anger.

Fiona linked her arm with his again. She didn't know what to say. 'They're making a move. Well, a swagger.'

Brody let out a sigh that had obviously been stuck at the bottom of his lungs for a very long time.

'What was that for?' she asked.

'It's complicated, Fiona. Family stuff.'

Fiona stared between him and the kids they were tailing. She shook her head. Family stuff – it sent ripples of jealousy through her as well as the desire to create her own. With Brody. But he'd already got a family. She didn't have anything to do with his ex-wife but the son had been a problem. She steered Brody round a couple of mums and their pushchairs. She wanted to remind him that she was here for him, but even by the second word, she regretted saying it. 'But you don't have a family any—'

'Don't you ever, ever say that to me again.' Brody swung round and grabbed her upper arms tightly, miraculously locating her first time. He pushed his face close to hers. Fiona caught the fry-up on his breath; the anger, the hate, the sadness mingled with the grease. They stood there, in the middle of the street in the lunchtime rush, stiff as boards, each waiting for the other to crack.

'I'm so sorry.' She felt wretched and meant it. It barely diffused things. 'I didn't mean . . .' But she stopped. Brody was already walking on, about to plough straight into a bench.

She ran up to him. 'I really am sorry.' She took his arm and guided him to the left. 'Bench,' she said.

'Just follow the boys.'

Brody instructed Fiona to take him right up to the school gates. In the past, he'd kept quiet enough about his family – a good thing, he now realised – and he doubted very much she would figure out that this was the school Max had decided to attend after eschewing private education, of which, Brody had to admit, he was not a fan. When Max was eight years old, it was something he'd just gone along with, trusting Carrie's motherly instincts to make the right decisions for their son.

Brody's heart beat heavy in his chest. Max skulked in here every morning, pack weighing him down, life making him stoop even more. He couldn't see the place, of course, but the blackness in his eyes was representative of how Max must feel to act so rashly. Where did he go when he truanted? Brody wondered. He'd had four phone calls from the school so far, a meeting with the head threatened if the absences continued. He'd tried to bring the subject up with Max – what parent wouldn't? – but the time had never been right. In his head, Brody had run through the conversation they might have but reckoned the damage to their tenuous relationship would be too great. Max was living on a knife edge as it was, adjusting to the new routine post-boarding school, coping with his mother, who Brody knew would have been livid about Max's decision to quit Denningham. He couldn't do it to the boy. Not yet. So what if he missed a few lessons.

But it was the messages last week that finally caused Brody to take matters into his own hands. It would kill the boy if he knew. *Watch yer back, you freakin' loser . . . We're following you, lowlife scum . . . Say anything and we gonna shank yer ass in school . . . We know you fucked yer own mother you ugly shitface . . .*

'What's going on?' he asked.

'Nothing. They've just gone back into school like good little children.'

Brody imagined Fiona's face, squinting and peering through the school gates on his behalf. He realised in all the time they'd worked together, he'd never once asked what she looked like. In his world the visual took a back seat. If pressed, he reckoned she was a redhead – a petite but feisty little thing with freckles all over her nose that she covered up with powder. He could sometimes smell it.

'Can you still see them?'

'Brody . . .'

He didn't reply.

'Is this to do with Max, by any chance?'

Silence.

'Is it?'

'Why?' He'd really not wanted to talk directly about his son.

'Because he's walking right towards us.'

Brody pulled his arm from Fiona's. Damn. Damn a thousand times. He hadn't reckoned on running into Max.

'Hello, Max,' Fiona said a certain way. Cautious, Brody thought.

In meetings or when they came across colleagues, she would take the introduction initiative – stating names, angling her voice so he got a sense of position. It gave Brody immediate know-ledge. She was his missing sense. She was good at it. He couldn't argue with that.

'What are you doing here, Dad?' There was an indignant wobble in Max's voice.

It was Brody who made the awkward teenage noise. Caught red-handed.

'Are you checking up on me?' Max found it in him to laugh. If they switched places, Brody reckoned he would be angry too. 'Thanks a lot, Dad, for parading around here like a . . .

'Stop. Don't say it.' Brody held up his hands, palms out. Kids could be so cruel.

'Your father and I have just had lunch. We were walking back to the car,' Fiona intervened.

'Right,' Max said sourly. 'I'm OK, you know, Dad. I'm at school. English next, then double physics. We're doing sound waves.'

'That's good.' Brody picked up the scuff of his son's trainer on the tarmac. 'You at your mother's tonight?'

'Guess.'

'Come round for some food if you like. I'll cook.' Brody put on his best father-son voice – one that promised a takeaway, a beer, a movie, silly banter. They could talk.

'Nah. Already got plans.'

Brody wanted to ask what. Was he doing something with his mother? He doubted that. A girlfriend. Was he taking her out? That would be a good sign. Or maybe he just had loads of homework. But then how could he if he was skipping as many lessons as the head had told him?

'OK, son. Well, let's—'

'Brody. He's gone.' Fiona's hand clamped round his forearm. It was little comfort. Every time Max went away, Brody knew there was less of his life left in which to get things right.

'Sure.' Brody walked off and Fiona pulled him round in the correct direction. 'Take me back to the car.'

'Of course,' she said. 'But only if you tell me what that was all about.'

When he'd strapped himself into the passenger seat, Brody felt along the dash for the air conditioner. It wasn't that warm, but he was sweating. 'What's with all the blackmailing, woman?'

He heard her laugh. Something that didn't happen very often. Fiona was quite intense. 'Are you going to fire me?'

Brody didn't reply. He heard the crunch of first gear as she drove off. She always did that, never quite depressed the clutch enough. Once, he'd forced her out of the driver's side and got in himself. 'Just be my eyes. Left or right. Fast or slow.' They didn't make it out of the university car park before Brody had crumpled the left wing on the gatekeeper's booth.

'See what you've done?' Fiona had said, running her hand over the impacted front panel.

Of course I didn't see, he thought, but he did now. As Fiona forced the gear stick into third then fourth, he saw quite clearly what was happening. He imagined Max veering off from the school entrance as all the other kids reluctantly went back to lessons after the lunch break. He would take a detour down to the canal or the railway for a smoke, to think, to ponder the car crash that was his family, his life.

'What this is all about,' Brody said slowly, 'is saving my son.'

'From what?'

He heard the indicator ticking as they sat still at a junction, the whir of Fiona's thoughts. Was she working it out – his obsession

122

with the lads in the café, the book on bullying he wanted her to read to him, hanging around the school?

'Never mind,' Brody finally replied, thinking that, apart from the bullies, what Max needed saving from most was his parents.

FRIDAY, 24 APRIL 2009

By mid-afternoon, Carrie had managed to change into a pair of trousers, a plain sweater. She was in the kitchen. Why were there so many people in her house? Everything was fuzzy. She didn't understand. Someone had made her a cup of tea.

She found herself opening her laptop, feeling strangely serene. Her fingers tingled and her skin danced as if she'd been out in the sun, whereas her heart beat slowly as though it was on ice. She thought she might be hungry. Did a part of her not realise?

'They say this happens, Carrie. Just go with it.' It was Leah's voice, prising apart the shroud. 'Why don't you sit somewhere more comfortable?' A hand on her shoulder, another on her waist.

'But I want to check my emails.' Perched on the kitchen stool, one foot hooked over the rail, Carrie tried to log in. 'I eat a snack and sometimes check my messages here. It's what I do.' She sighed and nodded, entering her password. The computer made a noise and rejected the log-in attempt.

'But today I think you should take it easy. Come and sit over here.'

'No.' Carrie entered the password again. Log-in failed. She turned her head and looked at the woman beside her. It was definitely Leah, but she was all misty, like a photo taken through a filter. She thought Leah looked beautiful.

Carrie smiled. 'Why can't I remember my password?'

'Because you're in shock. Your emails don't matter. I wish you'd come—'

'I want to remember my fucking password.' She punched in more keys, but it just didn't feel right, wasn't the familiar pattern her fingers made every morning to get things going, to see who was going to be on the show, to find out from her agent about the week's bookings, interviews, appearances . . . 'Leah?' Carrie gripped the worktop. Words were grit in her mouth.

'Do you remember the phone call from school, Carrie? Being at the hospital?'

Carrie felt Leah wrap around her, the tickle of her hair as it brushed her face.

'Yes. I think so.' Everything was blurred. Carrie pulled away and stood up. She went for more coffee, but it was all gone. It had made her heart beat faster; made her blood plump up her veins.

'I'll make some more.' Leah refilled the machine. 'Dennis wants to talk to you. He *needs* to.'

'Yes.' Carrie walked around the kitchen, her shoes clicking on the tiles. 'Why?' She felt it was right that they should talk; there was always so much to discuss. Sometimes they even spoke about when they were lovers, but for the most part they skirted around their brief affair. 'Is it about Max?' Carrie allowed her feet to fall sideways out of her shoes.

'Yes. About Max.' Leah guided her towards the living room. It was filled with police. 'Talk to Dennis about Max, honey.'

She was used to everyone falling silent in her presence. She adored it when all eyes were on her. Being guest of honour at receptions, opening shopping centres, being interviewed on late-night chat shows, hosting *Reality Check*, Carrie Kent was never happier than when she was the centre of attention. But this wasn't right.

'I need to ask you some questions, Carrie. And I need your permission to take some of Max's things away for analysis.'

'Sure,' she said. 'That's all fine.' She felt better sitting down, her long back supported by the white leather of the chaise, her head not so crazy. Whatever Dennis wanted.

'First of all, I need to ask you if Max had any enemies. It may seem obvious but it could make things incredibly easy. Anyone he'd fallen out with.'

Easy? Things didn't feel as if they would ever be easy, though her mind wouldn't allow her to know exactly why. She thought her lips might be swelling up.

'He didn't have any enemies.'

'Are you certain?'

She felt the nip of a frown. 'He was a quiet boy.' Carrie recalled telling him to stop making a din when he played that guitar. He had obeyed immediately and the house had once again become peaceful. She thought she might have heard a sob but that was all. 'I don't think he had any enemies.'

Something snagged in her heart.

'What about at school?'

'School?' Carrie allowed her eyes to close. She saw a little boy aged eight, posing in his new uniform. They'd just bought it. He'd wanted her to take a photograph of him in his blazer and cap. Maroon and green. 'He went to boarding school when he was eight.' Then an image of a taller Max, a young man with a smattering of stubble and close-cropped hair, unlike the frizz of his boyhood; an image of him shouting, thumping the wall, yelling that he couldn't go on there any more, that he was leaving.

Was blood leaking from her vessels, seeping into the tissue, bursting from under her fingernails?

It hurt so.

Carrie counted six people in the room apart from her. She wasn't even sure she was actually there. Her soul felt loosened from her body, detached from reality. She wouldn't have minded if they'd separated completely. She counted the panes in the Georgian windows. Thirty-six.

'Tell me about his school.'

There was so much. She summed it up. 'He was average.' Why did she settle on that?

'How long had he been at Milton Park High?'

Carrie had to think what month it was now. April. Not long since her birthday. Max had given her a garden shredder. He'd wrapped it in pink paper. She'd left it in the garage for the man that came on Thursdays to use.

'Since last September. Two thousand and eight. He left Denningham the previous term.'

'How come?' Dennis sat close to Carrie. She sensed the urgency in him, smelt it on his breath. She looked away.

'There were some kids, he said. Mean kids. That kind of stuff.' Carrie swept back her hair. Her voice was a whisper, barely there. Did saying it mean it was suddenly true? 'Max was different. Sensitive.' She'd never introduced Max to Dennis the few times he'd stayed over. Either Dennis had left before Max got up, or the other way round. Max would have caused a fuss.

'Was he being bullied?'

Carrie thought about this. She'd met some bullies in her time on the show. Parents who bullied their children, employers who made their workers' lives hell, deranged men who drove their wives to seek refuge – they came in all shapes and sizes.

'No,' she replied. 'Definitely not. He would have told me.' She felt sick.

'But you just said there were mean kids—'

'I didn't say they were bullying Max, did I? There's a difference.'

Dennis pulled a face which told Carrie that he didn't think there was.

'And how was he getting on at the local comp?'

'It's not *local*.' Carrie briefly covered her face. 'The school is in Harlesden near where his father lives.'

Carrie saw clearer than ever the precipice upon which she existed, that precarious place between the two realities of her life. Hampstead and Harlesden, only a short bus ride or chauffeur-driven limo apart. The desperate people she had on her show and her own privileged existence were at opposite poles of the universe but she couldn't do without either.

Then there was her and Brody – a marriage doomed from the start.

Mother and son.

Her life then. Her life now.

Her life yesterday. Her life today.

Black and white.

'Did it happen at school?' A seepage of truth, of realisation. Sudden clarity.

Dennis nodded.

'I want to see.' She'd never even been to the comprehensive.

Dennis looked at his officers. A series of nods were exchanged. 'When we're done.' He continued. 'Carrie, was your son involved in any gangs? Perhaps since he moved schools he might have fallen in with the wrong crowd. Did he take drugs? Was he a drinker?'

'Why are you asking me these things? Of course not. Max was a good boy.' Carrie pressed her fingers against her temples. The pain between them was unbearable. Max would never be in a gang. He wasn't like that.

'Shall I get you a painkiller?' Leah stood up from crouching beside her and soon returned with some pills.

Carrie took them. She began to rock. 'This wasn't meant to happen. He was my son. No one takes my son.'

'Carrie . . .'

She stood. She strode to the kitchen and opened the lid of her laptop. Her fingers typed the password and her computer flashed to life. 'My son's first words,' she said to the detectives following in her wake. Then the tears fell as if they had been waiting in her eyes all her life. 'I was the only one who heard them.'

Unable to hold herself upright any longer, Carrie folded on to the floor, wondering who had been there to hear Max's last words.

No one noticed when Dayna left the house. Kev had got back in a bad mood and lashed out at anyone in his way. He'd been laid off again. No more work, he said. All the jobs dried up like dog shit in the sun. He'd still been able to afford a slab of beer and a bottle of whisky, she noticed, as she slipped down the stairs. She put on her jacket and went out. Her mother and Kev were bickering in the kitchen about the police sniffing around earlier. They were worried about their benefits. Lorrell whined on the floor.

Outside, the air was cooler than this morning. She couldn't believe he was *dead*. It was crazy. Her feet marked urgent strides and her head went dizzy. The walk that she'd done twice a day for the last few years suddenly seemed unfamiliar. She'd never particularly thought of her neighbourhood as ugly, but today it seemed apocalyptic, otherworldly, as if she was the only one left alive picking through the grey rubble after a nuclear war. Racks and rows of pebble-dash and iron-framed buildings spanned the horizon as far as her bloodshot eyes could see. The only relief, the only colour, in the entire scene was a bright red crisp packet blowing round in circles. Dayna picked it up and put it in her pocket. She didn't like to see litter.

Ten minutes later, the top storey of the science block came into view over the rooftops. Endless lessons, pointless, she thought, chin in hand, backside sore from those stupid wooden stools, a desire to mix up all the colourful chemicals to see what havoc could be wreaked; to teach them all a lesson.

There was still some kind of fuss going on at the school. Once she rounded the corner she'd be in full view of whoever was at the main entrance gates. As it was, she could already see the bright yellow jackets, the luminous tape blowing in the breeze, the neon-blue pulse of a police light.

Staying in the shadows, she took small steps. She strained her neck. Within the boundaries of the tape was a kind of tent thing. Four white-suited men were on their hands and knees just inside it. Looking for remnants of Max, she thought.

Dayna had wanted to take a closer look, to revisit the exact spot to make it real, because right now she didn't think it was real at all. The only thing she knew for certain was the taste of the bile in her throat. Was the blood still fresh or had they washed it away? she wondered, getting closer. Picking up her pace, she bravely walked past the railings. She might just get a glimpse. No one would notice her; no one ever did, except when they wanted to beat her up.

She marched past, but there were too many people in the way to see anything clearly. She glanced sideways again at the spot where she'd left Max with the ambulance men.

Take time back, she thought. Rewind.

She cradled her belly. It ached. She wanted to throw up.

The door of a parked car opened wide across the pavement. Dayna darted out of the way. A woman got out.

She squinted at her, staggering sideways.

Didn't she know her?

Dayna walked backwards for a few paces, hugging her coat round her. She stared at the woman as she was escorted into school by the police. One of them was that cop from earlier. Dayna thought the woman looked empty, lifeless, so very, very sad.

Then it struck her.

'Oh,' Dayna called out involuntarily. Wasn't she the one off the telly?

The blonde woman stopped and turned. She lifted her dark glasses and stared at Dayna. She'd been crying. The woman's mouth opened but then she dropped her glasses down on to her nose again and allowed herself to be led through the school gates.

It's *her*, Dayna thought. It really is. Her heart sprinted and stumbled in her chest. What was Carrie Kent doing here? Was she making a show about it already? Was Max going to be on telly?

'Oh no,' Dayna whispered. She felt her feet breaking into a run. 'No, *no . . .*' she called out, charging down the street. She'd seen what that woman could do to people.

Dayna headed for the shed. She needed to be alone, near Max. Today wasn't real and she would just wait for it to pass. When morning came everything would be all right.

Dennis wanted her to see the blood. The scene had, according to forensics, already been photographed and was now being thoroughly searched. Various items found there had already been sent away for analysis. Rain threatened and, even though a tent had been erected over the incident area, they had to work swiftly. They couldn't have evidence washed away.

'Is this it?' Carrie asked.

Dennis nodded. He could almost believe they were checking out the scene for filming. He was so used to production tech-niques and hearing about camera angles, lighting and such, he had to remind himself that this was Carrie's tragedy, not some stranger who would go on to become yet another statistic.

'Whoever did this fled in a hurry. We know there were several of them.' Dennis noticed Carrie turn away, bow her head. 'Unfortunately we haven't recovered the weapon. But at least there was a witness.' How useful she would prove to be, though, was beginning to concern Dennis. The girl had so far been unhelpful. Whether she was lying or still in shock and unable to think coherently was as yet undecided. His experience told him it was the latter.

'There was?' Carrie whispered.

'We'll be interviewing everyone. We hope to get fingerprints, DNA, CCTV footage.'

Dennis felt himself detaching as Carrie nodded, walked up to the tape, teetered on the edge of the crime scene as if taking one step closer might send her over to the afterlife.

'He died here?'

'Yes.'

'Just this morning. I don't understand. This morning isn't long ago, yet it seems a lifetime away. As if I never even had a son.' Her voice was thin. 'All those years together.' Carrie lifted the yellow tape. She wobbled. 'Just gone.'

'You can't go in there.' Dennis was quick, his hand on her shoulder. 'I'm sorry. We have to observe from here.'

Carrie nodded. 'Is that blood?'

'It's where the paramedics helped Max.' It was easier to say it like that.

'Max's blood?'

Dennis was forced to say yes. He wanted her to show anger or vow revenge. He wanted her to remember something helpful, a lead, to swear not to rest until they'd caught the killer.

'It's so dark. Like treacle.'

Dennis felt Carrie's cold fingers searching for his until they settled in his fist. He held her hand tightly, thrown by her vulnerability.

'There's so much of it. Did he suffer?'

'He was stabbed, Carrie. Repeatedly.'

It was as good as saying yes, he suffered an agonising, drawn-out death and was left for dead in the dirt. Dennis didn't like doing it but he wanted a reaction. He needed Carrie's help.

She swallowed and said blankly, 'OK. Thank you.'

Dennis turned her to face him. This wasn't the woman he knew, the woman he had worked with for years, the woman who commanded a prime-time television slot and shocked, appalled or incited outrage. Carrie Kent didn't say *OK*, and rarely did she say *Thank you*.

'Who did it, Carrie?' He made her look at him. 'Who did this to your son? He must have had friends visit, talked about who he liked, disliked. You're going to have to help me here.'

'I . . . I . . . work long hours. I wasn't always home.'

Dennis could almost smell it, the guilt seeping out. He found himself wanting to cup her face, push back her hair, draw her to him. It had always been on her terms.

'Let's hope his computer and phone throw up some answers. Meantime, I've got detectives interviewing every pupil and member of staff here.'

'Will you go to his old school?' Carrie asked quietly.

'If necessary, yes. Depends what we uncover here. Tragic as this is, it could just be a case of Max being in the wrong place at the wrong time. Kids carry knives. They use them.'

Carrie nodded and walked back to the waiting car. Dennis thought how small she looked. He would take her home then get back to the incident room for an update.

As they drove away from the school, raindrops smacked against the windscreen – slow at first but then urgent and heavy. The dark sky had come from nowhere. He prayed that forensics had made good progress.

'Jess.' Dennis nodded a greeting. She sat down on the other side of his desk. They'd talk things over between them first, before releasing an updated brief to the rest of the team. 'Anything?'

DI Britton dutifully handed over a couple of reports. 'The first of the school interviews. To sum up, Max wasn't a particularly popular pupil. His classmates said he kept himself to himself and hadn't really bothered making friends since he'd joined the school in September. It was almost as if . . .'

'What?' Dennis leant forward on his desk but then retreated when he saw the piles of other cases that needed dealing with. He couldn't face them.

'It was as if the other kids enjoyed slagging him off, even after he was dead. Like it made them feel big.'

'Pack mentality,' Dennis added. 'Anyone in particular?'

'A couple of names kept coming up. Gang-related stuff. Blake Samms and Owen Driscoll were mentioned. They're both off the Westmount estate. If they're not directly involved, I reckon they'll know something. No one was particularly willing to talk, but that's normal.'

'Have we paid a visit yet?'

Jess nodded. 'I'm expecting the guys back soon.'

Dennis bit his lip. He drained cold coffee from a plastic cup. 'I'm going to see the father after the brief. Want to come with me?'

'Most definitely,' Jess said, already standing. 'Should be interesting.'

'How come?' Dennis put on his jacket. His right shoulder ached.

'Because he lives on the Westmount estate too.'

He'd sent Fiona away. He wanted to be alone, utterly and finally drenched in solitary darkness. He wanted to gouge out his ears so he was deaf; cut out his tongue so he'd never speak again; slice up his skin so that nothing could be more painful.

Brody's heart had been ripped out.

Never before had such an image been so cruel. His son – tall and skinny with stubble and piercings – was still a toddler in his mind, yet a man as he lay cool and still on the morgue slab. His hands had driven over the landscape of Max's face, his body – the gentle mound of his chest, the fuzzy warmth of the hair on his legs. The doctor had told him to stop, not to touch any more, that he could be disturbing evidence.

His son had become nothing more than a mind full of memories and a zipped-up body bag of potential clues. Minute traces of skin under his nails, a globule of spit on his cheek, a stray hair caught up in his clothing. Brody knew that there wouldn't be a square inch of his son's body left unexamined. At the end of it, the forensic pathologist would know Max better than he had.

Brody tensed. He knew someone – more than one person? – was approaching his flat. The kitchen window always rattled when anyone heavy-footed came along the concrete walkway outside. He just wanted to be alone.

As expected, there was a knock. It wouldn't be Fiona. She obeyed her orders and would stay away until he called her. The only other person to ever visit was . . . was Max.

'Police. Professor Quinell, if you're in there, we'd like to speak to you.'

So he was right. More than one.

Brody hauled himself to his front door. He'd never seen it, of course, but Fiona told him it was dirty and grey and looked as if it belonged in a prison cell. Brody didn't care. It kept the world out. He stood still.

'Hello? Is anybody home?' More knocking.

It had to be done. Brody opened the door. Male and female, he thought, catching a vague whiff of perfume.

'Professor, I'm Detective Chief Inspector Dennis Masters and with me is Detective Inspector Jess Britton. We'd like to speak to you about your son.' A pause. 'We are so desperately sorry about your loss.'

Brody nodded and allowed them in. He sensed the hesitation in their footsteps, probably because the place was a shithole. That's what Fiona and Max always told him.

'In here,' Brody growled. His voice was hoarse. Tears stung his useless eyes. 'Please, sit.' He swept his hands along the sofa, sending papers and CDs and clothes to the floor.

'Thank you.'

Brody heard the creak of the old springs as they took a seat. He sat in the armchair opposite.

'My detectives are working round the clock on this case. I'm hopeful that we'll catch the person who killed your son, Professor. I can't begin to imagine what you and your ex-wife must be going through.'

Carrie. He'd not gone back to her at the hospital, couldn't face what their reunion actually meant – that they had failed as parents. What, he wondered, was she doing at this exact moment? Same as him – her body barely functioning, every breath a struggle, her eyes burnt out from crying, her heart sluggish in her chest. He felt an overwhelming desire to hold her, like he'd done just after she'd given birth to Max. He'd never felt so close to anyone as his new son and his beautiful wife.

'No,' Brody replied. 'You can't imagine.'

He would call her. When the police had gone. They should be together at this time, in spite of everything. Nothing mattered now.

'I need to ask you a few questions.'

Brody nodded. His head pounded.

'Do you know if Max had any enemies? It may sound obvious but if there was anyone who had a grudge then we need to speak to them.'

Brody nodded again. 'There were three boys at his school who were giving him trouble.' Brody stopped for a breather, recalled the shouting match he'd had with his son when he'd tried to discuss things. 'Irony is that he left his last school for the same reason.' He could still recall the last message on Max's phone verbatim . . . *don't want no dirty shit like you round here . . . We're gonna make you drink bleach . . .*

'Why do you think kids picked on him?'

Brody could have spent an hour talking about how his son was different from other teenagers, how having a recluse for a father and a famous mother set him apart, that he never quite fitted in. How liking maths and knowing how to program a computer in six different languages since the age of eight had won him the disrespect of his peers; how having a passion for entering competitions – not just a couple, but dozens and dozens a week – had driven him further away from those who should have been his friends.

'Max was different. He was quiet, thoughtful.' Brody heard the scratch of a pencil on paper.

'Why would that upset anyone?' This time the woman's voice.

'Kids pick on anyone different. Makes them feel good about themselves, I guess.' Brody suddenly felt a wave of nausea cramp through his guts. It was simple. He'd not been there when his son needed him most. His hands shook as they gripped the side of the armchair.

'Can you give me any names?' Masters asked.

'No, but I can give you a description and a mobile phone number.'

'A description?' The detective was incredulous, having obviously noted his disability. 'How come?'

'Last year, when I learnt about the kids that were giving Max a hard time, I tracked them down. It was easy enough. Fiona, my assistant, came with me and told me what they looked like. It could be nothing of course . . .' He stopped, hating himself for not pursuing this.

'The descriptions, Professor?' the woman said.

Brody rattled off a mobile phone number from memory and repeated the exact words Fiona had used in the café. It was a start, albeit too late.

The detectives mumbled to each other, their words obscured by the yells of youths outside, but *matches* and *Westmount* were in the mix.

Westmount? Had Max run into trouble on his estate?

'Did your son have a girlfriend, Professor?' Masters asked.

'He always denied it,' Brody replied. He recalled Max's coyness. It was as good as a yes. 'But I think there was a girl.' He remembered her cheap scent.

'What about best mate, someone he was close to?'

Brody thought. 'I don't think so.' He suddenly felt desolate, empty, perhaps how Max must have felt knowing there was no one for him to talk to. 'He would chat with me occasionally.' Not enough, Brody thought.

'Did Max have a bedroom here?' the woman asked. 'Could we take a look?'

'When Max stayed with me, he slept on the couch.' What kind of father was he, he wondered, that his son didn't even have a space to call his own? Max had a room at his mother's of course, but when he was here – which had been more often recently – the couch was where Max crashed after they'd watched a movie or played chess. 'This is a one-bedroom flat.' Brody was justifying the arrangement. 'But he kept some stuff in a drawer. Over there.' He indicated the dresser.

'Do you mind if we take a look?'

'Go right ahead.' Brody didn't care about possessions. They could take what they liked. None of it would bring his son back. He heard the drawer open, paper sliding, the clatter of something else, the drawer closing again.

'There are some leaflets I'm taking, if that's OK with you, Professor. We need to build a picture of Max.'

So do I, Brody thought as his empty heart ached. *So do I.*

Back in his office, DCI Masters found that several interview reports had already been emailed to him. CCTV footage from the area was being scanned. Initial pathology findings concluded that the blade of the murder weapon was around twelve to fifteen centimetres long and clean-edged.

'No shit,' Dennis said, enlarging the photograph of Max's naked torso. He twisted his head round. Half a dozen or more wounds cross-hatched his skin – neat mahogany gashes in his dark skin. Dennis speed-read down the rest of the initial report. Blood tests had revealed moderate levels of THC present but no alcohol. A more detailed document would follow after an extensive examination of the body. 'Ghastly,' he found himself saying, perhaps thinking more about Carrie and her future than the faceless torso on his monitor. He switched screens. At the bottom of one of the school interview summaries there was a recommendation that Samms and Driscoll be brought to the station for further questioning.

Dennis reached for his phone and glanced at his watch. 'Get the little sods in here,' he ordered. It was going to be a long night.

THE PAST

Carrie didn't think she'd been born angry. She didn't think, either, that she'd been born with an ambition to fix things – to fix the world. *Nature or nurture?* her mother used to ask when Carrie came home from university and sprayed their quiet semi with fury and outrage.

'I don't know where you get it from, Caroline Kent. Certainly not from my side of the family. You used to be such a quiet little girl.'

Carrie didn't remember herself as a quiet child at all. Inside her head, from an early age, there raged a torrent of morals battling out issues over which she had no control. At school, if there was ever an argument, if someone was hurt or left out or being too pushy, Carrie would step in to sort things out. It won the respect of those she helped, but lost her many friends in the process. She grew up with other kids either in awe of her or hating her.

It was, if she was completely honest with herself, all about being in control.

'And not losing it,' she told Leah during their first year at university. It was 1986 and they were both studying Broadcast Journalism.

'I don't get that,' Leah said. They were sunning themselves on a grassy bank, both of them on their backs staring up at the intensely blue sky. A plane left a trail thousands of feet above. 'I have absolutely no control over my life whatsoever. And that's fine by me.'

Carrie sat up and leant on her elbow. 'How can you say that? Why are you even here studying then?'

'Because my parents made me.'

Carrie flopped down again. Her turn not to understand now. She'd known Leah for seven months. They shared a flat with two other girls. That Leah wanted life to just *happen* to her both fascinated and angered Carrie. It was such a waste. Things should be steered, manipulated, taken care of.

'So you don't want a say over your own destiny?'

'Nope.' Leah flung her arm across her eyes. The sun was so bright.

'That's shameful.'

'I like to go with the flow. See what happens.'

Carrie thought about this. 'But how can anything happen to you if you don't orchestrate it?'

Leah never had a chance to answer the question. She suddenly doubled up, moaning in pain. A ball had hit her right in the stomach.

'Oh, I'm so sorry . . .' A girl came running up, all flustered and apologetic. She reached down and picked up the ball, tentatively touching Leah on the shoulder.

'That's OK. Really.' Leah grimaced and stood, smoothing down her T-shirt, trying to smile at the pretty girl, even though Carrie could tell she was still in pain.

'Want to join us? We're having this silly game.' The other girl with her sweet face and long hair had already taken control of easy-prey Leah, Carrie noted with a pang of jealousy, and her friend had absolutely no idea what was going on.

'Sure,' she replied, giving a quick glance back at Carrie.

Carrie forced a smile and lay back down on the grass.

I would have said no, she thought, watching the cloud above morph from a cat into an elephant. A big emphatic no. Then I would have told her to chuck her stupid ball around somewhere else unless she wanted it thrown right back in her stomach to see how she liked it.

She heard Leah's squeals as everyone in the game cheered. Carrie turned her head sideways and squinted. Leah was having fun.

'Going with the flow,' she whispered, wondering what it was in her past that prevented her from doing exactly that.

'You don't talk about your folks much.' It was spaghetti again. Boiled within an inch of its life and blanketed with grated cheese. Leah handed the dish to Carrie.

Carrie was already on her feet. 'Nope. Sorry. Can't do this three nights in a row.' She scooped the food into the bin, ignoring what Leah had said.

'What are you doing? We can't afford to throw food away.'

'I swear I will die if I eat one more plate of pasta and cheese.'

'Tell the guys next door to stop nicking our food then.'

Carrie halted, plate hovering over the sink. She always locked their door in the halls of residence. 'They stole our food?' It annoyed her that no one else ever bothered to lock up.

'I bought chicken and salad earlier. I reckon—'

'Don't move.'

But Leah did move. She followed Carrie as she stormed round to the flat next door and banged on the door.

'Carrie, don't. It's no big deal.' Leah tried to pull her back, but when no one answered, Carrie barged right in. Clearly locking their door wasn't a priority either. A couple of lads glanced up at her from cushions on the floor, nodded and ignored her as she went straight to their fridge and helped herself to the contents.

'Is this it?' she said, holding up a packet of chicken.

'I . . . I . . .' Leah pulled a pained face. 'We can't do this.'

'Wanna bet?' Carrie removed the salad drawer and marched back to their flat with the food. 'Now we can eat.' She took a chopping board and knife and began to hack up the meat. 'It's only fair,' she heard herself saying, but by this time she'd fallen into a kind of trance – chopping automatically, tears filling up her eyes, anger welling in her heart.

Carrie was back at the military base. She smelt the musty walls of their bungalow, which she'd once believed were made of cardboard. She heard the rumble of army vehicles as they hauled equipment around the base. She heard the familiar claxon marking the start of manoeuvres, and she saw herself reflected in the impossible gleam of her father's boots.

Charles Ernest Kent joined the army when he was sixteen. He met Carrie's mother, Rita, while on leave aged twenty-two and they'd married almost immediately. Rita gave up nursing and followed him from base to base, watching, admiring and adoring her husband as he progressed through the ranks. She never complained about the lack of stability, or having a home of her own, or leaving newly made friends, or the loneliness that she felt bringing up a baby as if she was a single parent.

As a child, Carrie's earliest memories involved only her mother – her soft hazel eyes, the red spotty apron she always wore in the kitchen, the way she carefully placed her wedding ring on a saucer on the table before tackling any chores. *Don't want to scrub away the love*, she'd say. Then she'd sigh with relief as she put it back on. *Daddy will be home soon. One hundred and twenty-three sleeps to go.*

When she was old enough to know why, Carrie counted those sleeps too. While her mother couldn't wait for Charles Kent to lie in bed beside her, to return from faraway places smelling of the sun, the desert, of oily tanks, Carrie breathlessly awaited her father's return for different reasons. She was dreaming up new ways not to exist.

She would eat her tea in the garden if it was fine or hide out in her bunk if not. The dolls and books and jigsaws that lay strewn around the bungalow when he was away would all be tidied up days before his return. It was as if he could *smell* the mess. Noise, chatter, friends, television and any sort of physical contact – a hug, a handhold, even an accidental brush of arms – were all out of the question. Major Charles Kent was a man who lived life by his own set of rules, with strict policies. Quite simply, he had to be in control.

'He never wanted me. He made that quite clear. In fact, he hated me.'

'What?' Leah had started to prepare the salad. She'd locked their flat door. How would she ever face the blokes next door again? Perhaps they didn't have much money for food either. Surely it was only fair that they should share.

Carrie stuck the knife point down into the chicken. It missed her finger by a millimetre. She squinted at Leah, frowned and shook her head. 'Nothing,' she said, tossing the chicken pieces into the frying pan along with some oil, garlic and peppers.

To hell with him, she thought, watching the chicken turn white, the garlic aroma opening her nostrils. Her mouth watered at the thought of a decent meal.

AUTUMN 2008

The likelihood of Max getting a snog was waning. At one point during the film, he'd hoped that Dayna might cling on to him out of fear. As it happened, all she did was lean over and whisper, 'I saw that coming several scenes back.' He was thankful it was dark. He'd opened his lips, truly believing she was going to plant a kiss on his mouth, and now he was sweating with embarrassment.

He should have realised, he thought while waiting in the corridor outside the ladies' loos after the movie, that Dayna wouldn't do that. She wasn't the kind of girl to scream and jump and grab him for comfort. He doubted she was the kind of girl to throw kisses around freely either. He liked it that she wasn't easy, unlike most girls in school who virtually kept a daily scorecard.

'All done,' she said. She wiped her wet hands on her jeans. 'Shall we go back to your place?'

Max froze. That was the last thing he wanted. 'The shed? Sure.'

'No, dummy. Your real house. I want to see your room. I could meet your mum.'

Oh, Christ. What was he to do now? Perhaps she really was interested, after all. Whatever Dayna's intentions, it was too good an opportunity to pass up. A girl – a girl he really liked – wanted to see his room. This might never happen again in his entire life. Even if they just sat at opposite ends of the bed, that was fine by him. In fact, he didn't really want to rush it the first time. He wanted it to be special, to get to know her first, to take things really slow.

But how could he let her meet his mother? Everything would change. In Dayna's eyes, he would become someone else and, while at first it might seem amazing and unbelievable to have a mother whose show was watched by millions each week, the size of her fame would sooner or later come between them.

There was only one thing for it. They would have to go back to his dad's flat. He couldn't possibly take her to his mother's house. Even if she wasn't home, the sheer opulence of it would be mind-blowing for Dayna.

'Sure. But it'll have to be Dad's place.' He thought for a second. ''Cos Mum'll be pissed or something.'

They crossed the road and waited at the bus stop. Max pulled his phone out of his pocket and toggled through some texts. *Away till Sunday at conference. Dad.* They'd have the place to themselves. Max wondered if he ought to clean his teeth when they got back, just in case, but the flat was so small, the walls so thin, that Dayna would be bound to hear. He reckoned there might be some gum or mints in the drawer.

The bus was crowded so they had to stand. Max liked it that Dayna kept getting shoved against him, even though she scowled and grumbled at the man who kept lolling into her. They leapt off at the nearest stop to the estate where Max's dad lived.

'Brace yourself,' Max said. He automatically tensed as they crossed the threshold from the High Street filled with second-hand shops, grocers with unidentifiable vegetables parked in boxes on the pavement, barber's shops and all kinds of takeaways, to the colourless world of the Westmount estate.

'Why?' Dayna seemed quite at ease, despite the surroundings. Max knew she'd grown up in a similar place – a world apart from his life at boarding school.

'It can be a bit rough.' Max instinctively hung his head and shrugged his zip-up top further up his neck.

'What you on about?' Dayna was laughing and Max didn't like it.

'Things happen, right?' He kicked up the pace as they walked through the concrete tunnel that led to the bowels of the estate. Nearly two thousand flats arranged in square blocks five storeys high occupied the western periphery of Harlesden. Residents referred to it as the local slammer. Max reckoned they were about right.

'What things?' Dayna pulled out the last of the sweets they'd bought. 'Want one?'

Max shook his head. 'Stuff.' He didn't want to put her off by telling her about the gang rape a couple of weeks ago or the burglaries – just about every flat had been broken into at some time – or the cars that were squealed around the estate on a Saturday night before being set alight, still glowing and smoking and stinking of rubber the next morning.

'Stuff happens everywhere. My street isn't exactly Paradise Row.'

Max wasn't listening. Up ahead, at the stairwell entry, was a group of lads. Maybe there was a girl there as well, he couldn't be sure. He considered diverting, but they'd already been spotted.

'Eh, there's da skinny bastard.'

Dayna drew breath to answer back, but Max pinched her.

'Don't say anything. We need to go up those stairs. Just look down.'

'Like hell I will.' They were blocking the opening. Their concrete hideout smelt of urine, marijuana and sweat. There was a pile of dog muck in the corner. ''Scuse me,' Dayna said. She attempted to pass, but one of the boys stretched out his arms. They were tattooed from wrist to shoulder – violent green-blue swirls of anger and hate. 'Can we get past?'

'S'all right,' Max said. 'We can go the other way.'

'What you got for us today, fuckhead?'

Max mumbled something. Their faces flashed through his mind, along with the computer. The youth stepped away from the stairs and went round behind Max. 'You ask dat whore if you can fuck her?' The rest of the crowd laughed. 'You know what I got in my pocket, little halfie boy?'

Max shook his head. He could smell the boy's sour breath – fags and lager.

'I got summat that want to slip inside ya skinny black ass until it comes out ya mouth, right?' The youth pushed a finger into his belly. 'This is my patch, yeah? You come through it, you ask my permission, right?'

Max nodded. The boy spat down his front.

'Wanna sweet?' Dayna shoved the bag in between Max and the youth. He grinned and took the whole bag. 'Remember this,' he said, beckoning to the others who lurked in the shadows. 'You fuck me off, man, and my blade gonna shank you so fast there's gonna be two of ya.'

Max watched them walk off, hoods up except for the girl whose short skirt showed the curve of her buttocks below it. Dayna still didn't latch on to him for comfort – in fact, the opposite. She was already holding open the door to the stairwell.

'Come on,' she said. 'Show me your palace.' She let the door swing shut when Max took the stairs two at a time. He hated this part of visiting his dad. No wonder he never had any visitors. The gangs were his personal firewall.

They walked along the concrete balcony, which was strewn with washing and plastic toys, and Max tried to stop his legs from shaking. He took the key from his pocket and unlocked the door. His heart was still racing. 'It's a bit messy,' he said before opening it. 'And sometimes Dad forgets to wash up.'

'Stop making excuses.' Dayna opened the door and went right in. 'Where's your room?'

Max was about to say that he didn't have one, that there was only one bedroom and that was his dad's, but he didn't want to risk Dayna leaving because he didn't have a room to hang out in. Besides, questions would be asked. 'This way,' he said, turning down the dingy corridor.

'Nice,' she said when they went in. 'Not much stuff though.'

Max exhaled. Clearly Fiona had sorted things out before they'd left. When Max was younger, he used to go with his dad to the various conferences he attended each year. He got to stay in posh hotels and got food brought up to the room – anything he liked – while his dad spoke and presented and impressed other mathematicians with his work. He couldn't afford to think about all that now.

'Has your dad got a job?' Dayna smoothed out the sheets and parked herself on the bed. 'My stepdad's a twat and doesn't work mostly.'

'He's a mathematician. A professor at the university.' He was so relieved that Dayna believed this was his room, he completely forgot to make something up.

'He's a what?' Dayna was incredulous. She pulled a face.

Max swallowed. 'He works in the maths *department*, I mean. Nothing special.' He looked away to hide his embarrassment and sat next to her on the bed. She sank towards him a little.

'If he's a professor, it doesn't sound like nothing. What's he live here for then? Is your dad loaded?' Dayna whipped a smile across her face. Max thought it made her look so cute. He wanted to tell her everything, truly he did, but what would that do to them apart from open up a chasm?

Guess what, Dayna? My mother's a multimillionaire award-winning television star and my father's a world-renowned mathematician. That they choose to live the oddest of lives an entire universe away from me is something I'll never understand . . .

He would lose the only friend he had, for sure. Things would break down, little by little. She just wouldn't get it.

'Nah. He's just, you know, the cleaner. Dad likes to big himself up.' Max lay back on the pillow. It smelt of his father.

'I don't see my dad. He and my mum split up a few years ago. Lorrell's my half-sister.'

'Sucks, doesn't it?'

'Mmm.' Dayna lay back, too, but the opposite way round. 'Do you have any brothers or sisters?'

'Nope. Just me.' Max spread his arm across the bed. It accidentally found Dayna's leg. When she didn't flinch, he left it there. 'Do you ever wish they were back together, your mum and dad?'

'Hell no,' Dayna said immediately. 'They'd kill each other. You?'

Max paused. His fingers walked up on to the hillock of Dayna's knee. 'All the time.' And while his hand sat there, too terrified to do anything more, he dreamt up the crazy world that was him, his father and his mother all living under the same roof again.

FRIDAY, 24 APRIL 2009

Leah followed Carrie everywhere. She sat on the edge of the bath while her friend peed.

'There was so much blood. Spread so wide.' Carrie's face was paler than white. It was translucent, mapped with veins and bone. She virtually fell off the toilet and ended up on all fours on the floor. Leah was beside her, knowing that she was beyond sobbing.

'Bed?'

Carrie nodded and allowed herself to be led to the comfort of her darkened bedroom. Leah pulled back the sheets, removed Carrie's shoes and unfolded her on the mattress. The woman who commanded the attention of millions of viewers each week, the powerhouse that had brought justice to hundreds of families, victims, women, children who would otherwise have suffered their plight, the businesswoman who kept the show fresh, under contract, and most of all the woman who followed up on each and every one of her show guests to make certain they were receiving the help they needed from the show's counselling team, was dissolving before her eyes. Leah pulled the sheet across her, leaving only messy hair and a cheek visible.

She sat bolt upright, her bleary eyes betraying that sleep had finally come. Leah must have been watching over her.

'What time is it?'

'Five,' Leah said, looking at her watch. 'You slept for nearly an hour. Are you thirsty?'

'No.' Carrie whipped back the sheets and sat on the edge of the bed. She straightened her blouse and ran her fingers through her hair. 'There are things I need to do.'

'All in good time,' Leah said, supporting Carrie when she staggered, dizzy, over to the window.

'There is no good time,' Carrie replied. Her voice was dry and determined.

'What things? There's nothing for you to do right now. And Brody will help when the time's right.'

It seemed that the mention of her ex-husband's name set off a chain reaction. Carrie swept back her hair in a ponytail and secured it with a band lying on her dressing table. She went into the bathroom, Leah following, and doused her face in cold water. Leaning on the sink, she watched as the drips fell off her nose. She didn't – perhaps *couldn't* – look in the mirror.

'I'm going out.' Carrie tore off the skirt she had slept in and thrust her legs into rarely-worn jeans. She rummaged in her wardrobe and pulled out a pair of shoes – not the usual heels, but a sensible pair of canvas lace-ups.

'You probably shouldn't . . .' Leah ran out of the bedroom after her. Carrie was moving at speed. Voices in the kitchen became louder, although none belonged to Dennis Masters or any of his immediate team of detectives, they discovered, when Carrie burst in.

'Where's Dennis?' she ordered.

A young WPC answered. 'Gone for now, Miss Kent. We're here to answer any questions and update you on—'

'Right. Answer this.' Carrie leant forward across the worktop, making the policewoman step back. 'Who was with my son when he died? Dennis said there was a witness. I want to know who. A name and an address.'

'I'm so sorry, Miss Kent, I don't know, and even if I did I couldn't . . .'

But Carrie had already left the kitchen.

'Where are you going, Carrie? You're not thinking straight.' Leah was horrified to see her pull her car keys from the hall table drawer.

'To find Dennis,' Carrie called out. 'To find Brody, the witness . . . anyone. To find the person who killed my son.'

She dashed down the internal steps that led to the garage. At the bottom, she punched in the security code and the steel door slowly swung open. As soon as it was wide enough, she slipped through and marched into the garage. Leah followed, swinging round the corner, struggling to keep up.

'At least let me drive,' Leah said as Carrie got into the car. 'You're in no fit state.'

'I'm absolutely fine. I have things to take care of,' she said unconvincingly.

'I'm coming with you then.' Leah got in the passenger seat.

Carrie pointed the remote control at the automatic garage door and waited for it to open, edging the car forward little by little. Leah wondered if Carrie even remembered how to drive. She was chauffeured everywhere or, at the very worst, took a cab.

Leah covered her eyes as they roared out of the underground garage and up into the daylight. 'Slow down, for Christ's sake.' But Carrie ignored her and ploughed relentlessly through the traffic as she headed out of Hampstead. 'Where are we going?'

'Brody's place.'

Leah didn't recognise her voice. It was as though someone else had got into Carrie's body and was telling it what to do. There was no sign of the real Carrie who had been live on television only that morning. It was unfathomable, what had happened to time. Not even a day had passed since they were on air. Distracted by Carrie's untimely disappearance, she'd met with the executive producer, discussed future ideas with Dennis, and taken a call from the States about a slot for Carrie on the *Late Show* next month. In this new, altered state, it might as well have taken place last year.

'Do you even know where he lives?' Leah was certain that Carrie had never actually been there. In fact, she pretty much knew that in the last nine years the pair had spoken exactly three times, usually if Max was ill.

'I have an address on my phone.'

Carrie's hands tightened on the wheel as the neighbourhood transformed from pleasant, expensive, desirable housing with delicatessens and boutiques and trendy Nepalese restaurants into boarded-up shops, nineteen sixties grey-fronted flats and weed-strewn petrol stations that had long since closed down.

'Jesus,' Leah said. 'Are you sure you're going the right way?' The vehicles on the road had also changed from Range Rovers and BMWs to hotted-up Fiestas and Corsas. Carrie didn't reply. 'You were in hospital only a few hours ago. Why don't you at least let me—'

'Just leave it, Leah!'

Carrie revved the engine and cut through several lanes of traffic to get to the lights. She turned left on red and sped down the road. She was going the wrong way down a one-way street. A minute later, she pulled over and broke down in tears.

'I have no idea where I'm going.' Her head fell on to the wheel, causing the horn to sound. Leah got out, went round to the driver's side and eased Carrie from the car. She buckled her into the passenger seat and pulled up the satnav on her phone. A few minutes later, they were turned round, grinding their way through the traffic and heading into an even more depressing neighbourhood.

Leah's hands shook as she drove – not entirely from grief, not entirely from uncertainty, mostly from never having seen Carrie, in the two decades she had known her, not be as strong as a rock.

'Do you think the satnav got it wrong?' She changed down into second gear and peered up at the tenements. 'I don't think we can be near Brody's place.'

'It's so . . . so close . . .' Carrie said in a way that belied an altered state, as if she could suddenly see things that she had been blind to before today. 'All this . . . so close to where I live.'

Leah was convinced they'd entered the postcode wrong. 'I don't get it. This is Westmount Road.' She pointed to a street sign, barely legible through the graffiti that was daubed over it. 'I can't believe Brody lives round here.' Leah drove on. Even the car seemed hesitant as it juddered slowly in third.

Looming in the distance, like an otherworldly city – grey concrete, a mix of broken windows and boards, colourless washing flapping from tiny balconies, an occasional splash of red where someone had fixed a pot plant to a railing, more graffiti and plenty of unsavoury and downright terrifying groups of youths huddled in pockets – was the notorious estate, the place Brody had chosen to live. She didn't understand. No wonder Carrie had decided to block it all out.

Leah pulled on the handbrake. 'This is as close as I can park.' She prayed Carrie would change her mind about needing to see Brody, although she could understand why she would want nothing more than to fall into his arms and be close to Max's father, whatever their differences had been in the past.

Carrie opened the door and got out. Leah followed. Two lanky boys wearing hats pulled low and tracksuit tops were suddenly inches away from the car. They'd appeared from nowhere.

'Wannus to look after it?' His face was thin and mean, with spots encrusting his forehead. His eyes were cold.

'Fuck off,' Carrie said calmly. 'It's insured.' She walked off. 'Number three four nine.'

The two women approached the estate. It appeared sealed off

from the rest of the world with its ugly back turned to reality. A small opening between the ground floor flats led to an inner area the size of several tennis courts. They stopped for a moment and stared up. They were in the middle of a quadrant, bounded on all sides by five storeys of concrete.

'No one would choose to live here,' Leah said. The grimness of their surroundings was a temporary distraction from the day's events and she was sure that Carrie's irrational behaviour by coming here was fuelled by grief.

'My ex-husband did,' Carrie snapped back. 'And my son when he visited his father.' Leah understood the anger in her voice. Carrie's mind would be forming links – Westmount estate, gangs, knives, her son killed. Brody's choice. Blame was a natural emotion. 'I had no idea it was like this,' she said, breathless as they marched on.

They scanned the signs at each corner of the quadrant, showing which stinking concrete staircase they needed to go up to find flat three forty-nine. Most signs had been burnt off or spray-painted over, but eventually they found the right one and ascended three floors. They held their breath and Carrie grabbed on to Leah as they went along the concrete balcony, stepping over rubbish bags, bikes and toddlers put out to play like unwanted puppies. Leah knocked on the door of Brody's flat.

Brody yelled out that whoever was there should just come in. He didn't think his body would be capable of hauling itself to the door, greeting yet another team of detectives, reeling off and picking apart his son's life until he believed that Max had never existed at all.

It took him three seconds to determine that this wasn't the police.

'Hello?' Brody stood. He listened. He smelt. He felt for vibrations. Women.

Oh my fucking God were the words that told him Carrie Kent, his ex-wife, was standing in his living room surveying the devastation that he called home. That he and Max had once called home.

Brody fell back into the armchair. He didn't give a shit what she thought. Despite this defence, despite years of imagining this most ghastly of scenarios – his ex in his flat – he was filled with the most immense swell of relief that she was actually here. And however she chose to display it, whatever public exhibition of pandemonium and journalistic mayhem the death of Carrie Kent's only son would produce, beneath all that he knew they shared the same raw emotion: absolute and utter emptiness.

'We failed him.' Her words were emotionless.

'Carrie . . .'

That was the other woman, her sidekick from the show. He'd spoken to her once or twice. Brody never forgot a voice.

'Fine job we did of raising a son who fell in with gangs and knives and . . . and . . .' Brody imagined Carrie staring around his flat, speechless – and that was rare – at the state of it. But she concluded with a simple, 'Why?'

'Why indeed.' He heard the sofa being sat on.

'How did this happen to us?'

'Any of it,' Brody replied. They both knew the comment ran deeper than that day's misery alone.

'I don't think I can live without him,' Carrie confessed.

The tone was, Brody thought, more akin to one of her beaten-down studio guests. 'Could you live *with* him?' It was confrontational, he knew, but he didn't know what else to say. Max had cried for help and they hadn't listened.

'Brody—'

'Don't,' he snapped at Leah. He didn't want her interfering on such a raw day. Someone needed see that justice was done. *See* that justice was done, he thought, blinking at the irony of it.

'We have to help each other,' Carrie continued.

'Bit late, don't you think?'

'You two, please don't do this . . .' Leah trailed off.

'We're in this together, Brody. From the minute Max was created, we've been in this together.' Carrie surprised them all with her clarity. 'However far apart we might have grown.'

Brody laughed inappropriately. 'Together? Far apart?' he repeated. 'Do you honestly understand any of that? Have you ever, once, in your precious, self-absorbed life that consists only of Carrie Kent and more Carrie Kent, have you ever really once considered how universally shattered and distant the three of us actually are . . . were?'

The effort was too much. His body wouldn't take sitting down peacefully any longer. Brody paced the room, wishing he had a clear-cut aim of a vase or ornament to smash against the wall – except that he didn't possess any ornaments or vases.

'This isn't the time for us to fight. We need to find out what happened. Who did this to our son.'

'She's right.' Leah's voice prevented the response Brody was about to hurl back.

'Have the police interviewed you?' he said instead.

'Yes. You?'

'Briefly. Don't think they have much to go on.'

'There was a witness,' Carrie continued. 'Do you know who it is?'

'No.' Brody was thoughtful.

'I want to speak to them. I *need* to.'

Brody could tell she was fighting back tears. 'Don't you think the police are taking care of that?' He bumped into the wall. He'd lost his bearings for a moment.

Carrie didn't reply immediately – collecting herself, Brody thought. She wouldn't want to cry in front of him.

'We can't just sit back and wait for something to happen,' she finally said.

Even though her voice was broken – he imagined her small, frail, red-eyed on his couch – Brody could still detect the power of Carrie Kent behind her words. He knew she had connections in the Met and, if he was honest, he didn't think he could wait for news from the police either. If they still had one thing in common, it was that they each had a need for answers in their professional lives.

'Max brought a girl here a few times.' Brody doubted Carrie knew.

'Who? When?'

'It started last autumn. He didn't say much.'

'Do you know her name? She might know something.'

'No.' Brody hadn't pried. It was only because he caught a foreign whiff in his bedroom once or twice – a smell not of perfume, but of hairspray, make-up, laundry detergent – that he even suspected a girl had been in his flat. He'd wanted Max to tell him when he was ready.

'I must go back to the school,' Carrie said.

Brody knew that she thrived on action. Doing nothing wasn't an option for her. He imagined them together again, at their house, their beloved family home, with Max pedalling round the garden on his trike. If something went wrong in their lives, Carrie leapt in to fix it. *You make things right before they've even gone wrong*, Brody used to joke.

'Will you come with me?' she asked.

'Carrie, is this wise today?' Leah sounded doubtful.

'Yes, I'll come,' he said without hesitating.

The Mercedes was still in one piece when they got back to it. Leah drove while Brody sat in the passenger seat. Carrie had shown him the door, pulled out the belt for him to secure. She was surprised at how easy it came, even though they'd only had to adapt their marriage to blindness for a short while.

'Tell me which way to go,' Leah said. Carrie leant forward and frowned. She had no idea where they were.

'You need to head towards the station. Take a sharp right before you get there.' Brody spoke clearly, as if he sensed exactly which direction they were pointing. Five minutes later, they were in the school car park.

'I'm not sure I can stand to see . . . I was here earlier. It was awful.' Carrie buried her face in her hands and allowed a moment of comfort from Leah.

On many occasions, she had accompanied victims' families along with her film crew to the scene of the crime – usually where a loved one had died in a car accident, or been in a pub brawl that had ended in tragedy, or been mugged or raped. The cameraman knew what to do: a wide pan of the scene, the bunches of flowers, the notes, the teddy bears, followed by a close-up cut of their immediate reaction. It was essential to capture that first horror, the raw emotion, the distilled grief. But nothing, she believed, had been as dreadful as seeing her son's blood spread over the ground. To get through it, she had forced herself to detach, to make-believe she was filming for yet another show, that really her son hadn't died this morning at all. *This morning* . . .

'I'm sorry, you can't go any further.' Two policemen stepped forward at the gate that funnelled visitors in from the car park. 'There's been an incident.'

'It was my son,' Carrie whispered. 'The incident was my son.' Brody was between them. Carrie could sense his reluctance at their guidance, but also that he needed their hands on his sleeve. 'This is his father. We have to see the head teacher.' Carrie swallowed it all back down.

The policemen glanced at each other and slowly realised

who she was, as if the famous Carrie Kent was now only recognisable because of tragedy. They nodded. 'Follow me.' One of the officers turned and led them into the drab building.

Why, oh *why* had Max left boarding school for this?

Jack Rushen, head of Milton Park, was deep in conversation with two other staff members. For a school that would normally be closed and empty at this hour, it was humming with low talk and crisis management. They looked stunned when they saw Carrie shaking in front of them. It was clear they didn't know what to say.

'We're Max's parents. We need to talk.'

'I was going to contact you, of course, Mrs Kent, but I thought you'd have enough on your plate today.' Rushen was insipid. He stood up, offered a useless handshake and mumbled his name. He didn't know what to do with them.

Carrie already hated him. Wasn't it his fault, after all, that her son was dead? She knew it had to be someone's. 'What, I want to know, happened this morning?' The words came out automatically. Her body was in overdrive.

'The police are working on it, Mrs Kent. It's a tragic situation, but believe me—'

'I don't see one good reason why I should believe anything you tell me. My son attended your school in good faith and now he's . . . now he's . . . dead.' A sob forced its way out.

'Carrie, stop.' Brody's words were oddly soothing. That was how it used to be, wasn't it, when they were a team? 'We'd like to know who his close friends were. So we can request they come to the funeral.'

Silence as Brody's words sank in. *Max's funeral.*

Carrie looked at Brody. How he'd been able to think of this so quickly, she had no idea. Of course the head wasn't going to give out details of witnesses, if he even knew. The police wouldn't be likely to divulge that information either at this early stage, and

161

Rushen knew it was more than his job – if he had one any more – was worth to give out confidential details.

One of the other men spoke. Carrie had no idea who he was, but he seemed more in control than Rushen, more able to appease them, more able – by one tiny ounce – to add a glimmer of warmth to their frozen, aching hearts. 'Max was a popular boy. I'm so sorry.'

No one said anything. Popular, Carrie thought. Was he? He never brought friends home. At least she didn't think he did. And when they'd spoken, it was never about a Tom or Jack or Sarah or Mike. No gossip about who was dating who, or who made the football team, or who'd got detention.

'Popular?' she heard herself repeat.

'So who should we contact?' Leah asked. She'd taken a pad and pen from her bag.

The same man shrugged. 'I think many of the pupils will come to the service. We'll do an announcement when the time is right. When school reopens.'

'His closest friend, then?' Brody said. 'One name.'

The staff glanced at each other. 'It's a big school. To name names would be hard.'

In other words, they didn't know. 'What about a teacher? Did he have a favourite?' Carrie felt that swell of grief again, the one that wouldn't allow her to stand upright. She fell against Brody's arm, latching on to his sleeve. He tensed, supporting her.

'Tim Lockhart. English,' the third man said quickly as if he shouldn't, as if he actually cared. 'He's a mate of mine. Lives locally. Twenty-four Denby Terrace.'

The head glared at his colleague. 'I'd advise waiting for information from the police before contacting staff.'

'Of course,' Leah said, putting away her pad. 'Let's go,' she said to Carrie and Brody.

They left the office. Carrie felt utterly exhausted and just wanted to go home to sleep, even though she knew that would be impossible. But she couldn't do any more today. As they trudged down the long corridors, she felt like a schoolgirl leaving the head's office after she'd just had a good telling-off. What, she wondered in time with the stabbing pain in her heart, was she supposed to have done wrong?

They'd come in kicking and screaming of course. Each had a mother, smoking outside the station door, spitting curses at the desk sergeant, threatening legal action – all the usual crap. They couldn't be bothered to sit with their sons who were in the interview room alone, looking an awful lot younger than their teenage years betrayed. One of them rubbed his eyes.

'How old are you boys?' Dennis asked.

'Thirteen,' they said in unison, both pronouncing it *firt-een*.

'So that makes me twenty-one, right?' They knew the law.

They shrugged. One picked a spot on his forehead. His hair was greasy.

'Are we arrested?'

'You know you're not arrested. I've already told you that.' Dennis glanced across at Jess. He thought she looked good for someone who'd been at work eighteen hours straight. 'I want you to answer some questions that might help us and then you can go.'

The pair smirked at each other.

'Just confirm your names for me. Blake Samms and Owen Driscoll. Say yes, please.'

'Yeah,' they both said.

'Do you know anyone called Max Quinell?' Dennis and Jess were both taking notes. The tape recorder whirred on the table. Neither of them expected to get much out of the boys.

'Dunno,' Driscoll said. 'Maybe, maybe not.' He grinned. His teeth were yellow.

'He was stabbed earlier today.' Masters glanced at his watch to make sure it was still today. 'To death.'

'Yeah,' Samms said. He wasn't quite as bright.

'So you do know Max Quinell?'

'Mebbe.'

'Do you know who did it?'

'Nah,' they both said together.

'Was Max in a gang?'

At this, Driscoll laughed. 'No way, man.'

'Oh?' However he phrased the questions, however on their level or on their side or friendly cop he tried to be, Dennis knew they'd happily kick his head in. 'How come?'

'Dunno,' Driscoll said. 'Just a guess.'

'Right.' Dennis had had enough of this. It could go on for ever. 'Owen, you come with me. Blake, stay here with DI Britton.' Dennis led the boy to another interview room. He'd hoped that they'd fuel each other. Not so. It had gone the opposite way and, for the most important question, he wanted them apart.

He sat the boy down but remained standing himself. 'Where were you between ten and eleven this morning?'

Driscoll shrugged. He frowned and his eyes flicked to the ceiling. 'School, man,' he said.

'What lesson?'

He pulled a face. 'I can't fucking remember. Science.'

'But you were definitely in school.'

'Yeah. Course. I'm a good boy.' He smirked. 'Ask Warren Lane. He's me mate.'

Dennis nodded and left him with the attending officer. He went back to Samms and asked the same question. Jess stood wearily beside him.

Samms bowed his head. 'Me and Owen bunked off school, man.'

164

'You and Owen Driscoll skipped school this morning?' Dennis asked. 'What about this Warren character?'

'Yeah. We went to do some . . . to do some shoppin', right?'

'All morning?'

'Yeah,' Samms replied.

'Stick them in a cell for an hour,' Dennis said privately to Jess. He gripped her arm before she could protest that they really shouldn't be doing that.

AUTUMN 2008

He wasn't sure how long they'd been lying on the bed. An hour, two, four, ten? Or maybe just a minute or so, but it was still long enough for his entire childhood to rush through his mind in this timeless, beautiful moment with Dayna. He thought he might be falling in love.

Max stared at the nicotine-stained ceiling of his father's room and went back to that place he could barely remember. He held on to the precious memories as though they were crafted from the thinnest crystal glass or spun from pure silk.

Surely he'd had different parents back then, right? His father – younger not just in age but in the way he swept Max up from the floor with hands so strong they could hold steady the entire planet. He'd liked it best when they'd come down on his ribs, tickling him hard before lifting him up over his shoulder and carrying him out to the garden for a kick-about with a football.

Those same hands now, well, they mostly guided the cigarette between his lips or felt his way along the wall to the bathroom or the kitchen. Sometimes they were dusty with chalk from the many lectures he gave to his students and Max had been impressed at the speed with which they typed on his specially adapted computer. Other times Max saw them gesture wildly to Fiona or his associates on the days he'd been allowed into his dad's work. It broke his heart to think about those hands now, that all they held, really, was despair.

'You OK?' He thought Dayna might have drifted off. She was making little contented noises.

'Yeah. Just thinking.'

'Me too,' Max said. It was harder to remember his mother from back then – perhaps because out of the two of them, she'd changed the most, even though it was his father who had gone blind.

He'd never thought of her hands as safe or fun or, even, frightening. She wasn't one for smacking, but then neither did she dish out hugs or play or . . . well, anything, apart from the prescribed meals and clothing and bathing. His mother delivered what was necessary in such a way that no one could ever say she neglected her son. Their house was clean and welcoming, and his mother was pleasant and cheerful; always in control.

'Is there ever, you know, fuss in your place?' Max asked. It was really hot underneath his hand now, still attached to Dayna's leg.

She laughed loudly. 'God, yeah. Is there ever *peace*, you should ask, and the answer would be no. Only when Kev's passed out and Mum's at bingo. Me and Lorrell just play. I read to her. That's true peace.'

Dayna wasn't like the other girls he'd met. 'You can have too much of it, you know. When things are just too . . .'

'Good?' she finished.

'No . . . not good.' Max thought. He so desperately wanted to sit up, pull Dayna against him, hold on to her. 'Too *perfect*,' he finished. By the little grunt she made, he figured that Dayna didn't get what he meant, that he was – although she didn't know it – referring to his mother. His perfect mother.

He swore a promise in his head that the two of them would never meet.

'I've got to go.' She stood up, causing Max's hand to fall off her leg. It tingled, sending shock waves up his arm. Max knew,

167

that for the briefest of moments, he'd just experienced perfection too.

He decided to go home too, feeling rather empty now that Dayna was leaving. He opted to walk rather than take the bus. Thankfully, there had been no trouble getting off his dad's estate – they didn't see the youths again – and Dayna didn't comment on where his father lived or how horrid it was. Probably because her place wasn't much better. Deep inside, though, Max still thought about protection – that it wasn't just him now risking a confrontation on the estate. If he brought Dayna here again, he vowed to protect her, make her think he was a proper man. If there was trouble, he wanted to be ready next time.

They'd parted after ten minutes or so, her veering off down towards school, towards where she lived, and him making an excuse that he was going to meet some mates. It made him sound as if he had some, while really it was cover for going back to his mum's place in Hampstead. *His mother's eight million pound house.*

Max shoved his hands in his pockets and stared at his trainers as he walked briskly home. At Denningham, his last school, everyone had known exactly who he was. Carrie Kent's son . . . *Reality Check* . . . Britain's sexiest TV personality of the year, the woman who dominated the screens of the nation every week, the star of the show everyone talked about, the name that filled the gossip magazines regularly. She was as famous as Oprah and as polemic as Jerry Springer. But then, he thought, he had been rubbing shoulders with the sons of corporate millionaires, lords and foreign princes. Had his mother not been famous, he would have stood out for being ordinary.

'Hello?' he called out as he went through the second security door. The first was a reinforced steel grille blockade; if the code was entered incorrectly more than three times, the police were automatically informed. That was if anyone had managed to get past the face recognition cameras. Max yelled out again from the hallway. He never knew who would be in the house. Generally it wasn't his mother, rather an assortment of domestic staff, security guards and maids.

'Hello,' came back at him from down the long white corridor at the end of the vast marble-tiled reception hall. Martha. 'There's some food for you if you like, pet. Your mother's gone to Charlbury. She'll be back on Sunday.'

Max went into the kitchen. He felt small in the huge room. His mother had had the back wall ripped out and a glass structure added. It made the space about twenty times bigger than they needed. Everything was white; dazzling.

'Thanks.' Max sat down at the table and tucked in to the plate of food Martha set in front of him. He smiled at her. Had she been waiting all afternoon for him to come home? He liked to think so. He reckoned he spoke more to the housekeeper than he did to his mother. Max ate greedily. He liked Martha. She was kind.

Charlbury, he thought. It made his stomach knot. He'd not been to the country house since New Year when his mother had thrown a cocktail party. He knew he'd let her down by getting drunk and throwing up in a stone urn. She had the staff deal with him then, too, escorting him away, locking him up in some faraway bedroom so that he didn't embarrass her further in front of the celebrity guests.

'This is good. Thanks, Martha.'

She smiled in reply. He'd wished that Martha was his mother, slightly shocked at the sudden feeling but also relishing the warmth it brought.

'You seen that brilliant father of yours recently?' Martha wiped her hands. The kitchen gleamed.

'He's gone away too,' Max said. 'Conference.' Had either of

his parents actually realised that he would be on his own for the weekend? 'I'm an orphan, me.' He grinned.

'Well, I'll be around until seven. Give me a shout if you need anything, love.'

Max thought she was going to pat him on the head as she went out of the room, but she didn't. He pressed a button on the remote and a television rotated out of the wall. Some Sky channel. A phone-in competition. *How many days of the week are there? Your chance to win five thousand pounds cash. A) One. B) Seven. C) Three hundred and sixty-five.*

Max's mouth went dry. His palms began to sweat and his heart kicked up a gear. He dialled the premium rate line and listened to the lengthy message. When it was done, he left his details and said clearly that the answer was B. Then he did it another dozen times. He forked up the rest of his meal, left the plate beside the pristine white sink, and walked out of the kitchen. Apart from feeling dirty against the brilliant white of everything, he didn't feel much else at all. Only that somehow, this time, he knew he wasn't going to win.

Max desperately wanted to see Dayna again. He couldn't forget the real live person he'd felt warm and solid beneath the fabric of her jeans, and neither could he get out of his head that she really seemed to like him. So far, they'd shared a picnic, she'd seen inside his hut, he'd given her a present, they'd been to a movie together and spent time on their backs on his father's bed. It virtually made Max do a backflip.

He hadn't spoken to anyone since Martha had left the day before. She'd huffed out of the house with sackloads of his mother's clothes to take to the charity shop. Today it was raining. He took his Coco-Pops into the drawing room – the space his mother reserved for important guests, for pre-dinner cocktails, for important meetings – and parked himself on the damask-covered salon suite while he ate. He splashed chocolate milk on the fabric and wiped it off with the hem of his towelling robe.

It was a boring room, he thought, gazing around. No television, not even any books. He stared at the paintings his mother had chosen. Huge canvases with chunks of bold colour, abstract forms – a naked body? he wondered – hung in every nook and niche. Above the fireplace was the largest of them all, a chocolate and blue striped mass of crusty paint forming an image of . . . of absolutely nothing at all. Max knew how much they'd cost. He didn't understand his mother one bit.

He went back to the kitchen and opened the fridge. He stood staring at the contents. There was nothing he liked. Punnets of berries, trays of salad, cuts of unusual meat wrapped in wax paper piled up next to cheeses that appeared too bizarre to eat, and the usual assortment of patés, fish and unrecognisable fruit. He was still hungry. Max really fancied a pasty. Or sausage and chips.

He pulled his phone from his pocket.

Want 2 meet?

The text came back in seconds. *Yeah. Where?*

Chippy nr school

OK x

She'd put a kiss. A *kiss*. Max wouldn't delete that one for ages. He raced up to his room and threw on jeans, a T-shirt, a zip top. He scrubbed his teeth, fingered his hair with some spray stuff, decided to leave the spot on his chin well alone, and took the stairs two at a time back to the kitchen.

He suddenly felt giddy, as if today could turn out to be the best day of his life.

They would have chips, maybe take a walk down by the stream, throw rubbish at the trains as they sped past. Then he would suggest they go to the hut, sit next to each other on the car

171

seat, shoulders nudging . . . and then . . . he so desperately wanted to kiss Dayna that it hurt low down in his throat.

In all his muddle of thoughts, beneath the desire, the excitement, the fear that he might blow it, say something wrong, Max wasn't surprised to find that he had opened the kitchen drawer. It glided out smoothly, exposing a clean wooden interior with perfect slits housing a dozen of the highest quality knives. His mother only bought the best.

Just a small one, he thought, useful for cutting open the packaging on his winnings, if nothing else.

He ran his fingers along the backs of every knife. His heart beat faster, as if he was playing a lethal xylophone, his fingers softly brushing every iridescent handle.

This one.

He withdrew it from its slot.

He skimmed his thumb sideways across the blade. It was so bloody sharp.

He nudged the drawer closed with his hip, gazing intently at the six inches of high-grade glistening steel. Already he felt better; safer.

Max put the knife in the zip-up compartment of the brown leather bag he wore slung across his back. He left the house feeling more of a man than ever.

FRIDAY AND SATURDAY, 24 AND 25 APRIL 2009

Dennis had the two boys brought back to the interview room. The scabby little pair of sods sat at his table kicking each other's feet and letting out pseudo-manly growls that made them seem a lot younger than the fifteen or sixteen years he reckoned they were.

'Decided to remember anything interesting then?' Masters looked at his watch. It was ten forty. Three hours past the end of his shift. If he'd even bothered to go home from the last one. He couldn't remember. 'Like who stabbed Max Quinell?'

The youths shrugged.

'But you were there, right?'

'Nah.'

'What if I said I've been speaking to someone who could confirm that you were there?' Dennis wanted to know more about Warren Lane. He reckoned these two could give him a reason to bring the boy in.

They shrugged, but not before glancing at each other. This is why Masters wanted them together. 'Then they're lying,' Driscoll said. His teeth clamped together.

'Even if they were prepared to swear that in court?'

'Yeah,' Samms said, egged on by the other boy's cockiness. ''Cos we didn't fucking hurt no one.'

'What if it was Waren?' Dennis asked, turning to Owen.

The boy paled and looked at the floor. 'If he said anything then he's a fucking liar. Warren doesn't know nuffin.'

Dennis glanced at Jess who'd just come into the interview room. Maybe worth following up but not a priority. As it was, they were probably wasting their time with these two.

'Are you in a gang?' Masters asked. Jess handed him a coffee.

'Everyone is.' Owen Driscoll spoke this time. 'Otherwise, you know, man . . .' He drew a line across his neck. 'It ain't safe not to be.'

Masters nodded slowly. 'Does your gang have a name?'

The boys reverted to shrugging.

'The quicker you tell me, the quicker you'll be out of here.'

'We have rights, you know.' Samms kicked the table leg. He was picking the paint off it.

'You reckon?' Masters turned to Jess. 'Another hour in the cells, detective.' He got up to go.

'Wait . . .' It was unexpectedly Driscoll's voice that cracked. 'Blade Runnerz. With a zed. But we ain't hurt no one, all right?' The boy stood up.

Dennis made a face at Jess and swung back round. 'Sit down, you.' He put his coffee on the table, sloshing it as he sat opposite the boys. 'Blade Runnerz,' he repeated. 'And you carry knives, right?'

The pair just stared at him. It was as good as a yes. Of course they'd been searched when they were brought in, but they were clean. No doubt there had been enough time to get rid of weapons or hide them at home before they were escorted out. Dennis recalled the amnesty he'd instigated last year. Thirteen hundred knives of all kinds had been brought in to police stations in the area. He remembered sifting through them with a broom handle. The large container was brimming with lethal metal, some of which had probably already inflicted injuries.

'Why?' Dennis had to ask. 'Why do you carry them?' He

174

knew, of course, he just didn't understand. It was going to be a long night, even after he let these two idiots go home.

Samms and Driscoll stared at each other then at Masters. ''Cos if we don't, then we're dead,' Driscoll said. 'Tha's all.'

It was late but Dennis desperately wanted to call Carrie. He still couldn't believe that her son was dead. He'd never met the boy; never met the father before today either. He'd ended up staying at Carrie's place on several occasions but had either been ushered out before or after Max had gone to school. In the light of what had happened, he felt even guiltier for dipping his toes in the water of a very turbulent, brief relationship with one of the most famous women in Britain. The only good thing to come of their time together was that they'd agreed to continue with their professional commitments, even if their personal ones had fizzled out.

The phone made him jump. The detectives going through the CCTV footage thought he should come and look at something.

Dennis hadn't eaten for hours and couldn't recall the last time he'd slept. He stopped at the coffee machine in the hallway. He put in a pound, pressed the buttons, but nothing happened. He kicked the machine and walked off.

'What have you got?' He pulled up a chair next to the two detectives whose job it was to scan through the hours and hours of footage captured from the streets in the vicinity of the school. The bank of monitors glowed in an otherwise darkened room.

'Take a look at this,' Deb Curry said. She'd not been with Brent Met long but had already proved her worth. She was diligent, caring, but also wickedly tough. Dennis had heard a few of the lads suggest she was a man in drag.

She jumped back to a certain spot on the footage and slowed the fuzzy grey image down to a frame a second. The time stamp on the bottom right corner of the screen showed it to be

10.34 a.m. on 24th April 2009. This morning. Or yesterday, Dennis thought, not knowing which side of midnight it was.

'See? Those five youths have come from the direction of the school where the stabbing happened. They go down Bottle Road and can be followed all along there up to Acton Lane. I've tracked them right to Harlesden Station.'

Dennis leant in to get a better look. He could only see the backs of the boys. They all wore hoods. 'Any faces?' he asked. They were running, virtually tripping each other up in slow motion.

'Not a one. Not clear, anyway. I've sent some frames off to be enhanced to see what we get. I've also requested the station's CCTV, but I won't get it until tomorrow morning.'

Dennis nodded. 'That tracksuit top, the one with the white stripes on the sleeves . . .' He paused, squinting. 'I've just been up close and personal with it.' He allowed a small grin. 'Get someone to find out where it's from. How common they are.' Identifying these youths was one matter, but proving they had anything to do with Max's murder was quite another.

Dennis's head hit his pillow at 3 a.m. Five minutes later, he was up again, in his boxers, sweating, pacing, unable to sleep. He wondered if she was awake and considered calling her. Was she alone, sobbing on her bed or curled up in the arms of a loved one, weeping intermittently? Perhaps she was rampaging around the streets of London, wielding a knife, lashing out at gangs of youths, slashing justice back into her life.

He decided that Carrie Kent would be doing none of these things. Knowing her the way he did, he reckoned she would be sitting by herself, silent, staring at a wall or whatever happened to be in her way. She would be sipping water from a glass, having eaten nothing all day, and, on the outside, she would appear serene and in control, as if nothing very much was wrong. Inside her head, however, there would be a torrent of crazed thoughts and blames and what ifs and should haves and, yes, in the mix of utter regret, would be the seed of revenge. Knowing her as he did, Dennis was sure of one thing: she wouldn't rest until she found out who had done this to her son.

No one, she had once said when their bodies were spent and knotted in sheets, *no one will ever make my life not perfect.*

Carrie sipped a glass of water. It was the middle of the night. Several hours ago, she'd insisted everyone leave. With people around her – Leah, the police, Brody, and later that woman Fiona – it was just all too real, too sore, too unbearable.

Alone, she made up her own reality. She spent a few seconds believing that she'd woken in the night from a stomach bug – why else would her belly be churning? – and she'd taken some medication, choosing to sit by the open window to breathe in the cool night air. Then she was a kid and it was Christmas Eve and, again, she was unable to sleep because of the butterflies in her tummy.

The next lie she invented involved Brody. Somehow, she thought, if we were still together, this wouldn't have happened. She imagined she was waiting up for his homecoming after a week-long conference in the States. She couldn't sleep, knowing that his warm body, the body that he cared for so well by exercising and eating all the right things, would soon be pressed along hers. And even if they didn't make love because he was too tired after the journey, they would just hold each other and be thankful that they had one another, that they had Max, that they had a nice house and good jobs and really, it was already the perfect life, wasn't it?

Carrie's body shivered and every muscle contracted, causing her to cry out in pain.

Max was dead.

Her son had been murdered.

Nothing was perfect. Nothing ever had been.

When her eyes opened, it was both light and unbearable. Her neck was stiff from dropping sideways on to the arm of the chair and the rest of her was sore from shivering. Then she remembered. It was a flood of wretched realisation although, through the intermittent dozing, she hadn't completely been able to escape the horror.

Carrie stood up. She didn't want to eat but knew she had to. In the kitchen she peeled a banana. She glanced at the clock. Six fifty. Normally, she'd be up and would have done twenty minutes on the treadmill. A shower followed by coffee, fruit, toast, whatever Martha had put out, would precede time catching up with emails and show briefs . . . just as she had done yesterday. Nowhere in the grand plan did it say anything about this.

'*Why!*' she yelled out, throwing the banana skin across the room. She fought to keep the fruit in her stomach. She was a mother, goddammit, just like any other mother, but now she had lost her only son. Why was she feeling this differently? Why was she separating from her grief, unlike all the other mothers and fathers and siblings that she'd interviewed over the years when they'd lost loved ones?

Carrie thought of the dozens of times she'd sat in grim houses and tried to prise coherent words from a bereft mother. Lorraine Plummer, she thought. *I'm so lucky*, Carrie recalled, *and you're not*. It was that separation that had kept her going. Feeling good about her life wasn't wrong, was it?

Perhaps, she thought, I'm not so very different from any of them after all.

She heard the key in the lock. Who was it? Brody home from work . . . Max off to school?

Shit.

'Oh, my love,' came the voice in the hall. Then it was in the kitchen and Martha was sweeping across the tiles with her arms outstretched. 'Oh Carrie, my pet, I'm so desperately sorry. I got over here as soon as I heard. It was on the radio news. No one told me. That's the first I knew of it.'

The gap that was never crossed between the two women was bridged by Martha's outstretched arms. They wrapped around Carrie's shoulders and she was surprised at how strong they felt. How *good* they felt.

'Don't,' Carrie heard herself say, when what she really meant was yes, wrap me up and hug me tight until this pain goes away.

Martha withdrew immediately. 'I'm sorry. It's just that . . .'

'I know. I know.' Carrie allowed her hands to drop to her thighs. She slid on to a stool. Martha went for the kettle and filled it. All the while she was shaking her head.

'Do they know who did it?' Martha leant on the worktop opposite. She had been crying. Carrie was suddenly so glad she was there.

'Not yet.' Carrie couldn't stand it if they weren't caught.

'I lost a son.' It was as if Martha had used all her courage to say that; as if it had worn her thin and pale over the years.

Carrie looked up and raised her eyebrows. She had little energy to speak.

'My son. Stillborn. That was years ago now. I only had him for the nine months he was inside me. He was born with his eyes open. Conned the lot of us for a few moments.' Martha almost laughed. 'He never stopped kicking, that whole time. Then . . . nothing.'

The two women, separated by several decades, by huge amounts of money, by looks, by fame, were now threaded together in a mini-flash of understanding. Carrie had never considered that Martha might have suffered such loss. It made

179

her think, but only for a moment, before her own troubles took over again. 'I'm so sorry. I had no idea.'

Martha came round the worktop and grabbed Carrie's hands. 'And I won't have any of this crying alone. I'm here, right? I'll move in. Max was a good boy. He was a nice boy. This is terrible and he would want me to be with you. Max liked me being here.'

'He did?'

'Of course. Sometimes this house was as empty as a cave and I'd see the look on his face when he knew I was here, pottering in the kitchen.'

Christ, Carrie thought, reeling. How would she survive the guilt? *More* guilt. 'I wasn't here for him.'

'You were a good mother.' Martha's voice echoed in the vast room. They both knew that what she really meant was no, Carrie hadn't been a good mother, but for now we must pretend she was. 'I'll make you some tea.'

Carrie nodded. Her mobile phone rang.

'Dennis,' she said. 'No, I didn't sleep.'

She kicked her bare feet against the stool rung. Her toenails were painted. Her mind screamed out that she'd had that pedicure when Max was still alive, that each of her toes had been painted pink while her son was still drawing breath.

'You did?' Carrie suddenly stiffened. 'Did you arrest them?' She flushed then paled. 'Why not?' She wilted, her shoulders falling forward under the weight of a false alarm. 'No, oddly, I don't know what I'm going to do, detective,' she snapped. 'What would you suggest? A little holiday perhaps, or a week at a health spa? Or maybe straight back to work and forget about the whole thing.' She was salivating with anger. There was a pause, Carrie listening, followed by, 'Just catch my son's killer, Dennis,' and then a string of expletives. She hung up, slamming her phone on the worktop.

She sobbed continuously for an hour.

Martha insisted Carrie change her clothes. A shower was too much effort but a clean blouse, some comfortable linen trousers, a soft sweater gave her the tiniest amount of a normality that seemed both long gone and unattainable.

'Now, pet, I want you to eat this.' She delivered a plate of scrambled eggs and toast to Carrie, who stared at it as if it were poison. 'You can't expect to function on thin air, can you?' A cup of tea was placed on a mat and sugar that Carrie never took was stirred in. Martha was a good woman. Carrie felt ashamed she'd never noticed.

'Thank you.' She ate. She felt queasy.

'What are they saying? What are they doing?' Martha had kept mostly silent, allowing Carrie time and space to eat and talk when she felt like it.

'They brought two boys into the police station last night.'

'That's good.'

'Then they let them go.' Carrie curled her fingernails into her palms. It hurt and she liked it. 'They caught them and then they let them go free.'

'But, pet, maybe it wasn't the right lads, y'know. Maybe they were just helping them with their inquiries, eh?' Martha placed a hand gently on top of Carrie's, but Carrie pulled away. It didn't feel right.

'They also saw a gang of boys running away from the direction of the school. On CCTV. They're having it enhanced.'

'Well, that's good then. All these things happening, see? They'll catch him in no time. The police are amazing these days, pet.'

Carrie nodded, remembering all the behind-the-scenes bungles Dennis had told her about when his guard was down. When his pants were down more like, she thought, pushing her head into her palms. 'I need to speak to that teacher. Max's

English teacher.' She stood and fetched her bag and keys. Things had to be got on with. She didn't trust Dennis and his team to get inside the case, to pursue the *story* behind this – the emotions, the reasons, the cause. That was what, she believed, would ultimately lead them to Max's killer. It was her speciality; what she did every week of her life. She got results.

'I'd like it if you stayed here,' she said to Martha, smiling briefly. 'And Max would have liked it too.'

'I'll fetch my stuff from home then.' She stood and collected the crockery as Carrie left. 'You be careful now, pet.'

Denby Terrace was unremarkable. Redbrick two-up two-downs curved down the gentle slope towards the railway beyond. These few streets didn't seem nearly as rough as the triangle of roads that encased the school her son had chosen for himself.

There was nowhere to park so she bumped the car up on to the kerb on double yellow lines. She didn't care if she got a ticket. The air smelt of kebabs and hot spicy sauce – perhaps a leftover from last night's post-pub fallout or maybe preparation for the evening. It made Carrie feel even queasier. She doubted her stomach would ever feel normal again. It was swimming with adrenalin, tea, anger.

She knocked on number twenty-four. She was about to knock again when a young woman answered. 'Yeah?' She was wearing a short robe and her bleached hair was messy.

'Is Tim here?' she asked. 'Tim Lockhart?'

'Who wants to know?' The woman was abrasive. She clearly didn't like being disturbed by a stranger, although there was a flash of a frown, a quick glance up and down Carrie as if she was wondering. A quick shake of her head convinced her that no, TV celebrities didn't come knocking on doors down this street.

'I'm the parent of a boy he teaches. Taught.' There was no smile. Carrie couldn't manage it.

'Come in then.' The woman made Carrie wait in the hall while she went upstairs. A moment later a man came down, bleary-eyed with his hair sticking up in tufts. He rubbed his face and squinted at Carrie, also disbelieving what he thought he saw.

'Mr Lockhart?'

'Yes. How can I help?' The man appeared well-mannered and led the way to a small sitting room.

'I'm Max Quinell's mother.'

Mr Lockhart's face suddenly became expressionless as if that was the right thing to do in front of someone who had just lost their son. He swallowed audibly and then exhaled. He flopped down on to a brown settee and indicated with a loose sweep of his hand that Carrie should do the same. His head was now in his hands, but still his face showed nothing other than he'd had a rough night's sleep.

'I'm so sorry, Mrs Quinell.'

Carrie didn't correct him about her name. She thought that every time she heard someone say they were sorry, the lump of grief in her throat would just get bigger and bigger until she couldn't breathe.

'I want to talk to you about Max.'

'Of course.' The woman walked past the door, dressed now, glancing in to see what was going on. Tim edged forward on his seat. 'I was off sick yesterday, but got the call from the head in the evening.' He coughed as if that was evidence enough to confirm his illness. 'And of course it was on the news.'

'I didn't watch it.' She'd seen the journalists outside her house, waiting for a statement, a glimpse of the broken star at the window. Leah had said a few words to them; Dennis had closed all the blinds and curtains and instructed her to keep them shut. 'Yesterday was a blur.' Carrie's voice was weak. She tried to focus on why she was here. 'What was Max like in class, Mr Lockhart?'

Tim shifted, as if it was a parent-teacher meeting and he had

183

to deliver bad news about grades. 'He could have been one of my brightest students. He showed a real interest in literature.' The sentence finished with a high tone, as if there was more.

'But?' Carrie knew it was coming.

'But he was prone to skipping lessons. The GCSE year is an important one and—'

'He missed lessons?' Carrie was shocked. 'Why didn't I know about this?'

'That's something the head would have dealt with, Mrs Quinell.'

Carrie tried to stick to what she'd come for, but it hurt so. Every breath rasped in her chest, every syllable she spoke ulcerated her tongue. 'Why did he miss lessons? Where the hell was he?' The idea of her son playing truant was as foreign as the notion of him not being alive. Denningham College wouldn't have tolerated this kind of behaviour. 'I mean . . .'

'He's not the only pupil to decide that hanging out at the shops or down at the park is better than school. They smoke, drink, eat, get high. That kind of stuff.' Tim Lockhart was cavalier and seemingly comfortable with this idea. He was still young, in his late twenties, Carrie guessed, and clearly not that far removed from a time when he did exactly what he had just described.

The teacher continued. 'Look, I know he'd not been at Milton Park long, and I know that he was finding it quite hard to fit in, but if it's any comfort, he wasn't totally alone. I saw him hanging out with a girl quite often. She is in the same English class. Another bright spark. She used to try to make him come to lessons, get him to do his homework.'

'Who?' Her son had a friend that she knew nothing about. A girl.

'It's not normal for me to give out pupils' names—'

'Do you think it's normal for me to be sitting here discussing

184

my dead son?' She half stood, staring intently at the man. A small piece of Carrie Kent took hold of the situation.

Mr Lockhart nodded. He pulled his robe closed around his chest. 'Dayna Ray. She lives somewhere on the Gorse Vale estate. If you're going to visit, I'd take someone with you if I were you.'

'Thank you.' Carrie made to leave. She needed some air. The house was stuffy.

'Wait.' The teacher rose and went through a frosted door to the dining room. The table was stacked with books and papers. He flipped through a pile of what looked like handwritten essays. 'I think you should have this. Max's last essay.' He hung his head and handed over the two A4 pages of blue biro scrawl. 'They're studying *Romeo and Juliet*. I gave him a top mark. His insights were, well, both disturbing and brilliant.'

Carrie took it. She closed her eyes for a second, nodded and left, knowing it would be a while before she could bring herself to read it.

Gorse Vale was infected with tearaway kids, most of them not much older than six or seven, spiralling around the streets on bikes and scooters while their mothers were, no doubt, inside with a fag, a beer, watching daytime TV. Carrie stopped walking and closed her eyes. Was she, somehow, fuelling the social fire rather than quenching it?

'Why are you doing this?' Brody's voice was worn out. She'd picked him up half an hour ago, insisting he come with her to talk to Max's friend. He hadn't wanted to, thought it was pointless, contrary to how he'd been the day before. He was coping OK, he'd told her, by lying on his back and smoking. He couldn't do anything else.

'I have to do something,' Carrie said. Their arms were linked. 'Max was a part of this and I never knew.'

'You think it will help, being here, finding this girl?'

'If you could see this place, you'd know what I mean.'

Brody yanked his arm from his ex's. 'It looks fine to me.' He put his hand against his forehead as if shielding his eyes from the sun he couldn't see. He squinted.

'It looks a lot like the dump you live in.' Carrie began walking again. She knew Brody would follow the sound of her footsteps, but he wouldn't know where the kerbs were or where the discarded bikes lay on their sides, wheels spinning. 'Except you have a choice.'

It was Brody's turn to halt. 'You just can't stand it, can you?' Several of the kids nearby stared at them.

'What?'

'That someone you used to be married to lives in a housing tenement. That the father of your son lives in a shithole.'

'You're being ridiculous.' Carrie pulled him along by the arm. They needed to find out where this girl lived and she didn't much fancy approaching the groups of kids and grilling them alone.

'Admit it.'

'There's nothing to admit.' Her voice gave way. She didn't want this conversation now. Ever. Brody's feet were stuck fast to the pavement. Carrie sighed. She felt weak. Normally, she wouldn't let this pass, but nothing was normal any more.

'Tell me that it's nearly killing you to have seen where I live.'

Carrie swallowed. She knew Brody would have noticed the hesitation. A plane rumbled low overhead. 'Is that why you did it? You've spent years living in that place just to piss me off?' She laughed cruelly and yanked him by the wrist. 'You were born blind, Brody Quinell.'

Carrie stepped up to a group of girls to ask if they knew Dayna Ray. She was surprised she had any feeling left to notice that Brody was actually right – that yes, of course it had got to her, and it certainly angered her to know where Max had been staying when he was with his father. Brody spun her roughly round. His face was close.

'No, *you're* the only blind person I know, Carrie Kent. You've been blind to everything that's been right under your nose your entire life, yet you're too stupid to see it.' He shook her hard. His voice slipped from rage to misery. He was sobbing. 'Nothing in this life is flawless, woman. *Nothing.* And you, it may surprise you to know, are no bloody different to the rest of us.'

Carrie screwed up her eyes. She couldn't stand to see the truth.

AUTUMN 2008

Dayna had been thinking about him when he texted. *Psychic,* she thought, grinning, rolling about on her bed. He wanted to meet at the chippy.

She put away her books, clipped her essay into the ring binder and crept along the landing to the bathroom. Kev was asleep on his bed. If she woke him, there'd be hell to pay. She allowed a trickle of water to escape the tap and attempted to wash the ink off her hands. She stared in the mirror. Her eyeliner had smudged so she licked her finger and rubbed at it. Now it looked as if she'd been crying. She forked her fingers through her hair, wishing she could afford to go to a hairdresser, just that little place on the corner, or at least get a box of dye to do her roots.

Dayna went quietly down the stairs and slipped into her jacket. Lorrell stared at her from the lounge. Her eyes were big and pleading: *don't go.* In the kitchen, she saw her mum leaning against the sink, smoking, talking in a hushed voice on the phone. That in itself was odd. She only ever shouted.

In a flash of madness, Dayna beckoned Lorrell with a flick of her head and a forefinger to her mouth. *Shhh.* Max probably won't like it, she thought, but there was no way she was leaving Lorrell behind for a beating or a day of starvation when no one bothered to feed her.

Dayna pushed Lorrell's feet into shoes that were too small and slipped her arms into the sleeves of a grubby coat. Her face shone and was alight with wonder.

'Adventure,' she whispered in her big sister's ear. It sent shivers down Dayna's spine. She nodded and took Lorrell's hand. Yes, they were off to see Max. They were off on an adventure because, when she was with him, Dayna felt as if anything might happen.

He was waiting outside the chippy. He wanted to treat her, he said. She smiled coyly, thinking she was going to get a kiss because he'd kind of leant towards her as she approached. He stopped short, distracted by Lorrell's presence.

'Hey, you,' he said to her. He didn't seem at all annoyed that she was tagging along. The opposite, in fact. He was fascinated.

'Lorrell, this is Max. Can you say Max?' Dayna thrust out the child's hand in a pretend introduction. When Max tried to take it she pulled away and shook her head at the same time. 'She's not normally shy.'

The three of them went into the chippy and stared up at the menu. 'What've you been up to?' Max moved closer to Dayna, brushing against her. Her fingers tingled, desperate to slip into his but not having the courage to make the first move.

She shrugged. 'Did a bit on that essay this morning. My stepdad came home drunk at two in the morning and shoved my mum down the stairs. That was . . . interesting.' She tried to smile.

Max shook his head and Dayna noticed that his eyes were sad.

'Don't worry about me. Happens all the time.' She laughed. She didn't want things getting miserable. 'They should go on that show and get sorted out. What's it called? *Reality Check* or something.' Then Lorrell was tugging at her arm, pulling a face that was only too familiar. 'Oh God,' Dayna said. She glanced around. 'She needs a wee,' she whispered to Max, but he was frozen stiff, unmoving as though he'd died on the spot. 'Back in a mo.'

Dayna knew there weren't any public loos nearby so she nipped Lorrell over to the park. 'You going to water this tree for me?' She glanced around. She had to look out for her kid sister now, too. This place attracted all sorts of weirdos. Someone from school had been gang-raped here last week, although a rumour was going around that she'd pretty much asked for it. How were four boys supposed to keep it to themselves, everyone was saying, when she was dressed like that?

Dayna shuddered as Lorrell squatted at the base of the tree. 'Hurry, babe.' The tree she'd chosen was away from the main road to give her sister some privacy. It was behind the lopsided swings and rusted-up roundabout. Dayna glanced around. There was a woman with a dog the other side of the grassy area. Some other kids were hanging around outside the chippy now.

Lorrell pulled up her knickers. 'Done,' she said proudly. Dayna took her hand and was about to walk away but, a second before it happened, her spine fizzed, as though she knew what was coming.

'*Oi, you!*'

The voice stopped Dayna in her tracks. Her breathing quickened and she dug her nails into her palms to slow the panic. She squinted across at the chippy. She could make a dash for it, but Lorrell would never keep up. Slowly, Dayna turned round. There was a hand on her shoulder.

'Oi, emo bint. I'm talking to you.'

A little column of sick pushed up her throat. Bony fingers clawed at her arm. The other three boys surrounded her. Lorrell clung to her leg and whimpered. Dayna stroked her hair and shrugged. She swallowed, refusing to sound scared even though she was panting from fear. 'My kid sis just peed there. Watch where you tread.' Dayna hoped it might send them scarpering. It didn't.

'Ain't you gonna piss then?'

A peal of chesty laughter rang out. One of them lit a fag.

'Yeah, go on. Have a piss.'

'Pull her knickers down.'

'If she's got any on, the dirty little emo.'

''Scuse me, I'm off.' Dayna gathered all her strength and hoisted Lorrell on to her hip. Her cheeks were flushed and she could hardly breathe now. The child clung round her neck as she made to walk back to the chippy.

'You ain't going nowhere.' That bony hand again, caught round her arm, her throat, her life.

'Wee wee wee wee . . .' More laughter and more hands on her, spreading across her back, her bum, her hair . . . they were tugging at her studded belt . . . her zip . . .

There was a scream . . . *hers* . . . and then she was on the ground and the cold grass smacked against her cheek. She felt her jeans being pulled off her, her bag being torn from her shoulder. She had grit in her mouth. Where was Lorrell?

'Fucking leave her alone and piss off.'

Suddenly everything was still.

Dayna squinted up at the sky. Red, breathless faces loomed above. She pulled herself upright, dizzy, staggering, and there was Max, come to save her. She stared at him, hardly able to believe what she was seeing.

'Calm fucking down, man. It was just a game, weren't it?' The boys grouped together.

'Piss off and don't come back.'

'Max?' Dayna was suddenly by his side, her eyes enormous. She reached out for Lorrell's hand as the child crept closer. She'd been hiding behind the tree. 'What're you doing?' Her voice shook.

'Saving you,' he said. He ruffled Lorrell's hair. Dayna noticed his hands were shaking.

'No . . . I mean, what are you *doing*?' She glanced at his other hand. 'With . . . with that?' She'd thought he was different from the others.

Max didn't say anything. He just tucked the kitchen knife back in his bag.

They walked over to the chippy and bought food. Sitting on a wall outside, Dayna asked, 'Would you have done it to them? You know . . .' She pretended to stab herself with the little wooden chip fork. She stopped when Lorrell glanced up.

Max's face fell serious. He hadn't shaved, she noticed, as the sun picked out soft fuzz on his upper lip. He stared straight at her and nodded. 'Yes.'

Dayna's stomach did backflips. The feeling was way better than any kiss.

Fiona often speculated where it all went wrong for Brody. Of course, she'd wondered about the lives of other men in her life too – men who really *were* in her life, those disastrous relationships that typically lasted half a dozen dates before she couldn't stand them ruining any chance she might one day have with Brody – and her guesses had been wrong as often as half right. Never, though, had she drawn quite such a blank as she did with Brody. She'd always been able to come up with something – miserable childhood leading to an inability to commit, three marriages already and he's never going to settle down, he should just admit he's gay and only after friendship, serial cheater. Fiona was a realist, had been trained to think straight, rationally, and always relied on proof to reach her conclusions.

With Brody things were different. It was as though he wanted everyone close to him to be blind too, she concluded. He was like a toddler playing hide and seek, she decided one day, as she ate her usual sandwich while Brody sat in his office hunched over his keyboard.

'Eyes tight shut and you believe the rest of the world can't see you either,' she said to herself.

'Second sign,' a colleague called out from the adjoining desk. The maths department was unusually quiet this lunchtime.

'What is?'

'Talking to yourself. Second sign of madness.'

'What's the first?' Fiona laughed. Pete always cheered her up.

'Working for *him*.' Pete was grinning.

'All these years,' Fiona said, 'and I haven't any more of a clue about him than the day I started working here.' A bit of cheese dropped on her trousers. She picked it up, wiping the mayonnaise off with a napkin. 'He never talks about how he went . . . you know, how he went blind.' It was hard even for Fiona to say the words. University staff and students alike knew to keep quiet.

'They say it might have been an accident,' Pete said.

'I heard that too,' Fiona agreed. She kept watch over her boss through the glass wall of his private office. The door was closed, a sign he was working on something confidential. She would be allowed in, but only after knocking and Brody confirming it was her. She wasn't interested in spying on his work, she just wanted to get inside her boss's mind.

She saw Brody pick up his phone. A second later, her phone rang. 'We're going out,' he said.

'Where?'

'To the country.'

Bemused, Fiona watched as Brody shut down his laptop and put on his navy wool coat. He knew exactly where everything was. He wrapped a checked scarf round his neck and came out to Fiona's desk. It was cold for the end of October and Fiona had left her flat that morning with only a light mac. She shrugged into it and grabbed her purse and keys. 'See you later, Pete. I'm off on another mystery tour.' She pulled a face but found she'd been talking to herself. Pete wasn't there. 'Definitely going mad, then,' she concluded, taking her boss's arm and guiding him to the lift.

The drive to Cambridgeshire was pleasant. Being inside the car with Brody, the drizzle outside, made Fiona feel cosy and special – a feeling she relished while also being somewhat wary of. The hot coffee Brody insisted they buy at a service station lightened her introspective mood and took her mind off the fact that the man she'd known longest in her life – longer than the disaster of a relationship which had ended badly just before she took the job with Brody – would never notice her. In over ten years, he hadn't given her a second glance.

'You going to tell me yet?' Fiona braked. Red tail lights flashed on and off ahead. All he'd given her was a postcode for the satnav.

'Ah, Fiona,' he said as part sigh and part what she thought sounded a lot like despair. 'It's complicated.'

'Isn't everything?' She imagined he was thinking of their relationship, working it all out. He wasn't, of course.

'Not in mathematics, no.'

She decided to stay silent, just in case.

'You've never been married, have you, Fiona?' he continued.

Her heart skidded and she gripped the wheel tightly. How could he know about Daniel? He'd never asked anything about her personal life before, apart from the cursory 'What are you doing for Christmas?' or 'How was your long weekend?' and she'd never divulged anything to him about her previous disastrous relationship. Too much detail and he was more than likely to lose interest. That she didn't want.

'No,' she managed to say. 'I don't think I'm the marrying sort.' She wanted to kick herself for that.

The level of polite familiarity they shared was not exponential

194

to the intimacy of her place in his life. She was often in his bedroom, for Christ's sake, sorting out his personal stuff. She chose his underwear, cleaned out his fridge, filtered his emails and watched him grow older. None of these things were in her job description, yet she didn't begrudge any of it.

'If you're ever tempted,' he finished, 'then don't.'

She dug her nails into the steering wheel for the rest of the journey and remained silent, just the way Brody liked things.

It was only when the dual carriageway gave way to country roads slipping narrowly through pretty villages, only when they passed beneath the golden shroud of the autumn trees lining the college driveway, only when Fiona read the navy and gold sign that welcomed them to Denningham College that she realised their mission was all about Max again.

SATURDAY, 25 APRIL 2009

They found her by accident. The small puddle of what they thought was a child curled up beneath a tree at the edge of the Gorse Vale estate – pretty much the *only* tree in the area – turned out to be a cocky-looking teenage girl when she unfurled herself at the sound of their voices. They asked if they knew where Dayna Ray lived.

'You being funny, or what?' She prickled with defensiveness – a girl clearly used to fending off. She glanced up at them. Her heavily made-up eyes were smudged and wet with tears. Snot bubbled at her nose.

'No,' Carrie replied more gently than she'd intended. 'We just need to find her. The other kids said she lived at this end of the estate.'

The girl squinted at Carrie. A glimmer of recognition, although outweighed by sorrow, flickered in her eyes. She turned to Brody, gave him the once over, and then dropped her forehead on to her knees again. 'She lives over there.' Her arm came up and pointed behind her.

'Thank you,' Carrie replied, walking off.

'She's not home.'

Carrie stopped and turned back. The girl was standing now – a skinny thing in a black leather jacket and grey jeans. Her hair was frazzled at the ends from too much dye, but pale and childlike at the roots. Carrie reckoned that she was trying to look eighteen or nineteen but in reality was probably fifteen. The same as Max. She felt her stomach cramp.

'What do you want her for?' The girl wiped her nose on her sleeve. She hiccupped back some sobs.

Brody spoke, his suddenly loud voice causing the girl to recoil. 'We want to talk to her.'

Carrie's hand latched on to Brody's arm. She wasn't sure if it was to guide him or take some comfort. 'Just to ask her a few things.' Carrie felt herself swallowing back sobs. Nothing felt real.

'What things?' The girl pulled a packet of Superkings from her pocket and lit one with shaking fingers. She exhaled through tight lips.

'It doesn't matter.' Carrie bowed her head. She was hardly capable of talking, let alone telling a stranger everything. 'Thanks.' She turned and led Brody away.

'Wait.' The girl was suddenly in front of them. 'Aren't you that woman off the telly?'

Carrie offered a minimal nod. In truth, she didn't know who she was any more.

'I saw you.'

'Yes.' Carrie smiled weakly – a foreign feeling – and continued walking. She was shocked when the girl's hand clamped round her arm. 'A lot of people do.'

'No. I *saw* you.' She sucked hard on the cigarette and exhaled. 'Yesterday at the school when it was closed after . . .'

Carrie shook her head. 'We have to go.' She tugged at Brody's arm but he was reluctant to move.

'I was walking past and you were getting out of your car with someone. You . . . you looked sad.' The girl chucked the remaining half of her cigarette a few feet away. 'Are you making a show about . . . what happened there?'

A pause, but then Carrie replied. 'About what?' If she'd been thinking clearly, she'd have realised that it wasn't odd for this girl to know about the stabbing. The school was local and she probably went to it. The whole area would be buzzing with the news.

'About Max. About the stabbing,' the girl finished.

The name hung thickly between them, as if her son was actually there. A car revved along the street. Some kids wailed on the other side of the road.

'You knew him?' Carrie's hand came up, grasping at the air between her and the girl. There was a thread, a tiny wisp of a connection and it hurt so deep she felt as though she'd been stabbed in the heart herself.

The café was empty apart from them and one old man sitting in the corner. They were seated with coffees and a Coke that no one really wanted. This girl knew her son. She wasn't going to let her go.

'It's me. I'm Dayna,' she said.

By then it should have come as no surprise to Carrie, but she became still, her fingers hooked through the mug handle. She gave a small nod.

Then, when the waitress walked by their table, stopped and backed up, offered a familiar greeting to Brody, it should have made her ask: how come she knows you? But it was taking all Carrie's concentration to piece together what the schoolgirl opposite was saying.

'It's empty,' Dayna commented. She glanced up at the clock. 'There'd always be a group of kids in here on a Saturday morning.'

Carrie frowned. The girl was staring at her feet. 'What do you mean?'

'It's like everything's dead now.'

'Shit.' Brody's voice was deep and resonant and broke the

word into two syllables. The coffee machine behind them steamed and hissed.

'Do you know who I am? Really am?' Carrie asked before adding, 'Know who *we* are?'

Dayna shook her head. 'You're that woman off the telly.'

That she was sitting in a café with one of the most famous women in the country should have at least ruffled the teenager enough for her to be texting some friends or asking for her autograph. As it was, they sat awkwardly as if Carrie was an impatient aunt or teacher that Dayna had bumped into while out shopping.

'I'm Max's mother, Dayna. This is his father.'

Slowly, the girl's eyes narrowed as she took it in, wondering, Carrie thought, why Max hadn't introduced her or brought her home. Did she even know that Max was the son of a celebrity? A tiny patch of fog cleared in Carrie's mind before the mess in her head occluded her thoughts again: Max hadn't *wanted* his friends to meet her.

'You're . . . you're Max's mother?'

'Yes.' Carrie held her hand out across the table. Dayna tentatively pressed her fingers against the older woman's – the teen's nicotine-stained skin and bitten-down nails a contrast to the milky whiteness of Carrie's pampered hands and French manicured fingertips.

'But . . .'

'I know.' They stared at each other, each caught up in the realisation of who the other was.

'I . . . but he said . . .' Dayna let out a little hiccup, stunned by the legacy Max had left them. 'It's all been so horrid. Like life's just been blown out.'

Carrie reeled from the girl's honest words. She nodded and briefly shut her eyes. 'It only happens to other people,' she whispered in return. The irony was lost on Dayna, Carrie knew, as her entire career filled her head at the speed of light. Just as fast, it was gone, and there was a void so terrifying she didn't know how she would cope. *Other people*, she thought, refusing to acknowledge that as of yesterday morning that was exactly what she had become.

Brody was convinced she was the same girl that Max had brought to his flat on several occasions. He'd already visualised her from the traces she'd left in his bedroom – a faint scent of hairspray, a touch of leather from a jacket or some heavy boots perhaps, and the unmistakable aroma of teen lust; nothing that could be smelt exactly, he thought, rather *felt*. A vibe left lingering in his bedroom. He'd been transported back to his own boyhood, suddenly envious of his son's age and opportunity.

'Did he ever talk about his old school?' Brody asked.

'He didn't like it,' Dayna said. 'We had that in common. Not liking school.'

Brody heard the fizz of her can as she sipped and put it back on the table.

'Were you . . . you know, going out?' Carrie asked. Brody could have answered that.

'No. Yes. I dunno. Doesn't matter now, does it?' She let out a snort, one that told the world she didn't care what it threw at her because nothing could be worse than this.

'He mentioned you a couple of times.' Brody knew that whatever colour the girl's eyes were, they would now be wide as saucers. 'He was fond of you.'

'Yeah,' was all she said. Brody sensed the judder in the word; how it was filled with desolation.

'Dayna, do you know who could have done . . . it?' Carrie's voice, on the other hand, cut insensitively through the café buzz. A group of four young mums had come in with pushchairs and whining toddlers.

'It's not fucking show time, Carrie.'

'Brody, please.' Then the predictable hand on arm. He shrugged it away. 'Dayna, if you know anything, you have to speak up,' she continued.

'No one liked us,' was all she said. Brody imagined all the anger and depression strung up behind those few words. Kids these days battled for acceptance, and hearing coldly, truthfully, that his own son hadn't been liked hurt badly. Carrie just didn't get it.

'Why?' Carrie demanded. 'What was wrong with you? What was wrong with my son?'

Brody heard the scrape of the chair opposite.

'No, wait . . .' Desperate words from Carrie.

'*Wrong* with us?' Dayna said from somewhere near the door. 'What's wrong with you, more like, that your own son never once mentioned who his mother was?'

And she was gone, leaving both of them reeling from the truth that neither of them was ready to face.

Dayna went back to the tree. There was nowhere else to go. She rested her back against the bark of its narrow trunk and slid down, not caring if it ripped her jacket. Her bum hit the ground hard, sending shock waves up her spine and into her skull. She liked the feeling of controlling the pain.

She resumed the position she'd been in when those two idiots had found her, lured her into their sick lives, just so they could probe her about Max. Well, whatever she knew, she wasn't telling. That bitch. What must she have done to Max for him not even to mention his mother. Fucking Carrie fucking bloody Kent.

Dayna tried to cry but couldn't. She pulled a fag out of her pocket. It was her last one. She lit it, making sure she hardly paused between drags so that none was wasted. Her lungs seared, not from the dry smoke but because they were right next to her burning heart.

'Oi,' came the call across the scrubby grass separating the rows of council houses. 'Catch this.'

Dayna instinctively lurched sideways. The dog shit hit the tree inches from her shoulder. She retched at the stink. 'Fuck off, toad.' She picked up a rock and hurled it back at the nine-year-olds who were looking for another pile of mess to scoop up and chuck from a polystyrene container. The rock missed and, in return, the boys rained a load of names at her, one of them sending her into a blind rage. 'That's it,' she said, scrabbling to her feet. 'Come here, you little fuckers.'

Dayna tore across the littered area and managed to grab one of the kids by the collar. He choked as she yanked him round. The other boy fled on his bike.

'Give me what you've got,' she spat at him. He just stood there and shrugged, a smirk breaking his sallow face. She smacked him round the head and got a glimmer of joy from it before digging her hands into his jeans pockets.

'Err, get off, you perv,' he squealed. Dayna held him firmly and pulled out his cigarettes. She grinned. 'I eat little shits like you.' She brandished the fags in his face. 'Now piss off and tell your mate it's his turn next.'

Her heart thumping, paced by the surge of power she'd got from fighting back, even if it was with a nine-year-old kid, Dayna marched off, fag in mouth, to the only place she felt safe.

When she was inside the hut, when the candle was lit – the one that only recently had scented the air as Max traced the freckles on her arm with his finger – she pushed her face hard against her knees and cried until she fell asleep.

It was all on the internet. Time at the computer was rare but, if she was lucky, Kev would fall asleep after a lunchtime session down the Dog and Gun and not bother staring at naked women and videos of teens getting it off.

Sure enough, as she'd hoped, when she got back from the hut – had she inherited it now? she wondered – Kev was sprawled out along the length of the sofa, the dog draped over his legs, both their tongues showing long and dry. He made her feel sick.

The computer was in the same room, tucked away in an alcove under the stairs. It was old, nothing as flash as the modern machine Max said he'd been going to give her. The monitor was huge and caked in a layer of dust. The screen was smeary from Lorrell's eager fingerprints as she pointed at her favourite cartoons with a strawberry chew in hand, or surfed toy websites wishing for things she knew she'd never get. The keyboard was yellowed from too many smoky fingers passing across its worn-out keys, and the mouse pointer juddered and jerked over the screen as if it, too, was fed up with being old and overused.

Dayna waited for it to boot up, watching Kev sleep, aware that the dog had one eye on her, his short tail giving a half-hearted thump, too lazy to move off his owner's warm legs to greet her. Eventually, after connecting to the internet, she arrived at the TV station's website and she clicked straight through to the 'watch again' section. Dozens of shows from dramas to chat shows to current affairs programmes scrolled across the page. *Reality Check* was at the top of the popularity list.

'Why?' she whispered to the computer.

Why had Max not told her that his mother – his *mother*, for God's sake – was Carrie Kent? She still couldn't believe it was true.

As the show page resolved, Dayna hardly recognised the woman she'd sat opposite only a couple of hours ago. Airbrushed and preened to perfection, the glamorous Carrie Kent smiled seductively from the screen, her fingers making her famous gesture that heralded the start of every show.

Dayna chose a show at random. One from last month. The old computer took ages to buffer the stream and Dayna turned the volume on the speakers right down so as not to wake Kev. She leant in to hear what was going on. When the video player sputtered to life, Carrie Kent was centre stage, dressed in a tight scarlet skirt, black patent heels and a cream blouse that showed more cleavage than any other daytime presenter would dare to reveal. She held her audience captive from the start. She's amazing, Dayna thought.

'Today on *Reality Check* I will be talking to Britain's youngest mum. She's now sixteen but Jody Burrows gave birth to her first child, Krystal, when she was just eleven years and ten months old. Since then, Jody has gone on to have two more children, each by different partners. She still holds the record of being Britain's youngest mum. Her own mother, Stacey, is just thirty-two and a grandmother three times over.'

A pause – partly from the jerky buffering of the video stream, and partly from Carrie Kent working the audience, who were gasping in their seats at the facts. Carrie allowed the ripples of shock to percolate the studio before bringing on her guest. The teenager swaggered on stage and sat proudly in one of the blue chairs arranged on the set. She chewed gum as if she hadn't eaten for a week – revolting, Dayna thought, to do that on the telly – and crossed one ankle up over her knee. Dayna tweaked up the volume a tiny bit. Eleven years bloody old, she thought.

'Jody, welcome to my show.' The audience applause settled down and Carrie Kent approached the girl. The teen's doleful eyes, ringed with a sallow grey colour, tracked the presenter as she parked herself in the chair beside her. Carrie crossed her long legs. The girl said nothing. 'I invited you here today to talk about your experiences of motherhood and sex and to try to put out a message to other youngsters who might be thinking about having an intimate relationship at a young age.'

Jody Burrows shrugged and chewed. She half nodded to indicate her compliance. Carrie Kent didn't faze her one bit.

'Bet she's being paid a fortune,' Dayna whispered. 'Why else would you make a twat of yourself?'

'Tell me, Jody,' Carrie continued. 'Did your mother ever talk to you about sex before you got pregnant?'

'Nah,' the girl replied. She laughed. 'We didn't do it in school neither.' She sat up a bit. She was wearing jeans, a denim jacket and a tight T-shirt beneath it. Dayna thought her tummy was flat for someone who'd had three kids. Her own mum spilled over the top of her jeans from having just her and Lorrell.

'Was the father of your first baby your boyfriend? Had you talked about having sex before it happened?'

'Nah. We was drunk. Too pissed to know what was happening really. It was at a party. Everyone had been drinking so it was OK. It just kind of happened naturally.' Jody Burrows sat up straight, enjoying the attention. Dayna shook her head. She bit her lip.

'How old was the boy, Jody?'

'At the time, he were fourteen.'

'And what happened to him?'

'They tried to charge him with rape. He got some time in the juvy but he's working in a garage now.'

'Do you ever see him?'

'He's a good dad. He brings me some nappies and fags and takes Krystal out so I can study.'

Dayna snorted. 'Get wasted, more like.'

'I'm training to be a beautician at college.'

'Where are you living now, Jody?'

'At the moment I'm with my mum, but it's crowded because—'

Kev groaned and sat up.

Dayna quickly shut down the window. She'd had enough of

teen pregnancies. She'd not had enough of Carrie Kent. Her spine stiffened as she thought of Max. She gulped back a sob.

'What you doing?'

'Nothing.'

'Where's your mother?'

Dayna shrugged. Kev shoved the dog off his legs and stood up.

'Ain't you got nothing better to do?' He lit up and went into the kitchen.

Yes, thought Dayna, I have. It's just that I'm too scared to do it.

THE PAST

Carrie had just returned from the cinema with Leah and their flatmates. Was she the only person in the world who hadn't enjoyed *Cocktail*? There was a note with her name on it slipped under the door. She picked it up. Leah flopped on to the saggy sofa while Jenny and Tina made the drinks.

'It was implausible and sickly. Made my skin crawl.' Carrie hung up her coat, while the others chucked theirs on nearby furniture.

Leah threw a cushion at her friend. 'Oh shut up, Miss Spoil Sport. We loved it.' She kicked off her shoes and pulled open a bag of corn chips, even though they'd eaten their way through buckets of popcorn at the cinema.

'Here, get this inside you.' Jenny handed Carrie a tall vodka and tonic, the glass stuffed full of ice and lemon to make it last longer. It was their Friday night treat. Girls only. Pizza or a movie or ice skating followed by the cheapest bottle of gin or vodka they could buy diluted with slimline tonic. The week's gossip followed until three or four in the morning, and then the prescribed hangover for the next day. The only cure was to go out dancing on Saturday night and forget about lectures until Monday.

'I'm in heaven,' Tina declared, sipping on her drink. She lay back in the bean bag. 'What's Mel up to tonight?' she asked Leah.

'Studying, of course.' She attempted a smile while thinking of her girlfriend, but was only saddened by her absence. 'I was going to invite—'

'I have to call home.' Carrie's voice was stiff and cold. She scrunched up the note and stuffed it into her pocket. She dug in her purse for some change and walked briskly out of the door, running down the stairs to the payphone in the hall.

She tripped on the last few stairs, saved herself by grabbing the banister rail, broke a nail and lunged at the sticky phone handset. She grabbed it by its tangled wire. She was shaking. In her heart, she already knew.

She pushed the fifty pence into the slot and dialled. 'Come on . . .'

Call home. Urgent was all the note had said, in some unfamiliar scrawl – probably one of the lads who lived downstairs, the same one perhaps who always left his bicycle blocking the corridor.

'Hello? Mum?'

Carrie listened. She nodded. She sat down gently on the small wicker chair that the landlord had placed beneath the telephone. Her cheeks went scarlet as a motorway of images sped through her mind.

He didn't suffer, she heard. *It was over instantly.*

'By the time the ambulance came, honey, it was too late.'

Carrie coughed. She thought it might turn into a sob, but it didn't. Her mother quietly expunged herself of the details. About how his face had grown violet; about how they massaged his heart; about how they pumped oxygen and medication into him. She took it all in, trying to recall when she'd last seen him, what they'd said – or not said.

'Will you come home?' her mother asked.

'For the funeral, yes,' Carrie replied. She almost saw the tight nod of approval. Her mother would rather be alone for the next few days, Carrie knew, to ponder the passing of her husband, to begin the dwelling on things and the solitary existence that would become a lifelong task – no more fun or indulgence or frivolity, not that there ever had been. There would be the sorting, the clothes, the arrangements, all perfect for her to deal with, to occupy her, Carrie thought coldly.

'Bye, Mum,' she said eventually.

She slowly climbed the three flights of stairs, barely out of breath when she opened the door to the flat. The sweet smell of alcohol pulled her inside, along with the warm banter of her friends. But they stopped when they saw her.

Carrie pulled a face, not concerned that her heart felt like a bloodless stone inside her chest. 'Well, that's a bloody nuisance,' she said, knocking back her drink.

She was missing lectures for the funeral. 'The Dynamics of the Live Interview' was being delivered by Glen McGowan, a silky smooth Channel Four presenter renowned for his late-afternoon chat show watched by millions of bored housewives. Carrie was really pissed that she couldn't go. 'Of all the days for a funeral,' she said.

'Carrie, that's awful. It's your dad.' Leah flung a black sweater at her friend, but Carrie chucked it right back.

'Black sucks at funerals. I'm going to wear this.' She pulled a bright pink shirt off its hanger and slipped it on.

'Carrie, you can't. It's not respectful.'

'He never respected me.' She buttoned her cuffs and pulled on her only coat – navy wool with giant buttons and a chunky collar. October had given way to November. The air was freshly chilled with the nip of autumn. 'I'd still rather be at the lecture. Glen bloody McGowan speaking.'

'All we're doing after that is research crap.' Leah helped her friend tie her scarf. She held her shoulders and stared at her, clearly wanting to say something but quite unable.

'I might be back by then. Take notes for me. McGowan's

good, but I know I can be better. When we're rich and famous, we'll invite him on our show.'

'Oh, Carrie.' Leah exhaled. She rested her head gently on Carrie's shoulder. 'When we're out of this place we'll no doubt be one of thousands applying for jobs while we hone our burger-making skills at McDonald's.'

'Speak for yourself.' Carrie tucked a strand of Leah's wayward hair behind her ear. 'You might be satisfied with riding the tide for the rest of your life, but I know what I want.'

'Maybe I'll hitch a ride in your great wake, then,' Leah said, closing her eyes as Carrie planted a fond kiss on her head.

'Nice pun,' Carrie said, grabbing her bag and leaving. She heard Leah gasp for breath when she realised what she'd said, on today of all days. Carrie laughed as she went down the stairs. It was borderline hysteria by the time the chilly wind cut across her face outside and she realised she would never see her father again.

In the taxi, Carrie thought back over her childhood days as if they'd happened to a different person. That child couldn't be her, could it? The one peeking between the banisters, the one who scuttled in from the garden at the sound of clicking boots, the one that hardly spoke? She thought back as the streets flashed past.

No one could accuse Major Kent of being cruel to his only child. His wife and daughter were both kept warm and fed; they were clothed and, when he was on leave, they took holidays in Dorset and Wales. One day, he promised them, they would go to France. On the hovercraft, or the ferry, he said. They didn't make it across the Channel, but Caroline Kent never forgot that promise – one of the better ones. She added it to her list, scribbled in a tatty notebook, and scored it out of ten.

'Eight,' she reckoned, chewing the end of her pencil. She

totted up the numbers written beside the other promises. They totalled seventy-two. Sixty-nine the second time she added up.

She'd wanted a pet rabbit. Carrie recalled the day she'd finally mustered the courage to ask.

'Wait until he has food in his belly,' was her mother's advice. 'And his weekend sherry.'

Little Caroline nodded. Other kids at the base had pets. Simon had two rats. Kelly a horrid spider thing. She reckoned a rabbit wouldn't be any trouble.

'Don't be stupid,' he said. He didn't look up from the newspaper.

She wondered if she should have waited until he'd changed out of his uniform, hoping he'd transform into a milder, gentler father once he peeled off the stiff layers of green and brown. 'Can I have one then? A rabbit?'

Charles Kent was immersed in the day's news, his brow closing together with each turn of the page. The air was scented with the heavy tang of newsprint. Carrie read the headline of the front page. *Bomb Blast Rocks Northern Ireland.*

'Will they come to the base?'

Her father flattened the newspaper against his stomach and asked, 'Who?' He wasn't unpleasant or impatient, but his voice was cold, as if it was already decided that she was a nuisance.

'Those bombers.'

'No.' He pushed his reading glasses back up his nose and re-furrowed his brow. One finger tapped lightly against the edge of the newspaper as he read. Caroline watched it, wondering if he was thinking about the rabbit.

'I'd look after it all by myself.' She was standing beside him now, tall and upright and with her ankles pressed together and her palms against her thighs. All the best soldiers stood like that. She knew her dad was important in the army.

'Fine,' he said. 'Have a rabbit.' This time he didn't lower the newspaper or look at his daughter.

'Really?' She wondered if she ought to add 'sir' when speaking to him. She wanted to hug him but didn't. It wouldn't be right.

'I said so.'

Caroline ran off to tell her mother. Her arms were elbow-deep in soapy water. 'Dad says I can have a rabbit. He did!'

No one mentioned the rabbit for a few days, not even Caroline for fear of pushing her father one step too far.

'When I'm a grown-up,' she said later through her toothbrush and foamy paste, staring into the mirror, 'I'm going to do whatever I want.' She swilled and spat. 'Have a hundred rabbits.'

Next day at dinner, Major Charles Kent surprised his daughter. Caroline held her knife and fork, ready to tuck in to the stew her mother had prepared. Her father said grace as always and then stared straight at her.

'You wanted rabbit,' he said with more warmth than Caroline had ever seen on his usually tight face.

'Oh yes,' she replied, her mouth now bursting with food. Was it outside, she wondered, sitting in a cage, waiting to be cuddled?

'Bon appétit,' Charles Kent replied and he didn't say anything else for the entire meal.

AUTUMN 2008

They pushed Lorrell on a swing. As Max shoved the plastic seat, fearful the little girl might fly off, Dayna stood in front of her kid sister and made faces every time she drew close. Lorrell hooted with excitement.

'Tummy funny,' she squealed.

'Hold on, Lorrell,' Max called out. He'd not had much to do with little kids before. He remembered some cousins from way back, when his parents were still together. His dad's sister's kids, he thought. He hadn't seen them for years, not since they'd visited from Jamaica. His lasting memory was his mother rushing around after them wiping up the sticky fingerprints they left around her immaculate house, or insisting their parents control them more. No wonder they hadn't come again, he thought.

'Do you ever see your dad's family? You know, since your folks got divorced.'

Dayna shook her head. 'Nah. Weeeee!' She clapped her hands against Lorrell's.

'Me neither.' Max missed a couple of pushes. Lorrell, he thought, was going high enough. When he had his own kids, he wanted things to be different.

He stared at Dayna. Her pale cheeks were crested with a pretty shade of pink – far too delicate for someone who wore biker boots and a leather jacket. He wondered who would be the mother of his kids and how old he'd be when he had them. He wanted a job, a house, all that stuff first. Maybe thirty, he thought, and he hoped that he still knew Dayna then. 'You're a good mother to her,' he called out.

Dayna winked back. 'No one else is.' She pulled on the chains to stop the swing and lifted Lorrell off. Lorrell immediately ran over to the red and green roundabout. The wooden boards were sprayed with graffiti and the rails rusty and chipped.

'Get on,' Max told them. He grabbed a rail and began to run. 'Hold tight!' He got dizzy himself and, as soon as they were whizzing round at speed, Max leapt on next to Dayna. Lorrell clung on to a bar in the centre. Her face was frozen – her mouth wide open and her eyes bursting with so much fun. Her wispy hair trailed behind.

Max wobbled and grabbed on to Dayna. 'Craaazy,' he called out, grinning. Their faces were close and he could focus on her even though they were spinning wildly. The world whizzed around them while they, at the eye of a terrifying storm, held their breath in the calm.

'It's all like spilt paint,' Dayna said, waving her arms about. 'But you're still perfect.'

Max could hardly believe it.

Perfect, she'd said.

Was she thinking the very same thing as him – *feeling* it? Emotions transferred across the electric air between them. With his mind pressed against the side of his skull, Max seized the moment. He cupped Dayna's face and pushed his mouth against hers. Her lips were salty from the chips they'd eaten; full and soft from all the things they would say to him. Her eyes were wide and still, he noticed, as the world flew out of control behind them.

She responded. Her lips parted. She put a hand on the back of his head.

Nothing was real.

They were spinning. Together. Untouchable.

214

Everything was perfect.

'Yuk!' Lorrell cried. 'That's yukky.'

'I'm so sorry,' Max said, his mouth still stuck against Dayna's.

That's OK, she vibrated into him. He felt the coy smile form against his chin. He hoped he didn't feel prickly. It was the first time he'd ever kissed a girl. He prayed he'd done it right. He felt the tip of Dayna's tongue nudge his teeth. He allowed her in. He felt something bashing his legs.

It was all over. The world was back and they were laughing, looking down at Lorrell who'd jumped off the slowing round-about. She was beating them both with a twig.

'Ice cream,' she said, pouting.

Dayna hauled her back up on to the roundabout. She hugged her and turned back to Max.

'No one's ever done that to me before,' she confessed. 'It was nice.'

'Yukky.'

Max smiled. Inside him everything was mixed up. He had no idea how he would ever sift through these new feelings. He had kissed Dayna. She had kissed him back. This was a huge deal. He needed to go away, to be alone, to lie on his bed and think what it all meant; to decide if it had really happened.

But then, he never wanted to leave her side.

Did he look different? he wondered. He touched his face as Dayna drew away with Lorrell, who was now whining about ice cream. His chin was wet.

'Better get her one,' Dayna said. 'Don't forget your bag.' She led Lorrell across the grass towards the shops. It suddenly felt a lot like nothing had happened.

'Wait,' Max called out. He ran back to the swings and hooked his bag over his shoulder. He suddenly remembered the knife tucked inside it and wondered how just a couple of hours could be filled with such extremes. Dayna was halfway to the shop when he caught up. She stared straight ahead, chastising Lorrell for whingeing so much.

Max pulled a face and touched Dayna's arm. He thought she jerked away but couldn't be sure. 'What's up?'

Dayna glanced round at him, her eyes dark and stormy. 'Got any money?' she said in the voice she used at school – her tough voice, the one that both threatened and defended. The one that said she didn't give a shit about anything.

Max dug into his pocket. 'Sure. But why are you—'

'Thanks.' Dayna took the coins. She led Lorrell into the corner shop and waited while she chose a lolly. Max stood behind them, staring at the way Dayna's hair brushed the edge of her face.

'Hurry up, Lorrell,' she said, shifting from one foot to the other.

'Dayna . . .' Max pulled up close. There was a group of kids from the year above them trying to buy some cider. They didn't have ID. He ignored the brewing grumbles as the shopkeeper refused to serve them. 'Dayna, I'm sorry. OK? I didn't mean to—'

'Just fucking shut up, Max.' Dayna grabbed the lolly from Lorrell's hand as soon as she'd pulled one from the misty depths of the freezer. She slid the door closed and marched up to the checkout where the boys were still arguing about buying booze.

The shop man caught Dayna's eye and reached out for her item. He scanned it.

'One forty-nine, love,' he said over the heads of the bickering boys. Dayna reached round them and handed over two pound coins. Lorrell was jumping up and down at her side, desperate to get her hands on the ice lolly.

'Why, Dayna? What's the matter with you?'

'She's a fucking miserable bitch, that's what's wrong wiv her . . .' The boy trailed off into fits of laughter.

Max's fists clenched round the strap of his bag. He stared at the youths. He knew them from school. They were trouble. Always drinking, starting fights. He reckoned one or two had been banged up before. He felt the worn leather of his bag, reminding himself of what was inside. But he couldn't, not in here. He glanced up behind the till. There was a security camera pointing right down at them.

The boys finally skulked out of the shop when they realised they weren't going to get served. One of them punched Max in the back as he went past. Lorrell peeled the paper off her lolly and dropped it on the ground outside the shop. 'No, Lorrell,' Max said. 'Go and put it in the bin.' She did as she was told, running the creamy pink lolly between her lips. Max took hold of Dayna's shoulders and turned her to face him. 'We kissed,' he said flatly. 'And now you're unhappy. I'm sorry.'

Dayna's eyes filled with tears. 'Don't be sorry,' she whispered. 'It's nothing you've done.'

'Then what?'

Lorrell scooted up to her big sister, pushing the fingers of her free hand into Dayna's.

'It was like . . . like . . .' She stared up at the sky and sniffed. 'I felt something so hot in my heart I could hardly stand it,' she continued. 'But it made me angry too.'

'And?' Max hardly dared breathe.

'And,' she let out a huge sigh, 'it made me realise that we're unloved, people like you and me.'

'People like us?'

Dayna squinted up at Max. 'My entire life I've had to deal with crap. I'm numb to it all now. Except . . .'

Max wondered why she'd included him in her summation. He had to admit, he liked being *us*. He understood exactly what she meant about being numb. 'Except?'

'Except now I'm not quite so numb. My heart is tingling.' And with that, Dayna reddened, tugged Lorrell, and the pair ran off down the street.

Max watched them go, stunned. He touched his lips. He put his hand inside his jacket, cupping his heart. He felt it too.

The hut had been leaking. Several boxes were wilting and soggy. Max stripped off the cardboard and examined the contents. He removed the plates one by one and set them on top of the dry boxes. They were a bit ugly, he thought, like an old lady would use. A sort of mottled cream colour with grapes and apples painted around the edge. He picked one up and threw it across the hut. 'Twelve-piece dinner service now fucking eleven,' he said, reaching for a bowl. He smashed that too, shards of ugly porcelain raining around the small hut.

Soon the whole set was broken. Max kicked the box outside the door. The rain had started again. He slumped down on the car seat and lit a fag. He felt better, more normal. 'Numb again,' he said. 'People like *us*.'

He closed his eyes and drew the smoke deep into his lungs. All he could see was Dayna's face as they stood on the roundabout, the world licking past behind her lovely face.

Baffled by the new feelings, by the way Dayna was working it out, Max ran his hands over the other boxes in the corner. He would have to move the tarpaulin. Stuff was getting ruined. He lifted up a Morphy Richards steam iron. He'd asked around, but no one wanted it. There was a juicer and a craft set. He moved them out of the way, peeling the soggy cardboard off both. The craft set he placed on the car seat. He could give it to Lorrell. It would be an excuse to visit Dayna, to see where things stood.

Max punched his code into the security pad. Once through, he turned the key in the Georgian front door. It had been recently painted and still smelt oily and new, somehow less familiar every time he came back. The big brass handle and knocker shone, thanks to Martha's cleaning skills and, as he pushed it open, he got a whiff of the fresh lilies that his mother insisted were placed on the hall table, fresh every three days.

He kicked off his shoes and shoved them in the walk-in cupboard. His mother would go spare if he wore them in the house. 'You're bringing other people's dirt inside. Why would I want that?' Max, if he was honest, found it difficult to call the place home.

He stopped and listened. Martha would have left by now. His mother – well, she could be anywhere from New York to Selfridges or her office at the television station. He didn't really care. Seeing her would only remind him how much of a freak he was and, while he was glad that it had brought him closer to Dayna, he didn't want to be different. No one did, did they? Least of all a teenager like him who'd struck unusual in the looks department. He took the stairs two at a time, thankful at least that his scrawny legs allowed him to get to his room quickly.

'Max? Is that you?' It was shrill, commanding and made him freeze on the landing.

'Yep,' he replied.

'Come here a minute.' If he didn't go, she'd only come to his room.

'What, Mum?' He ran back downstairs. Surprising himself, Max caught his breath when he saw her. He thought she looked beautiful today. He couldn't recall ever thinking that before. What had Dayna's kiss done to him? His mother was in her study, sitting at her desk, some website or other on her monitor, her brown leather briefcase spilling out papers at her feet. Her hair cast a golden glow around her face and her lips seemed shiny and new, the bow of their smile setting something off in his heart that took him back. Way back to when things were good.

She smiled. 'I just wanted to say hi. See how you are. Sit

down.' She pointed to the reclining chair the other side of the room. Max moved a mohair throw before sitting, praying that his jeans were clean. He'd get it in the neck if he left grime on the leather. 'How are things?'

Oh God, he thought. It was one of those catch-up guilt conversations, more of an interview than mother and son having a chat. He couldn't even recall the last time he'd actually seen her – maybe briefly this morning, out of the window perhaps, or maybe last week when she had guests for dinner. Yes, that was it. The house had been filled with raucous old men spouting off about Viagra and Polo. They'd put on some dreadful pop music way past midnight. Max couldn't stand it. He'd thrown on some clothes and cycled over to his dad's house. His old couch was way better than listening to his mother living it up all night with her stupid rich friends.

'Max?'

'Yeah. Things are all right.'

'How's your new school?'

He heard the tension in her voice as she mentioned the place that had caused so much trouble between them. *Carrie Kent's son goes to Milton Park.* Oh yeah, he loved it.

'It's great.'

'Are you learning lots?' His mother crossed her legs the other way. She was wearing a bright pink skirt and a paler pink blouse. He'd seen her on telly in that outfit. She was really pretty, he had to admit. A couple of lads from Denningham had told him 'they would' when referring to her. It had made him want to die and kill them in equal measure.

'Yeah. Lots.'

Carrie sighed. She pulled a sorrowful face, one filled with remorse, Max thought, because she wasn't getting anything out of him. Not like those poor suckers she strung up on her show.

'And what about friends? Have you made some new ones?'

Max straightened. Did she know about Dayna? He stared into her eyes. They chilled him, but even more so now she had mentioned this. He shrugged.

'You must miss your old chums,' she said. Now he knew where this was going.

'They were tossers.'

'Oh, Max . . .' Carrie leant forward. At last, she had got something out of him, something to build on. He knew the way she worked. 'How about I talk to the head back at Denningham? It shouldn't be you who had to leave if there were problems.'

'Mum, it's OK. I like it at Milton.' He swallowed, praying she couldn't read him too well. 'There are plenty of nice kids there and the lessons are cool. Stop worrying. I'll take my GCSEs next summer and then think about A levels. Perhaps go to college.' He could already tell by his mother's face that she wasn't buying it.

'God, Maxie, I didn't bring you into this world to mix with chavs and pot smokers. Heaven knows, I see enough low-life scum on my show without having you caught up in it. Those places are a breeding ground for drugs, alcohol, violence. Before you know it, you'll be in trouble with the police or have some girl preg—'

'Stop!' Max stood. His mother stiffened, not recoiling exactly, she'd never do that, but she was clearly surprised by his outburst. 'I can look after myself, Mum.' He was calmer now. 'Nothing's going to happen to me.' He thought he saw the gloss of a tear in her eye.

'Fine,' she said, swivelling her chair round to face the computer again. 'I just want you to be happy.'

There was something in the way she said it that made a small part of Max believe her; a little bit of love resonating in her words that brushed close to his heart. He plodded upstairs to shut himself away. Was it, he wondered, all because of Dayna? Was he, because of the kiss, a little less numb now, even though he'd tried not to be? He picked up a Sharpie marker and hurled himself on to his bed. He pushed up his left sleeve and wrote *Dayna* all over his arm.

SATURDAY AND SUNDAY, 25 AND 26 APRIL 2009

'She knew him, Leah.' Carrie couldn't feel the chair beneath her. The nerves in her body had shut down. 'That girl Dayna knew Max. She probably knew more about him than I did.'

'That's not true.' Leah had got the whisky out. She sloshed more into their tumblers. Neither of them felt in the least bit drunk even after several shots.

'She said no one had liked them.' Carrie tipped her face to the ceiling. The tear escaped anyway. 'No one *liked* us,' she repeated. 'Was that "us" in the *us* sense, you know, like they were together, or "us" as in they were just the unfortunate sods who got picked on?'

'Stop analysing, Carrie. You'll drive yourself mad.'

'My son was stabbed.' Carrie worked out each syllable. She sipped whisky. 'I will analyse what the fuck I like.' She knocked the rest of the drink back. Her throat seared.

'You're reading between the lines, that's all, and I'm worried for you. It was good that she was his friend, surely.' Leah shifted closer on the sofa.

'You didn't see her.'

'No.' Leah tightened the cap on the bottle of bourbon and set it on the table. 'But it wouldn't have made a difference if I had.'

'You're not getting this, Leah. She said no one liked them. Them. Them bloody them. And I didn't know.' Carrie reached for the whisky but Leah intercepted. Carrie fell sideways on to

223

her. The sobs were bitter, unreal, saturated with anger. 'This doesn't happen to *me*!'

Carrie felt the gentle touch of Leah's fingers stroking her head, her shoulders, her neck, until, somehow, she slept away one more hour of her life.

'Detective Masters, this girl needs talking to.' Composure had come at a price. Lying prone across Leah's legs, accepting comfort, allowing the whisky to wash through her, Carrie had woken with a bad headache. She didn't care. In fact, she welcomed the pain between her temples. Her phone beeped. The battery was running low.

'She's been interviewed, Carrie. Twice.'

'And?'

'She doesn't know who did it.'

'For fuck's sake . . .' There were no more words. Nothing would ever be the same again. She wasn't Carrie Kent any more. She was the woman whose son was stabbed. Just like all the rest.

'Look,' Masters said. 'Why don't you and Max's father come down to the station in the morning and I'll update you on progress. I'll be here from eight.'

'Progress?' Carrie whispered. Progress, he'd said. That was a positive word, as if they'd found something. She couldn't stand to ask what. She wanted that little bit of hope, that little bit of progress to carry her through the dark hours of the night. 'OK,' she replied and hung up.

Leah drove. 'I don't care,' she said. 'I'm your friend. I'll be here as long as it takes.' She'd stayed the night, insisting that Carrie step into the shower before they left for the police station the next morning. She had set out some clothes for her, just regular Sunday stuff – an attempt at normality way before it was due – and borrowed something from Carrie's vast wardrobe for herself.

While Carrie was drying, Leah prepared some food. She cut up some fruit and made toast. Neither of them wanted it but ate a little anyway. Leah poured coffee. 'Do you think Brody will turn up?'

Carrie shrugged. 'I left a message. What more can I do? He has that woman to ferry him about. Just because our son is dead doesn't mean we're best buddies again.'

'Carrie, don't get hung up on what Dennis said. Progress can mean all sorts of things. We're used to dealing with the police, so don't—'

'It's Max, Leah. *Max*.' Carrie dragged her hair back and secured it with a band. She had no make-up on. Best that way, Leah thought. She didn't want her to be any more recognisable than she already was. 'Not some *Reality Check* trash no-hoper.'

They stared at each other. *That's the difference between us.* Leah shook her head. That's why you're in the limelight, the one scissoring open the scars of strangers, of criminals, of victims, of people who are so desperate and hopeless that they have nowhere else to turn; the one exposing raw wounds on live television every week. Leah couldn't possibly think of the people they had on the show as trash. Trash was rubbish. Trash was to be got rid of. Trash was stuff nobody wanted or had a use for any more. However grim or unscrupulous or morally askew the families were that they lined up on stage, each had a story to tell and somehow, after Carrie had got their stories out, one or two of them made it with the help of the show's aftercare team. As far as Leah was concerned, that made it all worthwhile.

The roads were clear. Leah drove out of Hampstead and headed west. Remnants of a ferocious Saturday night littered the streets – bottles, takeaway cartons, cans, an occasional group of lads leaning on railings, smoking, one or two girls in short skirts and heels stepping out of an unknown boy's flat into the bright morning light of Sunday.

'Thanks, Leah. For sticking with me.' Carrie touched Leah's hand as it pulled through the gears. 'Not just now, but you know, forever.'

Leah glanced across. She hardly recognised the woman she had known since university. 'You'll get through this. Not yet. But in time, you will.'

After they'd parked at the police station, as they were walking up to the entrance, Leah's heart clenched as she saw Carrie mouthing the word progress over and over. As on *Reality Check*, all anyone ever wanted was a bit of hope.

Brody never usually tripped, but he stumbled up the steps to the police station and Fiona had no chance of catching him. He went down, his hands splaying out for unseen ground, his head hitting the sharp edge of concrete. Fiona squealed and lunged at him, turning his head as he lay there, on his side, so that she could see what damage had been done.

'Oh God, you're bleeding.' She reached into her bag and pulled out a packet of tissues. 'Don't move. I'm so sorry, Brody. I wasn't thinking—'

'It's not your fault that I can't fucking see anything.'

Fiona frowned. 'But it's my job to keep you out of trouble.'

'No. It's your job to get me out of it.'

Fiona kept quiet. The cut was jagged and lined with grit. She pondered what he'd said in the short time it took to dab the wound. 'I'm sorry,' she repeated.

'I wasn't . . . looking where I was going.' Brody's voice was deadly serious, his words slow and measured. Fiona dabbed at his red-streaked temple. They both knew he wasn't just talking about the fall.

'I think it needs water. Antiseptic.' She tugged on Brody's arm, a signal that he should stand. He grimaced and rubbed his knees.

'I'm getting old,' he remarked, groaning and straightening his back. At forty-six, Fiona didn't think he looked old. She wished she could hold a mirror for him to see his face – the way his eyes stared straight ahead no matter what he was doing. She sometimes watched his mouth as he worked – his lips curling and thinning with concentration – and her own eyes widened as she shocked herself by wondering who had kissed them last.

'Wait,' she said, folding another clean tissue. 'Hold this here.' She wanted to take all his pain away. She knew she couldn't.

Inside the station they were taken to an interview room. Coffee was brought in and set on the large round table. There was a plate of biscuits. As if they would want to eat, Fiona thought.

'It's grim in here.' Brody refused to sit but rather paced the square room while they waited for DCI Masters.

And your flat's not? Fiona thought to herself. She knew he'd have an impression of the room just by the click of his heels and the residual stink of overnight antiseptic sloshed around by cleaners. 'It's depressing.' She went up to him. Blood was seeping through the tissue, but he had refused further help. 'Want to sit down? There's coffee.'

'Nope.' Brody was drawn to the window. There were bars across it. 'They bring criminals in here,' he commented. 'To question them.' He'd got the place to a T.

'I think so, yes.'

Suddenly, Brody turned. His teeth flashed at Fiona, although not through a smile. 'We're the criminals,' he said. 'Carrie and I, for letting this happen.' He reached out, as if to grab her shoulders, but stopped. Before she could reply, the door opened and they weren't alone.

'It's Carrie and another woman. There are two detectives,' Fiona whispered to Brody. She guided him up to the group but he shrugged her away.

'What happened to you?' Carrie squinted at Brody's face and pulled out a chair opposite him. He didn't reply. Carrie's friend, the woman introduced as Leah, sat beside her. No one spoke until DCI Masters broke the silence.

'It's been a long forty-eight hours. Gruelling and ghastly for all concerned, but we're making progress.'

Carrie suddenly sat upright. Her head tilted in anticipation and her fingers were clasped tightly together on the table, Fiona noticed. She was nothing like she was on the television. Her poise, confidence, aggression – it was all gone. Carrie Kent was a brittle shell, devoid of colour or life. Fiona was intrigued by just what kind of woman Brody had once been attracted to.

'CCTV footage from the streets surrounding the school has been analysed and some promising images sent away for further enhancement. A group of youths was tracked leaving the area at around the time of the stabbing.'

No mention of Max's name, Fiona noticed, just *the stabbing* as if the incident itself had become an entity. She glanced at Brody. He stared straight ahead. He'd removed the tissue from his wound, which had thankfully stopped bleeding. White bits of lint were stuck to his skin.

'Who? What group of youths?' Carrie said with a waver in her voice.

'Five of them, Carrie. They were on camera running away from the school area, although we can't be sure they were ever on school property unless we can get a positive ID from the witness. Unfortunately at the time of the stabbing, the school's security system was down. There's no money to fix it.' Dennis sighed – exasperated, apologetic, resigned. 'We're tracing some clothing and, when the enhanced images come back, we'll show them to the witness.'

'The witness . . .' Carrie stiffened. Fiona noticed Brody's shoulders pull back.

'Yes. As you know, there was a witness at the scene. A girl.' Masters was scant with his words. 'On top of that, we're searching the area for the murder weapon. The autopsy report will be with me by the end of the day. Forensics have a number of leads to report on, hopefully by—'

'A girl?' Brody stood, knocking the table and sloshing the coffee as he did so. 'What's her name?' Fiona's eyes flicked across the detectives' faces. For Brody's sake, she had to remember everything.

The other detective spoke. 'We've been taking statements from a young female witness. She was at the scene and we believe holds key information. However, she's in a fragile state and we have to be careful not to push her too far.'

'Fragile?' Carrie was also on her feet. She circuited the table to stand beside Brody. Fiona felt a line of sweat break along her top lip. She could see how they'd been a couple, both striking in their own broken way. What they would have looked like once, strong, together, a family with Max, momentarily took Fiona's breath away.

'Sometimes witnesses can suffer a kind of post-traumatic stress,' Dennis continued. 'They block out what they've seen, especially children and adolescents. It's a protection mechanism. The girl is reacting beyond her control. She saw a catastrophic event. Life-changing. Some people aren't equipped to deal with the consequences and their brains shut off everything as if it never happened. But we'll get her to talk.'

Carrie's cheeks burnt red. 'That's all very well but—'

His hands came down on her shoulders. 'I've dealt with this kind of thing before. She needs time. If necessary, I'll get a child psychologist to work with her.'

Fiona's eyes flicked between Brody, Carrie and the detective. 'What's the witness's name?' she asked, probing on Brody's behalf.

Dennis frowned. 'I'm sorry. I can't tell you that.'

Carrie loomed in front of him. She was close to tears. Her eyes begged him for details – anything to keep the hope alive. She was shaking, waiting for a snippet of information to show her that things were progressing.

'Her name's Dayna,' Dennis said reluctantly. 'But I can't tell you any more than that.'

THE PAST

Each knew what the other was thinking. They held back smiles – knowing flickers of understanding that only they would pick up on – and they turned to face the altar.

'Do you, Caroline Elizabeth Kent, take Brody Nathan Quinell to be your lawfully wedded husband, to have and to hold from this day . . .'

They'd done it at rehearsal; God knows she'd read it to herself a thousand times in her bedroom, gleaning every last drop of meaning from the words she was now hearing in the chapel. But what did it all really mean? She looked up at Brody. His eyes sparkled and occasionally he gave a small nod. Carrie thought that his collar looked too tight round his neck.

For better for worse, for richer for poorer, in sickness and in health . . .

The man who would be her husband in just a few minutes listened intently to the chaplain as he recited the service. He would have delivered these words a hundred times before; they would hear them just the once. It was a contract, she knew that much. A promise that whatever life threw at them, they would suffer it together. They would ride the storm side by side and, without wanting to be too maudlin on her wedding day, Carrie also knew that it was an exciting agreement to share and delight in each other's minds and bodies for ever. It was nineteen ninety-three and for ever seemed a long way off.

A peal of anticipation spiralled through her as she longed for the reception to be over with so they could be tucked away in the honeymoon cottage.

Till death do you part . . .

There was a void so huge it filled her entire soul, sent a line of inexplicable fear from her head to her feet, to the earth. It cut straight through her heart. She was suddenly freezing in the simple white dress she'd chosen.

'Caroline?' The chaplain's voice was filled with warmth and calm.

She thawed and smiled. 'I do,' she said sincerely, recognising her cue. And she meant what she said as she stared into Brody's eyes – dark eyes that bound their world together. How she loved waking up next to him, watching his lids flicker through beautiful dreams. Brody was a secret man, an intelligent man, a man who spent his life dreaming, whether asleep or awake. He was ambitious yet careless with the consequences. Carrie adored this about him – the myriad surprises his creative genius brought home.

Brody Nathan Quinell, do you take . . .

How they danced. Neither of them had much in the way of family present, even though Brody had a plethora of cousins and uncles and aunts still living back home in Jamaica.

His parents had come to England when he was a baby and done well for themselves as market traders. They'd owned their own home in a respectable neighbourhood, had many friends, built up a solid fruit and vegetable business, and worked hard all their lives. It saddened Brody greatly that they weren't with him to celebrate his marriage to Carrie. He wanted a bond with her like his parents had shared, even to the very end. They'd died within a week of each other – his father falling down at the stall one morning, succumbing to a massive heart attack. His mother had also suffered from heart problems, her friends said afterwards. A broken one.

Brody pulled Carrie close. They were the stars of the show, the spotlight on them as they swirled alone around the spangled dance floor. He loved her tiny waist, her strong legs turned him on more than he could stand, and her arms wrapped around his neck while her painted nails toyed gently with his tight collar. It made him want to lose his clothes right there and then.

'I love you,' he growled against her ear. In response, Carrie nipped his lips with her teeth. Their friends, all clustered round the edge of the dance floor, laughed and clapped for them. Weddings were like that – they reminded everyone about precious relationships, whether it be with a partner, a child, a parent. It was a day full with emotion, with hope, and an insight to the future.

A happy future. On days like today, everyone believed the best.

There was a buffet and Brody grudgingly made chit-chat to people he didn't know, mostly Carrie's work colleagues. He piled his plate with sea bass and mango salsa, feta tarts topped with roasted figs, and chicken baked with lemons and rice. He ate and smiled and made comments and watched his new wife skirt around the hall that she'd had decorated with white lilies because his mother was called, he'd told her on many occasions, Lily-Mae.

'The house needs work,' Brody said to the tenth person at least who asked him about their new investment. 'But we'll get there.' What he really wanted to say was he didn't care if the house was a rundown mess for the rest of their lives, as long as he could live in it with Carrie.

He manoeuvred his way to her side. 'You're so beautiful,' he said. He plucked a prawn off the plate she'd been holding for the last hour and yet hadn't taken a bite of the food. Brody popped it in her mouth. 'Eat. You're going to need all your energy.'

Carrie's eyebrows rose and her eyes widened. She poked him in the ribs but said nothing. She didn't need to. Everything was all set, their stage perfectly prepared. Fine, so ask him a year ago and he wouldn't have guessed at any of this, but even Brody Quinell had a heart to be played with.

'How's the work going, mate?'

He turned reluctantly. From the corner of his eye he noticed Carrie slip away into the celebrating hordes of their friends once more. The sleek lines of her simple dress left a white flash burnt on the back of his eyes.

'Got it all added up yet?'

'Nick. Good to see you.' The men exchanged hearty slaps on their backs.

'Congratulations. She's beautiful.'

Brody nodded. 'Didn't expect all this, to be honest.'

'You surprised us all.' Nick handed Brody a drink. 'For the groom,' he said. 'So where are you working now?'

'I'm still at the university. I'll probably die there. You?'

'Same old same old. Still chugging it out with aerospace. The pay's good, though, and I might just be following you down the aisle soon.'

The men stared at each other for a moment, wondering what it all meant, trying to fathom – even though they knew it was impossible – how things could change in what seemed like only days since they were undergraduates together.

'Doesn't add up at all really, does it, eh?' Nick laughed too loudly.

'Never heard that before.' Brody pulled a face and raised his glass. They drank silently together. The days when he and Nick shared a poky flat during their years of study seemed long gone. This was real life now.

'What does she do?' Nick trailed Carrie with his eyes as she swept between her guests, being the perfect bride and hostess even though Brody knew she just wanted it to be over, for them to be alone.

He felt a tinge of jealousy; healthy, he told himself. 'She's a journalist.' He didn't want to expand, even though he could have gone on for hours about how good she was at her job, how she cared about researching her stories almost as much as she cared for him. That she was making a name for herself with the local BBC news team and how she hoped, one day, to work in television.

'Nice,' Nick said. 'Well, take it easy then. I'd better go and speak to . . .' And he trailed off, raising his pint at a woman across the room who had clearly caught his eye. Brody didn't think Nick knew her but reckoned he would by the end of the night.

'You too.' And Brody retreated to the edge of the flower-festooned hall to lean against the wall. He looked at his watch. It wasn't long until his life began.

Carrie wasn't sure who caught her bouquet. She couldn't, in all honesty, remember much about her special day, as everyone kept calling it. It was all over so quickly, yet would fill the rest of her life. She meshed her fingers with Brody's as they left the reception for the Cotswold cottage they'd taken for a few days. Brody had work commitments and couldn't spare any more time off. Besides, a lavish, overseas honeymoon was out of the question financially, what with the house they'd just bought and all the work that needed doing.

The stone cottage just outside Chipping Norton was owned by one of Brody's colleagues at the university. 'It's so peaceful here.' Carrie stood at the leaded window and stared out at the dark fields beyond. She swept the curtains closed. 'But I think I'd miss city life.'

'Bob comes here most weekends. No doubt brings a pretty young student along with him too.'

'Brody, that's a terrible thing to say on our wedding night. Is that what you plan on doing when I'm old and grey? Have fun with one of your bright young things? Give them a bit of personal coaching?' Carrie was laughing as she slipped off the grey cardigan she'd worn over a new silk blouse and black trousers when they left the hotel reception.

'I don't even need to answer that.'

Carrie shivered as Brody's large hands deftly undid each of the tiny buttons down the front of her blouse. The fabric shimmied from her shoulders as he released her bra clasp, causing her to catch her breath as the cool air fanned over her skin. They moved closer to the log fire that Brody had lit as soon as they'd arrived. The cottage owner had made sure there were plenty of logs and kindling in the grate, as well as champagne in the fridge.

'We have good friends,' Carrie said. Brody's hands were all over her, his face buried in the mass of hair she'd let down around her neck. He didn't reply, rather let his mouth travel over her skin as if she was someone new entirely just because they'd got married.

Later, wrapped in blankets beside the fire, sipping the champagne and hungrily eating the boxed canapés that had been delivered earlier that day from Oxford, Carrie rested her head on Brody's shoulder.

'It's for ever, all this, you know,' she said. She chewed and sipped, utterly contented. 'You, me, the house, the kids, the dog, the holidays. Nothing bad will ever happen to take that away, right?'

Brody looked down at her. He kissed her forehead. 'I'll make sure of it.'

AUTUMN 2008

Dayna had overheard the other girls talking about who they'd had loads of times. It was what they talked about between lessons, if they bothered to go – the number of lads they'd scored with, how they'd had to take the morning-after pill, how much they did or didn't remember because of how pissed they'd been, if they'd caught anything, how big he was, or how small, and if they'd gone down on him.

None of their talk was driven by love – not true love, anyway, Dayna thought. Immunity to such emotion had pretty much swept through everyone in her generation, and she believed that probably included her. Or so she'd thought. They'd all been brought up tough, because of the way things were in the world, because of the way they lived, because of their families – or lack of – as well as their prospects. They lived life in line with that, surviving one day to the next. At least that's what it was like round her estate, anyway. Neither Dayna nor any of the other kids had knowledge of anywhere else, anything better.

'What you staring at, ugly?' It was break time. The girl was tall with straightened hair ending in cropped strands of white-blond.

Dayna shrugged. 'You.' She didn't care if she pissed her off. Nothing much mattered, the way she was feeling. She kicked the heels of her boots against the wall she was sitting on. She was hoping to see Max. They needed to talk.

There was a peal of high-pitched laughter. Someone spat. The group of five girls, all looking so similar they could pass as sisters, opened up and circled round her. Dayna swallowed, cursing herself for tensing up, for giving away her fear. What the fuck had she gone and said that for? She knew to keep her head down and hadn't.

'You staring at me?' the tall one said again, eyeing Dayna up and down. 'What are you, a dyke then?' The posse of girls laughed.

'She looks like a dyke,' another said.

'You don't fucking stare at me, right? I don't want your filthy dyke eyes on my body, yeah?' The girl lit a cigarette. Her nails were pink and sparkly, quite unlike Dayna's bitten-down stumps. 'Speak, dyke.' She crossed her arms and jutted out one hip. Dayna would never look like any of these girls. She would always be different.

'I'm not a dyke,' she said so quietly she wondered if it had even come out. She wanted to hang her head in shame, accept her torture, then be allowed free. But a bigger part of her wanted to kick and punch and bite and rip and tear the life from the girl standing in front of her.

'Speak up. We can't hear you.' The girls moved in closer.

'Which one of us you got the hots for then, eh?' More laughter, more cigarettes, someone's mobile phone beeped from a text, one chewed gum, another swished back her hair.

Dayna shrugged. She felt a surge of adrenalin inside her chest, then the short, sharp breaths as the fear took hold. She stared at her feet, knowing that in a minute, two minutes, an hour, the rest of her life, it would all be over. She thought of Lorrell, knowing she had all this to come. What could she tell her? How could she make sure her little sister didn't live through this shit every single day?

'I said, you emo lezzie, which one of us do you wanna snog?'

Dayna lifted her eyes. She shuddered, trying to keep control of herself. It was the tall blonde one again. The ringleader. The one she'd inadvertently been staring at, thinking about Max and the kiss they'd shared. Nothing to do with the girl.

'Maybe it's all of us,' another girl said.

'I don't like any of you,' Dayna found herself saying. 'I think you're all disgusting.' She held her breath, hoping it would prevent a full-blown display of panic. She saw their eyes all widen in unison, their mouths drop in shock.

'Fuckin' get her!'

Dayna leapt off the wall and ran for the school gates. Unlike the other girls, she was wearing flat boots, allowing her to charge off at a speed the others couldn't match. The adrenalin made her fast.

'Come back, bitch!' Dayna heard as she charged from the school. 'We'll get you!' She ran on and on, across the disused car lot, across the scrub ground and down towards the stream where she'd shared the picnic with Max. At the water's edge, she stopped, panting, leaning forward with her hands pressing just above her knees.

Dayna sobbed. Tears of anger burnt tracks down her sweaty cheeks. She hated them all. Why couldn't they leave her alone? She'd done nothing to them. She bent down and picked up a rock, hurling it into the water so it clattered on to an old shopping trolley. She imagined pushing the blonde girl's head deep into the sludge at the bottom of the polluted stream, watching as the bubbles and her thrashing limbs slowly subsided. More than anything else in the world, she wanted to hurt someone – anyone – to get it all out; to leach the pain that had built up inside for so long.

She decided not to go back to school, but rather to go on to Max's hut. She knew he wouldn't be there, but she could sit and wait. She might even text him if she had any credit left. It was English this afternoon and she'd been looking forward to getting her essays back. Those girls, they changed everything in her life. From the route she took through the school to get to lessons – careful she didn't go down corridors where she could be headed off and surrounded – to whether she ate in the canteen or skulked behind the science labs with a spliff and a Coke. They governed every breath, every blink, every heartbeat.

A train rattled the air in her lungs as it sped over the bridge. Dayna wondered how the little hut had stood up so long, given all the vibrations directly above it. She went up to the door and twisted the padlock. It came away in her hand. She backed off slightly, scared of who or what might be in there. She thought Max was in school. There was a noise coming from inside. Had she disturbed burglars, someone nicking all Max's stuff?

She was about to replace the padlock when the door flung open.

Someone was there, brandishing a knife.

Dayna screamed and raised her fists. Then she let them fall limp as she registered who it was. 'What the hell . . .' She could hardly speak. She was shaking. She picked up the padlock that had fallen from her hands. 'I thought you were at school,' she said angrily.

'I was.' Max lowered the knife. He turned to go back into the hut.

'Oi, wait.' Dayna grabbed his shoulder and pulled him round. 'You've been crying.'

Max shrugged. 'So what.' He squirmed away from her hand and went back inside. Dayna followed.

'What's been going on?' She virtually pushed him down on to the car seat, beside which sat a half-smoked joint and a can of ale. She lit the smoke and passed it to Max. She took a swig of the beer and winced. 'Tell me.'

Max stared into her eyes. She could hardly stand it.

*

Max's heart took fifteen minutes to stop racing. He'd tried not to show how scared he'd been when he heard someone outside the hut, but Dayna noticed everything. Adrenalin had set light to his fingertips and his hands shook as he took the joint back from her. How had she known he was in there? Had word got round that quickly?

'Please tell me,' Dayna said again.

Out of all of them, Max knew she would understand, but after what had happened at the park – their kiss – how could he risk blowing it with the only girl he'd ever truly liked? There'd been a couple of others at his last school, but none like Dayna. Anyway, they were part of the reason he left. It had all been a set-up, a hoax, a big prank to ridicule him. The staff had turned a blind eye, almost as if they condoned such obnoxious behaviour between pupils, as if, until you'd been mercilessly bullied, picked on, spat at, beaten up, belittled, mocked and robbed, you just weren't part of the Denningham community.

Max turned away from Dayna. He retched, but nothing came up. He could still taste it. 'Really, it's nothing. Just having a bad day, that's all.' He remembered saying the same words to his tutor at Denningham. Shrugging off all the shit as if he'd just tripped over or broken the lead of his pencil. 'What's up with you, anyway? You look as if you've been running,' he said, trying to change the subject.

Dayna's eyes went wide and she sighed. 'Yeah. Running from them bitches.' She sneered as if she didn't care. Max knew she did.

'What did they do?'

'Usual. They came after me but I'm faster.' She laughed in her chesty way. She pulled the smoke from his fingers and took a draw. He liked it when she gave it back and it was faintly damp, just a hint of Dayna. 'But I want to know what upset you. You act all tough when I know you're not.'

241

For some reason, Max's entire childhood condensed into the next few moments, probably, he thought, because of what she'd said. *I know you're not.* It was all muddled and crazy in his head, but he clearly saw – no, *felt* – that gang in the shower at Denningham, the boot in his temple as his cash card was swiped from him, the five-year-old who pulled the chair away as he was about to sit down and the peals of laughter from the other kids in the kindergarten, the way his parents were always too busy to listen, the taste of his school dinner after the pot of salt that had been tipped in, the broken ankle from when he was shoved down the stairs, the stolen property – calculators, books, his wallet, his lunch money, his phone, the watch his dad had given him – the teachers that called him names and cuffed him round the ear, the jibes and comments everywhere he went, the way no one had wanted to be his partner in class, ever.

'Max?'

He felt Dayna's finger on his cheek. She was wiping away a tear.

'What is it? Tell me.'

'Just tired of everything. You know how it is.' He grinned and swigged the ale. Even that didn't get rid of the taste of piss.

SUNDAY, 26 APRIL 2009

DCI Masters didn't recognise the pain inside his chest as anything but indigestion after Carrie had left the station with Leah. Max's father and his assistant had gone first, leaving him and Marsh to placate the most implacable woman in the country. In a flash, his working relationship with Carrie Kent had dissolved into a mess of cop versus victim – ghastly at the best of times. This, however, was the worst of times. A boy had lost his life. The son of a famous person. A person with whom his department had formed close links. The television coverage that Carrie gave the Met at least once a month, with a police crime special aired every three, was invaluable in terms of leads and arrests. Plus, if he was honest, he enjoyed the glamour of the studio. In the past, working with Carrie had been known to have its benefits.

'It's fucking awful,' Alan Marsh said as Carrie's waif-like form was escorted away by Leah.

Masters stared at the detective. He spoke abruptly. 'It's a disaster for the borough. We need an arrest.' He placed his hand on his chest. Not indigestion, he realised as he went to his office to fetch his keys, rather something akin to regret.

'I need to speak to your daughter again, Mrs Ray.' It was habit to flash his ID. The woman ignored it.

'Hasn't she said enough?' She flung the door wide – an invitation, Dennis supposed, to come in. 'Day-na,' she screamed.

'That cop's here again.' She pointed to the living room where a man was sprawled on the sofa. A dog was splayed across his legs. There was nowhere else to sit. Before he could speak, he heard the girl behind him.

'Hello,' she said, almost sounding pleased to see him.

Dennis offered a broad yet sensitive smile. 'Dayna,' he said, nodding. 'I'd like to talk to you again, if that's OK.' He glanced at the man, who was showing no signs of moving. 'How do you fancy going for a walk?'

She shrugged. 'Sure.'

Dennis watched her struggle into a jacket that was clearly too small for her and wondered if the black eyeliner around her eyes was actually tattooed in place. He noticed how she kindly yet firmly resisted when her younger sister begged to come along. 'Grown-up talk, Lorrell,' she said, stroking the child's hair.

Now, walking along the pavement, heading east through the estate, Dennis could see the sadness and pain stitched into her face. The make-up – black and harsh, making her look tougher than he suspected she really was; her hair, again black, cropped on top but reaching down to below her shoulders in angry choppy strands of black and burnt orange. Her nails were short and grubby, the fingertips stained yellow from smoking.

'Want one?' Dennis always kept a pack in his pocket. He didn't smoke himself, but most of the people he dealt with did.

'Ta.'

Dennis clicked the lighter at her mouth. 'I know it's the last thing you want to talk about, love, but we need to get things straight while they're still fresh in your mind.'

Dayna nodded and sucked on the cigarette. 'Yeah.' She looked up at Dennis, one hand pushed deep inside her jacket pocket, the other at her mouth.

'You are the only witness we have. Max needs your help. It's your chance to do one final thing for him.' He could see the girl

244

was thinking about this, the way her eyes narrowed. She sniffed.

'Yeah, all right. What do you want to know?'

'Start just before you met up with Max on Friday.'

'I'd been to get chips.' She paused, as if she might get told off. 'I was bunking off. I hate science because those girls are in my group.'

'Where did you get the chips from?' They walked slowly.

'The chippy down from school. Everyone goes there.'

'And after you'd bought the chips?'

'I went back to school. I was going to eat them on the wall. Thought I'd wait for Max. He didn't like science either.'

Dennis was thankful that Dayna seemed more willing to talk. Twenty-four hours could make a huge difference. 'So did you sit on the wall?'

'Yeah. Kids smoke there all the time. No one really gives a shit.'

'How long did you have to wait until Max arrived?'

Dayna thought. 'Maybe ten minutes or so. I hadn't eaten all the chips.'

'Did he sit right next to you?' Dennis watched as the girl ground the butt beneath her boot. He wouldn't offer another just yet. She knew he had them; she could wait.

'Yeah.'

'How did he seem? Was he troubled? I've heard that he was a bit . . . well, different.'

Immediately, Dayna let out a throaty hoot of disgusted laughter. 'A bit *what*?'

They walked in silence for a few minutes, Dennis annoyed with himself for having touched so obvious a raw nerve.

'You just don't get it, do you?' Dayna finally said.

'What?'

'How it all works? The gangs and stuff. The other kids and what it's like if you *are* different.'

'One day you can enlighten me. For now, I just want to talk about Friday. Get things straight. So you sat on the wall, ate chips, and then what?'

Dayna let out a huge sigh. She thought carefully, swallowed, then spoke. 'Then they came. Like from nowhere.'

'Who came, love?' Dennis fully intended on taking her down to the station after this. He knew she would never speak freely there, but once it was out, the truth purged, it would be easier to get it down in a statement.

'The gang. Eight, nine, ten of them. All, like, suddenly having a go at Max.' Dayna stared at the pavement, concentrating on each of her footfalls as she spoke.

'That must have been scary.' Dennis thought of the CCTV. Only five youths.

'It was.'

'What were they doing or saying?'

Dayna seemed to clam up. 'I dunno. Like making comments and stuff.'

'Why?'

She stopped and turned. 'It was only fucking Friday that he died. I've hardly cried yet.' Her hands flapped about. She was distraught.

'Here.' Dennis rationed out another cigarette.

'It was the same old shit. They wanted his money. His phone. They tormented us.'

'Did Max give up the stuff?'

Dayna faltered, then spoke. 'Not this time. That's why . . .' She let out a hiccup and a puff of smoke. 'That's why it ended like it did. They say you should just hand it over, right?'

Dennis nodded. 'So Max refused to give them his phone.' He tried to picture it all. 'And were you two still sitting on the wall?'

'God, no,' she said. 'They'd knocked the chips from my hand and dragged us off. I got grazes on my legs.'

Dennis recalled the crime scene. He knew the wall she was referring to. It was ten feet at least from where Max was stabbed. The chips were bloodied, lying right beside the body.

'They dragged you both off?'

'Yeah, a couple of them did,' Dayna said. She paused and frowned. 'Max by the arms and me by the hair.' She was nodding vigorously.

He gave a cursory glance at Dayna's head but he wouldn't know if there'd been trauma. He would check the autopsy report for bruising to the boy's arms.

'Then they surrounded us. One of them groped my bum. I was shaking. I was so scared.'

'It must have been horrible.' No more questions. Just let her talk.

'Then suddenly there was a knife. They said they'd heard Max liked a fight, that we were going to get it. It was one of those switchblades or butterfly knives. It came from nowhere, like one of those magic tricks.' She took two drags of the cigarette in quick succession then stopped. 'I never thought they'd use it though. They were, like, always just threatening us and stuff.'

'So you knew them?' Dennis had wanted her to keep going, but this had to be asked. 'They'd threatened you before?'

She shrugged. 'Yeah, but I don't know their names.'

'Were they from your school?'

'Maybe. Don't reckon they go to school now. Dunno.'

'But you could identify them if you had to?'

Dayna shrugged again. She looked pained. 'They had their hoods up. All pulled tight round their faces.'

Dennis nodded. That's what he'd seen on the CCTV.

'Do you remember what their clothes were like?' They were walking slowly again. He was following Dayna's lead.

'Usual stuff. Tracksuit bottoms. Really white trainers. Hoodies. One had stripes on the sleeve, I think.'

Again, Dennis thought of the CCTV. When they were back at the station, he would show her some pictures. It was going to be a long evening, but he was sure of one thing. Dayna Ray wasn't going home without making a statement and giving them a damn good description of who stabbed Max.

She was freezing, even though it wasn't actually that cold. Her mother had been furious she couldn't look after Lorrell that night while she and Kev went down the pub.

'We always fucking go,' she'd screamed at the cop when he'd told her he was taking Dayna to the station and did she want to accompany her daughter. 'What am I s'posed to do with her?' She pointed at Lorrell, who was rolling about on top of the dog. 'I can't leave her.'

But Dayna knew that's exactly what she would do. She felt desperately worried and sad for her little sister, but the cop had said no when Dayna had asked if she could bring her along. 'It's serious,' he'd told her. 'We need you to focus.'

Dennis told her to call him by his first name and she felt a tingle of importance. It was good to have something blur the sadness for a while. Before she'd left, Kev and her mother were arguing about money and there was the bang of a pan as another horrid meal was slopped from a can. She was glad to be out of it. Especially with missing Max as if someone had butchered a piece of her heart. She reckoned being sad at the police station would be better than being sad at home. No one there cared, whereas these cops had probably given her more attention in the last twenty-four hours than she'd ever got from her mother.

'What's that?' she asked when they were on the way to the police station.

'The radio,' Dennis replied. 'So I can talk to all the other detectives.'

'No Radio One then?' She trailed a finger over it. Max would

248

have thought this was exciting; riding in an undercover cop car when you hadn't done anything wrong. She'd never been arrested, but plenty of kids at school bragged of nights in cells for being drunk on the street and fighting or busted for drugs. It made them big.

On the way, Dayna thought about what she was going to say. Dennis had already told her she would have to tell him and some other detectives the whole story again while he wrote it down. They'd make a recording, too, he'd said, so they didn't get anything wrong. Her fists balled and her fingers grew numb and sweaty. A voice crackled through the radio and Dennis answered, but she didn't understand what they were saying. Was she going mad because of it all, she wondered, as the bloodied body of the only person who had ever understood her swallowed up her thoughts?

'I can't believe he's dead,' she said quietly. At first, she thought Dennis hadn't heard because he was silent.

'Neither can I,' was his eventual reply.

Dayna was left in the care of a woman who, when they arrived, appeared stern, uninterested and cold. But she quickly softened when she spoke to Dayna. Masters disappeared with two other detectives and called out that he'd be back shortly.

'I'm Jess Britton,' the woman said. She put her hands on Dayna's shoulders. Her breath smelt of tea. Her hair was dark and cropped. 'I'm a detective like Dennis. Come with me and we'll get you a hot chocolate if that machine's working.'

'Thanks.' Dayna followed her. What she really wanted was a fag. They were the same height, she noticed, glancing sideways. She wondered if Jess had a gun tucked on her somewhere, but couldn't see where. She was wearing a white blouse and slim-leg black trousers. Not a cop uniform exactly but it made her look tough, slightly manly, even though she was pretty.

They stopped along a corridor – grey lino floor, shiny grey walls half-height with dirty cream above – and Jess stuffed two coins into the drinks machine. Everything smelt of disinfectant, like at school on a Monday. Jess kicked the machine and out came a plastic cup of frothy chocolate that Dayna could hardly stand to hold it was so hot. She found it in her to smile in place of a thank-you. Being in the bowels of the police station had wilted what little strength she had left. How she would survive the next few hours, she didn't know. What was it Dennis had said? *It'll be gruelling, but you'll get through it.*

What, she wondered, was *it*?

'In here, love,' Jess said, holding open a door to a room that was bigger than the entire downstairs of her house. 'Have a seat. The others'll be along soon. We're just going to go over, you know, what happened.'

Dayna didn't reply. She simply stared at the slim woman with her radio clipped to her belt and gold chain glinting at her elegant neck. She was, Dayna reckoned, like what she wanted to be when she grew up. She might not be clever enough to be a cop or a nurse or an air stewardess, but from when she was Lorrell's age, she'd hoped to be a strong woman, a confident woman, a career woman – a person that others would look at and think: *I want to be like her.*

Thing is, they'd beaten it out of her.

'Can I have a fag?'

Jess went to the window and opened it. 'Lean out then.'

Dayna stood stupidly in the middle of the room and slapped her hands down her sides. 'I haven't got any.' She pulled a face.

There was a desk against the wall and Jess rummaged through the drawers. Eventually she pulled out a packet of Lamberts.

'Catch.' She tossed over some matches too.

Dayna lit up and leant as far out of the window as she could, thankful they were on the ground floor.

The cops were going to ask her about Friday, that was all. She just had to tell them what happened and then she'd be able to go. The police would handle the rest, right? Everything would be fine. Except that Max would still be dead and her life would be shit again without him. She started to weep, but Jess didn't see.

Stop it, stupid, she mumbled with the fag shaking between her lips.

Tell them what happened. Tell them the story.

Was it really so hard to do? Didn't she want to see those bastards locked up for good? Max would want them sent down. Serve them right for everything.

'Come on, love.' There was a hand on her back. Dayna sucked the last of the smoke and tossed the butt out on to the grass. 'Time to begin.'

Jess sat her at the table in the centre of the room. Dennis came in with two other men. She recognised one of them from when he was at her house.

'See you're enjoying a cup of our finest sludge then?' Dennis said. No one laughed.

'It's all right.' Dayna had thought it was really nice, actually. Too hot still, but it was a bit of comfort other than the fags.

'We're going to make a recording of this interview, Dayna, and we'll be writing down your statement, too.' Dennis glanced at the others.

'Yeah. Whatever.'

'It's going to sound as if we're going over and over the same stuff, love, but we're at such a crucial stage of the investigation, we don't want to mess up.'

Dayna didn't want things messed up. Not any more than they already were. She couldn't stand it that Max had suffered everything for nothing. Had he lived his life a victim just for it to fizzle out and them lot get off scot-free? This was way more than bullying. Bullying, Dayna knew, was something that schools had to harp on about and have written policies for. It was something that parents talked about in the primary school playground but then closed their eyes to at high school. Bullying was a bit of a nuisance if your kid came home with a ripped sweater or complaining that they'd lost their lunch money again. Bullying was a chat with the headmaster, a promise it was just a phase, being sorted.

In all of it, they'd done nothing wrong, her and Max. Just chatted, smoked, snogged, been friends and . . . and stuff.

'I'll help in any way I can,' she said loudly. The detectives looked up from their papers. 'I want you to catch them. I will help you.' She sipped her chocolate; for brown sludge, it tasted mighty good.

Carrie couldn't go home. It wasn't a place for her any more. There was Max's stuff to face – the food he'd shoved in the refrigerator that she moaned about and chucked out, his toothbrush in the bathroom, his coat and spare trainers lying in the hall, and his bike in the garage. Martha would have to deal with it. She could see no time in any of her bleak future when she would feel strong enough to take care of these things. It wasn't just that he was dead – hell, she'd dealt with enough bereaved families to know that a tiny semblance of normal life eventually returns. Eventually. No, it was more that he *shouldn't* have been dead, that if she or Brody had paid more attention, had noticed even the tiniest clue about their son and who he was mixing with, the kind of life he was living, he would still be alive. She felt sure of it. They'd both been utterly blind and she couldn't stand it.

'Take me back to that girl's estate. I want to see her again.'

'Carrie, I don't think—'

'Fine. Then I'll drive myself.'

'That's not a good—'

'Leah.' Carrie's voice bit out. 'Do you remember when we were at university and my father died?'

Leah gripped the wheel tightly as they stop-started through traffic. 'Yes. You were a mess after the funeral. Trying to act as if you didn't care.'

'And I didn't even love my father.'

'You had issues.' Leah edged the car forward. 'I helped you come to terms with a few things.'

'Yes, you did.' Suddenly Carrie was sitting sideways, facing Leah, speaking urgently as if she had everything to live for. 'You sat through the long nights with me, talking, going over and over my childhood, trying to help me figure out exactly what it was I'd done wrong, why my father went out of his way to pretend I didn't exist.' She reached out and touched her hand. 'Then you took me back to the places we'd lived, arranged to go inside the old army accommodation. Hell, do you remember when we went to that caravan park in Wales so I could face everything, work it all out? It was all about knowing what I'd done wrong.'

'But Carrie,' Leah said, braking. 'You hadn't done anything wrong. You know that. You accept that now.'

A year of therapy had seen to it that some kind of conclusion and peace had been reached inside a head scratched out by her father's nit-picking nails. And Leah had helped more than she could know.

'Yes, yes, exactly. But don't you see? This is the same, Leah. Except this time I *have* done something wrong.' Leah shook her head. Carrie continued. 'And if I don't get to the bottom of it, I think I will give up and die myself.'

Carrie knew that Leah didn't completely understand but she wisely decided not to argue. In the end, she agreed it wouldn't do any harm to drive through the estate and see if they could spot the girl or find her house. It took a while to get there, even though the journey through the depressing streets was only a mile or two.

'Look at them,' Carrie said, breathless, as if it was the first time she'd ever witnessed unsavoury-looking youth. She had them on her show most weeks. 'Really look at them.'

'They're just kids, Carrie. Just people like you and me but with less luck in their lives. It's not their fault.'

Carrie was agitated by what Leah said. It was the first glimmer of emotion other than grief that she had experienced since she'd learnt of Max's death. 'It's not bloody luck, Leah. How can you say that?' She knew she'd said that line many times on the show, last time to some hopeless woman who was moaning about the five kids she'd had by different men, beginning when she was fifteen.

'It's not down to luck to keep your legs together, is it?' she'd shot back when the mother had said women like Carrie were plain lucky. 'And it's not luck's fault either that you didn't turn up at school most days. Neither is luck to answer for you neglecting your children or not bothering to leave your house to find a job, however menial, to pay your way in the world. What is lucky, though,' and Carrie almost regretted saying this, 'is that I won't have to think about you and your drug-dealing partner once you've left the studio. You, darling, will. For the rest of your life.'

The audience had stood and both booed and clapped and, when they reacted this way as they had on many occasions, Carrie was often unsure who the boos were directed at – her for being so hard on the studio guests, or the guests for living such hopeless lives. Either way, she didn't care. Her skin was rhinoceros-thick. A wired audience meant similar viewers at home and that's what kept the show going. It was all in a day's work.

'It was around here.' Carrie's voice was barely audible. Every syllable hurt as if she had tonsillitis. Every little sound battered her ears, and every painful breath slowed her heart more. 'We found her over there, up there by that tree.'

Leah cruised past but there was no one in sight apart from a group of very young kids playing with a crisp packet and a stick.

'Do you know which house she lives in?'

Carrie shook her head.

'We could ask those kids,' Leah suggested. 'They shouldn't be out on their own.' She wound down the window. 'They're so young and it's getting dark. Hey!' she called out. 'Do any of you know where a girl called Dayna lives?'

Four pairs of sullen eyes stared back at the car. There were three boys and one girl, anywhere between the ages of three and six. The girl, who was holding the stick, brandished it at the car and, for a moment, Leah thought she was going to scratch it down the side of the Mercedes.

Carrie leant across. 'A girl called Dayna lives around here. I'll give you fifty pounds if you can take me to her house.'

The girl stepped forward. 'I know it.' Her voice was babyish and her cherry-red lips curled innocently round the words.

'Hop in the back,' Carrie called out.

'Carrie, we can't!' Leah was horrified when the little girl actually heaved open the big car door and scrambled on to the leather seat. She brought the stick with her.

'Which way?' Carrie asked, leaning round. The girl pointed straight ahead and prodded the roof. Then she squealed with delight as she saw her friends racing alongside the car on their bikes. 'Do we keep going? Do you know a number or an address?' She didn't think the child understood.

'Over vere,' she suddenly said.

'Dayna lives there?' Carrie asked, pointing at a house, and the girl nodded, leaning right forward between the two front seats so

255

that Carrie could smell her sickly sweet breath from the grubby chew she was clutching.

Leah parked. 'Are you going to go in?' she asked incredulously.

'Of course.' She turned to the back to thank the child and give her the money, but she was already getting out of the car. They'd only come a hundred yards or so from where they'd picked her up. 'Am I going in alone?'

Leah sighed. 'No, of course not, although I don't know what you expect to achieve.'

Carrie got out of the car without replying. The little girl had disappeared, clearly not old enough to understand bribes. Resting on the front wall of the house were what appeared to be several bunches of flowers. Carrie pulled back the paper on one of them and gasped.

'Oh God,' she said. 'Oh no, look.'

Leah locked the car and joined Carrie. 'What is it?' She peered inside the paper wrapping. When she saw that all the heads had been cut off and it was just a bunch of stems, she put her arm around Carrie. 'It's nothing to do with Max. You're hypersensitive at the moment.'

'*You next*,' Carrie said, reading the note stuck to the paper. 'What do they mean?' She was underwater, on the moon, dead . . . anywhere except real life.

Leah reached for the other cone of newspaper. When she opened it, nettles and weeds and something revolting spilt out. They had been bound together with soggy toilet paper. It stank. 'Nice,' Leah said, trying to sound casual. She brushed her hands together. 'Amazing what people leave lying around. They're idiots. It'll be kids messing about.'

Carrie closed her eyes. She was about to rip up the note but knew that Dennis would need it. Carefully, she placed it in her bag.

'Carrie, I don't think we should . . .' Leah trailed off. Carrie was already at the front door, knocking, her head bowed.

'Yeah?' The woman was wearing jeans, a T-shirt, and an angry expression. A child appeared beside her legs. It was the girl they'd just picked up in the car.

'Oh, it's you,' Leah said.

'She been bad again?' The woman clipped the child round the head, sending her scuttling back inside. 'What do you want?'

'The stuff on the wall, was it—'

'What fucking stuff?' The woman peered out, squinting through cigarette smoke.

'Do you know who left it?' Carrie asked.

'Course I don't. All sorts of shit gets dumped round here.' She was about to shut the door.

'Wait. Is Dayna home?'

The woman pulled a mean face. 'I reckoned you was the cops. Is it that stabbing again? Anyway, you're too late. They already took her down the station. Been gone a while now.' She made to close the door.

'Who took her?' Carrie asked.

'That Masters cop. He can have her, for all I care. All the stupid girl does is lay about.'

Carrie glanced at Leah, who made a *come on, let's go* gesture with her head. The two women went back to the car with the angry words of Dayna's mother ringing in their ears.

Thank God, Dennis thought, as she spilt out everything she had already told him loud and clear for the others, and the tape recorder, to hear. Away from her home environment, off the street, the young girl suddenly seemed much more mature and sensible, knowing full well what it meant for her to make an accurate statement.

'They weren't going to let up. Not till something bad

happened. Then one of them just had this knife, like, suddenly in his hand.'

'Would you be able to identify the knife if we found it?' Dennis asked.

'Oh yeah, I reckon. It was one of those flick ones. It came out so quick.'

'And so the boy with the knife threatened Max?'

Dayna paused to think. She pulled a face, thinking back. 'Well, kind of. They'd all been jeering and threatening, like I said. Then it got nasty.'

'In what way?'

Dennis watched the girl's features as she recalled the events. He could see the trauma written on her young face. He hated making her relive it – she reminded him a little of Estelle, with her innocent eyes and that wanting-to-please look. He'd grilled his only daughter, too, when he suspected Kaye of playing away; hadn't been proud of the way he'd reduced his daughter to tears to get the truth, not letting up as he pounded her for details of the new man.

'They, like, they started poking and threatening and kicking us really, really hard. We didn't have anywhere to go. Max and I weren't doing anything wrong. Just eating chips and . . . and talking.'

'Was it the boy who first took out the knife who stabbed Max?'

Dayna's expression switched to a poker-faced stare and her eyes hardened to glass.

'Dayna?' Dennis pressed. 'Did you see? Was it him?'

She looked straight at Dennis. 'Yeah.' Her eyes filled with tears as her mind regurgitated what it had blocked out. 'Over and over,' she whispered, gripping the edge of the table. 'The knife went in once and everyone screamed, although not Max.' Dayna stared at the ceiling. 'It went in like butter and came out in slow motion. When . . . when he realised what he'd actually done, it was like, well, he had to keep doing it. There was no way back.'

'And what about Max?'

Dayna shook her head. 'He just stood there for the longest time. His eyes weren't like his eyes, even though they stared at me the whole time like was trying to tell me something. Blood just spurted out.' Dayna released the table and allowed her forehead to drop forward. 'And then he fell to his knees and, finally, he went down.'

'At what point did the gang of boys run away?'

Dayna lifted her heavy head. 'It was after he was on the ground. I screamed out and, like, even those boys were yelling and screaming. Then they ran, when they fucking realised what had happened. Can I have a smoke? I need a cigarette.'

Jess went to the desk to fetch an ashtray. This was no time to break Dayna's flow by making her puff out of the window.

'So as soon as Max went down, the youths ran.'

Dayna nodded and exhaled.

'Which direction did they go?'

'I don't know. School gates, I reckon. I wasn't watching. I was trying to help Max.' She let out sobs that wouldn't resolve into full-blown tears. Instead, she snuffled through the cigarette. 'I felt so useless. Like, he was dying in front of my eyes. I called the ambulance and tried to remember first aid.'

'You did well, love,' Jess said. 'We've interviewed lots of people from your school. While no one else actually saw what happened like you did, one or two claimed to have seen the youths running away. Is it possible, and think carefully about this, that they could have left school a different way?'

Dayna frowned and stared at the ceiling. Dennis glared at Jess. What was she doing? That was as good as telling her they'd had conflicting statements.

'What Jess means is are you sure they went out the front school gates?'

'Yeah, pretty sure.'

'And was the boy who did the stabbing, was he holding the knife when they ran away?' Dennis continued.

'Must have been.' Dayna shrugged as if she wasn't really sure.

'Did they say anything when they left?'

Dayna sniffed and coughed. 'They didn't exactly call out goodbye or anything.'

Dennis felt stupid. It wasn't what he'd meant, of course. 'Anything, Dayna. If you can remember anything at all.'

'One of them screamed twist. *Fucking twist.* I didn't know what he meant.'

'You said they taunted you and kicked you and Max,' Jess continued, making notes.

'Yeah. It was horrid.'

'Where did they kick you?'

'Everywhere. Like on my legs and stuff. My shins.'

'Do you have any bruises?'

Dayna sat still for a moment then shrugged. 'Probably. Dunno.'

'Can we take a look? Is it possible just to push up your trousers?'

Dayna blinked and hesitated.

'It would help,' Jess said.

Dayna bent forward and lifted one trouser leg to the knee. 'It was around here. And on the other leg.'

'Can I see that one too?'

Dayna obliged. As she was bending down to straighten her clothing, Dennis caught Jess's eye. He shook his head, indicating she shouldn't press things.

'I don't see any bruises there,' Jess said.

Dayna picked up the cigarette from the ashtray and clamped

it between her first two fingers. 'My legs still hurt though.'

Dennis shifted in his chair. He could see what Jess was getting at, but at this rate, she was going to do irreparable damage. 'Perhaps it wasn't hard enough to bruise,' he said, trying to diffuse things. She was getting tense, he could tell.

The girl nodded. 'Yeah.'

'But you did say that the youths kicked you,' Jess continued.

Oh, sweet Jesus, Dennis thought. 'Let's just forget about kicking at this point, shall we?' But both Jess and Dayna ignored him.

'Are you saying I'm lying?'

'Not at all. I just want to get it straight. It's important. You said that the youths kicked you really hard. But I can't understand why there are no bruises. Now you're saying it wasn't very hard.'

'I dunno. Maybe it wasn't that hard then. I'm really trying to remember everything properly. Really I am. I want you to catch them. My best friend is dead.' She ground the butt into the ashtray and let her head drop forward.

Nice one, Dennis mouthed at Jess who completely ignored him. She turned to a fresh page on her notepad.

'Let's go back a bit in time, Dayna. I'm interested in knowing who Max's enemies were and, as his best friend, you're probably the one to ask.'

Dayna was laughing before he'd even finished. It was borderline hysteria as she fished in her pocket for a tissue. When she couldn't find one, Jess plucked one from a nearby box and passed it over. 'You lot just don't get it, do you?' She shook her head and blew her nose. 'I mean, no one liked us. We were hated by everyone.'

'You say *us*, Dayna. Do you think you were hated before you knew Max?'

'God, yeah,' she replied. 'The same people hated us both. In fact, it was almost as if poor Max inherited everyone who hated me just by being my friend. He'd not been at the school long. I'd had a few years for everyone to, well, you know . . . know I was different and didn't fit in. A freak.' She spat out the last word in verbal self-harm.

'Why?' asked Jess. 'Why do the other kids pick on you?'

Dayna didn't need time to think of her reply. 'Because I look different. I'm not in a gang and I'm not a chav or an emo or whatever. Everyone likes to label everyone else.'

'So what are you?' Jess asked.

Dayna shrugged. 'I'm just . . . me.' She reddened as fast as she said it.

Dennis cut in. 'Did Max fit into a group? Was he in a gang?'

'God, no. He'd come from this weird school. It was a private one and cost a fortune. I don't think he told many people, but word got out anyway and that was, like, you know, petrol on the fire.' Dayna swallowed. 'He was good at lessons and stuff. He tried to work hard, but it's a zoo, not a school.'

'So would you say he was a loner?' Dennis asked.

She nodded. 'We just wanted to be left alone.'

'What made Max happy, Dayna? What did he like to do for fun?' It was necessary to build a full picture of Max. He couldn't press Carrie for details – he didn't honestly think she was capable of answering. Dayna would have to do for now. Numerous detectives and officers were out in the field, interviewing, scouring, door-knocking, piecing together the events of Friday morning. He and Jess were best placed here for now, with Dayna, unravelling Max's life bit by bit. Something, his inner voice said, didn't add up. He just wasn't sure what yet.

'He liked going down to the . . . he liked doing puzzles and stuff.'

Dennis noted the sudden change of tack, but didn't pounce. 'What kind of puzzles? Sudoku?'

'No. Not puzzles, exactly. More like competitions. He entered things.'

Dennis was surprised. 'Did he win anything?' Another reason for the boy to feel like a loser, he supposed.

Dayna shifted on her chair. She eyed up the packet of cigarettes and Jess pushed them across to her. It was a while before she spoke. 'He never won anything. Maybe a pen once.'

Dennis nodded. Just as he thought. The kid just wanted some escape. 'Was he into music or cars or gaming?'

'Yeah. A bit. He read books, like me, and we went to the cinema sometimes. He cooked me a meal once. Pasta.'

Dennis wrote fast. He stared at the girl. She looked utterly dejected, as if her world had fallen apart, which, even compared to how it usually was, it had. 'What did Max think of the gang culture in the area, Dayna? Was he ever pressured by local gang members to join?'

'There were these kids on his dad's estate. They used to hassle him when he went there. Not to join, but because he was dissing their territory by visiting his dad.'

Dennis rolled his eyes behind closed lids. It was all a mystery to him, yet he lived and breathed it every day. He suddenly had a huge need for Estelle and vowed he would call her later. 'Did they ever hurt him?'

'He had . . .' Dennis could see how much the girl was suffering. Tears pooled in her eyes and she tipped back her head to restrain them. 'He had a computer nicked once. He got beaten up. It was a present for me.'

'A computer for you?'

'Well, you know. Just a cast-off.' Dayna reddened.

It figured, Dennis thought. Carrie would have no doubt thrown it away otherwise. 'Anything else? Did he get gratuitously beaten up? You know, like for no reason.'

'Yeah. It hurt him inside as much as it hurt his body. He suffered a lot.'

Not any more, Dennis thought. Jesus Christ. None of this could move quickly enough. 'Did Max ever carry a knife?' he asked.

It seemed an age before the young girl answered and Dennis wished he could read whatever was flashing at speed behind those dark eyes. 'No,' she whispered, almost as if she was in a trance. 'No, he never did.'

Dayna wanted to run but her legs were paralysed. Someone had put lead in her boots or cut the tendons to her muscles. Her bones ached almost as much as her head and there was no way, after all those fags on the trot, that her lungs would power her at the speed she wanted to flee.

Damn that man. She leant her head on the loo wall. There was a window but it was high and too small to squeeze through. Why did she have to answer all these stupid questions? Over and over the same bloody stuff. Couldn't they just drop it, leave it all alone? Max was dead. End of. None of this shit was going to bring him back.

'Are you OK, love?'

It was that Jess woman again. She'd said she'd wait in the corridor but she must have come in when the toilet had flushed.

'Yeah. Won't be a sec.' She pulled a length of loo roll off and blew her nose hard. Then she did it again. She went out of the cubicle and washed her hands.

'I know it's tough, but we had to do it. We're finished now.'

'Can I go?'

'For now, yes. I'm going to drive you home.'

Adrenalin flooded Dayna's body and powered up her muscles. She walked briskly to the door. 'No need. I can walk. It's not far.'

'Are you . . .'

But Dayna didn't hear the rest of what DI Britton had to say. She was already scooting past the desk sergeant and the latest trouble to be brought in – she thought she recognised the sullen youth as his drug-heavy eyes watched her pass – and she burst out into the spring evening as if she'd been given a second chance; as if she'd been set free.

Set free from what? she asked herself, as she forced her pace to quicken.

Dayna was off to the hut. She should probably pack it all up, give the stuff to charity. The last thing she wanted was the cops picking through the remnants of Max's life. It was none of their business. She pressed her hands to her sides as a stitch gripped her, causing her to stop for a second, lean forward on her knees. There shouldn't be pain, just from walking, should there? She stood upright and noticed the big dark car pulling up beside her.

'Would you like a lift?'

Behind the dark glasses, behind the curtain of grief that hid the woman's features, Dayna saw Carrie Kent through the open car window. She took off her glasses and forked them on her head, exposing eyes that were sunken, puffy and red. Her cheeks were hollow and without make-up and her lips thin and colourless. If she hadn't spoken, even though her voice was a mere breath of its usual television tone, Dayna would not have recognised her.

'Where to?' she whispered. Any louder and she thought the woman might shatter. This was Max's *mother* she was talking to. The pain in her stomach grew worse. A lift anywhere was better than walking feeling like this.

'My house,' she said. 'Leah will drive us.'

Dayna glanced to the driver's seat where another woman sat. It was somehow a soothing proposition, to be cocooned in Max's world, to be taken care of by his mother in the big luxurious car. The shed could wait a while.

'OK,' she said. 'I'll come.' She opened the heavy rear door and got in. The buckle on her boots scratched the cream leather of the seat. The pain in her belly eased a little.

'I went to your house. Your mother told me that you were at the police station,' Carrie said, half facing backwards.

'Yeah,' Dayna said. Her lungs were already burning for another smoke. The fags got her through, minute by minute. 'They wanted to talk to me about what happened.'

'So do I,' Carrie confessed. 'But let's get home first.' She turned round fully and met Dayna's eyes.

Pure sadness, Dayna thought. She saw it in the mirror every day.

The first thing that struck Dayna wasn't the opulence or the expensive gadgetry that allowed them access to the grand house, but that Max hadn't ever mentioned the place or brought her here.

Dayna stared around in disbelief. Her mouth hung open. This was just the garage.

From inside the basement, Carrie pressed a series of remote controls and entered codes on keypads and they climbed up some white internal stairs. They were plastic and shiny and unlike anything Dayna had seen before. Almost white glass, she reckoned, hardly daring to place one boot in front of the other.

'This way,' Carrie said, and Dayna felt a hand gently on her back – the other woman, Leah, whoever she was. Probably a servant or something.

'Bloody hell.' Dayna couldn't help the exclamation as they emerged into a vast white hallway that had another staircase spiralling up one side. Everything was made of white marble and other stone stuff and there was crazy furniture that wasn't the right shape, yet seemed to hold huge vases and a massive display of perfect flowers in the brightest colours. Dayna reckoned they must be fake. 'It's different to my house,' she said.

Carrie smiled vaguely and took off her jacket. She tossed it over the graceful swirl that marked the end of the huge staircase.

'I mean, Max never said anything, you know, about all this.'

'That's why I want to talk to you, Dayna. To find out . . . things. About you and Max. He never mentioned you either, yet I get the impression you were close.'

They were in the kitchen, another homage to minimalism and purity with its glossy cupboards and sleek stone counters. The whole room was immaculate and immediately brought to Dayna's mind the kitchen back home – but only because of the contrast. Their entire house usually smelt of fat from Kev's chips and Dayna knew for sure there was a skim of it on the ceiling. Her gum had got stuck up there once in a silly game with Lorrell and, when she stood on a chair to peel it off, her fingers came away with a layer of green-orange grime. Her mother never bothered with cleaning.

'Max was a good friend.' Dayna suddenly felt giddy and wondered if she should sit down. There were a couple of stools on shiny legs that looked as if they would collapse if she put any weight on them. Instead, she gripped the stone worktop but then let go in case she left marks.

'Were you boyfriend and girlfriend?' Carrie asked. She had taken the lid off a kettle the likes of which Dayna had never seen – theirs was an old whistley thing that sat on the gas. This was like something from a spaceship.

Dayna shrugged. 'I guess.' She thought Carrie let out a little sigh but was unsure if it was from the effort of making tea – Leah had to take over as Carrie found the process too complicated in her state of mind – or because she was disappointed in her son's choice of girlfriend. Dayna already realised that, compared to all this, the way Max lived, his other, secret side, she wasn't a good catch at all. She felt dirty here and wondered if Max had felt the same way. He spent a lot of time at his dad's place and the hut. 'We snogged and that.'

Carrie closed her eyes and Dayna frowned. 'He loved me.'

'Did you love him?'

'Yes,' Dayna replied. 'But . . .' She trailed off, remembering who she was talking to. Just because she wasn't on the telly and she wasn't all dolled up and stomping about with a microphone didn't mean that she wasn't going to save it all up and use it on her show in the future. What had gone on between her and Max was private.

'How did you meet?' Carrie sat on one of the stools and indicated that Dayna should do the same.

'At school. In English class. It was our favourite subject and we were in the same stream.'

'I see.'

Carrie almost seemed surprised at this, Dayna thought, as if she didn't know anything at all about what Max liked. Mind you, she thought again, she doubted that her own mother even knew which school she went to let alone had any idea what lessons she liked. 'We're good at it. *Were* good at it,' she added, having no intention of setting foot inside school again.

'Max went to a decent school once,' the woman continued. 'He should never have left.'

'He'd probably still be dead.' Dayna instantly regretted saying this. 'What I mean is, some things happen anyway.'

'Max always thought he knew best. Even when he was really little.' She half laughed and Dayna thought this was a bit odd. She glanced around for an ashtray, supposing, really, that Carrie Kent would never smoke and she probably shouldn't ask. Everything was so white.

'He brought me nice food,' Dayna said. 'Leftovers and stuff like that.' She had already spotted the tank-like refrigerator set within the cabinets and imagined Max standing there, choosing what to bring in for their feast at the hut or by the stream if it wasn't raining. Smoked salmon, foie gras, hard-boiled duck eggs, fruit that she didn't recognise that was both musty and sweet. They'd tasted and laughed, spat out and gorged, kissed and smoked.

'He could have done anything, you know. Gone to Oxford, Cambridge, studied in the States.'

'Did he want to?' Dayna eyed the clear glass mug that Leah passed to her. It was filled with boiling water and had green leaves floating in it.

'It's not a matter of *wanting* to, is it?'

Dayna didn't think that was much of an answer but admitted that she'd done things she hadn't wanted in her life, so she kind of understood. 'I have to look after my kid sister all the time.' She tried a sip of the drink. It was minty and very hot. 'And I don't always want to do that.'

Carrie directly faced Dayna. The woman's skin was as pale as her surroundings, framed by a frail halo of hair that hadn't been brushed in a while. 'Who did it, Dayna? For God's sake, tell me who killed my son.'

Dayna swallowed and burnt her throat. She stared into the other woman's eyes, feeling like one of her show guests. She understood exactly why they crumbled and spilt their deepest secrets. Even with Carrie Kent a long way from her best, she was still a force hard to ignore. Dayna stared at the floor.

'I don't know,' she said quickly. 'And that's the honest truth. They were kids, like in a gang, and they had their hoods up and it happened so quickly. I just tried to help Max. Maybe I should have done more, but I was—'

'Did it take long?' Carrie asked coldly.

Dayna frowned and found herself caught up in the woman's eyes again.

'To die. Did it take long for Max to die?' she continued.

Dayna saw Max's face as it happened. Yes, she thought, and he knew he was going to die.

'No,' she whispered. Then she was shaking her head. She felt the dizzy waves behind her eyes as the shakes grew stronger, travelling down her neck, her shoulders, her back and arms and legs and everything was trembling and not her own and she thought she was going to throw up from the pain in her guts . . .

Dayna leapt up and ran across the kitchen – straight into the glass partition that separated Carrie's perfect interior from the outside world. She splayed her arms up against the glass, smearing her palms down the barrier while her face pressed against the cold.

She sobbed.

She slid down to the floor.

Then someone was holding her. Cold glass on one side. A warm person on the other.

Max's mother. A part of him.

He was everywhere.

His mother was rocking her, sobbing also.

Together they became one in their grief – Carrie Kent breaching her perfect white existence, and Dayna spilling over from the grim life that she would never escape.

Carrie looked up and swept back a strand of Dayna's hair. 'I loved him, you know. I really did. The tragedy is I don't think he knew.' Her eyes were ringed with red circles. 'I am so glad he'd found someone to love.'

And Dayna couldn't help but add in her head what she knew Carrie was thinking: *even if it was a girl like you.*

She couldn't have done it alone. Somehow, having her there made it more bearable, as if they were just looking for something, or waiting for Max to arrive home from school. Carrie went in first although she wanted nothing more than to shove Dayna inside, slam the door, and hope the girl would deal with the ghosts. She had clearly been close to her son, but the anonymity between herself and Dayna helped – as if she'd hired someone sympathetic to clean up the residue.

She needed to do it but couldn't have faced it alone.

She stepped inside. The girl followed behind, sniffing into her tissue.

The room smelt faintly sweet – a mash of dirty clothes, several plates of half-eaten food and lack of daylight. Carrie flicked on the light and screwed up her eyes – not from the pain of the bright bulb but from how it illuminated everything that was missing from her life; had *always* been missing.

'It's big,' Dayna said. 'And messy,' she added with another sniff that, in better times, might have been a laugh.

'I haven't been in here for . . . for ages,' Carrie said. It was easy to confess this to the girl. She probably wouldn't ever see her again.

'How come?'

'Does your mum come into your room?' Carrie stepped forward tentatively, almost wanting to reach out and take Dayna's hand. A pair of pyjama bottoms lay on the unmade bed, each leg bent in opposing directions. They reminded Carrie of the crime scene at the school, where Max's body had been marked out on the tarmac.

'Yeah. Sometimes.'

Carrie felt herself shoved down another rung of the parental ladder. Even this girl's mother was better than she'd ever been.

'Do you get on well with your mum?'

Dayna laughed. 'No way. She's a cow most of the time.'

Carrie felt both deflated yet somehow exonerated. She wanted to tell the other mother to patch things up, make friends, spend a day together – hell, no, a *year* together – not to waste any more time. All this flew around in her mind as she tried to absorb what her eyes were seeing. Her son's bedroom. She felt overwhelmed. She reached out and gripped Dayna's arm.

'This is so hard,' she admitted. The young girl put her hand on Carrie's. It was some comfort. 'It's not real.' They stood in silence.

'He had a lot of posters,' Dayna finally said. 'And books.' She turned her head sideways and scanned the titles. 'We like . . . liked the same things.' She pulled out a battered copy of *Romeo and Juliet*. 'We were doing this in English.'

'Is that why you were picked on?' Had sending Max to Denningham for all those years made him too smart, just too different for the real world? Although no one, surely, could ever label the dreadful institution that was Milton Park as the 'real world'.

'God, no. No one cared about that.'

'Then what? What was it?' Carrie's voice caved and crumbled. 'Max was a good boy. He didn't get into trouble. He didn't wear weird clothes.'

Dayna hung her head, shaking it slowly. 'He just wasn't like other kids. Neither am I.'

But you're still alive, Carrie thought, fighting off the urge to say it. 'Why?' It was a whisper.

'He just didn't fit in,' she answered. 'It's almost like they're scared of you. They see you as the enemy and fight back, even though we didn't do anything wrong.'

The shock of that admission hit Carrie square in the jaw. 'But—'

'It's gang culture. He was unlucky.'

'Unlucky?' The sharpness of her voice made the girl flinch. Carrie picked up the pyjama bottoms and pressed them to her face. She tried to draw breath through them, to harvest the last remnants of a son she thought she knew. But she was unable to breathe. There was a laundry basket in the corner of the room. She lifted the lid and let the garment fall on top of the other clothes. 'As if I'm ever going to wash them,' she said softly, turning away from Dayna.

There wasn't any point explaining further, Dayna knew that. She felt sorry for the woman, sure, but she felt sorrier for herself. She walked round Max's room looking at his stuff. It was as if he'd left her a legacy, another side of him for her to discover only now, after he'd gone, after it was too late.

'I already miss him,' Dayna said. 'We used to smoke and talk and laugh together.' She saw the look on the woman's face. 'It's all right. Everyone smokes. It's no big thing.'

Carrie Kent's eyes narrowed and Dayna thought she was going to explode out of them. But then there was nothing. Just such a deep sadness which made her want to throw her arms round her – something she didn't ever feel like doing to her own mother. She didn't think she looked very well. 'Why don't you sit down?'

She was standing with her arms slightly lifted away from her sides; a hopeless stance. Her feet were apart and she was swaying, as if she was hearing some distant tune.

'Sit down and look at all this stuff with me. He loved doing these, didn't he?' Dayna grabbed a bunch of papers lying on the floor. Why hadn't he ever brought her here?

'What are they?' Carrie gave in and allowed herself to sit on the bed.

'Magazines. Clippings from newspapers. Flyers and notes off the internet and telly.' Dayna leafed through them and handed over a couple of cut-out forms. 'You know, the competitions.' The magazines sat shiny and cool on her legs.

'What?' Carrie asked vaguely.

'He loved doing competitions. It was like he was addicted or something.'

'I don't know what you're talking about.'

Dayna watched as she leafed through the half-completed entry forms. Max's handwriting was spidery and he'd obviously used a pen that had been about to run out of ink.

'He won loads of stuff . . .' She trailed off, biting her tongue so she didn't say anything else. Another legacy, she thought.

'He won things?'

Dayna imagined the neat stash in Max's shed. He'd won all sorts. He'd told her that he'd had some of it for ages; that he didn't know what to do with it. 'He was just lucky, I guess.'

Dayna watched Max's mum think about it all. A hundred questions jostled on her lips, but she'd never ask her – she was just a kid, a wretch off a council estate that no one liked. What would she know?

A long silence hung between them until it was broken by remorse. 'It was horrid.' Dayna picked her nails. 'I'll never forget the look on his face when it . . . happened.'

'Do you think that makes you special?'

Dayna jolted and cried out as her head was suddenly shaken back. Carrie had her by the shoulders, digging her nails into her.

'Do you think that because you saw him die, that because you were there at the end, he loved you more?'

'No, I—'

'Well, I was there at the start. I was the one who made him and gave birth to him and the one who fretted at night when he wouldn't sleep. I was the one who worked myself to death so he could have the best of everything, I was the one who—'

'Stop!' Dayna yanked away, her eyes wide, her mouth tingling. It was all there again, screaming through her head as if the whole lot had been chucked in a blender. Flashing lights, sirens, kids wailing, the blood, the smell of chips, their white trainers, the jeering and jibing as the gang fled . . .

Before she knew what she was doing, Dayna raised her hand

and slapped Carrie's face. The rage, that liquid anger, was boiling over again. 'It just *happened*,' she screamed. 'There was the knife. It came from nowhere. Then it was over.'

Trembling, she stared at Carrie. One of her cheeks was scarlet.

'You will tell me who killed my son.' Each word was a threat; each syllable a direct hit. Without any of the persuasive skill she used on *Reality Check*, Carrie sent bolts of fear through Dayna. Carrie put her hand against her red cheek. 'You will tell me the truth.'

THE PAST

Carrie didn't think she'd ever felt nervous in her entire life. Unsure, certainly – her father's unpredictable mood had seen to that most of her childhood; apprehensive, of course – she'd taken a risk by ditching her career as a journalist and launching into television; anxious, often – she'd fretted constantly at the responsibility of caring for a son. But nervous – never. Except today. She was interviewing, live on national television, a man whom police suspected had killed his entire family.

They wanted a confession.

It was the end of the decade and *Reality Check* was only in its third month but the series had been green-lit way into the new millennium by executive producers and senior commissioners after only the fourth show. Ratings had already overtaken most other popular programmes aired at the same time and Carrie, a virtually unknown presenter, had become an overnight success. Her face was in all the women's weekly magazines, she'd been interviewed by the tabloids and told her story at either end of the day on breakfast TV and early evening chat shows. She was exhausted. She had a sore throat and her ankle was playing up – new-found fans had pushed and shoved outside the stage door, it was raining, she'd slipped; they'd bayed above her, pressing pens and paper against her, touching her hair and her face. *They don't know me*, was all Carrie could think as her bodyguard parted the crowd in a surge of swinging arms and barging shoulders. He hoisted her to her feet and tucked her inside the car. She had been too shocked to say anything, but on the journey home to her family, her ankle had swelled so that she had to remove her shoe.

'I can't possibly wear those,' Carrie told her stylist an hour before the show. The make-up artist flicked a huge soft brush over her cheeks. He caught her eye by mistake. 'Get me something flat.' It was the first time ever that she'd sounded even vaguely impatient. Carrie woke every single morning and counted her blessings and good fortune at having her show idea explode into such a massive success. She didn't want to blow it all by earning herself a brattish reputation. 'I just can't walk in them, that's all.' She coughed. It hurt deep in her chest.

She pulled off the cream court shoes with their impossibly high black patent heels. They were gorgeous, she admitted, but not what she needed for today's show. Earlier, she'd caught sight of the man she was going to interview – *interview?* Unravel was what Dennis had suggested. Her heart had pounded as she'd walked past the guest make-up room. Through the mirror, he'd stared at her blankly, coldly, a face without life or expression. But then his wife and two daughters had just been burnt alive.

'And I don't like the neckline on this. Isn't there something more flattering? I look like a frumpy school teacher.' Carrie waited as several pairs of hands swiftly undid the buttons on the pale silk blouse. They pulled at the necktie and slipped the garment off her shoulders. A robe was draped round her.

'How about this? Or this? Or this?' The stylist obediently held up half a dozen blouses and tops that would sit perfectly over the pale grey trousers she was wearing. The number of designers who virtually threw their latest clothes at the style department of the show had outstripped any other production that she'd worked on, the experienced woman had told Carrie. 'Makes my job easy,' she'd said. She selected a baby-blue blouse and held the hanger against Carrie's shoulders.

'I hate it,' Carrie said. 'I won't wear it.'

The stylist stepped back and frowned. 'But the colour—'

'Is horrible.' Carrie marched up to the rail that held over a hundred items. They were changed every week. She riffled through, shoving garments sharply to her right one by one with increasing speed. After a minute, she pulled out a black T-shirt. Further down the rail, she knew there was a pair of dark jeans. She'd worn them last week when she'd had to get some air and time away from the studio. She clutched both items against her chest and sighed.

'Pass me those boots. The grey slouch ones.'

The stylist moved in slow motion but did as she was told, staring all the while at Carrie. 'I don't think Leah will—'

'Leah *will*,' Carrie confirmed in a deep voice, nodding and striding into the changing cubicle. She emerged looking as if she was going to the supermarket or to pick up Max from school. The stylist gasped and ran after Carrie with a robe as she strode down the corridor. 'Drop it, Sue. I'm done.' Carrie flung her hands in the air, leaving a warning trail in her wake. Round the corner, alone, she stopped and spread her palms flat against the wall, the other side of which was studio four, home of *Reality Check*.

'Oh God,' she whispered. Her stomach churned and her limbs felt weak. She thought she might be sick. Dennis had told her how important this case was. He'd arrested the man last week but had had to release him without charge. He'd been in Europe on business when his wife and two daughters were shot and then their house set alight. Only dental records and bullet holes through their skulls gave a hint of the incomplete story. Bereft, the man had agreed to come on the show in the hope it might spur someone into giving up valuable information. He wanted the killer caught as much as anyone, he'd said.

But Dennis was still convinced the man was guilty; that

somehow he had orchestrated the death of his own family. They were heavily insured – the sums recently raised – and he was in financial trouble. Appearing on *Reality Check* was a smokescreen on his part no doubt, but it was also, Dennis hoped, the road to confession.

'He'll crack,' Dennis had said as Carrie read through the brief the day before. 'He's unstable. Been living on a knife edge since it happened. When we re-arrest, it's got to be for good. Do what you do best, Carrie. Just talk.'

AUTUMN 2008

Max called out to her as she left. She turned and gave him an expectant look. Did she want the kiss or not?

'What?' She clamped her arms round her body. She was skinny. He wanted to hold her close. Dayna frowned at him.

Maybe she just wanted to go. Had she had enough of him? Did she think their first kiss was revolting and didn't want another? If he just let her go now, it might be for the best. But when would he get another chance? He wasn't sure he could wait.

'Come here, yeah?' He held his breath. She was, what, ten feet away? Might as well have been ten miles. He thought there was the beginnings of a smile. The warmth on his lips leaked into his blood and moved quickly round his body. His fingers tingled.

'Why?' She tipped her head to the side. The smile grew.

Max held out his hands. That wasn't his doing. Something, someone, was pulling his strings. She walked towards him and suddenly her fingers were sitting inside his.

He froze. His mouth went dry. His fingers bent like brittle twigs around the softness of her hands. Something ridiculous came out of his mouth – half bark, half croaky explanation of why, in his heart of hearts, he needed her, desperately wanted her to be by his side, tucked in the crook of his arm. As he stared at her, his ridiculous voice making him break out in a sweat, he thought he might crumble to dust. They were exactly the same yet their lives were worlds apart.

I love you.

Had she heard? Did she understand those three nerve-riddled words? Had he even said them? Perhaps it wasn't his voice at all.

A train sped past on the bridge overhead. Max flinched. Dayna stood perfectly still, her hands set firmly within his. He'd be happy to stay like this for ever.

Then, like a knife through his heart, she was gone. Until it was over, he didn't feel the pain as the bond between their fingers was torn apart. Neither did he immediately register the look she'd given him when he'd said those words – *if* he'd said those words. He barely noticed her legs pedalling frantically over the rough ground as she sped away from the hut. Was that a glance from her – a smile perhaps, delivered coyly over her shoulder – or some subconscious yet cruel part of his brain teasing, trying to make him believe there was still hope?

He watched her clothes flap as she pushed past the bushes and up on to the path that led to higher ground, the route back to school. The pain in his heart spread through his body, as if each chamber had burst. It was hot pain.

He was going to kiss her. She had run away.

Something carried Max back inside the hut. Something gave him the strength to light the stupid scented candle and use the same match to fire up a half-finished joint. The same thing forced him to pick up a newspaper and continue with the entry he'd been working on.

Finish the sentence for your chance to win a pair of eighteen-speed mountain bikes with the latest suspension technology and the looks to kick any rocky road into touch.

One bike each, he reckoned, staring at the picture and trying to replace the image of Dayna running away. They were flash bikes and nothing like the old thing he used to get around London. They could go places, him and Dayna. Load up a couple of packs and get the hell out.

Life is good on a Sherano Rocky Road because . . .

Max chewed his pencil. He smoked the joint. He smudged away the tears. He hadn't a clue how to finish the sentence. Life simply wasn't good. He felt so alone. If he wanted to see his mother it was easier to turn on the television or open a trashy magazine than see her in real life. His father – well, things were better there, but the man was blind to pretty much everything except his job and that stupid genius kid he was always banging on about. Apart from having met Dayna, school sucked worse than when he was at Denningham. Nothing was as terrifying as the Milton Park gangs. The boys at his old school might have made his life a misery day and night, but at Milton there was underground evil – malicious violence wherever he went.

Just what was wrong with him?

. . . because it can't be rockier than the one I'm already on.

MONDAY, 27 APRIL 2009

Carrie woke feeling as if there was suddenly a radiant light waiting for her at the end of the black tunnel that she'd been trapped inside since Friday.

'I know it's the drugs,' she told Leah, who was sitting on her bed, watching her as she woke up.

Leah nodded. 'I made you tea.' She passed the mug to Carrie. 'There was a call,' she said, but Carrie ignored her.

'The last time tea tasted this good was after I gave birth to Max.' The crippling pain that would have gripped her the last few days at the mention of her son's name was finally dulled by medication. She didn't care what she took or how much, but when Leah called the doctor out late last night she'd begged him for help. He handed Leah three prescriptions. He told her to monitor Carrie's intake.

'I had a car take the girl home.'

Carrie nodded. It came back slowly. Dayna . . . Max's bedroom . . . the scent of him . . . the mess of him . . . what Dayna had said – or not said – it was all there, packed into her mind, but none of it was hurting as much.

'I think the girl's in shock too,' Leah continued. 'I tried to talk to her, but she was virtually silent. I can't help feeling she knows something.'

'Of course she does.' Carrie surprised even herself by the normality of her tone. 'Do you remember that guy who wiped his family out years ago?' Carrie propped herself up on the pillows. Leah was nodding. 'I was so bloody nervous about the interview.'

'But you nailed him.' Leah picked up the remote and lifted the blackout blinds. Sun exploded into the room.

'I just remember thinking, *he knows what happened. Get him to tell you.*'

Silence as the two women sipped their tea and recalled the show. Carrie's hands trembled as she brought the mug to her lips. 'I'm nervous as hell again,' she whispered over the rim. 'For the first time in as long as I can remember, I feel . . .' she hesitated, trying to identify how she was feeling. 'I feel out of control, Leah. This time last week, everything was just normal. It's not like we're given clues as to what's around the corner. If I'd thought even a tenth of this was going to happen, I'd have . . .' But she couldn't finish. She sipped her tea and burnt her tongue.

'It's called life, Carrie. If I believed in God then I'd say that he wanted us to live it to the full and enjoy every moment as if it were our last. To have no regrets.'

'I didn't do that with Max.' Carrie wanted to cry but there was nothing there. The pain in her heart was reduced to a dull throb. 'I wasn't a good mother, was I?'

'This is not the time to be reprimanding yourself. That won't bring Max back.' Leah handed Carrie her robe. 'Why not take a shower?' Leah hesitated before continuing. 'Look, Carrie. I came up to tell you that Dennis left a message overnight. There's been a development. He wants us down at the station by ten if you can manage it.'

Carrie wondered why Leah hadn't jolted her awake the moment she'd learnt this but in her new, calm state, she realised that Leah had wanted her to sleep, to absorb the drugs, to let a tiny fraction of normal life percolate her body.

'Fine,' she stated. 'I'll get up. But do you know how I did it? Do you remember?' Carrie's eyes swam and she went dizzy when she stood up. She leant against the wall. *A development?*

'Did what?' Leah steadied her.

'How I got that man to confess to killing his family? It turned out he wasn't even in Europe like the police had thought. He'd paid someone else to travel on his passport. A lookalike to con the CCTV at the airport. He stayed behind, shot his wife and kids while they slept. Then he set fire to the house.'

'Insurance scam, wasn't it?'

Carrie nodded, which she instantly regretted as her brain swilled in her skull. 'He had a mistress. He was living a double life.' She put on her robe and tied the belt. In the bathroom doorway, she stopped and turned. 'I became his friend, Leah. In those thirty minutes, I was the only person in the entire world that he trusted. It was as if the camera crew wasn't there, the audience was off his radar, and he wasn't thinking of the millions of viewers at home. He just couldn't live with the guilt. He couldn't stand to be the only one who knew. He had to tell someone. Me.'

Leah nodded slowly. 'I remember. You were amazing.'

Carrie stiffened. This time it wasn't for fame or glory. It was all about Max. Her face fell serious and her voice dropped back into its businesslike tone. 'I want the girl on the show, Leah.' And she turned, closing the bathroom door.

Brody was reluctant to call Fiona but he had no option. 'It's my job,' she said kindly. He knew that within twenty minutes she'd be pulling into the parking area of the estate. He didn't want her in his flat so he took the familiar route to wait for her.

'Whassup, man?' A couple of youths slammed a ball against a wall, allowing it to ricochet off the bricks from one to the other. A tired-looking woman with a towel round her head strained out of an adjacent window.

'Shut the fuck up wit dat ball. I been working all night long.'

She banged the pane closed and the youths just laughed, continuing with their monotonous game.

'My son,' Brody said. He scuffed the kerb. 'You know him? Well, he's dead.'

The beating of the ball stopped.

'No way, man.' One of the lads caught the ball under his arm and they swaggered up to Brody. They would know his face, Brody was sure of that, and he knew their voices. There were a dozen or so lads that he'd occasionally chatted to since he'd lived here. Gruff, belligerent encounters at first, followed by inquisitiveness that maybe he had some gear, some booze. They weren't bad, exactly. More defensive and out to protect their territory. They didn't like strangers. They didn't know any other way.

'He was stabbed at school.'

Brody heard the pair mumbling together and imagined them shaking their heads, staring at their feet, not knowing what to say.

'I told you that place ain't worth shit. Nowhere's safe these days, man.'

'Yeah. Well.' Brody strained for the sound of Fiona's smooth engine. He hadn't meant to talk about it, but they'd have seen Max hanging around when he visited. It would perhaps make them think.

'I do know your son. He dat skinny boy who don't say much to no one.'

'Probably,' Brody replied. He heard the hum of Fiona's Lexus.

Fiona wound down her window. 'Hey.' Her voice was sweet yet solemn. She got out and guided Brody to the passenger seat.

'He should have said a lot more,' Brody mumbled as he got into the car. Fiona asked what he was talking about. 'Then he might still be alive.'

★

'Get to the point, detective.' He knew Carrie would be on her way. He wanted to hear it before she arrived; avoid the hysteria. Brody sensed they were in the same interview room again. He could smell stale cigarette smoke, recognised the acoustics. Seconds later the door opened and he knew it was her before she even spoke. Was it her perfume? The little gasp she made? The way her bracelets jangled as her arm fell by her side or the sound of her footsteps as she approached the table? Brody tensed. She had that effect on everyone, he imagined, but it was all the more potent and alarming because he couldn't see her.

'What is it?' his ex-wife asked. 'What's happened?'

'Carrie,' Brody said, a little surprised by her unusually calm voice. He heard her pull out a chair, making four around the table. He'd asked Fiona to come in with him; didn't entirely trust himself not to react to whatever was said.

'Brody. What is it?'

Brody said nothing.

'Now that you're both here, I can tell you that one of my officers found a knife at first light this morning. They were scouring the area around the streams on the way down to the railway. It's a dismal, disused stretch of land about a quarter of a mile behind the school. It was wrapped in a plastic bag and hidden in a storm drain.'

'Hell, that's a breakthrough.' Brody needed a glass of water. His throat was dry and his lips cracked.

'We believe it might well be the weapon used in the attack on your son.'

'How do you know?'

Brody frowned at Carrie's monotonous voice. He could almost smell the drugs coursing round her body. He didn't blame her.

'Well, of course we don't know for certain yet. Forensics are running the usual tests. We should know in a few more hours if there's a blood match.'

'Blood?' Brody and Carrie said together.

'The weapon had blood on it, yes.' Dennis sighed and waited, which indicated to Brody that there was more. He was adept at reading the tiniest clues. 'The type of knife wasn't exactly what we were expecting, even given the initial findings in the pathology report. The youths round here tend to stick to one of a few blades, based on our survey of the knife amnesty haul and previous incidents. It usually follows a slight trend as well as what's locally available on the black market.'

'So what kind of knife was it?' Brody said and immediately heard a folder open, some paper being slid across a table. There was silence, followed by a brief gasp from Carrie.

'Oh my God,' she said.

'What the hell is it?' Brody demanded.

'It's a photograph of a kitchen knife,' Dennis said.

'One of *my* kitchen knives,' Carrie whispered.

Brody constructed the image in his mind – no doubt an expensive cook's utensil bought from the finest retailer. Then he added the blood; thick and dark after it had dried, perhaps peeling and cracked around the handle.

'Are you certain?' Dennis asked.

'I can show you the rest of the set if you like. They were specially imported from Japan. The handles are abalone and the blades the best steel available. Each one cost nearly three hundred pounds.'

'Hadn't you noticed one missing?'

'No, I hadn't,' she admitted. 'I don't cook.'

Brody grunted and shook his head. 'What the hell does this mean then?' He stood. His legs were aching. He couldn't sleep properly and when he did finally drift off, his body was contorted from alcohol and grief.

'I've been mulling over the same thing, Professor. Is it possible that Max found it necessary to carry a knife for protection? It's the most common reason. If so, then perhaps someone else, someone from the gang, got their hands on it during a scuffle.'

'Oh no . . . oh Christ.' Carrie's whimper was pitiful. It was pure sadness, dredged up from the core of her soul. 'He was killed with one of *my* knives.'

'We'll have to wait for forensics but it's likely, yes. I will say, however, and I know just how distressing this is for you both, but finding the weapon involved is a huge breakthrough. I am confident further evidence will be brought to light and lead to a quick arrest.'

Brody wasn't really listening any more and he sensed that Carrie probably wasn't either. 'Let us know the minute you have results.' Brody stuck out his arm – an indication for Fiona, who had remained silent throughout, to guide him from the room.

'Wait,' he heard Carrie say, followed by a chair scraping. The meeting was over. There was nothing more to be said. None of it would bring back Max.

The bonnet of the car was still warm and Brody leant back against it, knowing from the quickening footsteps behind that his ex had followed him outside. He lit a cigarette.

'Why would he do that?' Carrie said breathlessly as she approached. 'Take a knife.'

Brody shrugged. He sucked hard. 'Where the hell did it all go wrong, Carrie?' He imagined big plumes of smoke wrapping around her head; the disgusted look on her face.

'Last Friday,' she suggested quietly.

'What have they got you on?'

'I have no idea. Leah is taking care of it for me.'

Brody laughed bitterly. 'So we both need people to take care of us, right?' Fiona was already sealed inside the car, talking on the phone and rearranging his department meetings. Brody tapped the glass.

'I guess,' Carrie replied unexpectedly.

'And how did that happen?' Brody felt the heat of the cigarette approach his fingers. 'Was it when we fell out of love, do you think? When we realised that the world was a desolate place without the other but we were both too proud to admit—'

'Brody, stop!' Silence, then, 'I can't take this right now. Please.'

'As I thought,' he said, dropping the butt. 'The truth hurts.'

'You never could get over me leaving you, could you?'

Brody heard a tiny wave of anger welling in her. That's what he wanted.

'You never accepted that our lives were diverging so fast that . . . that . . .'

Disappointed, Brody listened as she trailed off. He reached out in her direction and found her arms. He gripped them. 'I was working it all out, Carrie. There was going to be a solution to it all but you never gave me a chance. You were the one that went off at a tangent with your career.'

'Life isn't all about mathematics, Brody. You can't work out a formula for love or happiness.'

Brody ignored the comment. He took a deep breath. 'I went back to Denningham last autumn.'

'What? Why?'

'I wanted to find out why Max left.'

'We know why he left. He was rebelling against us. Me.'

'That's not true, Carrie.' Brody could only imagine her face as he last saw it – fresh, honest and beautiful. With one little lift of her brow or pucker of her mouth, she could shift mountains inside him. He hoped she still had that about her. 'I spoke to some of Max's . . . classmates.' He couldn't bring himself to say friends.

'Oh?'

There. That glimmer of hope in her eyes; the tensing of tendons running either side of her neck that only showed up when she was anxious; the way she'd clasp her hands at her chest like a child. He knew it would all still be there. He reached out and felt her again. Her arms hung limply by her side and her shoulders were bent forward. She wasn't anything like the woman he remembered.

'He wasn't happy, Carrie.'

'Yeah. And?'

'I met the acting head. Turns out that Dr Jensen had to take extended sick leave due to stress. The current head teacher wasn't afraid to tell me that the school has had serious problems for the last decade. He'd been sent in to clear up the mess.'

'But Dr Jensen was so . . . nice.'

'But incompetent,' Brody added.

'This doesn't tell us much about Max, Brody, or why he left Denningham.'

'He was desperately unhappy, Carrie. I'm certain he was being bullied.'

'No . . . no, that's not—'

'It was no different for him at Milton Park either. His life was a misery there, too. But no one messes with the street gangs.'

'And you *knew* this?'

Brody lit another cigarette. He would smoke the whole packet in one go, then buy more and more and keep going until his lungs collapsed and he dropped dead. 'Yes,' he said while exhaling. The shame hit him full in the face. 'I knew.'

JANUARY 2009

It was during English that Max realised Dayna had somehow banished the thing that had haunted him all his life; perhaps replaced it. He also realised that it was that *thing* – the unnameable, dreadful force that had overpowered him all his life – that had made him the way he was.

Different.

He didn't like it that Dayna had ended up sitting next to Shane this term. It wasn't as if he could even hate the boy for bullying him. He was one of the few kids in the year that hadn't actually punched him, nicked something from him, or made his life a misery by spitting out soul-destroying comments every time he walked past.

Shane had his arm round the back of Dayna's chair. It was way worse than bullying.

Max couldn't take it any longer. He stood up. 'Need the toilet, sir.'

'Sit down, Quinell,' Mr Lockhart barked. It was unlike him to shout.

New ways for a new term, Max thought defiantly, ignoring the teacher and leaving the classroom. On the way past Shane, he lashed out and swiped his arm off Dayna's chair. He bent down close to Shane's ear. 'Get the fuck off my girlfriend.'

His insides shook as he stood in a cubicle, leaning back against the graffiti-covered wall. Risking a beating by Shane and his mates later was nothing compared to what he had just achieved. He'd just told Dayna, after all these months of skirting around each other, that they were properly together.

'What was all that about then?' Dayna opened the packet of smoked salmon Max had brought from home. She sniffed it.

Neither of them had mentioned the incident as they'd left class and headed down to the boiler room for lunch. It had been too cold to sit by the stream for a while now. Max had once suggested they sneak through the caretaker's store and eat in the warmth of the boiler room. The light bulb had blown on their first visit so they brought candles next time. There were no windows in the basement, but Max liked it that way and thought Dayna did too.

'I dunno.' Max shrugged. He was embarrassed now. He wanted to tell her he loved her. Properly this time, without it getting caught in his throat and her running off. 'It was Shane. He had his arm round you.'

Dayna laughed. 'You said I was your girlfriend.'

'Did I?' he replied far too quickly. His insides curled. Then, 'Maybe you are.'

'I'd like that. We've been friends for a long time, Max. We've kissed. We understand each other.'

'I'd like to kiss you again.' He couldn't believe he was saying this. Where had it come from? Was it because he'd stood up to Shane in English and ignored Mr Lockhart? Was it that being rude and foul-mouthed to people, not giving a toss about their feelings, sapped their confidence and handed it right over? If so, then he suddenly had a glimmer of insight into why everyone picked on him. He unwrapped the crackers and offered one to Dayna.

'There's no one else in the world like you, Max.' Then she laughed as she bit into a biscuit with salmon draped on top.

Max grinned. The sight of her, the sound of her, made his days worth living. Life was truly amazing.

The kiss was tentative at first – him leaning in but then backing off when she didn't respond. It never quite happened. She sipped her Coke and knotted her fingers. The bell would sound soon. He tried again, reaching out to the crook of her leg as it sat bent awkwardly under her other leg. They were sitting on dust sheets they'd found piled up in the corner. Like a bed, Max had thought as they'd spread them out.

He trailed his fingers down to her knee. Her muscles were tensed and her legs slim. She wore thick tights and he was touching her through the weight of her grey school skirt, but still the lines of her body made his mind spin as he imagined her limbs naked, pale and warm, wrapping around him.

He shook his head. She would hear his thoughts.

'I hate this uniform,' Dayna said.

Was that an invitation to take it off? Max wondered. He would never dare. Not in a million years. Their mouths were still a few inches apart. All he had to do was lean forward a little more, close his eyes . . .

'Kiss me,' she said.

Max threw back his shoulders and his eyes widened. What had she gone and said that for? Now he didn't know what to do.

'Not sex, stupid. Just a kiss.'

Max was trembling. He leant towards her again. She had already closed her eyes and was waiting for him. As he got closer, he smelt the Polo she'd just crunched. Her skin was lightly freckled, just a dash on her cheeks. He wanted to touch his lips on each one, working down her neck where the freckles disappeared beneath her school blouse.

'What are you doing?' Dayna suddenly had her eyes open.

Again, Max jolted back. What *had* he been doing?

'Sorry.' His voice was croaky. In an instant, he hated himself again. 'It's just that . . .'

His words were lost in Dayna's mouth as she pressed her lips against his. It was different this time – none of the coyness, wondering if he should or shouldn't. He knew he should, because Dayna was the one who'd started it. There was no doubt in his mind now that she wanted him as much as he wanted her. For weeks – *months* – they had danced around their feelings. They were preoccupied by surviving at school, by just getting through each day without being hurt, tormented or picked on. Max hadn't had the courage to take things further before. This was big. This was enormous.

Dayna's tongue prised apart his lips. God, he'd never felt like this before. She was amazing. Without realising how it had happened, Max somehow felt her shoulders against his palms – he was holding her, *touching* her. Even after their tentative, embarrassing, experimental kisses last year, he'd not had the courage to consider anything like this.

It beat everything, the years of suffering and ridicule and hatred and wishing he was dead. This kiss, this beautiful unending kiss, changed everything. He would suffer his whole life over again for a single moment with her. Max opened up and allowed himself to drown in the bliss. She was in control. She'd said she didn't want sex.

What?

Max turned rigid. What had she meant? He pulled away, leaving Dayna stunned, blushing, her pupils floating in her eyes like shiny buttons.

'What's wrong with me?'

'Max?' Dayna wiped her mouth.

'Why don't you want to have sex with me? What's wrong with me?'

Dayna's face relaxed again and the lips that had so recently been a part of his spread into a wide smile. 'Silly,' she said, hugging on to his arm. 'Just not yet. Not here. It needs to be right, yeah? Somewhere special.'

He didn't get her. He didn't get anything any more. 'So why do you like me?' he asked. 'When no one else does?' He heard the words echo a thousand times round the dingy room. It was no place for this to be happening, yet somehow it was perfect. It matched their lives, their inevitable union.

'Because,' Dayna said, cupping Max's face in her warm hands. The moment was electric. Max could hardly breathe. 'Because you're different.' She paused. 'And because you're just like me.'

Then she kissed him again. Max thought he had truly died and gone to heaven.

MONDAY, 27 APRIL 2009

'What d'you reckon?' Dennis was on his third coffee in the last hour. He'd spent most of the night pacing around his house – the insalubrious terrace that he'd just been able to afford once he'd paid off Kaye and made sure that Estelle had everything she needed. No one could accuse him of being a bad father, even though he'd not seen his daughter in over a month.

'They're playing us for a laugh, that's what. They get a lot of cred for spending time in a cell. They'll be right up with their mates now, you can be sure of that.'

Dennis wondered how Jess seemed so fresh, clear-skinned and, more annoyingly, clear-minded. If she wasn't newly married, he'd probably try it on. Carrie was way out of bounds, of course, and he couldn't forget her parting words last time he'd spent the night: *this never happened*. It did about as much for his self-esteem as having yet another stabbing on his patch and a series of interviews that, when viewed as a whole, just didn't stack up. Retirement seemed a long way off.

Dennis picked out Samms' and Driscoll's files. They'd been in trouble before, of course. Samms for joyriding and Driscoll for, well, pretty much everything except murder. 'I don't think it's either of them.' He dropped the papers back on the desk. His heart missed a few beats then caught up with itself in a flurry of tiredness and caffeine. 'God, I feel like shit.'

'So sure?'

'We can't be certain that the youths we've got on the CCTV heading to the station were even part of our gang.'

'Doesn't mean that these two weren't involved.'

'All we've got is a stack of statements from some manky school kids. Two of them reckoned they saw Samms and Driscoll hanging about. It's as good as speculation at the end of the day.'

'We can't rule them out. We've got nothing else.'

Dennis smiled as sweetly as he could manage. He was past being nice. 'Get the girl in again. I want her here within the hour.'

'Are you sure that's wise?'

'Nope.' Dennis drained his mug and headed off for the coffee machine again. 'But I can tell you one thing. She's not been telling us the truth.'

'Oh? Rather certain about everything this morning, aren't we?' Jess brought her herbal tea to her lips.

Dennis stopped in the doorway. 'Forensics confirmed earlier that the blood on the kitchen knife was indeed a match for Max's. Pathology also reported that the abdominal wounds were consistent with a fifteen-centimetre, unserrated blade. We've got our weapon.'

'There you go then.'

'There we go what? She was lying. Obviously. She said it was a flick knife.'

Jess shook her head. 'Would you have been cool-headed enough to notice what kind of knife was used? The poor kid watched her boyfriend get stabbed to death.' Her eyes narrowed.

'She knows more than she's letting on. She was there, for God's sake. Is she protecting someone? Is she afraid to speak out?'

'Yeah,' Jess replied. 'Protecting herself from the likes of us. The poor kid's traumatised, grieving for her boyfriend, has a shit life at home and is bullied at school. She was born cagey. I'll get her in again, but we need to be careful.'

'And *you're* telling *me* that?' Dennis grunted and walked off. Remembering a further email report he'd received earlier, he backtracked in time to see Jess giving him the finger. 'By the way, the wounds were consistent with someone shorter than the victim wielding the knife.'

'That would fit either Samms or Driscoll. They're both short-arses.'

'Max was six feet two. He was taller than most. And it went in underarm. Like someone who didn't know what they were doing might use a knife.' Dennis returned the finger to Jess before heading off to the coffee machine.

Dayna Ray said *no comment* to every question that Dennis put to her during the hour and a half interview. This time her mother accompanied her daughter to the station, obviously having heard of the free smokes they dished out. She puffed her way through at least ten cigarettes while telling Dayna not to say a word to *them pigs*. The girl left in tears, her mother dragging her by the arm, clutching the packet of remaining cigarettes. When they'd gone, Dennis turned to Jess, both of them sitting in the cloud of residual smoke.

'Nice lady,' he said, folding his chin on to his hands. He didn't think he'd ever be able to sleep again, he was so tired.

'I thought it was interesting.' Jess Britton didn't get a chance to explain why. A young officer poked her head round the door.

'Message for you, sir.' She handed Dennis a note from the switchboard, nodded and left.

Dennis read it. He handed it to Jess, who raised her eyebrows and blew out in a half whistle. 'What do we do?'

'Let her go to air,' he said. 'If anyone can get the girl to talk, it's Carrie.'

★

'This proves things were once normal.' Still feeling flat, calm, unreal, as if she would soon wake up, Carrie sat on the floor with a photograph album resting on her legs.

'Do you think it's such a good idea, you know, to be looking at those so soon after . . .'

'That's what they're for.' Carrie looked up at Leah. 'I didn't know it at the time, but when I took these pictures, they were really for the day when it would all be gone. If I'd ever once thought, when I was trying to stop Max crying as a baby, or when I moaned because Brody was late home, or when I was bogged down with work . . . if I'd ever once thought that one day it just wouldn't be there . . . that, bam, it would disappear just like that . . .' She exploded her hands in a limp gesture, 'I . . . I . . .'

Nothing. She couldn't say any more.

'Here, take this.' Leah crouched down with two tablets in her palm and a glass of water. 'I'm making some food if you're interested.'

Carrie shook her head. The pills would be enough. She swallowed them and turned the pages of the album. She'd labelled and dated every photograph, arranging the albums in order on the shelf. Brody had mocked her, preferring to keep his pictures in a shoebox under the bed.

'That's the difference between us,' she'd told him once. 'I like to be in control and you don't.' She'd always thought it odd that for a mathematician, Brody thrived on disorder.

'But there's nothing more chaotic than the science of maths. Come to one of my classes,' he'd argued a few months before they married. 'You'll be stunned.'

Carrie had slipped in at the back of the lecture theatre and prepared to learn about 'The Beauty of Mathematics'. She didn't understand a word of what her future husband was telling the thirty-eight bleary-eyed undergraduates during freshers' week, but she knew that he had convinced them all – all except one – that elegance and perfection were abundant within their chosen field.

'But is there any beauty in error?' the girl asked. She stood nervously, but Brody waved her to sit down again. Carrie liked the casual way he interacted with his students.

'Ah,' he said, flapping his arms in appreciation. 'A true mathematician in our midst.' Carrie noticed the girl blush as the other students stared at her. 'Our mistakes, Miss . . .'

'Caldwell,' she replied.

'Our mistakes, Miss Caldwell, are the most beautiful part of mathematics. It is only by making them that we are able, finally, to see the absolute elegance of the truth.'

The girl nodded slowly although a frown formed as she thought. 'So what if there weren't ever any errors?' She chewed her pencil. Carrie thought how young she looked.

'Then, Miss Caldwell, may you ever remain blind to the most dazzling, breathtaking experiences you are ever likely to discover during your time as a human being.'

'You know,' Carrie said to Leah, not realising that she'd been back to the kitchen and brought in a tray of soup and rolls. A glass of water quivered as she placed it on the footstool. 'A short while before he went blind, he went round measuring everything.'

'Brody did?'

Carrie nodded. 'I had no idea why at the time. He used precise instruments, mapping every millimetre of our house and garden, from the distance between chairs to the height of a light switch from the floor to the size of the holes in the colander. When he'd finished doing that, he went outside and did the same thing. He was obsessive, Leah. Only when he was satisfied that he'd got it all mapped out did his sight finally fail him.'

'Oh my God,' Leah said. 'That's weird.'

'Then, finally, when he couldn't see a single thing, he got a team of removals men in to rearrange the entire house.' Carrie eyed the soup and felt sick. 'He said there was beauty in error. That he wanted to discover as much of it as he could by making hundreds of mistakes every single day.'

'That's scary, Carrie.' Leah sat beside her. She picked up the bowl of soup. 'You should eat.'

'I wonder if he sees the beauty in *this*?' Carrie began to tremble as the tablets hit her empty stomach. 'It's his fault,' she whispered. Her teeth clenched together. 'He was too stupid to notice what was going on under his nose.'

'Carrie . . .'

'He said he *knew*, Leah.' Carrie stood but her legs buckled and she found herself dropping on to the sofa. 'Brody told me that he knew Max was being bullied but he didn't do anything about it.' Her voice was quiet yet piercing, each syllable laying blame on her ex-husband. It had to go somewhere. 'Max spent a lot of time with Brody in that shithole he calls a home.' She attempted to stand again. Her voice was an echo of her mounting anger. 'No wonder the poor boy fell in with the wrong crowd. What was Brody thinking, allowing him around there? It's his choice if he wants to live like that but he shouldn't have forced our son to be a part of it.'

'Carrie, calm down . . .'

Her hand suddenly came up beneath the bowl and sent an arc of tomato soup across the room. Leah gasped and reached out to pull Carrie into an embrace but she was shoved away.

'It's his fault,' she screamed. 'Brody killed our son!' She stood and charged from the room. She had to see him, to make him see what he'd done. 'Let's see how beautiful he thinks his mistakes are now.' She grabbed her car keys and pulled on her boots. She opened the front door and was faced with a thousand bright lights flashing before her. She raised a hand to her brow and squinted. They'd finally found out where she lived.

'Oh hell,' she heard Leah say behind her before she heard the barking questions.

'Is it true your son was in a gang, Miss Kent?'

'Is it true he was expelled from boarding school?'

'Was the stabbing because of a grudge against you?'

'How do you feel now that you've been hit by the very issues you've made your fortune from?'

But before Carrie could reply, before any coherent words could form in reply, she dissolved into a puddle on the doorstep.

JANUARY 2009

Dayna's insides were on fire. She wanted to sleep with Max. She'd never done it before. She wondered if he had.

'Most of them were appalling.' Mr Lockhart walked up and down the classroom chucking essays back on their desks. 'Of those that actually bothered to do any work, that is.' He hovered beside Dayna's desk. Again, her stomach swam as he leafed through the tatty pages to reach hers. He pulled it out of the small stack. 'This is your coursework, you bunch of losers. If any of you want to make anything of yourselves, in other words get a job somewhere other than the local burger bar, then you have to start working. That means writing something like this.' Mr Lockhart held up Dayna's essay before fluttering it on to her desk.

'Thank you, sir,' she said quietly. She felt her cheeks heat up as all eyes turned on her. There were a few of the expected comments about how she was a loser, how she must be fucking the teacher, how she'd stolen the essay off the internet. In all honesty, Dayna knew it wasn't that good. Her spelling was bad – she'd only learnt to read and write when she was nine – and her understanding of the play was patchy. But she was determined to get her final piece of coursework in by the deadline. She only wanted to get a couple of GCSEs, just enough to get on a course at college; something to take her away.

'Sad, isn't it?'

Dayna looked up. 'What?' Mr Lockhart hadn't finished with her yet.

'About those kids. You know, all that killing, all that feuding between their families.' He pulled a face and walked to the front of the classroom.

'Er, yeah.' Something hit her on the back of the head. She felt her hair. Chewing gum was stuck fast beneath the clip she had wedged in that morning. She left it there, knowing it would probably have to be cut out in the loos later.

'How does that relate to issues today? Anyone?' Mr Lockhart boomed. No one answered. 'Your next assignment then, if anyone can be bothered, is to discuss the differences between the relationships teenagers have today and the problems faced by Romeo and Juliet. Clear?' Again, no one spoke. Dayna would have loved to ask questions but she wasn't going to risk a bashing.

After she left class, she caught up with Max. 'What did you get?' she asked.

'D,' Max said. He didn't look at her. Instead, he trudged along with the crowds emerging from all the doors into the soulless corridor that led to the canteen.

'Me too,' she replied even though she'd got an A. 'Did you bring any food?'

'Nah. I was at my dad's last night. We ate Pot Noodles.'

'Wanna get chips?'

'Not hungry. See ya.' Max shoved his hands in his pockets and kicked up his pace, knocking into an older boy who lashed out and thumped him on the shoulder.

'Hey, wait. What's up?' Dayna was panting as she matched Max's pace. He'd left the building and stormed out into the freezing air. It took her breath away. 'Why are you angry at me?'

Max spun round. 'Don't you know? Can't you see?'

Dayna thought he looked beautiful, even though tears collected in his large dark eyes. She thought she saw the whole world and all its secrets reflected in them.

'No.' She caught his arm but he yanked it away. A bunch of kids flowed past, knocking into them and shoving them with their packs. One snarled something about sticking it up her.

'That's just it, isn't it?' Max said, staggering to catch his footing.

'Just what?' Dayna was close to tears herself now. After everything they'd shared the last few months, after the time they'd spent chatting and smoking and doing competitions instead of going to science, after all the hours they'd sat by the stream eating and throwing stones at the junk, after the afternoons they'd wandered round the shopping precinct buying sweets and feeling sick from stuffing their faces, she didn't think he had any reason to be like this with her. And they'd kissed.

'Just that we're never going to get to, you know, do it, are we?'

The fire swelled inside her again. He never talked about stuff like this even though she was desperate for them to get closer. Maybe the problem was her.

'I said I wanted to, didn't I?'

'Yeah, but you, like, never show me. I don't know where we stand any more.' Frantically, Max rubbed his hands through his hair. His face couldn't hide the anguish he was feeling. He half turned away, hoisted his pack further on to his back. 'They're right, you know. I'm just a fucking loser.'

Dayna's longing transformed quickly into anger. 'So having me just proves to everyone that you're not a dickhead, is that it? What you gonna do, put pictures up on Facebook?'

'Dayna . . .' Max bowed his head and dug his heel into the crumbling tarmac. 'It's nothing to do with anyone else. I'm, like, really into you but . . . I dunno . . .'

'Now,' Dayna said clearly. The school grounds were virtually empty again apart from half a dozen kids loitering around the gates. 'Let's do it now.'

'What you on about?' Something in Max changed, Dayna

thought, as if she'd flicked a switch inside him. His neck tensed and his cheekbones – she'd always thought they were so pretty – seemed to stand out even more, making him look dangerous, scared even. It was all there, tied up inside her. God, how she adored him. She was going to go for it. Wouldn't she lose him otherwise?

'Let's do it. Now. In the basement.' Maybe the switch had flicked inside her instead, because Dayna found herself pulling Max by the hand and running back towards school. They'd been on their way to science, but none of that mattered any more. Nothing in the world mattered apart from showing Max how much she loved him, even if she couldn't say it. She wouldn't have them become like Romeo and Juliet, torn apart because of other people. If one thing went right in her life, she wanted it to be Max.

'Hurry,' she whispered as they stumbled down the deserted corridor. She knew Max was shocked. 'I want you,' she heard herself saying as they pushed past the cleaning equipment that was always stacked up in the entrance to the basement. She knocked over a bucket, sending echoes through the space that would soon be the venue of her most cherished memories. Even in the dark, she could see the glint in Max's eyes. She trotted backwards, pulling him on by the hand. He swallowed and opened his mouth but nothing came out. 'Don't speak,' she said. 'It's going to be all right.'

Max surveyed the scene although he didn't really take in the litter that still lay strewn across the dust sheets from their last visit. Something smelt bad – probably the scraped-out tub of pâté, plus there was a sticky mess where he'd spilt his Coke the other day.

Were they about to have sex right here, now?

He felt himself being tugged towards the little sanctuary

307

they'd made on the floor. Pathetic really, but it meant the world to him. Since he'd known Dayna, she'd given out signals that were impossible to read. Some days he thought she was teasing him and asking for more and yet other times she was cold and distant. In Dayna, he saw himself. They were both messed up.

'What are you doing?' He sounded ridiculous.

'Max . . .' was all he heard her say. He knelt down when he felt her gently press on his shoulders. The concrete was cold on his knees. Her eyes never left his.

'I don't get you, Dayna Ray.' He wanted to be angry at her, for leading him on, because he knew they wouldn't go all the way. How many times had she cried on his shoulder or fallen asleep in the hut with her head on his lap as he figured out competition slogans?

'You don't need to.' The words floated like dust motes in the semi-darkness. Max felt his bag being lifted from his shoulder. She dumped it next to hers. 'We are boyfriend and girlfriend, aren't we?'

Max wanted to laugh but he kept quiet. He might scare her off. How he was torn between wanting her – she was so dainty and pretty beneath all that black eye make-up – and actually having her.

Would tomorrow feel any different?

'Of course we are,' he said. Was it really going to happen? 'Look, I'm sorry about before. It was those boys earlier.' Max remembered their comments. It didn't even hurt any more.

'You're with me now,' she said. 'Nothing bad's going to happen.'

Max felt something stirring, something he never usually allowed to surface. It was a longing so deep within his soul that it actually hurt his skin as it burst out.

'Dayna . . .' He lifted his hand. He was going to stroke her cheek but she caught his fingers and kissed them. Jesus, he

308

thought. Jesus Christ. This was real. This wasn't some snatched kiss at the park or a rushed snog during their lunch break. This was Dayna making love to him.

Love.

Even if she did nothing more than kiss those fingers, those lucky, lucky fingers on his right hand, he would be satisfied.

He went giddy. When he focused, he watched his hand being drawn down from her lips and on to her breast. The breast that hid behind her white school blouse, teasing him within the lines of the white bra he knew she wore.

But it hardly seemed like his hand any more, not when he felt the shape of her pressed against his palm. Even through the fabric, he could feel how warm and soft she was. They were a perfect fit. He daren't move. She let go of his wrist and his hand stayed there all by itself. Life didn't get much better, he thought, as he suddenly realised that she was staring down at his school trousers.

'It's not what you think,' he said. He hated himself all over again.

'I hope it is.' The confident laugh made Max wonder, briefly, if she had done this before. He didn't want to think about it.

'Well, yeah, it is . . .' He rolled his eyes.

There wasn't really much more talking, not that Max could recall anyway. Dayna reached round his shoulders – her face so close he could feel her breath on his chin – and she tugged his school jacket off. His mobile phone fell out of the inside pocket. Max felt himself sweating despite the cool, damp air of the basement. Should he take something off her in return? He gave an involuntary shudder as she tackled his shirt buttons and his top half was exposed.

'Oh, Max,' he thought he heard her say. She dropped his clothing and stared at his body. He knew he was skinny. Maybe she didn't like him. He'd been trying to put on weight but couldn't. He wanted to look like a man, not a kid. Shit. He should save himself now, get up, grab his stuff and run for it.

Dayna leant forward and left tiny kisses on Max's chest. They went straight to his heart.

Gently, yet leaving him no option but to obey, she guided him down on to the floor. It was cold and hard against his back, but he didn't care. He was shivering now – with both anticipation and fear. He would mess this up, of course he would, but he didn't think there was a way out now; wasn't even sure he wanted one.

Something was happening. In the half light, Max saw Dayna fiddling with his belt, his zipper, his trousers. Did she want him to lift up his hips so she could remove them, or would that make him look like a fool? He wished his first time could have been with someone he didn't care about, to practise.

Max felt the waist of his trousers loosen but then there was nothing. He closed his eyes and when he opened them he saw Dayna, beautiful Dayna, unbuttoning her blouse.

'You don't have to do this,' he remembered saying, but she ignored him. She swept a glance down his body, her eyes clearly showing that she wanted to. It turned Max on no end. He never thought he'd feel this way in real life; thought it was only possible when his mother wasn't home and he'd got a beer or two and some pretty pictures on the internet.

It was like watching a butterfly emerge, he thought, as Dayna's blouse slipped from her shoulders. One cuff got caught on her hand and she struggled to free it, trying to find the buttons. She glanced at him with big eyes, perhaps wondering if he might help, but Max was frozen. He was convinced that if he moved, it would all be over and he would wake up in bed alone.

Finally, Dayna pulled off her blouse. She gave a coy smile. Max's eyes dizzied in and out of focus at the sight of her almost naked top half. His arms stuck up in the air, beckoning her down on to him and she didn't hesitate, pleased at his invitation. A warmth spread over his skin as she melted on to him. Her arms threaded round his neck and he shifted, allowing her to settle.

'Hey . . .' he heard himself saying. She uttered a soft moan in return, busying her lips with his neck and working her way round to his mouth. Then they were kissing, tentative at first but Max quickly sensed her urgency and allowed himself to relax under her small frame. His hands swept across her back, one slightly bent round to her side so it could feel the first rise of her breast still nestled within her bra. He heard the clatter of chairs and footsteps in the classroom above, which made him absolutely terrified that they would get discovered. They'd never survive the aftermath. It would kill them.

'Oh, Max,' Dayna whispered. 'I want you.'

Max felt himself harden more, but it wasn't the same as usual. This time there was need, a desire, a promise at the end.

'You sure?' he asked. His voice was a muffled rasp all tangled up in her hair.

'I've never been more certain about anything,' she replied.

In one swift move, Max had rolled out from beneath Dayna's warm body and was hovering over her, getting rid of the rest of her clothes. With her breasts freed from her bra, he wasted no time in pulling off her tights and knickers. He left her skirt where it was.

He was really going to do it.

Something would go wrong. He thought he might throw up.

Max dropped down on top of Dayna. He didn't have much of a clue what to do or how to do it. He hitched up her skirt. Once he was in place, once Dayna's throaty, pained noises and the clenching of her nails in his back had subsided to tentative moans and scratches rather than gouges, Max found himself totally lost in a place he never thought he'd visit.

Then it was over.

He fell down on top of her, his weight making her gasp. His body had never felt like this before and his mind, for once, had been allowed to forget everything. He reached for his trousers and dug in the pocket. He pulled out the spare key to his hut; to his heart. He gave it to Dayna. 'What's mine is yours,' he said. He knew he was in love.

Dayna walked home by herself that afternoon, but oddly she didn't feel quite so alone. She felt that something, someone, was with her, would always be with her and that gave her comfort as she stepped inside the front door to witness her mother throwing a glass jar across the kitchen. It just missed Kev's head and smashed against the wall, splattering sick-coloured curry sauce everywhere.

'Where you been?' her mother yelled. 'Help me clear up.'

Dayna dumped her pack, not wanting the feeling inside her to wear off. Her feet crunched through broken glass.

Max had made love to her.

She took a dishcloth and wrung it out. They'd had PE after lunch but she'd sat out, claiming she had a tummy ache. Someone had spat on her head. Dayna scooped up as much of the mess on the floor as she could and washed out the cloth. She did this over and over. In fact, she convinced herself that she would happily do it all night long as well as any other jobs her mother threw at her.

Nothing mattered now. She had Max. They'd had sex. She was a woman.

She'd wanted to tell him that she loved him but hadn't quite been able to get the words out.

FEBRUARY 2009

Brody stopped and sniffed. Bleach. He slammed the door closed and let his bag slide off his arm.

'Stop now!' he yelled. 'What do you think you're doing?' He imagined a little Max standing on a stool at the sink, pink rubber gloves up to his elbows, pot scrubber in hand and bubbles flying everywhere. Try as he might, Brody had one hell of a job to see his son as the near grown-up man he was rather than a kid amusing himself with a bowl of warm soapy water.

'It's a shithole again, Dad. You can't live like this.'

'Just watch me.' Brody felt around the worktop for a glass. 'What the hell have you done with all my stuff?'

'Washed it. Put it away.' Max emptied the water and scrubbed the draining board. 'You can't let yourself go, Dad. It's been years.'

Brody refused to listen. 'I'm alive, aren't I? Doing OK.' If he knew where everything had gone, he'd swipe it all on to the floor just to show Max how little he cared about it all. 'Your mother. When we were together, she used to go on about this kind of thing—'

'Mum went on about housework?' Max laughed as he dried his hands. 'I've never seen her do a damn thing around the place. She has Martha and about a hundred cleaners come in each week.'

'I know, son, I know what your mother's like.' Brody sighed and leant against the wall.

'But you haven't seen her in years.'

'Nope.' Brody didn't admit to playing re-runs of Carrie's show on his computer. He'd listen to the same snippets of her voice over and over, remembering how things were, wondering how life had come to this. 'She's not happy, is she?' Brody reached out for his son's face, feeling him flinch as his hands landed first on his cheekbones then his forehead and hair. 'You're a handsome boy, Max. I'm proud of you.'

Max pulled away. 'I . . . I don't know if she's happy. We don't talk much.'

'And are you?' Brody heard the soft rustle of fabric, perhaps his son shrugging.

'What? Happy?'

A question with a question. Brody waited, hoping the silence would bring out what he'd been wanting to talk about for ages.

'Dunno. Yeah, I guess.' Max's voice was flat. It was all Brody had to go on.

'How's that girl of yours?'

'I told you. There isn't a girl.'

'Then all the women you bring back here wear the same perfume.'

'I don't bring *women* back here.' Max slammed a cupboard door.

Brody grabbed his son again. 'Max, why won't you talk to me? Why do I feel there's this huge *thing* between us?'

'It's not you, it's me.' Max stepped out of his father's grasp. He went into the sitting room. Brody followed his footsteps. 'It's just everything that's fucking going on . . . has always been going on . . .'

Brody heard the squeak of his old chair as Max slumped down.

'I'm a freak and everything's a mess and—'

'Did she dump you?'

314

There was silence apart from some kids outside playing on the concrete walkway.

'No.' Max was vehement.

'Is she seeing someone else?'

'Shut up, will you?'

'But it's about the girl, right?' Brody took the further silence as yes. 'You know, your mother used to make me feel like hanging myself most days.'

'Then why did you marry her?'

'Because she was different,' Brody answered flawlessly. It was what he had adored about Carrie from the start, but ultimately what had driven them apart. Carrie had instigated the divorce – irreconcilable differences, she'd said – and Brody hadn't put up a fight. He regretted that now but knew he couldn't struggle against what he couldn't see. Instead, he'd chosen to punish himself by moving to Westmount. That way, he would be reminded of what he'd lost every single day. He knew the shit was out there but he was too blind to see it. It kept his heart cold.

'Is your girl . . . different too?' Brody already knew the answer to this but wanted to hear Max say it.

He didn't. 'Why did you and Mum split up? Was it because she got famous?'

Brody laughed. 'So you think she left the geeky maths prof and his lowly pay cheque for the bright lights of stardom?'

'It's occurred to me.'

'Your mother is and always has been her own woman, Max. She likes to be in control of things and when . . .' Summing it up was hard, but he wanted Max to have some understanding at least. 'And if she ever felt she was losing control, she'd freak and ditch. You know, get rid.'

'So she lost control of you?'

Brody laughed. 'Maybe,' he replied, thinking back to the day his vision finally went, when the light went out. 'My blindness was hard for her too, you know. We were literally living in different worlds.'

Brody tried to see his son, sitting there, thinking, working it all out, but he simply couldn't. 'But I'm not blind to what's going on with you, son, so I suggest you spill all to me over a pizza.' He reckoned that would at least seal another couple of hours together. He was worried that Max hadn't been visiting as much as he used to.

'No thanks, Dad. I have school work.'

Wrong answer, Brody thought. 'We can talk more.'

Brody sensed it building up, felt the crackle in the air. He waited.

'Talk?' Max yelled. Something was kicked. 'Bit late for talking, isn't it?' Max let out a heartbreaking wail and tipped something over – the coffee table, Brody thought. He leapt to his feet and tried to find his son, but he tripped and stumbled backwards. 'Max, don't do this . . .'

There was more smashing and swearing and unintelligible growling. For a second, Brody caught hold of Max's arm and tried to pull him close. He didn't know what else to do. 'Please, Max, be reasonable. Please let's talk. I know there's been shit in your life . . .' Something was hurled across the room. 'I know about those boys—'

'You don't know shit! You're blind and you always have been.'

Footsteps were followed by the door slamming. Max was gone. Brody crunched through the wreckage. He bent down and felt around the floor. He sucked on his finger and tasted blood. Broken glass. He lit a cigarette but couldn't find the ashtray. Reluctantly, Brody opened a window and flicked his ash outside. He closed his eyes. It was the same. Why didn't he just go around with them shut?

TUESDAY, 28 APRIL 2009

Brody called the television station and left a message for Carrie to call him. He didn't have his ex-wife's number to hand. Several times since they'd divorced, he thought he should have phoned her, that they should have been parents together, but every time he'd put it off. Facing Carrie, acknowledging everything that she'd become, how far from their once happy lives together she'd grown, was incredibly hard. They'd failed each other and neither had ever been prepared to admit that. Except perhaps now.

'Hello,' he said into his phone when she rang back. 'Carrie?' He barely recognised her monotonous voice. 'Did the detective call you too?' A pause. She said nothing. 'Did you hear about the knife, that it was the one used to kill Max?'

More silence. Then, 'Brody, will you just come over?' She was crying.

'Of course.' Brody ran through the logistics – how fast he could get Fiona to drive him to Hampstead. 'I can be with you in about half—'

'Not London, Brody. I'll send my driver for you. He will take you to the airport.'

Brody went to airports often, attending conferences all over the world. Fiona was always with him, being his eyes, his carer, getting him through each day with precision. This time, though, he put his trust in Clive, Carrie's pilot, and allowed himself to be led from the car that had picked him up, through London City

Airport security, and out to Carrie's waiting helicopter. It felt oddly good to be out on his own.

'Should be a smooth ride, sir,' the pilot reported. Brody buckled himself in, not caring if it was smooth or if they spun out of the sky and splintered into a million pieces. He heard unfamiliar noises, technical banter between the pilot and the tower, and fifteen minutes later they were in the air.

As they flew, he thought of his son's short life. Sickness overwhelmed him and it wasn't from flying. Had neither he nor Carrie realised what they were doing? Max being flown to Denningham for the start of the school term by chopper . . . Max kicking a ball around graffiti-covered Westmount estate . . . Max spending weekends at Carrie's country house, which he knew would be opulent and lavish . . . Max kipping on the grubby sofa at his place . . . Max attending a thirty-thousand-pound-a-year boarding school . . . Max playing truant from one of the most crime-riddled schools in London . . .

What had they done to their son?

Another car took Brody to Carrie's country estate. He'd brought nothing with him and had no idea when he would return to London. He only knew that he'd been reacting to a thread of need in his ex-wife's voice and nothing – not now – would stop him responding. Fiona hadn't thought travelling without her was a wise idea, *not in your state*, she'd said. But he needed to be alone with Carrie, to reset something inside each of them because he knew, deep down, she would be feeling it too.

Carrie lay on the floor. She'd sent all the staff home or to their living quarters and insisted on not being disturbed. A cashmere throw was draped over her legs as she lay stiffly beside the cold, empty grate, remembering how Max used to repeatedly pull the logs out of the basket and build a house with them on the Persian rug. Was the rest of her life to be filled with fragments of pain?

Every time she turned a corner or opened a door, would she see Max standing there, eyebrows raised, silently asking her, *why?*

She had insisted that Leah stay in London and prepare for Friday's show. 'You're not thinking straight,' was all she'd said before Carrie hung up. No one wanted her to go ahead with the Dayna Ray interview; no one except her realised it wasn't what she wanted to do, rather what she *had* to do.

The old doorbell resounded throughout the downstairs of Charlbury. The dogs barked. There were no footsteps or warm greetings by the staff as Carrie was used to hearing. Slowly, she peeled herself from the floor. The dogs stuck at her ankles as she went through to the hallway, noticing someone had left the morning's mail on the oak table. She unlocked the heavy old door and pulled it open.

Brody was standing there, filling the space, with the driver standing patiently behind him waiting for further orders. 'Thanks, Tony. Take the rest of the day off.' Carrie automatically pulled her lips together which, in better times, would have been a smile and a nod. She turned her attention back to Brody. He looked awful, yet somehow as if he had come to save her. Maybe she wouldn't let him go. Maybe, if she harboured him here at Charlbury, Max would magically reappear as a little boy and they could do the whole thing again and get it right this time.

'Come in,' she said, standing aside. There was a pause and Brody stuck his hand out to his side, found the door and stepped forward, feeling for a step with his foot. 'Sorry, here,' she said, taking his hand. His skin was cool, she noticed. Not like it used to be. Brody had always been warm, a furnace to press against in winter as they lay in bed.

'Thank you.'

No objection, Carrie noted, as Brody allowed himself to be guided through to the snug.

'You have dogs,' he stated.

'Can you smell them?'

'It's their claws on the flagstones,' he said with a small laugh. She wondered how he managed even that.

'I should light the fire,' Carrie said, suddenly realising how freezing the house was. Until Brody arrived, it was almost as if she'd enjoyed the discomfort of being cold.

'Not something I imagined you doing yourself,' Brody commented. Carrie showed him where to sit and he eased down into the large maroon sofa. 'Someone like you surely has servants to do that.'

Carrie winced. 'They're not servants.' She screwed up her eyes. She was reining in annoyance. 'And I'm quite capable of lighting a fire.' She glared at her ex-husband as he tried to get comfortable in the oversized settee. They were perfect for an evening of sprawling, wine, laughter and movies, but not conducive to sitting on to discuss their dead son. In the end, Brody opted for perching on the edge and leaning on his forearms.

'There are plenty of logs.' She threw a pile of kindling on top of a couple of firelighters. The single flame quickly took hold and Carrie carefully placed a couple of dry logs on the stack. Within a few minutes, the grate began to radiate heat. Nothing, Carrie suspected, would warm their hearts.

'You wanted me to come.' Brody's words were accompanied by the crackle of burning logs.

Wanted me to come. Carrie realised that she'd sounded needy. It was a foreign, wrong feeling. 'I thought we should be together. There are things to discuss.'

Brody nodded slightly. She saw him swallow. So much to be said, yet she didn't think any of it would come out.

'Do you think they'll find who did it?' Carrie sat on the matching sofa the other side of the low table. She crossed her ankles.

'What good will it do if they do?'

'It's justice for Max. Someone needs to pay for what happened. Someone needs to go to prison.'

Carrie suddenly turned from freezing to flushed when Brody gave her a look that made her think he could see everything quite clearly. 'We're already there,' he replied.

FEBRUARY 2009

'Because . . . because . . .' She knew what she wanted to say, but it wouldn't come out right. She felt Max's stare on the back of her head. Even though she'd asked to sit at another desk, away from any boys, she could sense the tension between them. They'd not spoken all morning. In fact, she wondered if Max had been avoiding her for the last few days. He wasn't usually like that. Since they'd had sex in the basement, he'd been extra attentive, extra loving, extra thoughtful, as if they really were going out. Now he was suddenly like this and not speaking to her. She didn't know where she stood.

'Because they were in love and nobody understood.' Dayna reddened. It didn't matter because no one was listening or paying attention to her.

'Do you really believe that, Dayna? That the pair of them could really have fallen in love in such a short time? Or was it the fact that they shouldn't have fallen for each other at all, because of their feuding families, that drove them on? You know, being rebellious teenagers and all that.' Mr Lockhart expected a laugh but none of his pupils were listening so he didn't get one.

'Yeah, maybe that. Or maybe it was just because, like, they took one look at each other and that was it. You know, their eyes met and stuff at the ball. Sometimes you can't help it.' Dayna recalled staring at Max when he started at Milton Park. She didn't think he'd noticed her straight away, but she'd noticed him. She felt desperately sad for Romeo and Juliet. She suddenly felt desperately sad for herself and Max. Being in love was impossible.

'I'd like to believe that's true, Dayna. As for you lazy lot . . .' Mr Lockhart banged his book down on the desk. No one looked up. 'You can start planning your essays over the weekend. The final versions are due by the end of term. Two issues to examine. Firstly, the timescale within the play. Does the acceleration have an impact on the plausibility of Romeo and Juliet's love for each other and, secondly, I want you to make notes on how you think fate brought the youngsters together.'

Dayna twisted round in her chair and caught Max's eye. She offered a little smile, but he didn't return it. As she faced the front again, she frowned, let the smile go. What was wrong with him?

She caught up with him in the canteen. 'Hey.'

Max was beating his fingers on the tray, waiting for the dinner lady to catch his eye so he could tell her what he wanted. He turned away, angling his back to her, pretending to be interested in the slop in the metal trays. 'Pie,' he said. 'And chips and gravy.'

Dayna raised her hand and was about to place it on Max's shoulder, hoping a physical connection might get him talking. Something was definitely wrong.

'Ow!' Dayna was shoved hard from behind. She stumbled and her tray fell on the floor. The carton of juice exploded, soaking her ankles.

'Get out the way, emo bitch.'

Stunned but quite used to it, Dayna waited for Max to retaliate or say something or at least help her with the mess on the floor. He did none of these things. Instead, he just shuffled along in the line, allowing the dinner lady to add food to his tray until he finally came to the till to pay. The girl who had shoved Dayna took her place in the queue and sneered down at her as she picked cutlery. Another boy in her year drew up to the girl. He kissed her on the neck.

'Hey, Maxie baby,' the boy yelled out in a high voice, obviously pretending to be Dayna. She froze. The falsetto jibe continued. 'Can I suck your itty-bitty cock, Maxie baby?'

Horrified, Dayna waited for something to happen. She daren't breathe. Max's shoulders stiffened but he didn't turn. A few kids nearby sniggered.

'Oi, fathead, I'm talking to you.' The boy lobbed a bread roll at Max's head and it hit him cleanly. Max spun round.

'What the—'

'I'm talking to you, man.' The boy snarled and shifted his weight from one foot to the other. 'You not got that bint woman of yours under control yet, man? Dint ya hear what they're all saying?'

Max didn't move. Neither did Dayna. The canteen noise went on around them and it was as if they were freeze-frame characters caught up in a ghastly time slip.

What was he on about?

Suddenly, Max exploded into life. He picked up his tray of food and hurled it in the air. It spun round, food and cutlery and a can of Coke flying off and hitting the other kids. The pie landed next to Dayna and Max kicked it at her as he stormed off.

TUESDAY, 28 APRIL 2009

Somehow, Carrie managed to make two cups of tea. Charlbury seemed deserted without the staff but unnervingly more like home with Brody trailing her through the grand rooms. 'Mind the step,' she warned as they left the kitchen. They left the dogs slumped on the floor by the Aga. Their muddy paws overlapped and their snouts breathed wet halos on the tiles following a dash round the garden while the kettle boiled. 'The fire's still going,' she commented as if it was the only thing that mattered.

It had been four days since Max died.

They sat down again. This time Carrie was right beside Brody. She passed him his tea.

'Last autumn, Max left his mobile phone at my flat,' Brody said without prompting.

Carrie thought of the ghastly place where Brody lived. She didn't understand why he lived there but hadn't found it in her to ask. It wasn't as if he couldn't afford anything better. The foul smell that pervaded the whole estate was still thick in her mind – a fitting backdrop for everything else troubling her.

'He was forgetful,' she said. She'd lost count of the number of times she'd sent her driver back to Denningham with items of sports kit or books he'd not remembered to take at the start of term. She hadn't a clue if he'd forgotten to take things to Milton Park. If she was honest – which she couldn't entirely bring herself to be – she'd shown no interest in Max's school life from the day he quit Denningham last summer. 'Well, he used to be. I don't know what he was like at . . . at the new school.'

'Didn't *want* to know, you mean.'

Carrie swallowed. 'It's not like that,' was all she could manage. She wasn't going to confess to being a lousy mother to Brody after all these years apart.

'It was Max's choice to go there, Carrie. I told you, he was unhappy boarding.'

'And he's happy now? What did his new school do for him?' She felt justified finally.

Brody didn't retaliate. 'When Max left his phone at my flat, it started bleeping in the night. It was driving me mad. There was a message.'

Carrie mustered her full attention, which was hard. Concentration had been impossible the last few days.

'His phone's a different model to mine so I didn't know what I was doing exactly. I was tired and just wanted it to shut up.' He sighed heavily. 'I admit, though, that when I heard the voice message start, I listened to it. Or messages, should I say. I just wanted a night's sleep. I had an early start the next day.'

'And?'

'They weren't pleasant.'

'What did they say? Who were they from?'

Brody took a deep breath and let it go. 'From some sick kids. You know the kind of thing. Insults. Put-downs. Threats.'

Carrie was virtually speechless. Was he trying to protect her from the truth? 'No, I don't know. What threats? Why didn't you say something to Dennis?'

As she expected, Brody was suddenly defensive. 'I did. I gave him a description. And the phone number of the last boy to call. There was an option to redial, so I did. When the kid answered, I made out I had the wrong number. I'd woken him up and he was too stupid and groggy to be wary about repeating his number to me when I asked for it. I wrote it down.'

'How did you get a description? For God's sake, Brody, it could be Max's killer.' Carrie felt it welling up inside, despite the medication. The doctor had said the pills would only take the edge off, not wipe out the pain completely.

Brody drank some of his tea. Stalling, Carrie thought. It all came flooding back, how it used to be – the look on his face, the way his brow rose and the grooves formed. They were deeper now, years on, but his jaw still ticked nervously just as it had when he'd finally bothered to tell her he was going blind. 'You can't just ignore stuff like *that*, Brody.'

'I'll tell you. The school phoned me several times about his truanting. Max had given both our details. They'd not been able to contact you, apparently, so they ended up dealing with me about it. Anyway, I approached Max. We also talked about the messages I'd heard on his phone. You can't accuse me of not handling things.'

Carrie held her breath. This was her son. 'Well, what did he say?'

'He played it all down. Made out there was nothing wrong. That the kids who left the messages were mates just mucking about.' Brody stood up and manoeuvred his way to the fire, following the heat source. 'He went totally mad that I'd listened to his voicemail, even when I explained what I was trying to do. He said the truanting was no big deal. That everyone did it.'

'But who were—'

'He mentioned a couple of names. I calmed him down and we got talking, had a beer or two. Eventually, he told me about the café they hung out in. Max hadn't convinced me it was nothing so I took a taxi there several times. It was obviously impossible to figure out anything much by myself. That's when I got Fiona to help me, to see what they were like. I was going to fix everything, you know. Do the good parent thing. I bought a book on how to handle bullying. I thought I could work it out for him.'

Carrie didn't, *couldn't*, say a word. She stared up at her ex-husband. Should she pull him into her arms and allow the warmth to soak back between them or hurl the poker at him? She did neither. She let her mouth drop open. Then she saw that Brody was crying. Just a line of moisture at first, sitting atop his lower lids – it happened to her almost every minute – but then proper tears collected and rolled free. Brody made no attempt to hide them.

Carrie frowned. Her fingers tingled. Her heart raced.

'You bought a book?' She wanted it to sound incredulous but it didn't.

'Fiona read some of it to me. A lot of it made sense.'

'And you went spying on kids? Kids that were threatening Max?' Again, she was flat and factual when she hadn't meant to be. It was building up inside. She wanted to scream.

Brody simply nodded in agreement.

Carrie stood. She saw him flinch as she stamped her way to the fireplace. She began in a whisper. 'Why didn't you do more? Why didn't you call the headmaster? Why didn't you call *me*?' She managed to yell the last word.

'Because,' Brody said coldly, 'you were always too busy. I had no reason to believe things had changed there. Besides, things seemed to settle with Max. He got a girlfriend. I thought he was happy.'

Carrie halted. She felt a pain in her stomach. 'I don't know what to say.'

'There's nothing to say. It's too late to do anything now.'

She allowed herself to drop to the floor at Brody's feet. The rug was warm beneath her. Sensing her movements, Brody did the same.

They sat, silent, Carrie staring at the orange flames curling round the logs. Brody felt the heat flicker against his face. Both of them were freezing and it took a phone call from DCI Masters to temporarily set them free from the current wave of grief.

Dennis called Carrie at her London home first. The housekeeper answered and told him that she'd gone away. He rolled his eyes. When he called her mobile, it went straight to voicemail and, of course, he left a message telling her they'd made an arrest. He couldn't help the grin or the way his hand messed through his hair a thousand times with relief or even help the shot of whisky from the emergency supply as he waited for Max's father to answer. He'd rather tell Carrie directly, of course, but he didn't have the landline at her country house.

'Country bloody house,' he said incredulously. He considered himself lucky to have a box of a town house after what Kaye did to him in the divorce. 'Come on, come on . . .'

The boy had been hauled in earlier that day. 'Ah, bless him,' Jess had said grimly, peering through the viewing glass, watching him sitting there in his stained dressing gown and a pair of work boots.

'Doubt he's ever done a day's work in his life,' Dennis remarked as they went back to his office to discuss the interview.

'If I were his mother I'd . . .' Jess couldn't finish.

'What? Ruffle his hair? I doubt even *you* would produce offspring like that, DI Britton.' Dennis turned away but swung round quickly again. 'Aha,' he said. 'Gotcha.'

Jess wiggled her upright middle finger and pulled a face. 'So. What have we got?' She smiled and pulled down the hem of her skirt as she sat on the edge of the table. She'd caught Dennis looking at her legs. 'In good spirits, are we, sir?'

'You could say that. If we charge him, I'll die a happy man, Jess.' He glanced at her knees. The skirt refused to sit below them, however hard Jess tugged. 'They found a second set of prints on the knife. It took a while. There was a mix-up or something, but the results finally came in.'

'I know that. I can read emails too, you know.'

Dennis paused. 'We've got our man. If you can call him that.'

Jess frowned. She stood up and walked about, smoothing down her skirt.

Dennis continued. He sensed her doubt but refused to acknowledge it. 'Warren Lane's been brought in because of the print match.' No use wishing he'd hauled him in for questioning three days ago.

'I know that too,' she said slowly, still thinking. 'The database virtually overheated when we ran these new prints through. Is there anything our boy hasn't done?'

That was more like it, Dennis thought. 'His hand was on that knife. There must have been a struggle. An argument.' Whatever happened, he had to charge. Whatever happened, he needed a confession.

'. . . Come on, come on, answer . . .'

'Professor Quinell speaking.'

'Professor, it's DCI Masters calling. I have news for you. We've charged a fifteen-year-old youth with the murder of your son.'

It was late. Dennis translated the pause on the line to mean that he'd woken Max's father. That or the man was pissed. He wouldn't blame him if he was.

'Charged?'

'Yes, as in we have enough evidence to present to the Crown Prosecution Service. All being well, he should be in court in the morning. It's good news, Professor, in light of all the bad.'

'It is positive news. Hopeful.'

Dennis wanted to stand on the roof and shout out that they'd got the bastard. 'More than hopeful, I'd say, Professor. You can come to the station if you'd like a full brief. I assume you'll want to be in court tomorrow.'

More hesitation. 'I can't. I'm with Max's mother. In the country.'

Ah, Dennis thought. His mind fast-tracked. Marriages were usually blown apart by tragedy, not the reverse. He didn't like the feeling he got when he imagined Quinell and Carrie reconciling in the country. He'd not had a fair chance with her. But still, that was all outweighed by the arrest.

'She didn't want to be alone,' Quinell added.

'I quite understand. When will you be back?'

'Soon,' was all he said before hanging up.

Earlier, before they charged him, Dennis couldn't help thinking that Warren Lane's face looked as if it had been carved from wood with a blunt knife. That he came across as such a hopeless loser with a long criminal record given his age only served to help Dennis's purpose. He'd been arrested and charged twelve times in his pathetic life so far – Dennis was sure he recognised him – and had been in and out of juvenile detention centres since the age of ten. He was also currently on probation, most magistrates now wise to the fact that he just wanted a roof over his head and free food for as long as possible.

'Perfect,' Dennis said as he gathered the files and a cup of coffee. Jess took in some water.

The duty solicitor was fat, dressed like a man, and sat glum-faced next to the youth. She nodded at both Dennis and Jess when they entered. Warren sat pushed back from the table with his legs apart and his fingers picking at the tatty belt of his dressing gown. Slowly, he stared up at the detectives and then looked down again as if it was all perfectly normal. For him,

Dennis thought, it probably was. He started the tape and recorded the relevant details about the case.

'Do you understand why you've been arrested, Warren?' Dennis waited, but the boy said nothing.

'It's been explained,' the solicitor said. Amber or Saffron, Dennis thought she was called. Something yellow, anyway. Something stupid and inappropriate for the way she looked.

'Let's get started. Where were you on the morning of the twenty-fourth of April two thousand and nine?' He would keep it really simple to start. Then a few hours back in the cell.

Nothing.

'My client wishes to exercise his right to silence.'

Not unexpected, Dennis thought. This was murder, after all, an awfully long hotel stay courtesy of Her Majesty.

'Were you at Milton Park Comprehensive School on that same morning between the hours of ten and eleven in the morning?'

Again, nothing. The solicitor struggled to cross her large legs the other way.

'Did you fatally stab Max Quinell with a kitchen knife?' Dennis removed an image of the bloodied knife from the file and slid it across the table. Warren Lane glanced at it, whether involuntarily or not, and then continued with pulling the threads on his belt.

'Did you make obscene phone calls and send malicious text messages to Max Quinell's mobile phone between October two thousand and eight and March two thousand and nine?'

The youth swallowed and whispered something to his solicitor.

'Warren would like a glass of water, please.'

'Jess?' Dennis nodded at her. She rose and fetched a cup and filled it from the cooler.

'Do you belong to or are you the leader of a gang called Blade Runnerz?'

Silence.

'Do you know Owen Driscoll and Blake Samms?'

'No comment,' Warren Lane finally said. He sounded as if he had something in his throat. Guilt, Dennis thought.

'Did you actively recruit members into the gang? Were Driscoll and Samms your newest members?' Dennis hardly paused for an answer. 'Were you showing off to the younger members by causing a fight with Max Quinell? Were you showing off when you stabbed him?'

Thirty-six hours, Dennis thought, staring at the ceiling. Twelve already used up and here he was lying in bed. He was sweating so took off his pyjama top and flung it across the room. 'Pyjamas,' he said into the silence. 'Bloody pyjamas.' He stared across at the empty space on the other side of the bed. He'd often fantasised about inviting Carrie back, having her stretched out there, wondering what the celebrity magazines would make of that. It wouldn't do much for his career, but he could sell his story, he knew. Carrie knew that too. Probably why she finished things, he thought. Or probably because I'm a git.

Dennis got up and opened the window. He heard a siren in the distance and smelt the exhaust air from the kebab shop extractor fan a few doors down the road. It made him hungry so he dressed in jeans and a polo shirt and stepped out into the street. He fancied some grease and meat in his belly.

The light from Ken's Kebabs spilt out across the damp street. The pavement was lined with cars, double-parked in some places, and the air was warm for an April night. It felt more like June, Dennis thought. There was litter outside the shop despite the bin on the corner. A youth kicked a beer can into the gutter. One of his mates belched as he peeled the paper back further on his kebab.

'Y'all right, gramps?' someone from the gang said as he

stepped into the shop. The others laughed. Dennis stopped and stared at them. Doleful eyes peered out from beneath hoods. They had mean, chiselled faces, not unlike that of Warren Lane, whose expression would no doubt be all the meaner from being banged up in a cell for a few hours. The plan was to go back to the station at around 3 a.m., wake him up, and pummel him with questions all over again. One of the youths spat on the pavement.

Dennis frowned. 'All right, lads.' He went up to the counter and scanned the menu on the wall. He knew it by heart. 'Lamb shish with extra onions and chips please, Ken.' He reached into his back pocket for his wallet. He was aware that several of the youths had come back into the shop. They took Cokes from the fridge. They flanked him as he dug through his wallet for some coins.

'Five pounds thirty to you, Dennis,' Ken said. He wrapped the chips and put the whole lot in a bag. He set it on the counter. The youths closed in on Dennis, watching him as he delved in his wallet. 'Call it a fiver,' Ken finished.

But Dennis never got a chance to reply because the youth to his right suddenly reached deep into his pocket and pulled something out. Dennis swung round, arm already raised to defend. The boy was wide-eyed, probably high on something. Dennis recoiled and his heart thumped. He dropped his wallet and his change spilt everywhere.

'What the—'

'Hey,' the lad said, wiping his nose with the tissue he'd pulled from his pocket. 'Let me help.' He bent down and gathered up some of the coins and handed them back to Dennis. 'I'd better hurry. Me mum'll kill me if I'm late for me curfew.' The youth left a few coins of his own money on the counter and nodded at Dennis.

Stunned, Dennis could hardly speak. 'Thanks,' he finally managed to say. 'Thanks a lot.' The boy had pushed his hood back off his head. His hair stuck up in tufts and Dennis saw that he was about fourteen, slightly younger than Warren Lane.

'Don't stay up too late, gramps,' he rang out with a grin. The youths walked off.

'I'll try not to,' Dennis replied, wanting to laugh but not able to manage it.

He took his bag off the counter and walked slowly out of Ken's Kebabs. There was a small park opposite. He went and sat on a bench to eat. He stared into the bushes and laughed, shaking his head. A bit of lamb fell on to his jeans. He knew he wouldn't be going to bed that night. He would eat, shower and go straight back to the station. He would haul Lane out of the cell just when his breathing was at its deepest. He wanted to get it all over with; to prove, really, that there was some good still left in the world – to find out the difference between Warren Lane and the boy in the kebab shop.

THE PAST

'Aren't they beautiful, darling?' Carrie held Max on her hip, but he soon slid down. At six, he was a big boy and, as much as he loved being held by his mother, she couldn't hold him for very long. Max buried his face in Carrie's coat. 'Ah, honey, don't be scared. Look, they're so pretty. Do you want a sparkler? Brody, do you have the sparklers?' She turned to her husband who was staring at his feet. 'Don't tell me you're scared of the fireworks too,' she said, laughing. It was a good party. She was in high spirits. 'And why don't you bring out another couple of drinks while you're inside fetching sparklers. And one of those marshmallow cake things for Max. He adores them.'

Carrie had wanted to throw a millennium party herself but work commitments had totally undermined that idea. She'd been away the few weeks leading up to Christmas and knew she could never rely on Brody to organise such an event. Besides, their house was hardly up to impressing the kind of guests she was able to invite now that *Reality Check* was taking off. She'd spoken to Brody about moving, upgrading to something more impressive, but he'd shown little interest. In fact, getting him to show interest in anything had been virtually impossible the last few months or so. He seemed so . . . distracted, preoccupied, self-absorbed. Still, Carrie had been too busy with her career to sort everyone else's lives out. She wasn't superwoman.

'Darling. The sparklers?' Why was Brody just standing there?

So she was very grateful that Nancy and Preston – *the* Preston

Sykes off *Newsbox* – had hosted such a grand event and invited everyone who was anyone along, including their families, to their house near High Wycombe.

'Maxie really wants one, Brody.' Max buried his face further into his mother's coat and whimpered. Carrie knew he was tired and cold, but all the other children were enjoying the party and she couldn't understand why he wouldn't too. 'Darling, look!' She pulled Max by the arm and insisted he look up at the black sky. It rained pink and gold and green and blue and barely one bit of the universe was left without a rainbow of sparkles. 'Didn't Preston do a great job with the fireworks?' she said as a producer she knew from another channel walked past with his family.

He nodded at Carrie and indulged in some chit-chat but he was clearly the worse for champagne. They'd already done the countdown into the new millennium, which had been followed by this splendid display.

'And so generous with refreshments,' Carrie said, laughing and raising her glass at the man as he staggered off in search of his wife. 'Oh, for God's sake, Brody, shall I get the damned sparklers myself?' Carrie was reluctant to move from the terrace. They had such a fine view of the park-like grounds and she wanted Max to see the display. 'Do you have to be so bloody morose? It's New Year.'

'OK. OK. I'll fetch the sparklers,' Brody replied. He turned and walked straight into the huge glass door that separated Nancy's drawing room from the terrace.

'And do you have to make such a spectacle of yourself? People will think you're drunk.'

'I'm not drunk.' He turned to his left and felt his way along the glass, squinting every time there was a flash from the sky, until he was swallowed up in the crowd inside.

'They're in the reception hall,' Carrie called out. 'Nancy put out loads of stuff in a basket for the kids.' She turned to Max, exasperated. 'Look, darling, why don't you run after Daddy and help him? He's bound to get sidetracked by someone and you don't want to wait for ages, do you?'

'All right, Mummy,' Max said.

Carrie leant down and kissed him on his hat. 'Hurry after him now, darling.'

Max threaded his way through the bodies and Carrie saw him catch up with Brody, who was talking to someone in the drawing room. He hadn't even made it to the stack of sparklers. She watched as Max took his father by the hand and pulled him through the guests. Carrie turned to chat with Michelle and Jean, who had come over from Paris.

'Delightful party,' Carrie said, knowing that Michelle quite fancied herself as the most talked-about hostess, if the gossip magazines were to be believed. While Carrie had never been to any of their events in Paris, she could quite imagine the lack of taste with which Michelle would entertain her guests, judging by her dress sense.

'Mummy,' Max said, exhaling and grinning and pulling his father back by the hand. 'We've got the sparklers.'

'Oh good boy, Maxie, but don't interrupt while Mummy's talking.' Carrie turned back to the French couple, but Brody barged straight into her, causing her drink to slosh all down Michelle's coat. 'For heaven's sake, Brody, be careful. Look what you've done.' She was angry but managed to smile fondly as Max reached for his father's arm and guided him round to a clear space at her side. Michelle, dabbing at her clothing and pulling a face, moved on with her husband to chat with someone else.

'See what you've done, Brody? We could have had an invite to Paris. I'm convinced your father's drunk, Maxie. What will we do with him?' Carrie sighed and glanced around for someone else to chat to. More fireworks rained through the night in a cacophony of bangs and squeals.

Max covered his ears and yelled above the noise, 'Daddy's not drunk, he's blind.'

'So you didn't think to tell me? You thought that if you just said nothing, did nothing about it, it would all be OK, somehow get better on its own?'

'Isn't that how our lives work these days?' Brody sat stiffly on the chair. The waiting room smelt of lilies. He wondered if, after only four days without sight, his nose was already making up for what his eyes had lost. Would he, he wondered, hear a pin drop in the next room?

'Oh, don't be so stupid. You were driving this time last week. I just don't know how . . .' Carrie trailed off as someone else came into the waiting room and sat opposite. Brody was, of course, grateful that his wife had instructed her secretary to call the most renowned ophthalmologist in London, but all he wanted was to be assessed by the local hospital, be told that his sight would return in a few more days, that it was all a terrible mistake, that of course he'd see his son grow up and of course he'd see the look on his wife's face again when they made love. Things like this didn't happen to him.

Brody sighed and confessed. She hadn't been around much to notice if his car was in the drive or not. 'I've been taking taxis and the bus when it's been really bad. It just happened, right? Let's wait and see what the doctor says.' Brody scuffed his feet on what he guessed were shiny tiles. There was no vague outline of his shoes today, no silhouette against the floor, no fading impression of the world around him that he'd grown used to over the last few months. He'd thought nothing of it at first – just an annoying feeling that the night was closing in early, that a curtain was being eased shut in the centre of each of his eyes. Add to that a smear of grease – everyone at his age needs glasses, don't they? – and that was what Brody saw.

'If this guy doesn't cut it, I'm going straight to the local hospital.'

'That's all very well, Brody, but—'

'Professor Quinell, please,' the nurse announced softly.

Brody stood and wobbled. He felt Carrie's arm on his and he was grateful. She led him across the waiting room faster than he would have liked – it wasn't easy trusting someone so implicitly, even if they were your wife – and he heard her chatting brightly to the nurse about the clear skies and the snow that was forecast. He wondered if, when it did snow, the world would seem that little bit brighter.

It was two hours later when Mr Cleveland offered a diagnosis following an uncomfortable and lengthy electroretinography test on Brody. Carrie had sat in reception then gone for a coffee along Marylebone High Street. Several fans had asked her for her autograph. She sent them away with a swish of her hand.

'It's not good news, I'm afraid,' Mr Cleveland said, scanning over the results at his desk. 'We need to run some blood tests, to ascertain the genetic factors involved, but initially the signs are that you have a condition called choroideremia, Professor.'

'How's it treated?' Carrie immediately asked. 'Drops? Pills? What?' It was an inconvenience. Until he could see again, they'd need to hire help, have things adapted at home. She had precious little time to be attending to such needs and briefly cursed Brody in her head for letting the condition come this far.

'There is no treatment, I'm afraid. It's a progressive disease, which, if I'm right with my diagnosis, will have been hard-wired into you since birth by your mother genetically.'

'There,' Carrie continued. 'If you'd spoken up earlier, then you could have got something done about it.'

'No. No, you're wrong about that.' Mr Cleveland was patient but vehement. 'I'm afraid it's never curable. The sufferers, almost always men, are usually registered blind during their early to middle adulthoods. The faulty chromosome is carried by the mothers and passed down the male line.'

Carrie immediately thought of Max.

'But fathers never pass on the X chromosome to their sons. Your little boy will be fine. Had you had a daughter, or if you decide to add to your family, then genetic counselling will be in order.'

Carrie's mind whirred. She hadn't thought about having more children in a long while. *Reality Check* had only been running a few months but she was already becoming famous. She wanted to build up the show, branch out, travel – it all meant long days and nights away. The show was already in consultation for an indefinite run. Having more children was out of the question.

'We won't be having a daughter,' she said.

Brody's head whipped round to her. 'That's final, is it?' he asked coldly.

'Professor Quinell, you are going to have to make some big changes to your life from now on. I don't, in all honesty, comprehend how you've managed this far without needing assistance. There must have been a marked degeneration in your sight recently.'

Brody nodded slowly in agreement. Carrie reached out for his hand. She felt so desperately sorry for him, and for herself. This couldn't have come at a worse time.

'It's not unusual for sufferers of choroideremia to initially be in denial. Knowing that it's untreatable is particularly hard to take, as well as being aware of the final outcome. Blindness.'

'So are you telling me he can't see anything? Nothing at all?' Carrie glanced between the ophthalmologist and her husband. She blinked.

'From what I can determine, there's a minimal amount of peripheral vision remaining in the left eye and virtually nothing in the right. Would you concur with that, Professor Quinell?'

But Brody had left his seat and was walking tentatively across the room, arms outstretched, head bent to one side in a way that Carrie had noticed him doing recently – to use the minuscule amount of sight he had remaining, she now knew. He knocked into a plant stand, grabbed for it but missed. Soil spread over the pale carpet. 'I can see just fine,' he boomed. Then his voice gave way a little. 'It's the rest of the world that's got the problem.'

WEDNESDAY, 29 APRIL 2009

Clive flew Carrie and Brody back to London City Airport the next morning. Showing the utmost respect for his employer and choosing to wear a black tie rather than the usual green and gold one with the *Reality Check* embroidered logo, he made little chat during the hour-long flight. Rather he concentrated on flying them safely through the storm that followed them to the capital. Once landed and the engine cut, Clive produced two umbrellas for his passengers.

'Let me know if there's anything I can do,' he said solemnly once inside the terminal building.

'Thank you, Clive,' Carrie replied gratefully. It was a comfort to know she had reliable staff during such hard times. She instructed her driver to take them directly to the police station where she knew she would find Dennis and his team.

'I still can't believe you didn't ask details when Dennis called last night,' she said to Brody.

'We'll find out soon enough,' he replied flatly.

But it was those details that kept Carrie going from one minute to the next. How could her life have changed so drastically in such a short space of time? Details weren't something she was used to being caught up in or bothered with. She delegated and shifted the weight of them – to her stylist, her secretary, her producer, her housekeeper – all those people who were present in her life to remove annoying details.

But now, these last few days, she had become obsessed with

the minutiae of life and there was no one who could help her process the snippets of information that her brain churned over and over like wet washing.

Brody, too, had absorbed details during his overnight stay at Charlbury, picking up snippets of her life that he knew nothing about. Ironic, Carrie thought as she'd attempted to force sleep upon herself with pills and alcohol, that after all these years he finds me like this – lost, bereft, empty. Ironic again, she thought at 3.30 a.m., that they'd never, since they'd first met, been so similar in every way.

'Professor, Carrie,' Dennis said, nodding and guiding them immediately into his small office. It was hot and stuffy and Carrie gasped for air. It smelt of coffee and vaguely of sweat, she thought, imagining the detective up all night working on the case. 'Please have a seat.' He shifted a second chair into place the other side of his desk.

As she sat, Carrie was reminded of the last time Dennis had stayed over at her house. Perhaps it was the masculine scent pervading the office that brought the event to mind, or perhaps, too, the sombre, unreal aspect of the situation. Just as she didn't want to be here now, she hadn't wanted Dennis in her house either, not really, although she'd readily taken the comfort of his body to fulfil a need.

It was summer, an intolerably humid evening and Dennis had called her on the pretence of needing to talk about a woman she was having on the show that Friday. They'd already been over the details a thousand times and she knew the legal implications of getting it wrong, but still Dennis insisted they meet. Carrie recalled the flutter in her chest when she opened the door to him – seeing the way his pale shirt stuck to his back as he walked through to the kitchen, how his forehead was damp from the day's heat or, as Carrie imagined it, as if they'd already had sex. She remembered making martinis and knocking over the jar of olives, how Dennis grabbed her wrists and roughly pulled her towards him.

In the morning came the guilt of sneaking him out of the house, her pulse rate soaring as she tried to distract Max long enough for Dennis to escape unnoticed. It far outweighed the pleasure they'd shared in bed. Plus the potential scandal of being involved with the detective who had, on occasion, appeared on the show alongside her, was not something she relished. It was another detail. Another nuisance.

'We found his prints on the knife.' Dennis picked up a folder, half opened it, then dropped it back down on his desk. 'Details aside, they matched a boy called Warren Lane. He's a known offender and he clearly fits the description you gave us, Professor. I'm in no doubt he was one of the youths you spotted at the café.' Dennis's tone was measured and considered.

Carrie forced her mind to work. 'If Brody gave you a description . . .' She trailed off. She turned to Brody. She couldn't understand how it had taken so long to get to this point. 'You were actually watching Max's killer.' A noise came from her throat that she didn't immediately recognise as hers. It was a mix of incredulous laugh and a wail. 'You were *watching*,' she reiterated, realising the irony. 'Couldn't you have done something to stop him?'

'If I'd gone steaming in, Max would never have forgiven me. I was trying to make things more bearable for him. What parent wouldn't? I had no idea things would end like this.'

'But there's bad news, I'm afraid.' Dennis's voice cut through accusations and defence. Both Carrie and Brody turned simultaneously.

Bad news? Carrie thought. No. There was no more bad news left in the world. Anything he told them, as far as she was now concerned, could only be good.

'The Crown Prosecution Service decided not to charge half

345

an hour before you arrived. Warren Lane is to be released from custody.'

'What?' Brody slammed his hands on the desk. Carrie reeled and caught one of them between her palms. She was shaking.

'I'm sorry,' was Dennis's reply. 'It was out of my control. The evidence we produced was not strong enough in the view of the Crown Prosecution lawyer.'

'It sounds bloody conclusive to me.' It was Carrie's last burst of conscious speech. She broke down in sobs and fits of anger and rage.

'It was the quality of the fingerprints on the knife. They weren't a good enough match and, without a positive witness identification of Lane, it just wasn't enough.' Dennis paused, letting them take it in. 'Of course, I've already requested further analysis of the knife, to see if they can come up with something better. It's a travesty and I'm sorry.'

Dayna vomited. Hardly anything came up as she hadn't eaten properly in ages. Her stomach tightened and squeezed and fought to wring out her insides. It was horrible. She hoisted herself up from the floor, her hands flat on the cold loo seat, and stood feeling dizzy and weak. Her head swam as if her brain was floating through the universe with nothing but the rest of time around it. Her skin tingled and her mouth was dry one minute and salivating the next. She bobbed down and chucked up again.

'Bleedin' hurry up, girl,' came the voice through the door. It was Kev. He always went to the Working Men's Club on Wednesdays and usually soaped up his chin and shaved before he left. Dayna had no idea why he went there. He'd hardly ever worked in his life.

She flushed the loo and emerged on to the tiny landing. Her tongue was burning and the muscles in her belly ached. Kev scowled, pushed straight past her and slammed the bathroom door. In her room, Dayna lay on the bed. She had a weep. Max was dead. No more meetings at the shed. No more shared cigarettes. No more competitions. The thought of all that emptiness made her feel sick all over again.

She heard the knock on the front door. Then she heard an unfamiliar woman's voice. There were footsteps stamping up the stairs and then her door caved inwards. Her mother stood there. 'Some cop or other to see you. Get up.'

Dayna followed her mother downstairs. 'Who is it, Mum?' she asked quietly.

Her mother turned on the stairs. 'How the fuck do I know?' She shook her head and slammed back into the kitchen. On the front doorstep was a woman. Recognition set something alight in Dayna's recent memory.

'Yeah?' Dayna said. As much as she'd wanted to sound confrontational, she didn't. There was none of that left inside her.

'Dayna, my name's Leah Roffe. Do you remember? I work with Carrie. I'd like to talk to you. It's really important.'

She didn't tell her mother she was leaving. No one would notice she'd gone, anyway. Not until it came time to look after Lorrell, and even then her little sister would just be left in front of the telly with a bag of crisps.

'You know that Carrie has a television show, don't you?' Leah said with her eyes fixed on the road. She drove slowly, as if she didn't know where she was going, as if getting Dayna in the car and moving forward was simply a way of taking her captive.

'Yeah, of course,' Dayna replied.

'She's absolutely distraught about what has happened to her son. As is everyone,' she added. 'You must have seen how Carrie fights for justice on her shows. She's passionate about the rights of people just like you and tries to help the police and victims by giving airtime to cases.' Leah indicated left out of the estate. She slowed for a woman on a bike.

Dayna didn't say anything as she recalled Carrie Kent in action. Was that justice? she wondered. Was all that strutting about and poking into the lives of people worse off than her doing any good at all, or did it just make for good telly? Dayna wasn't convinced that the woman fought for anything other than fame and higher ratings. It was all about money in her world.

'So? What's that got to do with me?'

'Carrie has sent me personally to ask you if you would come on her show to help the police catch Max's killer. If you tell your story, people will phone in. I'm sure it would be the hardest thing you've ever—'

'No.'

The car swerved and Dayna grabbed the door handle.

'You need to think about this before you answer, love. You knew Max well and . . .' But her words were lost on Dayna as panic and more nausea swept over her. Dayna heard the studio audience baying at her, felt the heat of their wrath on her cheeks. She imagined Carrie Kent up close, her unwavering face only inches from hers, picking and picking away at the truth until she was left with no alternative but to stand up and confess the truth.

There was an arrest . . . she heard Leah say. The words blew through her head. *They let him go* . . .

'If Max could speak for himself, he'd want you to do it for him, love. We'll run a special crime line number at the same time. Carrie will be on your side. She'll ask you questions. You just have to go over what happened, how it felt for you, what you did to help Max. I'm in no doubt that the calls will flood in. Someone will know something that might just provide the piece of infor—'

'Stop!' Dayna cried. She fell forward as much as her seatbelt would allow and buried her face in her hands.

'I didn't mean to upset you, Dayna.' Leah pulled over into a bus stop. The engine ticked over.

Dayna prised her face from her hands and wished desperately that she could sob and sob until what she needed to say dissolved in all the snot and tears. 'I don't know anything, OK? I don't know who killed Max and I don't know what to say on the telly. Don't make me do it.'

Leah's hand was on her shoulder. 'Take this, Dayna. It's my card. Call me if you change your mind. The show is the day after tomorrow. I know this is a lot to take in but . . .'

Dayna couldn't hear anything more than fuzzy words echoing through a place she didn't want to be. When she glanced out of the window, she realised that they'd virtually come full circle and were only a street away from her house. Against her better judgement, she grabbed the woman's card and leapt out of the car. She ran and ran, away from the estate, away from the school, down to the stream and headed the back way through the industrial yard to Max's shed. When she got there, she leant against the rotting wood, panting, flinching when two trains went past overhead, one after the other. She was half crying and half hysterical.

What the hell was she going to do?

Fiona felt his agony. It gnawed and ate and upset her insides, her life, as if it were her own. She was watching someone she loved get hurt through a glass window so thick they couldn't hear her banging, couldn't see her lips crying out, wanting to help. Not when they were blind, anyway; not when they didn't know you loved them in the first place. She felt so desperately helpless; so very sorry for Brody.

Her flat was neat and tidy. In the near decade that she'd been working with the professor, he'd only been to her home once, years ago, and anyway, it wouldn't have affected Fiona's image of serenity, calm and organisation if everything had been flung from the cupboards and the place hadn't been cleaned in a month. Brody wouldn't have batted an eyelid. They'd been on their way to the airport, way back. Fiona had picked him up from his ghastly flat and they'd headed out towards Heathrow. She always liked to leave error time for traffic and breakdowns and other emergencies, not that there had ever been any. Except that day.

'Stop!' Brody yelled, banging his fist on the dashboard. If they'd been on a regular road, Fiona would have slammed on the brakes in a driving-test-style stop. The M25 allowed her only to switch lanes and slow to a speed which sent other motorists close to the car's rear before overtaking and hooting.

'What on earth's wrong?' she asked. Two years working for him and she thought she knew the maths professor pretty well. He'd never behaved like this before.

'I can't go to Boston,' he said.

'Why on earth not?' Fiona decided to pull over on to the hard shoulder. There was a junction coming up and if this was a real emergency, they'd need to get off the motorway fast.

'Because Max has a school concert.'

'What?' Fiona rolled her eyes and put the car into gear again. He was being ridiculous. A fast and steady stream of traffic prevented her pulling out. She rolled forward, waiting for a large enough gap to filter back on to the motorway.

'I want you to turn round and take me home. No, better still, take me to your place. It's nearer and I want to phone the school. We can sort out the other logistics there.'

'But you're the keynote speaker. Most of the delegates are only attending because of your speech. And you're the guest of honour at the banquet on Saturday.' Fiona was utterly disappointed. Five days in a hotel with Brody would surely have led to something. Did he think so little of her that he wouldn't have at least placed his hand on hers over dinner or kissed her cheek last thing at night, even if it was only to say he appreciated her? Something as small as that would have kept her going. She wasn't expecting anything more.

'I made a mistake. Max comes first.' Brody was calm, Fiona thought, for a man who was risking his reputation.

'Why don't you just call the school and ask when the next concert is? You could go to that instead.'

'Take me to your flat, Fiona. If you won't do that, then please drive me home.' He was acting perfectly rationally, as if he'd just decided not to go shopping.

Fiona couldn't argue with him. He was her boss. She was paid to do what he asked and if that involved turning the car round and damaging his career then so be it. That it gave her no opportunity now to talk a little more intimately on the long flight to the States than she'd ever dared before, or perhaps linger in his hotel room and help him unpack, maybe share a drink from the mini-bar, sat heavily in her chest. Tears welled in her eyes. Without saying anything, Fiona wove back into the traffic and exited the motorway at the next junction. She swung round the island and rejoined the M25 in the opposite direction. They would be at her place in less than half an hour.

It was as she guided Brody to the little desk under her window – the desk that had a telephone, her computer, some files from the university, a picture in a silver frame – that she realised there was something – *someone* – stuck right in the middle of any opportunity she might have with Brody. She almost wished he'd never been born.

'I'm calling about my son, Max Quinell,' he said into the phone. 'Yes, yes, that's right. He's performing in the concert. Can you tell him that his father will be there to watch him? Thank you. And wish him luck.'

Luck, Fiona thought, placing the photograph of Brody face

down on the desk. She was going to need more than luck to get him to notice her.

Now, years later, as Fiona sat by the phone willing Brody to call, aching deep inside, she wondered what had actually changed now that Max was dead. Wasn't he, in all this mess, still coming between her and Brody?

MARCH 2009

Dayna flushed the loo and picked up the blue and white box, the contents of which were strewn on the floor. She rubbed her eyes with toilet paper, knowing there'd be black crescents of mascara on her cheeks. Her eyes stung from crying. She blew her nose and breathed out deeply. It was a start, or an end, she thought, stuffing the instructions back inside the box. She hid it under her cardigan and emerged on to the tiny landing.

In her bedroom, she hurled herself on to her unmade bed. She lay for a while, staring at the ceiling, tracking the cracks in the plaster with her eyes and wondering if each one matched up with a mess in her life. Some people get born lucky, she thought to herself. Some don't.

She rolled sideways and opened her bedside cupboard. She reached out and hid the small box behind all the junk that had accumulated in there over the years. Broken Pez dispensers, an empty tissue packet, a few books, free CDs swiped from the cereal packets before anyone else could nab them. Old earphones all tangled up, a plastic bag of trading cards, a collection of plastic animals from when they were all the rage and swapped ferociously in the primary school playground, plus a few bits of old make-up in ridiculous shades of pink and turquoise that she'd never dream of wearing now – all these things incongruously shielding the most grown-up and un-childlike thing that had ever happened to her.

As an afterthought and glancing at her bedroom door to make

sure it was firmly shut, Dayna slipped the plastic wand from the box before closing the bedside cupboard. She pulled off the white plastic cap and stared at the pen-like object. There was no doubt that she'd done it right. She wasn't stupid. She'd read the instructions.

Hold the absorbent tip in your urine stream for five to eight seconds.

The hardest part was waiting three minutes for the result to resolve in the two windows. Her hands had been shaking, her vision blurry from all the crying and all the fear that the little wand contained. Eventually, the control window changed and showed a single blue line. Her heart thumped. That meant she'd done things right – for the first time ever, she added in her head.

Moments later, as the wetness crept further along whatever magic the plastic stick contained, the second line began to appear. A further single blue line would show she wasn't pregnant. A cross – symbolic? she pondered as the next minute time-slipped into a thousand years – would mean that she was.

Dayna stared at the result as it appeared before her eyes. She blinked a thousand times in the hope she would register what it all meant. Not pregnant or pregnant? she'd asked herself over and over before even buying the test at the chemist. She had no idea. Some women could tell, she'd heard, even from the moment of conception. At fifteen, she didn't understand her body enough to decide if there was another one growing inside. Her periods were irregular and puberty had come late compared to the other girls in the same year – yet another reason for them to jibe and make fun of her.

'Max. Good news. I'm pregnant,' she tried out quietly. Then, 'Max. Good news. I'm not pregnant.'

She imagined his face when she told him the result.

Happiness, regret, fear, shock? He'd been so weird recently, she wasn't sure she even knew him well enough to second-guess his reaction.

'But where should I tell him?' she whispered to her old bear. Battered and smelly, the threadbare toy had sat on her bed for the last fifteen years – the only thing her real dad had ever given her.

As if delaying the reality of it – would Max be disappointed whatever the result? – Dayna considered breaking the news down the alley behind the sports hall, on the roundabout at the park, in the school canteen. 'There's always the shed,' she said to the bear. The creature stared blankly at her with one eye glued back into its socket. The stitches of his lopsided mouth were coming away, giving him a permanent leer. Dayna knew exactly how he felt. 'I'll tell him at the shed.'

Not wanting to wait any longer, Dayna tucked the teddy under her duvet and texted Max. She spent ten minutes fixing her face. She didn't want him seeing her like this. A text came back a couple of minutes later.

Why? he asked in response to her request to meet. No kiss, no fond smiley face.

Why indeed, Dayna wondered in return, had everything gone so horrid?

It took half a dozen more text messages, but eventually Max capitulated and agreed to meet Dayna at the shed. In truth, he hadn't been there in a while. He'd got some recent prizes to take down – an electric toothbrush, a picnic set, a wind-up torch – but going there hadn't seemed right since he'd stopped hanging out with Dayna. Not since the phone calls; not since those vile messages.

Will u meet me @ shed? she'd put. No kisses at the end. He read it again as he waited. Perhaps she wouldn't even come.

Perhaps it was all a joke – like, he now realised, they had been. He'd been conning himself that she loved him.

After everything that had happened, he'd just wanted it all to go away, to forget, to move on. But now she'd gone and texted him, set his mind alight with possibilities and, anyway, what else was he to do? He had no other friends. His parents were always working and never interested in him. If he died, would anyone even notice?

So here he was, peering out of the window of the hut with sullen eyes, lurking in the cobwebby shadows because the last thing he wanted was for Dayna to think he was watching out for her. Adrenalin surged through him as a figure crowned the embankment. But it was just a man walking his dog. Max relaxed again and lit a cigarette to calm his nerves. He sat down on the old car seat and brushed ash off the space next to him. He didn't want Dayna to get it on her clothes.

'There you go again,' he said to himself. Smoke curled and spread as the wind kicked up under the ill-fitting door. 'Kidding yourself that you care about her.'

He pondered what caring about someone actually meant or, more specifically, what caring about *Dayna* had meant. What had it done to him? What would he be like now if he'd never got involved with her? Did his caring stretch as far as wanting to patch things up with her – if that's what she was coming to discuss – or was it only the kind of caring that meant he could brag about having got off with her in the boiler room?

He sat and thought and smoked. He had no idea.

'Fucking bitch,' Max said between tight lips. He snorted and coughed as he inhaled too deeply. How *could* she? How could she just go off and tell everyone? The looks came first – quick glances from a couple of girls in their year. Hands cupped to ears; giggles sprayed across the canteen. Then nothing for a day or two. Just that same warm feeling in his belly; the one he hoped she also had.

By the end of January the phone calls started. He was used to getting them anyway, but these were serious kicks in the gut compared to the others. The words were mean and harsh, mocking and cruel. Every syllable cut through his flesh and led directly to his heart.

He thought he heard footsteps outside the hut. His fists clenched with anger. There were so many things he wanted to say to her, yet saying nothing at all had been the easiest option these last few weeks. They'd kept out of each other's way – avoided seeing one another in the corridors, turned their backs in class. A few words had been spoken early on, but since those calls, Max hadn't been able to face her. It made it all too real, what she'd done. Over the years, he'd learnt how to fold inwards, how to dissociate. Never before had the skill been so useful. As far as he was concerned, nothing had ever happened between them. He'd already decided he was going to leave school as soon as he turned sixteen. After that, he had no idea what he would do.

Someone was banging on the hut door. Max drew on his cigarette and closed his eyes and it was all still there, haunting him, crippling him.

The first phone message was about screwing losers, that *he* was the loser. He was used to getting them, but these were different. They'd begun with *her*. They hurt more. The second was insulting about his body – stuff that only Dayna could have known. The next was about his performance, or the lack of, and the revolting voice spat it all out with sickening, degrading detail. Had she told them *everything*? The final message was about—

'Max, fucking let me in. I know you're in there.' She hammered hard, bashing her way into his mind again. He stood up. His hand reached out for the bolt. He slid it back and she was in. Right there in his heart again when he saw her small, pale face. He knew exactly why he'd loved her.

He closed the door. Thing is, he thought, watching Dayna pace nervously round the small space in the hut, he'd expected it to last for ever, not just a moment in time.

'Max,' she said. Her voice was deep and shaky, as if she'd only just mustered enough courage. He saw a flash of pain in her eyes. He wanted to take her, hold her, make it all better.

He just stared at her. Said nothing. What could he say that would fix everything?

'I'm pregnant.'

THURSDAY, 30 APRIL 2009

Dennis unwrapped a sausage roll. Flakes of pastry snowed on his dark trousers. He brushed them off with his free hand. The traffic wasn't going anywhere. 'I just don't know, Jess,' he said, biting into the unappetising breakfast he'd picked up at the corner shop. Jess had declined to eat.

'We can but try,' she replied, looking out of the passenger side window. Dennis knew she'd picked up on his desperation, sensed that nothing else mattered to him apart from securing an arrest in the Kent case. 'We can but try,' she said again, gently this time, surprising Dennis with her compassion. He held the sausage roll between his teeth and changed into first gear as the traffic moved forward. Their conversation dwindled.

There's a heart in there somewhere, Dennis thought, grateful for her company as they stop-started towards the station on their way back from court. Other cases had to be dealt with however much Dennis wanted to work round the clock on Max. This one was annoying but drawing to a close and they soon got back on topic.

'In all my time at the Met, I've never encountered such a . . .' Jess swung round to Dennis, her seatbelt preventing her leaning too close, although he sensed her proximity. He smelt her perfume. The one she always wore for work. Today it was more immediate, more urgent, as if her own body chemistry was reacting with the scent. It speeded up his mind, made him wonder what she was getting at.

'. . . such a mess, really,' she finished. 'A mess that just isn't leading to anything.'

'It's more than a mess,' he said, oddly calm. 'It's a fucking nightmare and there's nothing I can do about it. We had the little shit, you know, Jess, and they let him go.'

'No we didn't,' she replied. 'I don't think it was Warren Lane who stabbed Max.'

At this, Dennis spared a few seconds' glance sideways. Was she mad? Perhaps that perfume had done for her brain. 'Don't be ridiculous,' he found himself saying. 'We just need an arrest.' He realised how it sounded but didn't care.

'That woman called me earlier.'

'What woman?' It was stupid of her to hold things back. Probably still sour about the promotion, he thought, after all this time.

'The show producer.'

'Leah? How come?' Was everything slipping out of his control? Leah always called him.

'It's a woman thing. You know.' She pulled a face, her expression conveying everything in her coy smile, her glinting eyes, the quirky way her eyebrows curled, one up, one down. She laughed and put on a silly voice. 'She's cute.'

'For God's sake, Jess.'

'She wants me to have a word with Dayna. Convince the girl to go on the show tomorrow.' Jess was serious again. A moment's frivolity lost in the depths of the case. Dennis was almost pleased.

'Do you think that's wise?'

'Don't see why not. Carrie wants to give the case airtime. I mean, she would, wouldn't she?'

Because we've failed, Dennis thought but didn't say. He didn't need to. 'To be honest, I don't think she's in any fit state to . . .' But he stopped. Out of everyone he knew, everyone he'd ever met, if there was one person who could pull off an hour of live television, win the sympathy of the nation, get those hotline phones ringing only a week after her son had been stabbed, it was Carrie Kent.

'So why don't you cruise past the girl's house and let me have a word with her?' Jess glanced at her watch. 'We have time. Just.'

Dennis nodded. He chucked the remainder of the limp sausage roll at Jess's feet, did a U-turn at the next set of lights, put the siren on when the traffic ground to a halt, and drove Jess to Dayna Ray's house so she could work her new-found feminine magic.

MARCH 2009

Carrie knew something was wrong. It was a mother's instinct, wasn't it? It had been a crazy week, with a family of eight pulling out of the live show at the eleventh hour. She hated re-runs. Hated the complaints they got when repeats were aired. But what choice did they have? No guests. No show. They had a backup guest but he couldn't be contacted. Of course, they still had the pre-filmed segment which the single mother – single with seven kids under the age of ten – had signed off on for them to broadcast, but that was no good on its own. Carrie had wanted them, and the absent fathers, to have their say live in the studio. It wasn't a police-linked show. No crime had been committed. Not in the strictest sense of the word, anyway. Between her and Leah – and general public interest – they'd decided to devote a week to benefit fraud, to having kids for the apparent financial gain. *Pregnant For Profit*, they were going to call it.

But the woman had obviously got wise to the tack she was going to take – had a researcher given too much away? – and she'd pulled out with no hope of them changing her mind. Carrie was working from her office at home when the news came through from Leah. She was aware that Max was in the house, a rare occurrence of late, she'd noted, and she swept up from her desk and stormed into the kitchen for coffee. She felt like a chat with her son. She sensed something was wrong.

'Can you bloody believe it?' She saw the way Max's shoulders hunched and stiffened as he curled over his cereal bowl at the kitchen bar. Did the boy eat nothing else but chocolate crunchy stuff? 'I'm looking for a backup. Fancy being on the show?' It was meant to be a joke, a smattering of light-heartedness in what was turning out to be a bleak morning. It had barely got light, the day outside resembling a November afternoon more than spring.

Max shrugged. Or at least Carrie thought it was a shrug. It could have been a twitch. Was that his way of urging her to ask what was wrong? she wondered. She poured coffee from the machine and spilt some on the shiny work surface. Martha would tut-tut as she wiped it up, no doubt.

'What's up?' Carrie held the mug in one hand and draped an arm round her son's shoulders. He was still wearing his dressing gown. It smelled faintly of sleep, lightly of detergent, mostly of teenage boy. She pulled him close, but his body turned rigid. How thin you've become, Carrie thought as his shoulder blade pressed against her forearm. She blamed it all on that revolting school.

'Don't,' he muttered.

'Don't what? Hug you?' She released her son and, still in good spirits despite the annoying news, she ruffled his hair like she used to when he was younger.

'For God's sake, Mum.' He ducked away from her hand.

'Max . . .' She suddenly realised that she didn't know what to say. From the age of eight, he'd been someone else's problem at boarding school. In the holidays, nannies at Charlbury had taken care of him, or he'd been with his father. Those times, he always came back wretched and angry. Since he'd been at Milton Park, that same anger had surfaced again. 'If there's something bothering you, you should tell me.'

He swung round. Carrie saw his red, puffy eyes and nose raw from too much blowing. 'Get me on your stupid show then. Let your viewers decide what to do with your hopeless son.'

'That's rid—'

'Is it? Is it ridiculous, Mum?'

He hardly ever called her mum, she realised, as the single word hit her heart.

'I don't think it's fucking ridiculous. Just think, we'd get to spend a whole hour together.'

'What the hell is that supposed to mean?' She could get stuck into lecturing him on what a privileged life he led because of her work; that how, because of her spending hours, days, sometimes weeks away from home, she'd made sure they could have anything and everything they ever wanted.

'Nothing.' Max turned back to his cereal and stirred the brown rice bubbles into the milk. His face was a few inches from the bowl. His chest heaved a couple of times – almost a sob – but nothing came out. Carrie felt desperately sorry for him but at the same time angry as hell.

'When you were at Denningham we didn't have trouble like this.'

'You call this trouble?' He shot her a look.

He was her baby, her son, but at that moment she believed he truly hated her.

'It's not trouble, Mum, me sitting here looking a bit miserable and eating cereal.'

He was right, of course. On the surface there wasn't any trouble. But she knew that somewhere deep inside him something was brewing, festering, composting, *eating* away at him. It scared her because she didn't know how to stop it.

'Just tell me, honey. Tell me what's bothering you.' How she hated herself at that moment; hated the way she sounded, the way she couldn't break through to him. It was as if motherhood had slipped unnoticed right beneath her feet; as if she'd reached out for it, tried to have a go and missed. Here she was, asking him ineffectual questions when in her mind she was wondering if that email had come in yet from her agent, or if her stylist had managed to secure her favourite designer for the spring wardrobe. 'Nothing can be that bad, can it?'

'Nah, you're right. It's not bad.' Max shovelled a couple of spoonfuls into his mouth and ended up with chocolate milk on his chin. Carrie wanted to wipe it off. Max took care of it with his sleeve.

'How's school?' she asked, reminded again of the dreadful place by his lack of manners.

'You know,' he said, shrugging. 'Lots of work.'

'Really?' Maybe there was some hope. Perhaps, in her craziest and wildest of dreams, Max would leave the city comprehensive with eleven GCSEs all at A star grade and four A levels with similar stunning results.

'Yeah. Doing English at the moment. *Romeo and Juliet*.' Max snorted as if there was buried humour that Carrie simply wouldn't get.

'Well, you're going to be late for school if you don't get a move on.' Better leave it there, she thought. Quit while she was ahead, although she had no idea what she was ahead of. Certainly not the start of their conversation.

'Mum,' Max said fondly now, standing, placing his hands on her shoulders. A smile, slightly mad, spread over his face and those puffy eyes narrowed as they beheld her. Carrie half expected a kiss on the cheek. 'It's the fucking school holidays,' he finished, shoving her as hard as he dare before lifting the cereal bowl and hurling it across the kitchen.

The mess didn't matter. His mother would be neither hurt nor bothered by the lake of chocolate milk on the floor and the rivers of brown on the white, white walls. That was what Martha was there for. He wondered what he was there for.

In his room, Max lay on his bed. Not what most teenagers do, he thought bitterly, in their school holidays. How had she not even noticed? How had she not known that he'd been off school for the last ten days? He recalled, in her favour, that she had been in Paris for a while, then at Charlbury before spending virtually eighteen hours a day at the studio or out filming. And he'd been at his dad's, smoking, drinking beer, sometimes seeing him, sometimes not; sometimes sitting in the grotty flat alone, wondering what it would be like if he lived somewhere like that with Dayna . . . with the . . . the . . .

Max hurled himself over on to his belly. He pressed his face down hard into the pillow and bit on it. The wail forced its way out of his core.

. . . *with the baby* . . .

'Nooo . . .' he screamed, but wasn't sure if it was even audible. Nothing else that came out of his mouth had an effect on the world so why would this? Why would anyone take the slightest notice of his agony?

She'd told him; told him yesterday that she was pregnant. In the hut that was full of his prizes, in the space he'd called his own until last year when this girl with her crazy hair and long fingers and heart as big as a watermelon had come into his life and shared it with him.

'What?' was all he'd said. Then there was fifteen minutes of silence. He'd chain-smoked and she did the same. It hadn't occurred to him until later that, if she really had a baby in her, she shouldn't be lighting up.

Then, 'What?' came out again, a thousand times and it was as if she said 'I'm pregnant' a thousand times too, like when he stood in the bathroom and opened the mirror cabinet door. With the other big mirror behind, he could see himself stretch to infinity. Max for ever, he used to say when he was younger. Well, that was how he felt now, as if that baby inside her would make him immortal, that his genes would carry on for ever.

'How?' he said very quietly, slumping down on to the car seat.

'Is it . . .' It nearly came out but he stopped. He didn't want to ask if it was his. The vile phone messages from those shits at school made a little more sense now. They'd got it in for him, whatever happened.

'Is it yours, you were going to say.' Dayna wasn't stupid. He couldn't believe how thin she looked for someone who had someone else inside her. Had she been eating properly?

Max just shrugged.

'Well, it is yours,' she replied. Then she turned scarlet and stared at the floor, scuffing and kicking the leaves that had somehow curled beneath the door in the wind. To Max, it looked as if she was guilty as sin.

'People have been saying stuff,' he said. He just didn't understand how they, them, their . . . *relationship* . . . had gone from hand-holding to hating. If he was honest, he didn't actually hate her at all. It was the situation he hated. But self-protection prevented him from admitting that. He watched the crispy leaves disintegrate beneath her boot. 'Stuff about me. Bad stuff. Things no one should know.'

Dayna's leg heaved back and came forward at an almighty rate. It hammered against a box of baking tins until there was a hole in the side and they could hear the clanging of metal.

'What you gonna do with all this shit?'

Max laughed. 'We'll need it, won't we?' That's when he first imagined setting up home with Dayna. A little flat, like his dad's, probably on the same estate with raucous neighbours and gangs of yobs wreaking havoc every night. Would he let his son or daughter play out? he wondered. Probably not. How would his mother feel about him living somewhere like that? She would have nothing to do with him ever again, he reckoned. Leaving Denningham had virtually killed her; being a father at his age would finish her off.

He had become her worst nightmare. He was the kind of

person she had on her show. He had, comprehensively, let her down and he hated himself for what he had become.

Max's bedroom was large enough for him to pace around at speed. He ducked into his private bathroom and doused his head with cold water. That was not enough to take away how he felt so he stood under a scalding shower fully clothed. Dripping wet, he returned to the dark sanctuary of his bedroom and lay on the floor. Remembering it was there, he reached under the ebony chest of drawers and retrieved a virtually full bottle of vodka.

He drank.

He thought and thought what to do. Thought about consequences. There were so many. He focused on that one impulsive moment in the basement and how it had led to all this shit. If he could take time back, would he do it again?

No. Yes. No. Yes . . . no . . . I *dunno*.

He swigged from the bottle. The alcohol curdled the milk already in his stomach.

Dayna was pregnant. What if it wasn't his?

. . . catch anything from the emo bitch? She puts it around . . .

He remembered those particular words on his voicemail. He knew – he thought he knew – that they weren't true.

. . . I shafted her before you got to her, man . . .

Again, he was used to the comments. He'd grown up with them, become immune. Had Dayna been a virgin? He wouldn't know how to tell.

As the alcohol bled through him, he allowed some of the messages he'd received a few weeks ago to percolate his mind. Should he believe them? She must have said it to them, all that stuff about being together in the basement, how he'd been so unsure what to do, his size, or lack of, they'd said so cruelly, and how it had ended virtually before it began.

Max lay on his back. His hands swept up and down the plush

carpet as if he was making a snow angel. He needed an angel now, he thought, willing himself to see one. A guardian angel to take a message to Dayna. Tell her that he did love her. Does. Did. Does.

He sat up.

He would be a man. She would have to get rid of it.

Couldn't have a baby messing up his life. Not at fifteen.

What had he been thinking? Leaving Denningham.

He drank the vodka.

His mother would help him.

Get him back on the straight and narrow.

Try another school. Get away from all this shit.

Forget it.

For now, the vodka would help.

Dayna opened her phone. One new text message. From Max.

She squinted as she read it.

Get an abortion.

That was all.

Of course, since that little blue cross appeared as if by magic on the test kit, she'd thought about it. But that would be murder, wouldn't it?

Killing my baby . . .

She went into the kitchen. She needed to be near someone. Her mother was cooking chips. Nothing seemed real, not even when she lifted the basket from the fryer and pinched a scalding stick of half-cooked potato. She held it between her teeth. Closed her lips around it. She felt nothing.

'Get yer hands off,' her mother said.

How she wanted to hug her. How she wanted to push her face against her shoulder and sob and tell her everything and ask her what to do. How she wanted to be a little girl again, have another chance, have another family, another life. She would take Lorrell with her, scoop her up in love and keep her safe. What she needed was a guardian angel; someone to watch over her, tell her what to do, because she had absolutely no clue.

Get an abortion.

As if you could just pop out somewhere, come home without any mistakes. A clean slate.

What about if they had it? Got a place to live? She stared at her mother. She was tipping baked beans into a saucepan. What about if she told her?

Dayna ran out of the kitchen. She charged up the stairs and burst into Lorrell's tiny room. It was virtually a cupboard with a bed that converted from a cot. Lorrell's legs stuck out the end when she slept. She was sitting on the floor playing with some Lego that had been bought from a car boot sale. It was dirty. Dayna sat down next to her.

'Put your hand here,' she whispered. She took her little sister's warm hand and placed it low down on her belly.

'What?' Lorrell scowled as half her tower fell off.

'There's a baby in there,' Dayna whispered. She had to tell someone; hoped it would help. 'Sshh,' she said, putting a finger to her lips. 'Our secret, right?'

Lorrell's eyes became round in wonder. 'A real baby?' she asked.

Dayna nodded.

'Wheredit come from?'

'It was a present from Max,' she said, unable to help the grin. She knew it was a little boy.

'Why?' she said, turning back to her Lego. She scowled in concentration as she forced the bricks together.

'Because we love each other,' she replied, feeling so much better as she replied to Max's text with the words: *I'm going to.*

There was nothing more to be said.

★

370

Max's phone buzzed but he didn't look. He wouldn't be able to see it anyway, not with what the vodka had done to him. His head throbbed and he knew he was going to be sick. He would just do it on the carpet.

He thought he slept; not sure though; not sure how much time had passed. He lifted the bottle beside him. Nearly empty. Fuck.

He rolled on to his side and vomited. He shuffled his way out of the mess and hauled himself up on to his bed. That noise again; the same high-pitched tone that had cursed his unconsciousness. He plucked his phone off the floor. His eyes swam in and out of focus as he read the text.

I'm going to.

He chucked up again. Good, he thought. This crazy drunk unreal state was the way to be, he reckoned. Everything seemed much better; less biting, less cruel, less normal. Sense pervaded at last.

Max lay on his bed and drifted in and out of sleep for the remainder of the day, convinced that life was finally coming together. He didn't wake until the middle of the night, until it was dark, until the pain in his head had receded to a minor twinge when he stood up. He went into the kitchen and flicked on the light. Everything gleamed – so different to real life. He thought of Dayna. She was a tidal wave in his mind as he pulled open the vast refrigerator door. Nothing to eat.

Nothing to do except slide to the floor and weep. She was going to kill their baby.

THURSDAY, 30 APRIL 2009

On the one hand, Brody couldn't believe she was doing it but, similarly, if working out the world's entire unsolved mathematical problems would have got justice for Max, then he reckoned he'd have given it a go, too. So after he'd replaced the handset and returned to the warm, dented patch on the old sofa, he was able to understand, to a certain degree at least, why Carrie was acting this way. She was coping; doing what she could. He just couldn't grasp *how* she could physically do it. It hadn't even been a week. The difference between them, he assumed.

It was DCI Masters who had told him when he called for an update. 'Tomorrow?' Brody said. 'You sure?' Why hadn't Carrie mentioned the show? That was easy. She was worried he'd put up a fight.

'At first, the girl refused to cooperate,' Masters told him. 'But DI Britton worked her charm . . .' There was a noise in the background that Brody's heightened hearing told him was female and indignant. 'She's agreed to make the appeal. That's how it was spun to her. An appeal to the public for information. What I'm hoping is that it'll prompt a memory, get her to talk. I know it's a lot to ask of a young girl, but it's worked on young people before. If nothing else, it'll raise awareness of gang-related crime.'

Can't do any harm, were Masters' closing words. Brody half-heartedly agreed but still thought it was too soon for everyone concerned. But then he couldn't fathom when it wouldn't feel that way or when his ex-wife appealing on television about their dead son would seem right. There was no bringing back Max.

For the first time in a week, Brody opened his laptop. He checked his emails. His computer told him that he had three hundred and thirty-seven unread messages and five times that many in the junk folder. He listened to the most recent, organising the messages according to sender. He played the important ones first. There was nothing that couldn't wait. The one from his genius protégé, Ricky McBride, he played half a dozen times before he could take it in. The monotonous computer-generated voice recited the message impassionately.

Prof, I'm dropping out. I know you'll hate me for it but I can't do this any more. So what if I can do crazy things with numbers? It don't pay the bills. Fed up of being the odd one out. Sorry. Ricky.

Brody shut the lid of his laptop. He sat and thought, hearing nothing but the dripping tap in the kitchen. The estate was oddly quiet this afternoon, as if respecting his need for peace. The week had bombarded him with every emotion of which a human was capable. And he was tired, so very, very tired. He felt ill from fatigue, as if his immune system had packed up.

'Ricky's leaving,' he said. He nodded. He'd half expected it, to be honest. The kid had made quite a name for himself with his exceptional talent. If he truly wanted his bills paying then he was making the biggest mistake of his life by quitting university. Organisations worldwide would be lining up for him with their chequebooks when he graduated. 'Ricky's leaving,' he said again. 'He doesn't want to be the odd one out, so he's leaving.' Brody's words were measured and careful. There was nothing left over for chosen emotions, only the ones that crushed him involuntarily in the middle of the night.

'He's leaving because he has a choice. He doesn't want to be different.' Brody nodded. It was fair in a world where not much else was. Ricky had probably been different all his life, Brody thought. 'Just like Max,' he said. 'Not so different any more, son, are you?' he said, turning his face to the ceiling.

FRIDAY, 1 MAY 2009

For the first time in a week, Carrie slept for more than two hours. In fact, by her reckoning she must have soaked up at least four hours' continuous rest. Despite her insistence to the contrary, she had sent Leah home. Martha was ensconced in the staff flat, rushing around doting on Carrie as if she was terminally ill. Carrie thought she may well be, that her life had been cut short, yet cruelly she was still alive to experience the aftermath. It would be easier to be dead myself, she'd thought a thousand times a day during the last week. Whenever she had slept, she'd willed herself not to wake up.

'You're a gem, Martha.' It was nice, for the briefest of moments, to notice the good things.

'It's what you always have on a Friday, pet.'

Carrie sat down at the table and looked at the beautifully presented scrambled eggs nestled alongside several slivers of Scottish smoked salmon. A bowl of fresh fruit sat beside a pot of coffee and a pitcher of juice. Carrie didn't think Fridays would ever be the same again.

She ate a little and drank the coffee, allowing the warmth of it to seep through her frozen veins. It was still early and the sense of panic that she would normally have if it was six thirty on a Friday and she'd done no preparation whatsoever for the show would have had her barking down the phone at Leah and yelling at the researchers to find out what the hell was going on. Today, however, completely unprepared for what would occur when they went to air, Carrie sat calmly sipping her coffee and staring through the plate-glass window at a sparrow hopping about in her Spartan garden. It looked disappointed, she thought, with her slate and granite and marble edifices and pathways. It didn't much care either for the bamboo and specimen Japanese plants that her landscaper had convinced her were the only way to furnish an outdoor city space.

'Are there any crusts, Martha?' Carrie was beside the counter, scanning the worktop.

Martha turned from the sink. 'Crusts? Are you still peckish, pet?'

There was a smile. It still hurt. 'No. But the bird is.'

Martha said nothing but opened a white ceramic pot and pulled out a loaf of wholemeal granary bread. She cut a slice. 'Enough, pet?'

Carrie nodded and slid open the glass door as silently as she could. There were two sparrows now. One flew away the instant the door moved, but the other stood frozen, staring straight ahead but still able to see everything she was doing. She broke the bread into small pieces and tossed a couple outside. The bird didn't move. How can it be so still yet alive? she wondered. She envied it that. If she was able, she would freeze herself from the inside out and never move again.

The bird hopped closer to a piece of bread. Carrie broke up and threw out the rest of the slice. At her movement, the sparrow became rigid again. Carrie took a step outside. The bird hopped back several feet then flapped up on to an alabaster ball. Carrie and the bird stared at each other. It wanted the food; Carrie wanted it to eat. Why, then, were they both locked in this stand-off?

'It's OK, sparrow,' she whispered. The bird twitched its tail. 'I won't hurt you, even though you can't possibly know that.' Carrie skirted round the bread and leant against the side of the house. She tried to shrink into the bricks in the hope that the bird would take what it so desperately wanted.

Come to me, she pleaded in her head.

When nothing happened, when the sparrow flew up higher still on to the wall, Carrie scooped up the bread and tossed it further down the garden. 'I don't care if you don't want the bread, you stupid bird.' She kicked at the remaining crumbs, scuffing them into the damp paving. 'It was there for you and you didn't take it. Go hungry for all I care!'

She went back inside and hurled the glass door closed. Back at the table, calm again, she sipped her coffee and thought about the show. She prayed Dayna would keep her word and turn up at the studio. She prayed, too, that the girl would speak on air. Carrie refused to have much of a game plan. She wanted to allow the situation to unfold, making it all the more real for those watching. In reality, she hadn't had the mental energy to prepare. She would explain the unusual situation to her viewers, keep the emotions as flat as she could manage, and get the girl to paint a moment by moment picture of what had happened. Someone would know something. Someone would call the police hotline. They always did. It was usually the most insignificant comments from viewers that led the police to arrest.

Outside, the sparrow flew down from the wall and began tucking in to the bread. Soon there were half a dozen other birds pecking at the crumbs.

'All I had to do was let them know it was there,' Carrie said.

'What, pet?'

'Max,' she continued in a daze, watching the birds. 'I should have let him know I was here.' Carrie stood and gathered her keys and bag. She slipped on a jacket and faced the hall mirror square on. A stranger stared back. 'And I didn't,' she finished, turning and heading down to the car.

★

'I hope we're bleedin' getting paid for this, is all I can say.' Dayna's mother leant against the sink, forking bacon into her mouth.

'Well, no one asked you to say, did they?' Kev mopped up egg with a slice of white bread. He wasn't dressed. He had no intention of going to the studio with his stepdaughter. 'Something for nothing, these folk. Don't know why you're bothering.'

''Cos she bleedin' wants to help that lad, that's why.'

It was the first sympathetic thing she had heard her mother say in ages, Dayna thought, staring into her cereal. She couldn't eat, though. She'd be sick on the telly if she did. 'I do. Oh, I do,' she whispered, but only Lorrell heard.

'Here's my baby, Mummy,' she said, holding up a plastic doll. No one was listening. Her mother and Kev were still bickering about whether Dayna would get paid for appearing on *Reality Check*.

Dayna frowned at her little sister. She put a finger over her mouth.

'Sshh,' the little girl hissed back.

'I think it's got past money, Kev. Can't you see how upset our Dayna's been these last few days? She ain't eaten nothing and she's been chucking up every day, ain't you, love?'

'Mmm,' Dayna replied. She just wanted to get it all over with; to get to the studio, to be dazzled by the lights and Carrie Kent with her fabulous clothes and no-nonsense manner. She wanted to be torn apart in front of a baying audience and thrown to them afterwards, bloodied and bruised from their attack, just like Max had been.

Why had she agreed to do this?

Because she deserved it.

There was a knock at the door. Lorrell scrambled off her chair and ran to answer it. When Dayna glanced down the hall, she saw a man dressed in black wearing a cap. He was bending down talking to Lorrell, who soon came trotting back to the kitchen.

'That man has a car for Dayna,' she said. Her voice wobbled with excitement and she dribbled some of her breakfast.

'Oh no,' Dayna said in response. 'He's early.' She leapt up from the table and ran straight past the man who was still standing at the door.

'Ten minutes, miss,' he called out as she passed. 'I'll be waiting outside.'

Dayna tore up to her room to change for the third time, exhausting her entire wardrobe. Jeans didn't seem entirely right but were pretty much all she had. Seconds later, she was hopping back into the faded things and pulling on a clean T-shirt. Over the top, she wore a dark jacket. She looked OK, she thought. Just normal.

Whatever that was.

She didn't understand why everyone else in the world saw her differently. Was it because she'd dyed her hair with everything from boot polish to household bleach over the years that made them hate her? Was it because she'd pierced her own ears over a dozen times, some done with a compass point in the loos when things had got really bad? Or perhaps it was because of her blue nail varnish or armfuls of bangles or the way she smiled or smelt or spoke or laughed or cried, like she was doing now.

'Stop it, fool,' she snapped at herself. She stuffed some tissues in her pocket, grabbed her phone and ran downstairs. 'Mum,' she panted at the kitchen door. 'I'm going.'

'Not on your own, you're not,' her mother said. She dumped her empty plate in the sink, grabbed her old coat off the back of the chair, and shoved her fags and lighter into her pocket. She left a kiss on Lorrell's head. 'Be a good girl for Daddy, Los. And wave to sis on the telly.'

Squinting in the sun, as if the brilliance was guiding them to a better place, Dayna stopped before she got into the car. 'Thanks, Mum. Thanks for coming with me.'

'Wouldn't have missed it for the world, love,' she said.

Dayna used the silence of the journey, while her mother puffed smoke out of the window, to contemplate if that was because, like most of the guests who appeared on the show, her mother just wanted her five minutes of fame, her share of upside-down glory to tell the world how hard done by they were, or if, indeed, her mother really cared about the truth.

Carrie sat in the dressing room. Her stylist pondered the clothes rail in a less enthusiastic way than usual. The whole studio, in fact, had taken on a sombre air and Carrie appreciated that. While she didn't want people to treat her differently, she couldn't bear the noise and clatter of real life just yet.

'How about this?' the stylist suggested, holding up a slate-grey skirt with a dark striped shirt.

'I don't think so.' Carrie's hair was in rollers. 'It needs to be different today.' She was fed up with people choosing her clothes for her and she was sick of people swiping at her face, her hair, brushing things off her, adding bits to her and fussing over her as if she was a helpless child. She remembered the interview when she got the man to confess to killing his family. The clothes weren't important. 'I'll just wear what I came to the studio in.'

The stylist knew better than to argue, given Carrie's state of mind. The show would still be watched whatever she was wearing. The viewers tuned in for the edge-of-the-seat debate, argument and resolution. Today their sympathies would lie entirely with the presenter.

'Jeans and sweatshirt it is then.' She clapped her hands together, as if punctuating the beginning and end of a fight that wasn't going to happen. As the stylist left the dressing room,

Carrie thought she saw her pull a face at the make-up artist who was just arriving.

'I'm not trying to be awkward,' she called out, but the woman had already gone. 'I just want her to feel at ease, to be able to talk to me as if . . . as if maybe I was her mother.' Her voice was small and she didn't think the make-up girl was even listening. 'Just a touch. Nothing over the top.' The girl nodded, chewed her gum and took out her brushes.

'Is she here yet?' It was eight forty and Carrie was in Leah's office pacing about. She was shaking – one minute freezing, the next too hot. Her bones ached and felt brittle as they bore her weight, as if the sorrow of the last week had eaten away at them from the inside out. 'Has anyone bloody well seen the girl yet?'

'Calm down, Carrie. She'll be here.'

'But is she actually in the building?'

'Sally called the driver and they're stuck in traffic. They'll be here soon.'

At this news, Carrie paced more vehemently. 'What if they don't make it? I could interview her on the phone, couldn't I? Or we could take the cameras out to the car. Whatever happens, the girl is going on television.'

'Carrie, don't get your hopes up.' Leah stood from behind her desk. 'She could still back out. And even if she doesn't, the leads might not come in.'

'Does she have a mobile phone? Why didn't she have a police escort? Can't we get one?'

'Calm down. Please.' Leah grabbed her. 'You're getting in a state. You need to be in control for the show.' Leah swept a strand of hair off Carrie's face. 'Why don't you go and get changed and have your hair done.'

'I already have,' Carrie retorted. 'If I go on looking like I normally do, she'll be freaked and won't speak. I need to get on her level.' Carrie dropped on to a chair, barely perched on the edge. 'What if she won't talk to me? What if no one phones in?'

'Carrie, Carrie.' Leah handed her a glass of water. 'Are you sure you want to go ahead with this? It's not too late to pull out.'

'Of course I don't want to pull out. The simple fact is, I don't see any other way forward. If I don't do everything I can to get justice for Max then . . .' Carrie stopped. She couldn't imagine the emptiness her life would hold. She hated herself for only noticing the purpose of her existence once it had gone. 'Then I won't be able to live with myself,' she finished, not believing that explained a tenth of how she felt.

Dennis insisted that Jess sit and wait with the girl before the show. It was her, after all, who had got her to agree to the appeal and, in case of any last-minute second thoughts, he wanted Jess's persuasive skills on hand.

'She won't renege,' Jess said.

'So sure? She's not exactly been a reliable witness so far.'

'I told her about the Plummer boy. I told her how the mother had fallen apart after the kid was killed.'

'And she gave a hoot?' Dennis parked the car in the usual spot at the studio. He liked it that something was usual when nothing much else was.

'She thought about it deeply. She understood how the publicity had helped catch his killers. It was when I told her that a member of the gang involved had agreed to appear on Carrie's show, albeit incognito and with a disguised voice, that she changed her mind. I offered her the same anonymity but she refused. She's not like normal girls, Dennis. I only spent an hour with her but, well, she seems older than she really is. Wiser, in a sort of naive way as if everything she's been through has made her . . . different.'

'Different is bleeding right.' Dennis grunted and rubbed his neck, stretching and cracking it. 'There's something deep inside me been gnawing away about all this, Jess, and you know what? It's not so deep any more.'

'The only thing gnawing at you, Den, is getting an arrest. It's the pressure eating you up, not some sense of moralistic community duty—'

'Don't you ever, *ever* imply I don't care about morals, detective. This happens to be the son of a dear . . . a good friend of mine. Morals and statistics and appeasing the powers that be, let alone the community, don't even come close to watching Carrie suffer because some little shit decided to take out her son in the playground.' Dennis clicked off his seatbelt and flung open the door. His face was scarlet and his lips were sucking in air as if he was suffocating. Had Jess spotted it was all a ruse for how inadequate he felt?

'That dear, huh?' Jess closed her car door with a fraction of the force used by Dennis. He didn't reply as they walked side by side through the television centre's security and then on into the bowels of the building where he knew he'd find Carrie and her crew.

Yes, that dear, he thought.

Dayna wanted to slide her hand across the cool leather of the back seat of the car and reach out to her mother. She wanted to be pulled to her chest, have her head pressed against her shoulder and be told everything was going to be all right as she spilt the mess that was stuck inside her. She felt constantly sick and had a permanent headache. She couldn't sleep properly and when she did, her dreams were filled with Max dropping first to his knees – the blood silently coursing from his body – and then crumpling on to his side as he gave up on life.

'Mum,' she whispered.

'What?' She turned from the open window. Smoke escaped her lips as she spoke.

'I'm scared.'

Dayna's mother stared at her, shocked almost that her daughter could even be contemplating such an emotion. 'Think of the money, girl. It'll be all right, you'll see.' A hand did reach across to Dayna but it gave a playful pinch on her thigh.

'There isn't any money, Mum. You know that. I'm doing this to help Max.'

Her mother just grunted, not believing that there wouldn't be something in this for her.

As the traffic finally flowed again, Dayna turned and watched London transform from her grim neighbourhood into foreign streets filled with expensive cars and exclusive shops and hotels. When it came down to it, her mother was just like the bullies at school. They did what they did for gain, sometimes financial, sometimes to big themselves up, and sometimes, she knew, they did it because there wasn't any other way for them to act. It was kill or be killed. Simple. She wasn't aware of her mother ever having a sense of ambition or pride. Like the kids at school, she was just out to get what she could.

The television centre was the biggest building Dayna had ever seen. It was constructed from the same dreary nineteen seventies brick as her school, yet somehow managed to appear modern and cared for with two glass wings flanking the older curved central part. She thought it looked a hub of inform- ation and entertainment as she gazed at quick-paced men and women coming and going across the neat plaza where the car was now parked. How she wished she could be part of a world like this.

Slowly, she opened the car door. She emerged to the driver, who held the door and instructed her mother where to go. Dayna listened because her mother was too busy stubbing out her butt on the ground. The driver coughed and winked at Dayna. She felt sad and special at the same time.

'Bye and thank you,' she called out as she and her mother were swept through the revolving doors. Ahead of them was a long reception desk and already the woman behind was smiling in greeting. Minutes later, they each had a plastic wallet on a cord to wear round their necks and a floor plan to guide them to studio four.

It was when they were alone in the lift that Dayna said she couldn't do it. *Wouldn't* do it.

'Don't be fucking stupid. My girl on the telly.'

But Dayna began hammering buttons. She hit the emergency stop with her fist and banged her forehead on the wall. 'No!' she screamed and when the voice came through the intercom asking what the problem was, Dayna said quite clearly, 'Nothing. Everything's fine.' And the lift began moving again.

Carrie was told that Dayna was finally in the building. 'Not in the studio though, is she? Anyone actually seen her yet?'

Leah was on the phone and held up her hand to pause Carrie. 'OK, thanks. That's great.' She hung up. 'They've just arrived in the studio. Let's go.' Leah saw the change in Carrie's eyes – the way her pupils grew from anxious slits to black discs indicating her inner turmoil. She knew Carrie didn't want to be doing this show any more than the girl did, but the chances of the Met getting a call post-show were high, especially with such raw material as they were about to put out.

'Did you get the trailers sorted?' Carrie asked.

'Eight are going out this morning in the breakfast show and between news bulletins.' Leah glanced at her watch and offered a small smile. 'I hope it does the trick, Carrie, really I do.' Friends forever, Leah couldn't stand to see Carrie this way. There was a brief hug between the two women before they went off to find

Dayna, no doubt in the guest dressing room, no doubt biting her nails, no doubt wondering if she could run for her life.

Carrie had no idea what she would say, how she would open. No clue how she would conclude or indeed what would happen in between. It was going to be just her and Dayna, the stage to themselves, plus a fifteen-minute segment on knife crime in London, finishing up with the scene of the stabbing at Milton Park. The production team never failed to astound Carrie and this time they'd surpassed themselves. They'd put together the short film in just twenty-four hours. She wasn't alone in all this, she tried to tell herself, however much it hurt to lie alone – *really* alone – at night, waiting for the light to come. Having her team around her and Leah beside her gave some comfort. It was just that . . . she faltered in her thoughts as well as her steps as they entered the dressing room . . . just that she'd never properly noticed before.

'Thank you,' were Carrie's first words to the mirror that reflected an image of a very frightened young lady. She tried to smile at her but it came out as pity and agony. The girl shrugged. Carrie approached the chair in which Dayna sat. Her hair was swept back with a towelling band.

'I said I didn't want any make-up. That I already got some mascara on.'

'It's the lights,' Carrie explained. 'So bright you'll look dead if you . . .' She wished she hadn't stopped so suddenly. Dayna picked her nails. 'Just a bit of foundation, eh, to give you some colour.'

Dayna nodded. 'Do I have to do this?'

'Course you bleedin' do,' came a rough voice from the other end of the dressing room. It was Dayna's mother. Carrie remembered the woman from when she'd visited her house.

'Mrs Ray,' Carrie said. 'Good of you to come.'

386

The woman stood and strode to Carrie like a man. 'I won't have any of this not doing it lark. We need the money. I told her that.'

'I'm afraid there isn't any money, Mrs Ray. The show doesn't pay its guests.' Carrie nodded at the make-up artist to continue her work on Dayna. The mother hovered. She reeked of smoke.

'Then we're off. Come on, Dayna.' She pulled at her daughter's sleeve.

'Mu-um.' Dayna shrugged away. 'I'm doing it, all right?'

'On, off, on, bleedin' off. Make your mind up, girl.' The mother's vehemence that her daughter wasn't doing the show for nothing was simply serving to make the teen more convinced that she was.

'Mrs Ray,' Leah said, stepping in. 'Perhaps if you come with me, we can talk about the fee.'

Dayna's mother nodded triumphantly at Carrie as she was led off by Leah.

Ten minutes later, Leah said, 'I stuck her in the green room with one of the security guys. Told him that she shouldn't move until someone comes to see her. Should keep her quiet for a while.'

Carrie was grateful. All she wanted was to focus on Dayna and getting the truth from her. A second-by-second account of what happened would not only help jog the public's memory – someone's son must have come home with blood on his hands, someone's boyfriend must have seemed moody and detached – but, deep down, she hoped it would also give her a little peace. Not even recalling the last time she saw her son, not knowing how the last morning of his life panned out was, day by day, destroying her.

MARCH 2009

Dayna went to see her doctor. He barely looked up from his computer screen when she stumbled and tripped over the words as she explained how it had happened.

'I see it a lot,' he said, sighing through pursed lips. 'You won't be the last.'

'What?'

'Unplanned pregnancies. I'm sure I'll have several more today.'

'I won't?' Was he trying to make her feel better, she wondered, by not being the only one, by not being quite so different?

The doctor turned and looked at her. He was old, probably in his sixties, Dayna thought, and she didn't think he really cared if she had the baby or not. 'Are you sure you want an abortion?'

'Of course. Why would I be here otherwise?'

The doctor shrugged. 'Because you've been referring to it as "the baby" since you walked in.'

Dayna stopped and thought. Pink and smelling of talc, just like Lorrell had been not so long ago. A little wriggling bundle of tiny clothes and squirming fingers. Long eyelashes over deep blue eyes. The little pulsing soft spot on baby's head and a throaty comfort noise while feeding.

'I'm sure,' she said.

It was likely, she'd been told, that she could get a phone call at any time if there was a cancellation. 'Lots of girls get cold feet,' the nurse had said. 'So to save wasting the surgeon's time, we like to get others to take the slots. Would you be willing to go on a waiting list and be called in at short notice?'

Dayna nodded and signed the forms. She liked the idea of short notice more than she relished waiting days or weeks for the operation. It was an operation, wasn't it? she'd asked the nurse tentatively.

'Yes, love. You'll be asleep and won't know anything about it. When you wake up, baby will be gone.'

Gone, Dayna thought. Just as seamlessly as it came into her life, it would be taken away, yet without the passion, love or excitement that she and Max had shared getting it in there in the first place.

She wouldn't tell her mother or Kev, and Lorrell hadn't mentioned the baby again. All being well, she'd be in and out within the day. That's what the nurse had said. Her mother wouldn't have a clue where she was and wouldn't ask either.

'That's all then, chick,' the nurse said, ushering her out. There were four other girls waiting to be seen. They stared at Dayna as she left.

She fondled her phone and considered texting Max but decided that there wasn't anything more to say. He'd wanted her to have the abortion and that's what she was doing. At school, they managed to avoid each other so that by the end of term it had become something of an art form. Occasionally, she had heard him set upon by the usual troublemakers and she herself was also menaced, although she didn't have Max by her side to help fight her corner. She worked hard and was still determined to leave school at the end of the year with a few GCSEs. If she could get to college – ironically, a childcare course had taken her fancy – then she could get a job and get off the estate. She dreamt of working as a nanny for a rich family who took long holidays in tropical places. She'd have her own room and they'd give her a car to drive the kids to school. She'd be happy, meet someone, send a bit of money to her mum for Lorrell. All this was possible, she knew, if she studied and worked and got rid of the baby.

'I'm hoping that you're all pretty much ready to hand in your finished essays. The Easter holidays are only a few days away and I want all your efforts on my desk to mark during the break.'

The bell rang and thirty-seven chairs scraped and the same number of kids bolted for the door. All except two.

'Sir, mine's finished.'

'Thanks, Dayna. I'm impressed with your work this year. You're on target to get a good grade.'

'Here you go, sir.'

Dayna swung round as the essay landed on top of hers. She was greeted by Max's pack being hoisted on to his shoulder. It nearly hit her in the face.

'You finished as well, Max?' Mr Lockhart asked, but the boy walked off without reply. Dayna nodded at her teacher and followed slowly in Max's wake, making sure she didn't catch him up as she would have done once.

Life was desolate and he wasn't winning anything. He stared at the piles of stuff in the shed. There was no point in selling it. He had a generous allowance and didn't need the money. He wanted to make plans but, since he'd split with Dayna, he couldn't bring himself to do anything much. His arms hung by his side. He was cold and could neither sit nor stand for more than a minute at a time.

Max had hoped they'd be closer than ever after what went on in the basement. It virtually killed him that Dayna had chosen to spread gossip and rumours and vile heartbreaking lies about him, which, of course, the other kids in their year – no, the entire fucking school – delighted in furthering.

With all the stories circulating, there was no way Dayna could play dumb about what was going on. That she hadn't come to him to apologise or attempt, not a reconciliation, but some sort of explanation at least of why she did it was the worst to bear. Clearly, after everything they'd been through together, she didn't give a shit. She was, ultimately, just like all the others.

He should have realised sooner. The Thing had barked it at him every day of his life until Dayna got in the way. *You're different, Max. You're an oddball. A freak. And guess what? Everyone hates you.*

Max dropped on to the car seat and lit a fag. The smoke filled the huge space left inside him. His fingers were cold and so he touched one on the glowing tip of the cigarette. It didn't hurt but neither did it warm him. The crazy thing was, in all of this, what he really wanted was his mum.

She'd sowed the seed, all those years ago, with a throw-away comment at the start of term when he was ten, maybe eleven, and getting ready to leave Charlbury and head back to Denningham. His mother had not long owned the vast place and he hadn't nearly finished exploring the grounds when the holidays were suddenly over. His trunk was packed for school but he didn't want to go back. He cried and his mother had pulled him towards her – roughly at first, he remembered thinking, until he realised it was a hug – and then she'd whispered motherly things against his head almost as if she really was sad to see him go but was just too afraid to admit it. He'd closed his eyes and melted on to her, harvesting her scent, her touch, her words, in the hope that they would last the term.

'Everything will be fine once you get back there, Maxie. You'll be with your friends and fit right in like you've never been away.'

How he wanted to tell her that he wouldn't fit in and that he didn't have any friends. What would have happened if, back then, he'd stamped his feet and demanded that something be done about the kids who beat him up, about the teachers who ignored what futile complaints he'd made, about the long nights he spent sobbing in his dorm? He didn't want to think about that; didn't want to admit how things could have been different, that with one stubborn word he might have changed the course of his whole life.

'I've got something for you,' his mother said, sighing, reaching that place of patience where, just a moment later, either nothing more would be said or something would snap and words would be yelled. She went off briefly and returned to the hall with a few magazines and comics. 'I almost forgot to give you these.'

He took the magazines. 'Thanks, Mum.'

'Something for the long drive to Denningham.'

In those days, she didn't have the helicopter. He recalled thinking, *don't you know that I get sick if I read in the car?*

'And take this, too.'

His mother always insisted that the polished oak table in the centre of the old hall be laden with a bowl of shiny green apples. She offered one to guests on their way out. She passed him an apple, rubbing it against her sleeve before he took it.

'Do you know what my father used to say?'

Max saw his mother's eyes hardening and, if it wasn't for their glassy stare, he'd have thought she had tears in them. He shook his head.

'My father wasn't very good at telling me things, Maxie. He was in the army and away a lot. He had shiny boots and a stiff moustache.' She smiled a little. 'He would have been so proud of you.'

Max wondered if that was really true but listened anyway. He couldn't imagine his mother having a father.

'He told me that when you eat an apple and get to the centre, it's as if you're seeing light years into the future.'

392

'How come?'

'Just think about those apple pips, Caroline, he said to me. Each one has the potential to become a tree. And how many apples will each of those trees bear and how many seeds will those apples have?'

'It would go on and on for ever,' Max said, enthralled by what his mother was saying.

'Exactly,' she said. 'It made me excited when I was a child. The little things in life contain great hope if we bite deep enough.'

Max wasn't sure he totally understood. He kissed his mother and got into the car. On the journey back to Denningham, the driver humming away to the radio, he flicked through one of the magazines.

'Puzzle Tree,' he read out loud. 'Get all the words in the right order, solve the mystery riddle and send your answers on a postcard . . . winner receives fifty pounds . . .' Max's mouth dropped open. He stared at the apple and crunched deeply into it. Two more bites and he'd reached the woody centre. Several black pips nestled in pithy holes. Fifty pounds, he thought, wondering if that would be enough for a taxi home when he ran away from school. He took a pen from his blazer pocket and began solving the puzzle. He finished his apple. Five pips in all. Five trees. What if each tree had a few hundred apples and all those apples bore five trees? His maths wasn't that good. He'd need his father to work it out but he was in Chicago so, for now, Max made do with infinity.

You could go on for ever, he thought, winding down the window and chucking out the core. He kept one pip back, though, for himself, tucked in his pocket because he liked the thought of going on for ever too.

The next day, puzzle completed, he posted the envelope. Three weeks later, he got a letter back saying that he'd won fifty pounds. It was as easy as that. That same day, he noticed the first shoot from the apple pip he'd planted in a yoghurt pot of soil. He liked the feeling of being in control even when the odds were stacked against him. He liked the feeling of making something out of nothing. He liked the feeling of just a little bit of hope when everything else was shit.

And what of his father? What if he'd not gone blind? Max thought. He used to believe that it was his fault, that if he'd not messed about or cried at bedtime or kicked up when he'd had to go back to school, or if he'd even eaten up properly or tidied his room when asked then his father wouldn't have lost his sight.

Max sucked on his cigarette in the shed, his elbows resting on his bony knees as he pulled them in to his chest. The smoke drew up slowly in front of his eyes. Was that what it was like at the start? he thought. Misty patches of wondering if you'd seen that right, perhaps do a double take or stare a bit longer. He remembered his dad muttering about his eyes, about how he was going to need glasses and that he was turning into a typical old professor. He remembered his mother's shrill laugh, her arms slinging round his neck, telling his father that nonsense, glasses were sexy and he would never in a million years be typical. Then again, in those days, she was just as likely to ignore his father or snap his head off for no reason. His dad never went to the optician.

'Crazy adults,' Max said, puffing out smoke and suddenly feeling self-conscious for talking to himself. 'Fuck off, Thing,' he yelled at the shed roof. 'You're not real. You don't control me.' The very silence that followed, the disturbing and unnatural quiet in his head was reply enough. It was as desolate as the blackness his father woke to each day and as commanding as his mother on the television. There was no escaping it. He *was* controlled by the Thing and, as he sat alone, pining for Dayna, aching for his mother, feeling so sad for his father, he realised that all along the Thing had been him. He saw quite clearly, too, that he was the never-ending pip, the apple tree that soon died when he forgot to water it in its tiny yoghurt pot. But now even that line of infinity was over because Dayna was getting an abortion.

For hours, he sobbed for his unborn baby.

FRIDAY, 1 MAY 2009

It nearly killed Carrie when she saw Max. He was larger than life, giving her that half-smile that said, *Oh God, Mum, leave me alone*, while also screaming out that he desperately needed her. Except he hadn't been able to have her because, until now, she'd not noticed the way his mouth could be so expressive, his eyes so imploring and his skin belie his age. He'd always behaved much older, so mature – was that Denningham? she wondered – not to mention that tough act he put on; necessary, she now realised, to survive. He skulked home from his new school – she'd never got used to seeing his pack dumped in the hallway mid-term – and raided her refrigerator or put on his music so loud she couldn't think in her study. He left his stuff lying about the house and the whole of upstairs smelt of cheap body spray in the mornings. He hardly ever spoke and when he did, it was defensive and confrontational at the same time. Even a chat about school lunch could end in war.

'Oh God, I miss you so much, Max.' Carrie dropped to her knees in front of the massive image of her son that formed the backdrop of the *Reality Check* set. It crippled her to think that everything was normal this time last week. Then she'd received the call every mother dreads.

'Honey, don't.' Leah was beside her while the sound crew ran checks. Banks of lighting shone and dimmed around them as the engineers worked, just as they did every Friday morning, as if this was just any show.

'Then why put him up there?' Carrie was crying. Hopeless, she knew, with less than an hour until airtime, but she couldn't help it. Make-up could fix her face before they went live.

'We want the viewers to see him, honey. Someone might recognise his face, remember something useful. This show's not just about getting the word out there to stop this crazy violence. It's about catching his killer. You know how Dennis and his team work. They need us as much as we need them for the show.'

'I'm sorry.' Carrie straightened. She blew her nose. 'I'm being ridiculous.'

'Are you sure you want to do this?'

'If I don't, I'll never live with myself. I have to do everything I can to help.'

Leah nodded. 'Let's get you back to make-up. We're going to need you ready on set for sound checks.'

Slowly, Carrie walked down the corridors. Regular crew and runners and assistants and other members of the production team rushed past her. 'Hey, Carrie,' someone called out, until Leah waved them off with her arm. In the dressing room, she sat as if in a different world to everyone else. It was a surreal place and she had been in it for exactly a week. Glimpses of reality leaked around her, but as for being a part of it, she knew that would never happen again.

'I'm one of *them* now, aren't I?' she said into the mirror.

'Pardon?' the make-up girl said. Leah had been called off to the production room.

'Me. I've become everything I feared.'

The girl smiled nervously and swept a huge brush across Carrie's cheeks. She was only young, not much older than Max, Carrie supposed. 'I heard what happened,' the girl said. 'It's awful. My brother got threatened outside a club just before Christmas. He says he always sees people with knives. They do it, like, to be tough or something.'

But Carrie wasn't listening. She'd closed her eyes and allowed the faces of all the bereft mothers that she'd had on the show over the years to stampede through her mind. She apologised to each and every one of them.

THURSDAY, 9 APRIL 2009

Dayna took the bus. It would stop right outside the hospital. On impulse, as she was bumping along, rubbing shoulders with the old man to her left, not particularly listening to the other passengers – the squawks of kids, the chatter of women, the tinny sound of headphones – and trying to ignore the screams of fire in her belly, she texted Max.

Having abortion today.

She just wanted him to know. She wanted his heart to thump as madly as hers was doing; she wanted him to text back and beg her not to do it. She would ignore him, tell him when it was done, that it was too late, that he should have done something sooner, that she couldn't help all those things that they said about him and God, oh God, none of it was her fault.

She felt sick. Was it the baby? The bus ride? Or remembering how they beat her and pushed her face in the urinals until she told them all the details. None of what she'd heard going around the school was what she'd actually said. Despite all the bruises, the filth they made her eat, the stuff that got nicked, she never once meant to betray Max. She told them she loved him. Shame she hadn't told Max.

Then they'd spread the rumours. They created their own version of events; chucked around pieces of her time with Max as if they were trash. In her head, she ran about trying to collect them up, trying to tell Max what had really happened, but the looks he'd given her had nearly killed her. He believed them. He really believed that she'd said all those vile things. Was it, she thought, because he thought them himself?

The bus slowed and stopped. The infirmary loomed to the left, casting a shadow not of health and recovery, but of morbidity and finality. But she was bound to feel that way, she convinced herself, stepping off the bus. She placed a hand on her stomach, wondering if it knew or sensed her fear. She marched up to reception and handed across the form she'd been given at the clinic a couple of weeks ago. They'd called her yesterday, telling her there'd been a cancellation, telling her not to eat or drink anything after midnight. She sat on the loo for hours, thinking about it.

'Go to the third floor, love. Head for the gynae ward.'

Dayna seemed to float towards the lift. She got out at the correct floor, suddenly dazed by all the signs and porters and the whiteness of it all as if it had snowed in her head.

'Excuse me,' she said quietly. 'Do you know where . . .' *Do you know where the abortions are?* The words screamed through her mind. 'Where the gyn . . . the gyna . . .' She couldn't say it.

'Down that way. First corridor to the right.' The porter wheeled off a young woman in a chair. Her face was ghostly white, her fingers picking together nervously in her lap, her belly big as a hill.

She handed in her slip of paper. The nurse bit her lip and glanced at Dayna. 'On your own?' she said.

Always, Dayna wanted to say. She nodded timidly.

'Someone picking you up later?'

Dayna knew where this was going. 'Yeah, my mum,' she lied. The nurse relaxed and tapped away at a computer.

'Right, let's get you a bed and begin admission.' She took Dayna through the ward, past rows of women, many of whom were clearly heavily pregnant. After they'd passed along several more corridors, after the warmth and visitors and happy chatter had diminished, they went through a key-coded door and into a series of rooms that were filled with young girls and posters on the wall. *Stay smart, Stay safe . . . Rape, it's not your fault . . . Don't get caught naked . . .* There were images of condoms and packets of pills and other stuff that Dayna didn't recognise. She blinked slowly and passed it all by, following the nurse to her fate.

Fifteen minutes later, Dayna was wearing a hospital gown and was lying in bed telling the nurse her medical history. She was kind to Dayna and wrote everything down. She asked if she had a boyfriend. Dayna shook her head. Then the nurse said the anaesthetist would come to see her soon.

Four hours later, hungry and thirsty, Dayna was watching the ceiling lights, the ventilation shafts and the hospital signs whizz past above her as the porters wheeled her down to theatre. They chatted about their kids and wives over her head. She had a plastic bracelet on. She fiddled with it. She had a needle and tube in the back of her hand. It hurt. They'd made her wear paper pants.

It would all be over soon.

Max got the second text at twenty past five.

He'd imagined her asleep in the operating theatre, her legs up in those metal stirrups, the surgeon asking for instruments then chatting to the nurse about the restaurant he'd been to last night. The machines would be beeping steadily; everything normal. Occasionally the nurse would check Dayna's face, hidden behind the screen. The surgeon would do his work, hardly having to concentrate, he'd done it so many times before. Perhaps there'd be a comment or two, about the waste, the sadness, the circumstances. Their baby would be taken out, put in a metal dish. Then what?

Dayna would be cleaned and taken to recovery, given a cup of tea. The nurse would be kind but maybe distant. Had her sister been trying for a baby for years? Had she miscarried herself? Usually a day case, Max had read on the internet. In and out. She was on the bus home, she'd said, when she texted him.

It's all over.

FRIDAY, 1 MAY 2009

'Good morning and welcome to this week's *Reality Check*.' Her cheeks glowed. She stood tall and faced the camera. She took a breath and spoke slowly. 'I'm Carrie Kent and today we're broadcasting to you under rather unusual circumstances.' Another breath. 'It's no secret that my family was struck by life-stopping tragedy last week.' She swallowed. 'My dear son, Max, was stabbed to death in a cold-blooded attack in his own school grounds.' Carrie took a step backwards. Gone was her usual striding style, her flamboyant arm and head gestures. Her face was deadpan.

'Presenting this show today is the hardest thing I've ever had to do, but this morning I want to achieve two things. Firstly, someone out there knows something.' Carrie leant forward. The camera zoomed. 'Whether your son came home agitated or covered in blood or your boyfriend was bragging about what he did or mentioned something he witnessed, then I implore you to call in. You know something. You can help. The hotline numbers direct to members of the Met will be on your screens throughout the show. The information you give will be confidential and you don't have to leave your name.'

Carrie turned, a little of her stage presence resurfacing, and she walked towards the two chairs that were set at angles to each other beneath the huge photograph of Max.

'Secondly, I want to get the message out there to all the ignorant, misguided youths who think that carrying knives is a civilised way to act, that it simply isn't.' For three seconds, she said nothing. She glared at the camera and saw it not as a window to fame but rather an opening into the lives of the millions who watched her. It was her chance to help, to really do something good.

'Carrying a knife is not protection as some of you believe. It doesn't make you invincible or brave or manly. Neither does it make others look up to you.' The sob Carrie let out wasn't to gain sympathy. She couldn't help it. For now, she kept back the tears. She had to. The show had only just begun. 'Carrying a knife or any kind of weapon confirms you as the low-life scum you really are. It's a badge of cowardice and a licence to live with nothing but fear. If I can get just one person to do the right thing and call our team today, if I can make one person put down a knife, then standing here, my legs still shaking from grief, I will perhaps be able to carry on. My son's death won't have been totally in vain. As things are, I am finding it very hard. Thank you.'

Carrie turned and walked slowly to the rear of the studio, unable to get the thought of Max stealing her kitchen knife from her mind. She knew she was still being filmed but also that the remainder of the titles were scrolling on screen. There was usually a catchy theme jingle, but today there would be silence. The studio audience gave a tight, subdued clap as they had been instructed and, once quiet, Carrie faced the camera to commence.

'I want to introduce you to someone who's been rather brave throughout the last week. Until a few days ago, I didn't even know of her existence. She was Max's girlfriend and, teenagers being the private creatures they are, I knew nothing about her. Sadly for her, this young lady bore witness to my son's fatal stabbing. Sadly again, she is unable to identify the perpetrators. By getting her on the show, by listening to her story, I'm hoping that you, our viewers, will help. After ten years of doing this show, after ten years of interfering in other people's lives, it's time for you to interfere in mine.

'Ladies and gentlemen, please welcome, with the utmost respect for her grief, Miss Dayna Ray.'

Again, there was a ripple of restrained clapping followed by absolutely nothing. Carrie swallowed and waited by the wings to greet Dayna. She didn't care how nervous or tentative she was about stepping in front of the cameras, she just wanted her on air. Dayna didn't appear. Carrie pressed her earpiece. Nothing.

Finally, after another few seconds but what seemed like an hour, Dayna eased herself from the wings of the set. Behind her, Carrie caught a glance of Jess Britton. The detective nodded reassuringly, her hands on Dayna's back, gently easing her out into the brilliant lights.

'Dayna, my love, thank you so much for doing this.' It was a private moment, with Carrie holding away her microphone. She hugged the girl – a prolonged gesture which she hoped not only the viewers would recognise as a special yet unfortunate bond between the pair, but also as a genuine conveyance of her sympathy. Losing a close friend – she'd tried to imagine losing Leah – was not so far removed from losing a son.

Dayna blinked. She squinted ahead, obviously trying to make sense of what she saw. Carrie knew that she'd been brought on set earlier and shown around to get used to the lights, the crew, the cameras, and the hundreds of studio seats that would soon be filled with eager faces. For Carrie, it was all so easy to ignore. Dayna, she realised, would be shell-shocked from it. Even at the best of times, appearing on television was gruelling.

'Come and sit down here and we can talk.' Carrie involved the audience again, as if inviting them into their intimate chat. There was a low table in front of the chairs with two glasses and a jug of water. Carrie poured while Dayna settled herself. The girl seemed half her usual size, minimised by grief and fear. Her legs were pencil-thin in the tight grey jeans and the rest of her was swamped in the jacket she wore. She tried to make her face disappear beneath the collar with her shoulders hunched, her chin bent low. The girl stared at her feet as they shuffled within mucky plimsolls.

'We all really appreciate you coming, Dayna. There's no easy way to say what I need to ask you today. I hope you can take some comfort, as I am, in that by doing this we are making the most of this awful situation. Neither you nor I, nor the team of tireless detectives who are working round the clock on this case, want to be doing this, but we have to. For Max. For all the other kids out there who aren't dead yet but might be next week, next year . . . we have to try to stop it.'

Carrie took a moment to compose herself. She sipped some water, adjusted the way she sat and looked Dayna Ray straight in the eye.

'I want you to tell me, Dayna, in your own words, what happened at school on the morning of April the twenty-fourth.'

Dayna knew she looked nervous – all the squinting and fidgeting and fiddling with her hair – but she didn't care. She bit her nails, desperate for a fag, and could have done with a beer too, to get her through. On other shows, she'd seen some guests scream and kick and fight and end up storming off stage. That, or they were dragged off. Carrie used her charms to calm them down, bring them back, get down to business again. Could she do that? she wondered. Run away? She'd thought of it the last few days although it suddenly seemed much more of an option while sitting here with Carrie Kent, about to be taken to pieces because she didn't really know anything. She *didn't*.

'I want you to tell me, Dayna, in your own words, what happened at school on the morning of April the twenty-fourth.'

Carrie put down her glass. Dayna picked up hers. It would

prevent her having to speak for a few more seconds. Why had she come?

'In your own time,' Carrie continued, which obviously meant hurry up.

'It was just a normal day,' Dayna began. It felt weird being the only one speaking and all those people watching. Her voice didn't sound like hers. She could pick out faces in the audience; see them shaking their heads, shifting in their seats. 'I never thought anything like that would happen.' Her voice sounded vapid, as if she was simply talking about the bad canteen food or the way the PE teacher let them skive cross-country.

But it was true; she didn't think anything like that *would* happen. Even with everything that had gone before between her and Max, it still all seemed like a horror movie that she couldn't get out of her head.

'I got up early. I helped my kid sister get sorted and took her to school. Then I went on to Milton Park. It was all just normal.'

Dayna was aware of Carrie nodding. It was so hot in the studio. She wished she hadn't worn this stupid jacket.

'Did you talk to anyone when you got to school?'

'Nah. No one talks to me. Well, Max did but . . .' Dayna trailed off. Her heart thumped. She was already tip-toeing through broken glass in bare feet. 'I went to maths and, like, got really bored. I did geography next but decided to bunk off after that.'

The lights shone brightly in Dayna's eyes, dazzling her thoughts. She stared up at the metal racks with hundreds of spots aiming at her as if they were going to fire at her. Shots of light to make me spill the truth, she thought. She wouldn't. She couldn't. This was Max's *mother*.

'Was Max in either of those lessons?'

It was like the police interviews all over again, Dayna thought dismally. She'd wriggled through those somehow but not easily.

Had she come on the show to convince everyone, including herself, that she still didn't know anything? Or had she come to confess that she knew too much? She was on the verge of bolting and they'd only just started. God, all she wanted was for Max to be alive again. Surely that made them on the same team.

'He was in maths,' Dayna heard herself saying. She recalled his back curled over the desk, his fingers tapping at the calculator. He found maths hard, he'd told her once, as if, for some reason, he should be innately tuned in to the subject. Only bother with what you're good at, she'd said. Like the competitions, she'd continued, grinning. 'But I didn't see him in geography. We were doing stuff about fair trade. Max once told me that nothing was fair.'

She felt the burn of Carrie's stare, way hotter than the lights. The woman's silence made her continue talking. 'I went to the chippy. I hadn't eaten breakfast and I was hungry. I wasn't the only kid from school there. There were some girls bunking off from my year.'

Give us yer cash, Dayna remembered them saying. She saw the hatred in their eyes when she emptied her pocket. 'And the other one,' they said until she had no money left. They went in and ordered their chips. When they'd gone, Dayna hitched up her shirt and opened the money belt she wore. With a pound or two in her pockets to appease whoever chose to help themselves to her cash, she'd hidden the tenner she'd nicked from Kev's wallet in the pouch. She ordered chips and wandered slowly back to school.

'I was hoping to bump into Max. We'd got stuff to talk about,' Dayna continued. She felt a sweat break out on her top lip. Would all that stupid make-up smudge if she wiped her face?

'Such as?' Carrie said.

The two of them stared at each other. A frozen moment.

'Things hadn't been going too well between us.'

'Oh?' This was clearly news to Carrie. Dayna didn't speak to her mother about such things, and clearly Max hadn't confided in his either.

'It was just something . . . something I told him that he took the wrong way. I wanted him to know the truth. And kids had been mean to him at school because he was going out with me. They were spreading rumours and stuff.'

Carrie shook her head, looking concerned, lost. Dayna didn't expect her to hold it together after that revelation. She waited for the yell or the shake of her shoulders, demanding answers. But oddly she remained calm and professional. Dayna thought that was worse.

'So I went and sat on the wall and ate my chips. I reckoned Max would walk past. I wanted to talk to him. You know, clear things up.'

The lights flared in her eyes. Cameras rolled around her on big trolleys. There were so many people . . . so many people watching.

'Fucking hell,' he'd said when she'd called out his name as he'd walked past the wall. The first thing he'd said to her in ages. And she just held out her chips to him as if that would make it all better.

'He was . . . dancing around,' she told Carrie quietly. 'Dancing around and I didn't know why. His arms were everywhere and at one point I thought he was going to hit me. He was, like, really mad.'

Dayna heard a collective gasp. She noticed the ripple in Carrie's throat as she swallowed.

'I calmed him down and got him to sit with me on the wall.'

Dayna felt the cold grit of the cement beneath her school trousers. She was kicking her heels against the bricks, trying to make out that she was in control when really Max was. She ate the chips. The vinegar stung a cut she had from biting the skin on her lip.

'Had the gang arrived at this point? Was anyone threatening Max?'

Dayna heard Carrie's words in her head but she was back on the wall, burning her tongue, smelling Max's aftershave, feeling the sense of utter desolation inside from what she'd done.

'No,' she replied. 'The gang wasn't there yet.' She knew Carrie just wanted her to get to the point, identify the one who did it, get the phone lines buzzing. Blue eyes or black hair or a scar on their cheek? Adidas trainers or ripped jeans, a visible tattoo or description of a chain round their neck? Anything to help.

Could she make it all up? Would she be able to sit here, live on television, and lie? It was what she'd planned, wasn't it?

Dayna felt as if she was floating again. Everything had built up inside her the last week. She'd hardly slept or eaten and all she'd drunk was beer or Coke or whatever made her griping stomach feel full and the truth go away.

Was she standing, sitting? In the school grounds or at the television studio?

She took a step forward but the ground wasn't there. Maybe she was on the wall still. Yes, the wall. There was Max, jumped down now, looking all agitated and hopping about.

'I told him what I'd done,' Dayna said. Who was she talking to? Carrie? Max? She wanted to sob but couldn't. 'I was so angry that I screamed it at him. I told him I'd done what he wanted.'

'What had Max wanted?' That Carrie woman again, sticking her nose in. 'Tell me what you mean, Dayna.'

A long silence, broken only by a car going along the street outside school, the rhythmic thud of her boot on the wall, a cough from someone in the audience.

'About the baby,' she whispered. The shuffling chorus around her again. Shock and disbelief. Then the wide eyes of that

410

woman beside her, as if she, too, was walking in this strange, detached place.

'The baby? What baby, Dayna? For God's sake, you have to tell me.'

She felt a hand on her arm. Was it Max's or his mother's? Dayna remembered Max grabbing her. He was rough and angry.

'You killed our baby,' he said in such a way that Dayna didn't know if it was a yell or a whisper.

Then she was walking somewhere, anywhere, into the light. Someone was following her. She turned suddenly, her eyes wide and searching like a trapped animal. 'All this pain inside me,' she said. 'I just want to make it go away.'

'Tell me about the baby, Dayna.' A woman's voice – slight tremble, tightening fingers on her arm. Dayna stared into Carrie Kent's eyes, illuminated by the brilliance around them. Max's *mother*. Dayna smiled at that. Max was everywhere, wasn't he?

'We were lovers,' she said. A rumble from the audience but cut short. 'I loved him, but you know what?' Dayna heard someone laughing. It took her a moment to realise it was her. 'I never once told him.'

'You were having unprotected sex?'

Dayna was nodding, just as she had done to Max when he lay down on her. 'It's what you tell everyone to do, isn't it?' Dayna was vague, unreal.

'What?' Carrie asked indignantly.

'To use contraception.' Dayna shrugged herself from Carrie's grasp. She was sick of being pushed around. 'Well, we didn't, did we? And I got pregnant. I got pregnant with Max's baby.'

Oh my God . . . was all Dayna heard layered over the studio audience gasps of shock. She liked it that she had stunned everyone. A primer, she thought, for what was to come.

'You're, like, always going on about teen pregnancies and irresponsible sex. Well, guess what? Your own son was doing it

411

right under your nose.' Something was building inside Dayna. It was a similar feeling to when she'd stolen fags off that little kid. It was empowering, enabling her to stride across the studio just as she'd seen Carrie Kent do to intimidate her other guests. She spun round, the cameras tracking her, and glared at Carrie.

'How does that make you feel?' she spat out.

'I . . . I . . .' Carrie stopped. She touched her earpiece. 'When is it due?' she said so quietly that Dayna had to virtually lip-read. 'Max's baby . . .' she whispered.

'Thing is,' Dayna continued, staring down the camera lens that was aimed at her, 'it's not that simple.'

She remembered his face, the way it crumpled as he spoke, the utter loss and desolation. 'I didn't mean it, for fuck's sake. I didn't want you to get an abortion but you said those things about me. They said you'd slept with them all, that you were nothing but a slag. They told me you hated me. I hated you back.'

Dayna remembered shrugging. It was easier than hearing it. She'd wanted to tell him that they hurt her too, that someone had spotted them emerging from the boiler room. They'd forced lies out of her, that even if she hadn't said them they'd have made them up anyway. It's just what they were like, what they did. Her life and theirs. Combined misery.

'I've never had sex with anyone else,' was all Dayna managed to get out. Max didn't believe her. He made a face. One she'd never seen on him before. It was anger mixed with distrust wrapped up in such intensity it scared her. For the first time ever, she was afraid of him.

'What did it feel like, eh, having it ripped out of you?' He was strutting about, pacing up and down the length of the wall, panting like an animal, his head bobbing, his fists clenching.

'Max . . . please . . .' Then she remembered seeing them. Four or five? They were in her peripheral vision, skirting round the wire fence that separated school from street. She glanced at them then back at Max.

'There were a few of them. I dunno. Max and I were arguing when I caught sight of them,' she said clearly to Carrie. It was a clever shift back to what everyone wanted to know.

'Who?' Carrie asked. There were tears in her eyes. She'd had to sit back down in the chair. She sipped water.

'The gang. They were stalking about. Looking for trouble.'

'Did you see what they were wearing?'

'Usual stuff. Trackies. Trainers. Hoodies.'

'Did you recognise any of them?' Carrie leant forward. Dayna could almost smell the desperation on her. She suddenly felt as if it was her show and Carrie was the guest.

She turned to the camera. 'I'm not sure,' she said vaguely, narrowing her eyes. It was easy to bring back – she'd been doing it all week. Going over and over those minutes that seemed stretched into days.

'Max,' she remembered saying, trying to warn him with a nod of her head towards the gang. 'Behind you.'

Max had turned, momentarily released from his rage, but picking it up again when he spun back round to Dayna. He didn't seem to be bothered by the youths.

'You want to know something?' he said. He was up close now, crushing her legs against the wall as he stood squarely in front of her.

Dayna shrugged, glanced behind him again. They were almost through the gates. They'd clocked them; were staring in their direction. 'Sure.' She didn't like the way Max was behaving. She felt threatened. He hitched his bag up and patted it with his hand. She knew what he kept in there.

'I'm not scared any more.'

'That's good, Max.' Dayna played along. It had been a mistake to confront him. She had to accept that it was over.

413

She'd get her exams and get out of school in a couple of months. She picked up a chip and was about to put it in her mouth when Max grabbed the tray from her and hurled it across the tarmac. Chips sprayed everywhere. There was a lone slow clap from the gang by the school gates. One of them laughed and let out a lazy cheer.

'What you fucking staring at?' Max called out to them.

'Max, don't,' Dayna said urgently. 'Calm down. Let's have a smoke.' Her fingers trembled as she lit the joint. 'Here.' She passed it to him. He succumbed to temptation and sat on the wall next to her, squinting through the smoke at the gang. They were shoving each other around. *Yeah, you go to fucking school, man*, she heard one say.

'It was, like, really really scary,' Dayna told Carrie. 'All of them out there and just us. We were trying to act normal. To go back into the school building, we had to walk past them. We should have got out as soon as I saw them. It's all my fault.' She could see Carrie thinking it through. Despite this, the woman kept the show going. She stated facts and figures about knife crime that year so far. How many teens had been stabbed in London alone. How many arrests were made. Dayna could hardly believe it. Then she told the audience that they'd be back after the commercial break.

Suddenly, Carrie's face was in hers. She yanked her earpiece out. A woman was brushing at the star's make-up, another fixing her hair. She batted them away.

'What do you mean . . . the *baby*?'

Dayna didn't reply. She couldn't. Guilt was stuck in her throat. Silence would get her through the break. She stared emptily at Carrie before turning and walking back to the chair. She sat and sipped water, listening to frantic conversations between producers and camera crew and loads of other people all rushing about. She heard Carrie's voice among it all, saying

414

why, why, why over and over. Someone asked her if she wanted to continue with the show and she flipped out. *Thirty seconds*, she heard. More commotion and then silence. A countdown. Carrie stood centre stage.

'Welcome back to this week's *Reality Check*. I'm talking to Dayna Ray, friend of my son, Max, who was fatally stabbed last week. I'm appealing to you, my viewers, to phone the police hotline number on your screen if you can help in any way. It might be that you live close to Milton Park School and saw a group of youths hanging around on the morning of the twenty-fourth of April. Or perhaps your son has been acting strangely or you found blood on his clothes. Did you overhear your teenager talking to his mates on the phone about the incident? Or perhaps you were involved yourself. Whatever the connection and however small, I implore you to call in. The information you give will be strictly confidential and you don't have to reveal your name. But before we return to our guest, I want to show you a short film about knife crime in London.'

Everyone was motionless as the film also played for the benefit of those in the studio. Carrie stood proud and watched as images of her son flashed past to the most emotional music Dayna had ever heard. Other teenagers' faces – black, white, Asian – scrolled across the screen. All killed. All stabbed. All within the last year. There was footage of the school, of forensics doing their work, and even a picture of Max's bedroom. His leftover life. The film ended.

'Now.' Carrie took a deep breath. 'Back to Dayna.' She glared at her as she strode to the chairs. She sat down and, once her face was visible to the cameras again, she lost the stern look. 'At what point did you realise there was going to be trouble with the gang, Dayna? It must have been terrifying for you.' She'd obviously decided to lay off asking about the baby for the time being.

'Like I said, we were just smoking, sitting on the wall. I'd calmed Max down a bit. Then those lads came in the school grounds and began yelling things. Two of them had quite dark messy hair. It was sticking out from their hoods. One had terrible spots and the other had these horrid eyes. So scary. Max had told me how he wasn't going to give in to them any more. How he wasn't going to be scared. I was proud of him for that.'

At this, Dayna saw Carrie's face soften and her eyes shut for a moment. Dayna closed her eyes for a moment, too.

'Oi, fuckhead,' one of the gang called out. They were still hanging around the school gates, smoking, and one had a can of something.

'Hey, ow!' she said as Max bent her arm. 'What you do that for?'

'Murderer,' he said venomously, ignoring the calls from the gang.

'Stop . . . but you told me . . . no!'

Max pulled her off the wall, their arms tangled, Dayna trying to wrestle free from Max's vice-like grip. He'd gone mad. The joint was hanging from his mouth as he yelled abuse at her. Then there was cheering and clapping as three of the gang approached, drawn inside the gates by the scuffle, always up for a bit of trouble. The others had wandered off, bored. Dayna couldn't recall who she was more scared of, Max or them.

'Please, oh please stop . . .' She began to cry. This wasn't right. She wanted to talk to him, to reason with him, to make him understand what had happened. This was all so unfair. She'd not been given a chance. It should have been so simple but his eyes were scalding red and his teeth were chomping on the spliff like a monster.

Then she was on the ground, jolted and stunned. The tarmac grazed her palms. She stared up at him.

'I thought we were a thing, you and me. I thought you . . . thought you loved me.' Max was shaking, ripping off the bag that was slung diagonally across his body, pulling at his clothes, his hair. Had he taken something? This wasn't the Max she knew.

'Look, man, da skinny bastard's got one on 'im.' There was laughter. It fuelled Max's rage further.

It was slow motion. The world, fuzzy-edged. Unreal. Some crazy time slip.

Max reached into his bag.

'It was awful,' Dayna said to Carrie. She had to be careful. She had to get this right. She was on television. She thought of Max and prayed for his soul. The lights in the studio were so bright.

'What do you mean, Dayna?' Carrie asked.

'The gang, they'd surrounded him. One of the youths pulled out a knife.'

'Oh God,' she heard Carrie whisper. 'Then what happened?'

Total silence in the studio.

'There was shouting. They were calling Max names, really winding him up. Max got so mad I thought he was going to explode.' Dayna's stomach cramped with grief as she remembered. She leant forward and sobbed. It was all going wrong. She didn't care that she was on television. Didn't care who saw her or what she said. She didn't care about her story, either, because she was so confused and her insides hurt and it was nearly killing her that Max had died without knowing the truth.

It was all her fault.

'Oh please, no, don't,' she'd said. She tried to stand up again but Max pushed her back down with his foot pressed on her belly.

Then she saw it, glinting in his fist. The knife, drawn from his bag, pointing right at her.

'No . . .' she'd screamed, rolling sideways away from the blade. The youths formed a shroud around them, shouting out, always up for trouble. Somehow, she found her feet and backed away. Max followed her, the knife in his outstretched hand leading him on.

'Hey, easy, man,' one of the gang called out. 'Someone gonna get hurt with that thing.'

Max ignored them. He ignored Dayna, too, as she tried to spit out what she'd wanted to tell him. But his eyes were wide and staring, all of the soft velvet warmth they contained dried up and hardened. Max had had enough.

There was a hand on her back, stroking her. 'It's OK, love. Take your time. So the gang had surrounded you and Max. Did the boy threaten Max with the knife? What did he say? Can you remember what he looked like?'

Dayna lifted her head. There were tissues on the table so she reached out and took one as if she was just in someone's living room, not live on television. If she thought too hard about that, she'd be sick. She blew her nose. 'It, like, all goes fuzzy from there. This crazy stuff happened . . .'

Dayna had heard about the arrest from that detective, Jess; about how Warren Lane was taken in by the cops but then released again. Everyone knew Warren. He was a right loser. He'd been locked up loads before. He'd nicked cars, done some dealing, robbed the post office. And everyone said he was stupid to boot. Or was he so stupid, Dayna thought, as she remembered his face in the group of lads that awful morning.

He'd run away from more foster families than he could count and it was no secret he'd been living rough. The only time he bothered to come to school was when he needed a free meal or to use the showers and loos. Dayna knew it was him there that morning. His hood was up, shrouding his face, but it was Warren Lane all right. She also knew what he was up to by getting arrested. That wasn't any secret either. Get busted and get locked up. It was a roof over his head and free food for the next decade or two. Kids like him preferred it inside.

418

Should she tell them it was him?

In a flash, she caught Max's wrist in her hand as it came down towards her. She never once believed he was going to stab her. He wouldn't, would he?

'Max just wasn't himself,' she told Carrie. She could say that much. She cried some more and Carrie waited patiently.

Dayna screamed and scratched Max's face with her free hand. It gave him a moment's lucidity – the look of hatred transforming into a frown as he briefly wondered where he was, what he was doing, why the hell he was wrestling with the girl he loved.

His hand unclenched. He dropped the knife. It bounced and clattered on the tarmac.

'Hey, man, just cool it, yeah? Someone gonna get hurt.' Warren Lane stepped forward and picked up the knife. 'Nice,' he said, fingering the handle and running his thumb across the blade. 'You don't wanna shank ya girl, man. Take it from me.' Warren laughed and whipped the knife about, cutting at the air with speed. 'The slammer ain't no place for a skinny shit like you, man.' He laughed again, his smoker's voice making him sound ten years older than he really was. He lunged round at his mates, playfully stabbing at them. The other kids recoiled.

He turned to Dayna. 'You better take this then, yeah?' He held the knife out to her, handle first, as if he trusted her not to do anything stupid with it. 'And look after dat boy of yours cos he got some crazy shit in him today.'

'Max was really upset because, you know, about the baby and everything. He'd told me to get an abortion. I went to the hospital—'

'An *abortion*?' Carrie grabbed Dayna's wrists and pulled her round so they were facing each other. Their eyes were inches apart. Dayna saw the same sorrow in Carrie's eyes as there had been in Max's.

'You fucking killed our baby,' he'd spat out. The knife was long, so very sharp, and Dayna held it in her fist, pointing down the length of her leg. 'So tell me, what now? You fucking tell me what's left.' Spit was foaming on his lips. 'I got nothing in my life. Not even you. Not even any damned baby that we didn't want and now you've gone and killed it.'

'I was so angry with him when he told me to get an abortion. As if it was all so disposable. As if *I* was disposable.'

Carrie relinquished her grip. Dayna knew she couldn't be violent on television. But it was almost as if they weren't on television any more. Things had got past that. They were in their own private hell, one hiding from the truth, one searching for it.

'Max, just calm down,' Dayna begged. The other kids were heckling him again. It was just what they did; programmed into them.

'Don't fucking tell me to calm down.' The odd thing, she recalled, was that Max was entirely calm when he said this. For a second, in that beautiful moment before it happened, she'd believed she would be able to reason with him and tell him what she'd done and they could sit down again and talk and hug and forget about this shit of a drizzly morning. Hell, they could go down to the shed and do some competitions, have a smoke, eat some food.

'I had the knife in my hand,' Dayna blurted out to Carrie. There were gasps all around the studio.

'What? How?' Carrie asked incredulously.

It should have ended fine, it should have ended with Warren and his mates swaggering off to cause trouble elsewhere. It should have ended with Max's hand placed on her belly, his face pressed to her neck telling her his plans, how much he loved her. That was what she'd hoped as she lay on that hospital bed, the anaesthetist hovering over her, making jokes, trying to make her feel at ease before the operation. The lights above dazzled her.

The nurses were chattering. They lifted her wrist and said she would feel something cold in her arm and that she should count to a hundred.

'I didn't have the abortion. I couldn't go through with it,' Dayna said, suddenly standing up. She needed to move about. She went down the couple of steps from the studio platform they were sitting on. Her body was rigid with fear. 'But I never got to tell Max.' She spun round to face Carrie who was now also standing. 'He died thinking I killed our baby.' Dayna threw back her head and sobbed.

Carrie's eyes were wide and filled with something that Dayna should have been terrified of. Was she angry, happy, going to hit her, hug her?

'So you're still pregnant?' This news outweighed everything else. Carrie approached – cautiously, as if the truth itself was a weapon. 'And what do you mean, you had the knife in your hand?'

Dayna screwed up her eyes and covered her face with her hands. She let out stifled sobs.

It was a long knife, a kitchen knife. The sharpest she'd ever seen. It was the same one that Max had threatened those kids with at the park. It had sent them scarpering, all right. Max felt safe with it, in control. It was there when he needed it. Cold, infallible, certain.

Then another tussle, this time so fast she didn't know what was happening.

'Max, no! What the hell are you doing?' Dayna screamed. She'd thought it was all over, but he'd lunged at her, caught her off guard, made it all end wrong.

Dayna took a deep breath.

She didn't care about the cameras or the audience or the lights.

She was sweating.

421

'I killed Max,' she said coldly.

Everything was silent. Inside her head. Outside of it. There was nothing.

Everything gone as if it never even existed.

Carrie's face froze. Then her forehead and eyes drew together in a disbelieving contortion. She was reaching out, trying to grab someone, something. She didn't know what she was doing. She was staggering.

Then the tidal wave of shock from the audience.

No . . .

The single word was a bullet. Carrie slowly followed its path towards Dayna.

'I killed Max,' Dayna repeated flatly. 'And now I'm sorry.' She heard the words but it wasn't her saying them. 'So very, very sorry.'

Carrie crept towards Dayna. 'There is no *sorry*.' Flustered, sweating, red-faced, glassy-eyed, Carrie searched around her for help. She glanced to the wings. Leah was there, talking into her radio. Dennis was there too, whispering to that woman detective. Two bouncers came on stage and each stuck an arm under Dayna's armpit. They hauled her back to the chair and forced her to sit. They stood either side of her. She was shaking. So freezing cold.

'I killed Max,' she said again to make sure they all knew. She placed both hands on her belly as if to protect her baby from whatever she was now going to get.

Carrie stood in the middle of the stage, her arms dangling by her side, her neck barely able to hold up her head. She couldn't speak or cry.

Dayna swallowed and stared straight ahead. Any minute now that cop man would arrest her. She would tell them how she'd stabbed Max when he'd lunged at her for the knife, that it was self-defence, that she'd been covering up and lying all along. Her prints were on the knife. She had a motive – they'd been fighting about the abortion. There was no way out for her now.

She was ready to take her punishment. Max had believed that she'd gone through with the abortion. It was all her fault.

Before she knew what was happening, he'd swiped the knife from her hand. She lost her grip on the cold handle.

'Max, stop!'

He danced backwards. His face was contorted by the demons inside him.

The youths began jeering again, tormenting him, telling him he was a loser and should just piss off home.

Dayna circled him, her hands outstretched. She had to get the knife back.

Half crouching, half stalking, his legs apart, his back bent, Max growled and screamed. He yelled out stuff she didn't understand – didn't *want* to understand – and then he turned his face to the sky and begged for help. He was crying.

Dayna looked up, too, as if the heavens held the answer to everything they'd been searching for. Because it was a quest they'd been on, their pursuits converging for a few short months as they shared the agonies and the delights of being teenagers, of being alive, of being different when really, when it came down to it, they were just like everyone else.

Who is it, she wondered in those few short moments staring at the steel-coloured clouds, that decides our fate?

She lowered her eyes again, slowly, deliberately. Nothing was real any more.

Then everything changed when Max plunged the knife into his stomach.

His eyes bulged, swimming with tears.

He held Dayna's stare as he contemplated the pain.

A single wave engulfing him. All the misery of his life tied up in one deep wound.

'Oh God, *no!*'

Max pulled out the blade. Blood poured hot and angry from his belly.

Dayna screamed.

Max stabbed himself again and again and again and again. He was doubled up, both hands gripping the blade and plunging it upwards into his abdomen. His hands, his face, his clothes, his feet, the ground – within seconds, everything was covered in blood.

'Shit!' someone yelled.

'Fucking twist,' Warren Lane called out to his mates.

Dayna looked at him in a daze, wondering what that meant, hoping they were going to get help, make everything all right.

They didn't. They ran, their shiny trainers flashing through the murk. There was no one else about.

In slow motion, Max fell to his knees. Dayna screamed again but nothing came out. She watched, mesmerised, as beautiful, skinny, clever, hopeless Max folded to the ground. He hit his head.

Dayna rushed up to him. 'Don't die,' she begged. *Oh God, oh God, oh God . . .*

She heard pounding feet running away. She pressed her hands over Max's belly but she couldn't stop the blood. He gasped for breath and something inside him bubbled up then wheezed down.

'Help!' Dayna screamed out. She leapt to her feet. The school grounds were more desolate than she'd ever known. The gang had legged it. She fumbled for her mobile phone and called for an ambulance.

'I can't live without you,' she cried, trying to stop the blood pumping from him. Max was deflating. 'I *won't* live without you.'

It was all her fault. If she hadn't led him on, made him believe she'd gone through with the abortion to punish him, then he wouldn't have flipped out like this.

424

What had she done?

'Stop,' someone said. That woman Leah strode on to the stage.

Dayna looked up and her eyes widened. She bit her lip.

'Carrie, it's OK. It's OK,' she said. 'We're off air. We haven't been live since the film clip. I decided to go to a re-run when things got sticky.' She pulled Carrie into her arms. From over her shoulder, she glared at Dayna. 'The phones have been going mad. You did a good job.'

'I . . . don't understand,' Carrie said. Her voice was weak.

'You don't need to.' Dennis Masters was suddenly beside Dayna. She could smell sweat and coffee on him. 'Silly little girl,' he muttered. 'See to her, detective,' he said to Jess.

Dayna frowned. What were they on about?

'I killed Max. It's my fault he's dead,' Dayna said again. The words stung her lips. She saw Carrie flinch as she was guided off stage by Leah. Her face was a map of grief and despair.

'Nice try,' Dennis said to her. 'But you're too late. Warren Lane's already given himself up. He phoned in shortly after the show went to air. A car's on its way to pick him up.'

Dayna scowled. She didn't understand. What was he on about?

'Between you and me, love,' Dennis crouched down – Jess had stepped aside to take a call, 'I *know*.'

Dayna wanted to hit him and kick and punch him until he believed her. But all she could do was sit there, her shoulders rising up to her ears, her face dropping beneath the collar of her jacket.

'Those little squealers Samms and Driscoll decided that to save their mate Lane from getting into strife, they ought to fess up what really went on. They told me exactly what happened. It fits with the new forensics and autopsy reports.'

'I killed Max. It's my fault he's dead.' Dayna was robotic.

425

'No, love. No, you didn't.' Dennis sighed. He placed a hand on her arm. 'But Lane's confession is going to pave the way directly to the prison cell he's always dreamt of.'

Dayna's face reddened and paled and crumpled from shock. 'No . . . no . . . you don't understand—'

'But, you see, I have a bit of a problem.' Dennis shifted further round so his back was facing the crew. He got closer to Dayna. 'My officers are on their way to arrest Warren. The CPS will charge him and, after a quick spin in court, off he goes to the nick. It bangs up the little sod for a long time and gets him off my patch. It also appeases the powers that be as our violent crime statistics suddenly look a whole lot better. The only trouble is Samms, Driscoll and . . . and, of course, you.'

Dayna gasped. What was he saying? She couldn't take it all in.

'My advice to you, sweetheart, is, unless you want to get charged with wasting police time and obstructing justice, then you'll keep quiet. Why not just concentrate on being a good little girl at school and doing the best for your baby when it's born?' Dennis smiled – an attempt to conceal his fear in case she kicked up a fuss, Dayna deduced – and then he stood up, stretching out his back with a groan and a crack.

No . . . *no* . . . it wasn't meant to happen like this. If Dayna went to prison on Max's behalf, that was one thing. It was her personal hell; a fitting punishment. Going there because this cop had screwed her over was another matter entirely.

She thought hard. It would certainly be sweet justice for Max and her if the likes of Warren Lane went down. He and his gang had given them hell over the years.

'What about the other two . . . Driscoll and his mate?' Dayna asked. 'No one else saw what happened. The rest of the gang had already left.'

'Told them the same as you. They can get done for withhold-ing evidence or shut up and bugger off. Guess which they chose?' Dennis laughed. Dayna had never thought he was a mean man.

'What about Max's mum?' Dayna asked. 'Does she know?'

Dennis was about to walk away but he stopped and turned back. He stared hard at her. 'What do you think?'

Dayna suddenly felt about twenty years older. She didn't like it. She just needed to be a kid again. Her head hurt and she wanted out of the weird place that she'd been in for the last week.

She'd just wanted to protect Max and now all this had happened. How could she let him be remembered as the kid who flipped out and killed himself? She couldn't bear it that she was a part of the ugly mix that had driven him to it. During the last week, she'd certainly considered joining him, wherever he was, but knew she'd never have the guts; not now someone else was relying on her.

She screwed up her eyes but everything was still there, full colour, burnt in her head. It would never go away.

In a blind panic before the ambulance and cops had arrived, Dayna had slid the knife from beneath Max's leg. She shoved it under her cardigan. Then, suddenly, everyone was there. Paramedics, cops, teachers and kids – the mess and noise of it all. Mr Denton grabbed her arm, yelled questions at her, called the headmaster, and then she'd escaped unnoticed. She ran and ran, not knowing where she was going. She ended up down at the stream, panting, panicking, sobbing hysterically. She plucked a plastic bag from the water. She wrapped up the knife and dropped it down a drain. No one would find it there.

With hindsight, she knew it was Denton who'd told the cops that she'd been the one to discover Max. The only reason she hadn't stuck to her original spur-of-the-moment story was because one of the youths was bound to blab. But she'd been wrong. They hadn't. She should have realised that's what they did, the way they were. They stuck together, their kind. Clam up, say nothing to the pigs, or face the consequences. Simple gang law. Apart from Warren Lane, of course, who'd now decided he wanted back in the slammer. A part of Dayna totally understood.

The studio was buzzing with people, with talk, with rumour and speculation. Dayna didn't see Carrie again that day. It was Jess who drove her home.

The engine ticked over as they sat outside her house. 'Will you be OK?' she asked.

'Yeah,' Dayna said, meaning the opposite. Her house looked cold, dark, uninviting. 'I'll be all right.' She wondered if her mum was home yet. Apparently, she'd been escorted from the studios by security during the show.

Dayna stood on the pavement and watched the police car drive off. She placed both hands on her belly. She wanted to tell her baby all about its daddy.

From the moment he pressed the button on the remote control, he knew he couldn't spend another night in the place. The television fell silent. He heard kids roaring outside.

'I have to get to the studio,' he said quietly. He needed to be with Carrie. Hearing her on the show, listening to her question the girl about the death of their son, imagining the film clip, gasping at the statistics, wondering about the unscheduled re-run when the producer had decided enough was enough was even more painful than seeing it with his own eyes. He called Fiona.

When they got there, Carrie was in her dressing room. She refused to move, was unable to move, she told him, having sent everyone away. It was just the two of them.

'They shouldn't have let you do it,' he said. '*I* shouldn't have let you do it.' He hugged her close. He felt the warmth of the bright mirror lights near his cheeks.

'Yet how could I have done nothing?' Carrie replied. Brody shook his head as he pressed hers against his shoulder. He understood entirely, he thought, as he remembered his futile attempts to help his son. Both of them had been ineffectual. He wondered if, added together, the sum of them would have been enough to save Max, to make them see clearly what was needed.

'A youth has confessed,' Carrie said bitterly. It was news to Brody. 'But do you know what?'

Yes, he thought, I do.

'It doesn't change a thing. I don't care if the boy goes to prison. I don't care who did it.' Carrie levered herself back, held him at arm's length as if that would help him see the pain he knew would be written all over her face. 'The worst of it is, things like this don't happen to people like us, Brody. We're never ready. It's as if we have automatic immunity according to circumstance.' She waited and they both thought. 'But we don't. It's an illusion. We are, ultimately, all the same.'

When he left the studios, Fiona drove him to a motel. He refused to stay another night in his flat. He had once been convinced that living on the estate would make him feel part of a familiar world that had disappeared overnight; now he wasn't sure he could cope with the crystal-clear hindsight it had given him. He vowed never to go back. It was no place for him. It had been no place for his son. Things like this, as Carrie had said, didn't happen to them.

Leah found her alone in the dressing room, just a remnant of Brody's visit lingering in the air. The studio had cleared and the detectives had gone. Leah crouched beside Carrie as she sat in the swivel chair staring at herself in the bright mirror.

'It's time to go, honey,' she said.

Carrie limply held several pieces of lined paper. Fast-written scrawl filled both sides of the pages. There were round smudges blurring the ink at the edges – tears, Leah thought, when she saw the redness of Carrie's eyes.

'It's Max's essay,' she said. 'When I went to see his teacher, he gave it to me. I stuffed it in my bag. I couldn't face reading it straight away.'

Leah took it. '*Romeo and Juliet*,' she said, offering a small smile. 'Brings back exam memories.'

'Read it,' Carrie said. She turned her head as if averting her eyes would dampen the pain. 'Read the last paragraph.'

Are we any different then, today, in a world so far removed from that of Romeo or Juliet battling out their love? If a boy loves a girl, if he wants to be with her so badly that he has to hide half his life from her yet melts under only a moment of her gaze; if that same boy wants to scream out his love for her, yet gets crushed by the weight of others, is it right that his penance should be death? I say yes. I say that not even finality will get in his way. Not even fate will interfere if love, so raw and young and doomed from the start, is allowed to run its course. Our world is still made up of light and dark, of good and bad; us and them. Without this, we would live in a gloomy place. Without them, I wouldn't have lived at all.

'Oh, Carrie,' Leah said. 'Max was an amazing boy.'

That was all. No more words were necessary. The women embraced. They walked out of the television centre. Leah took Carrie home and left her alone, as she requested, to wait for the numbness to go; to wait, as she knew it one day would, for the light to come back.

JUNE 2009

Carrie was trying to concentrate but failing. Some days were better than others. Work had brought a little routine, normality, sanity, but today it was driving her mad. Those that had agreed to help with the centres weren't following up. 'That's what happens when you beg,' she muttered. The doorbell rang. It was Martha's day off so she answered it herself.

'Delivery for Max Quinell. Sign here please.'

'Oh . . .' Carrie said, catching her breath. She closed her eyes.

'Wrong address or something?' the courier said, holding out an electronic device for her to sign.

'No, no. It's the right address.' She spoke quietly. Mail still came for him. Ironically, last week a lad from Denningham had called to see how he was getting on at his new school. The GP had sent out a card about a routine vaccination and junk mail flooded in from various publications.

'I'll just fetch it from the van then. There's a lot.'

Carrie watched from the top step of her London home as the driver ran back and forth carrying large boxes. There were six in total and he left them in the hallway. Puzzled, Carrie closed the door and stared at them. They were all addressed to Max Quinell. One of six . . . two of six . . . three of six . . . was printed on each box.

'One in a million,' she whispered.

She fetched a letter opener and slit the tape. In the first box, she found a brand new Moses basket complete with bedding and stand. In the second there was a navy blue and grey fold-up pushchair. Then there was a travel cot and a car seat. By the time she'd delved into all the containers, Carrie had uncovered an entire nursery of baby equipment. She read the accompanying letter.

Dear Mr Quinell, Congratulations on your *Perfect Parent Magazine* win! We hope you and your family enjoy the quality baby equipment proudly supplied by ParentCare. With one hundred and thirty stores nationwide, ParentCare offers the best for you and your baby . . .

She didn't read the rest; couldn't focus on it. She went to the kitchen for a tissue. It would get easier by the tiniest bit each day, month, year, they'd said. Never easy, though. She knew that. She would call Dayna immediately and get her to come over. Show her what Max had won for her and the baby. Even after death, she was so proud of her son. She only wished she had taken the time to notice before it was too late.

Dennis sat in his car and watched the house. It wasn't the usual surveillance operation. Well, he thought, unwrapping the Danish pastry he'd bought from the shop round the corner, it was – just way more important. He was impressed that it was detached and clearly well cared for, even though it was a million miles from his shabby jammed-in terrace. There was a new model Ford in the drive and another car, too. He'd not been expecting that. Summer flowers cast a rainbow of colour either side of the front door, dangling lazily from baskets in a spectacular array which represented, he couldn't help thinking, familial contentment. It was in stark contrast to his usual operations.

'Bitch,' he said. He sipped from his takeaway cup of coffee and burnt his top lip.

'Oh, for God's sake, Den, do we have to sit here much longer?' Jess had opted for a bottle of water and an apple. Not much of a breakfast, he'd told her as she eyed his sticky Danish.

'You're free to go at any time,' he replied through a mouthful.

'And how am I supposed to get back to the station?' She crunched her apple and wound down the window. Even when they'd arrived at 7 a.m., they knew it was going to be a hot one. An hour and a half later and the hazy clouds had burnt off. The sky was now brilliant blue. Jess stuck her elbow out of the window and dropped her head on to her shoulder. 'Can't you just phone her or something?'

'I need to see for myself,' he said flatly. 'You, my dear, just happened to be in the car.'

'Great,' Jess began but quickly stopped when Dennis leant forward and grabbed the wheel. He held the Danish between his teeth. 'Her?' she asked.

There was a nod. He couldn't speak, not because of the mouthful but rather from shock. A teenage girl had come out of the house. She stopped on the driveway, looked puzzled for a moment before turning back towards the door. Someone opened it in anticipation – a man, Dennis noted – and handed her a small bag from within the house. The girl laughed, her white teeth flashing a signal of both her own forgetfulness and gratitude at the *man* who had aided her.

Dennis let out a growl.

The man beckoned her back and gave her a kiss on the cheek. Then that smile again, a swish of her long blond hair, the bag slung over her shoulder, and a skip down the drive.

Dennis started the engine.

'She's pretty,' Jess said. 'Can we go now?'

'Of course not,' Dennis said, chucking the pastry out of the window. He put the car into first gear and crept forward.

'So now we're stalking a teenage girl. You'll get us arrested, you idiot.'

Dennis saw the roll of her eyes, the exasperated look on her face that, really, they should be back at the station following up on last week's stabbing. The nightclub owner wasn't entirely guilt-free, he reckoned, when it came to security. None of the gang would talk. All he knew was that it was sport for them, hanging outside the club, waiting for kick-out time. A bit of gay-bashing was entertainment. This time it had gone too far.

'This is ridiculous,' Dennis suddenly said. He bumped the car up on to the kerb, yanked on the handbrake and got out.

'Glad you agree.'

'Wait here,' he ordered, leaving Jess sitting alone, watching as he walked briskly across the deserted road.

The girl was making ground, perhaps late for school. Her navy skirt and maroon blazer were impeccably turned out and her hair gleamed in the sun. Her purposeful stride spoke of a keenness to get where she was going, to open her books, to learn, to embrace, to socialise between lessons and be the most popular pupil. She certainly looked it, he thought. Suddenly, he was reminded of that girl Dayna, of Max, of their struggle through a world that refused to accept them. Not so his daughter, he thought gratefully, witnessing her as their antithesis. His heart warmed a little, knowing that she was happy, that she was being taken care of, that, even if it wasn't him kissing her goodbye at the door, at least someone who cared for her was.

'Estelle,' he called out. 'Estelle,' he shouted again when she didn't turn. At the sound of his voice, her pace increased. Only when she reached the bus stop round the corner was she forced to stop and wait. She hung her head.

Dennis was panting when he drew up next to her. 'OK, OK,' he said, laughing. 'You win. I'm an old . . .'

434

Estelle turned to face him. She squinted from the bright sun. Her eyes were full of tears.

'Estelle, honey, what's wrong?'

'Dad?' she whispered. 'What are you doing here?' There was an unresolved laugh, a sniff, a tissue pulled from a pocket and a frown.

'I . . . I came to see you. What's wrong? Why are you upset?'

'It's nothing,' she replied quickly. 'Mum'll go mad if she knows you've been following me. It's not visiting day.'

'It's never visiting day,' Dennis retorted. He didn't care about that. He wanted to know why his daughter – bright and cheery not two minutes ago – was now crying. 'What's upset you, sweetie?' His mind raced with possibilities – she was being bullied, threatened, teased by other kids. Or maybe a teacher was picking on her. The horrible possibilities were endless. Dennis reached out, his arms aching with unfamiliarity. His hands settled on her shoulders. She allowed him to draw her close. 'I won't let them hurt you,' he said into her soft hair.

'What are you on about, Dad?' Estelle drew away. She sniffed and laughed.

'If you have problems at school. You *must* tell me. I can help.'

'I don't. I love school.'

'Then what's bothering you, honey?' Dennis didn't understand. He tipped up her chin with his finger. Her blue eyes were so full of sadness that he felt weak from being drawn into them. Panic swept through him. She was lying.

In her young face, he saw a flash of Dayna, of the misery she bore with Max until it became a way of life – or death. Warren Lane was still in custody, his court case due in another month. On further analysis, the knife had revealed three sets of prints – one Max's, one inconclusive, and one most definitely Lane's. The weapon had been sent off for a new type of testing. The CPS was finally convinced.

'I miss you, Dad,' she said. 'I've learnt to block out that you're too busy to see me and you and Mum always argue. But when I heard your voice just now, it made me . . . sad.'

'Oh, Estelle,' Dennis said. He was so relieved he could hardly speak. 'I'm so sorry, honey. So very sorry. How can I make it up to you?'

'Easy,' Estelle said, smiling again. It warmed Dennis's heart. 'Be in my life.'

Fiona was surrounded by boxes while Brody worked at his makeshift desk. She was being orderly and capable when all he seemed to want to do was walk through the acres of park opposite his new house or immerse himself in work. She knew he didn't want to think too much. She also knew that everything still hurt – from cleaning his teeth to returning to lecturing.

Why, he'd said to her, when my world is as black as the night, do I see my son everywhere?

'I can have this unpacking done in a day if only you'd tell me where you want things to go.' His stuff had been in storage for several months. Brody had insisted on staying in a motel rather than take Fiona up on her offer of a room. She wasn't going to argue with him; that came later when she helped him choose a house.

'I would like quite the opposite,' Brody said. He shut the lid of his laptop and turned to her. 'Please go ahead and put everything away for me. Then I can have fun finding it.'

'Fun?' Fiona said. She stacked plates in a kitchen cupboard. The whole place was clean and modern and functional; if Brody knew just how functional, she'd thought when they'd viewed properties, then he'd have probably gone back to his old flat. 'It's quirky,' she'd told him. 'It has character and is perfectly placed for the university and only five minutes' drive from me.' She'd especially liked that.

'I'll make a deal,' Brody said. 'You unpack everything and I'll buy you dinner.'

'Dinner?' She remembered the last time he'd bought her a meal. 'Where?'

'Don't sound so ungrateful.' He chuckled – a take it or leave it laugh, knowing full well she'd take it.

'Thank you. Dinner would be . . . nice.' And she pulled the tape off another box.

She was showing now. At nearly six months pregnant, Dayna's trim body held in the firm bulge of baby well. Carrie had sent a car for her and she'd come straight round.

'It's just what I need,' she said, glowing, when she saw all the stuff. 'It's amazing.'

Then they both cried, ending in a brief laugh at the absurdness of it.

They had tea and talked. It wasn't the first time they'd met since the show. Carrie had come home one evening to find Dayna sitting on her front step. She was shocked at first, angry, too, but she took the girl inside. They talked. Carrie updated her on the case – when the trial was set, how Lane had been refused bail and it was likely he'd get life in response to his plea of guilty. Dayna had looked at her feet the whole time, Carrie noticed. The girl never said what was on her mind, but clearly something was.

'I don't think any less of you for what you did, you know. You're brave. Stupid for wanting to punish yourself, but brave. In fact, Max could have done with more friends like you.' There was no point, Carrie had decided, in blaming her. She was carrying her son's baby. She wanted to be a part of its life. Justice had ultimately been done. The killer had been caught. Her son had been the victim of a random act of violence. He was a statistic. She couldn't accept that now but hoped one day she might learn to live with it.

'So are you still going to help me with the Check Point project?' Carrie asked. She was setting up youth centres throughout the most deprived areas of London. Each one was in memory of the victim of a stabbing and the first one was to be named after Max.

'Of course I will. I'm taking my exams next week. I dunno how I'm going to do, you know, after all this, but I still want to try. Then when the baby's born, I'll be able to help you. You're gonna need someone who knows what kids want.' Dayna grinned and shifted in her seat.

'Forget table tennis and tiddlywinks,' Carrie had told her benefactors at the presentation. 'The Check Point centres will be an education for the street kids and gangs but disguised as cool stuff. Computers, a café, music, skate parks, counsellors to talk to, a bed if they need one.' It was all in the very early stages, but Carrie was determined to see it through.

Leah loved the idea of linking the centres to the weekly *Reality Check* show. By following the progress of disadvantaged kids, they felt they could really make a difference. And if Carrie didn't make a difference, she didn't think she could carry on.

'While you're here, love, I'd better give you Max's dad's new address. He moved last week. I know he'd love to hear how you're getting on.'

'Yeah, sure.' Dayna had made it clear she wanted to keep in touch with both of them, especially after the baby was born. They didn't know if it was a boy or a girl and no one cared. It was a part of Max and that was all that mattered. Dayna planned on living at home with her mum and Kev for a while. They'd grumbled about the situation but were eventually accepting. It wasn't a unique arrangement on the estate. Plus Carrie was going to make sure that Dayna and the baby had everything they needed.

'Not a moment too soon, right?' Carrie meant about Brody

moving, but Dayna was still trying to get comfortable. 'He's living out near the university now. Fiona persuaded him to get a decent place opposite a park. Between you and me, I think there's something going on between those two . . .' Carrie trailed off when she saw the pained look on Dayna's face. The girl's hands suddenly clutched at her belly. 'What's wrong? What's the matter?' Carrie was on her feet. Nothing would happen to this baby. Ever.

Dayna's face transformed from one of discomfort to one of pleasure. 'The little monkey's kicking me like a football,' she said. 'Here. Come and feel.' She reached out and took Carrie's hand. She placed it on the gentle mound of her stomach. Carrie was surprised at how hard and firm it felt. 'Just wait . . . wait,' Dayna said.

Carrie knelt down in front of her with both her palms spread flat on her belly. She held back the tears. She waited patiently, remembering the first time she'd felt Max kick inside her.

'There! Feel it?'

'Oh heavens, yes, I did,' Carrie said. She wouldn't weep. Not in front of Dayna. She'd save it until later when, alone in Max's room, she'd say a prayer for him, light a candle and remind him, as every mother should, that he was the best son in the world.